GORGON
The Crimson Witch

1

John North

ISBN (e-book): 978-1-7369249-1-4

ISBN (hardback): 978-1-7369249-0-7

ISBN (paperback): 978-1-7369249-2-1

ISBN (paperback color version): 978-1-7369249-6-9

ISBN (hardback color version): 978-1-7369249-7-6

Trigger Warnings

The content of this book contains material that may be sensitive to some readers, including mild to heavy depictions and themes of violence, gore, massacre, PTSD, and physical/child abuse.

ECHIDNA OCEAN

GENNOMY

ARBIRION SEA

ATLANTIS

ATALANTA O

ATHENS
OCEAN

SERRENIE

TRITO
OCEAN

ZEREX
ATHENS OCE
EDEN
Malt sea
VERONA
Alaxanderian Sea
DOMN
FERROW
ONA
GORGON

Contents

Prologue

If you had all the power in the world, what would you do with it? The question lingered in young Aurora Salem's mind as the boar sizzled over the crackling campfire. Blair asked her that after every public brawl they started. It was one of the few things Aurora didn't mind having repeated to her, so long as it meant she could continue to fight by Blair's side. Despite her young age, Aurora quite enjoyed the life of petty crime. After all, the criminal exploits of magic wielders often attracted other magic wielders, even those on the side of the law. It didn't matter if they had to steal, destroy public property, or pursue other magic wielders on the wanted list. So long as the pursuit resulted in a magical fight that could sharpen their skills.

Of course, Aurora knew the life of a wanted criminal was unortho-dox for a witch of her age. Still, if that life meant having nights end like this, under the dazzling stars, roasting a wild boar over a warm campfire, she wouldn't trade it for the world, or all the power it could offer.

A soft breeze rustled the leafy trees above, sending a light chill down the eight-year-old's neck. She hardly registered it, since she kept bouncing up and down in her seat with excitement. They'd easily defeated thirty armed guards in their most recent bank heist, and Aurora was in full celebration mode.

They each tore off a leg of the roasted boar and raised them to the sky.

"To the Salem Sisters!" They chanted in unison.

Aurora wasted no time chopping away at the steaming boar meat, outright trying to ignore the near burning of her mouth, and failing. She slowed her chewing in an attempt to let her mouth cool before she continued eating. Blair chuckled, making Aurora blush.

"You gotta slow down, kiddo! The food ain't goin' nowhere," Blair said mid-laugh.

After swallowing, Aurora stuck out her tongue in playful defiance. Still, she smiled all the same.

"Well, we hit another good lick, sis," Blair said between bites. "Hot damn! I don't know how we do it."

"But we didn't get any money, silly." Aurora giggled before taking another bite.

"We whooped some ass though!" Blair shredded more of the juicy meat with her teeth. She looked like a predator from across the fire, light reflecting off the juices all over her face. "Especially you, kiddo! Seven guards by yourself, all with your elemental magic? Someone's gettin' stronger."

"I didn't even pass out this time!"

Blair stopped munching, staring at the witch blankly. She swallowed before clearing her throat and wiping the juices off her chin with a napkin she found in her pocket. "Ya know, you may surpass me one of these days. I was never that strong at your age."

Blair showed her usual cheeky smile, and Aurora rolled her eyes at the compliment.

"Whaaat? Come on, Blair. You were in the Third Great War at eleven."

Blair averted her gaze from the young redhead, her trademark smile morphing into something she didn't recognize. Aurora bowed her head. How could she bring up such a sensitive topic when they should be celebrating?

"Don't fret, kiddo." Blair ran her hand through Aurora's natural scarlet curls. "The war toughened me up. I wouldn't be worth eighty million had I not."

"Yeah, but your parents would still be here." Aurora threw her hand over her mouth, but couldn't catch the words in time.

She didn't know why she'd said it, but Blair just blew air through her nose rather than seeming more upset. "True. But they weren't strong enough, so Medusa took 'em out. And then someone stronger than Medusa took her out. See where I'm goin' with this?"

Aurora scrunched up her eyebrows. "I thought you said your parents were strong magic users like you."

Blair stared into the fire intently, as if cycling through painful memories. "They were. But you'll learn out here that there will always be someone stronger than you. The road to being the strongest ain't easy for anyone. Even with rare magic like ours."

Blair pressed an open palm on a patch of grass on the ground. A purple misty fixation known as *aura* engulfed her hand, as the ground beneath her suddenly caved in. A thick cluster of shiny purple crystals spawned in the palm-sized indentation. Blair then picked the small, crystallized structure from the ground and quickly tossed it to Aurora. The young witch's emerald eyes sparkled.

"Amethyst! You live up to your name, Blair," Aurora said with an enormous grin. She looked down at the gem again and then back up at her companion. "Please, please, please teach me how to use crystal magic!"

Blair chuckled at Aurora's begging. "Honestly, I dunno if ya can, kiddo. Most elemental users manipulate forces around them using their aura and can only wield a single element. My earth magic is a...sort of mutation, since I can refine it to create crystal. Mutations like mine can't be taught. You're either born with it, or you're not."

Aurora didn't even try to mask her frown. Blair reached over and rustled the frowning young witch's hair.

"We need ya to focus on controllin' ya own rare abilities," Blair said quickly, her voice warm.

"Fine." Aurora sighed and then returned to the boar meat in her hand. "Even if we go to war again, it won't be like what you went through. We'll beat everyone. Even the Demi-Gods!"

Aurora giggled at this, basking in their shared strength, but Blair's face tightened as if made of solid stone. She lowered her head slightly, her violet curls obscuring her eyes momentarily. Aurora's excitement wavered once again. Had she overstepped a second time?

"Unless we have all the power in the world, we'll always be bottom feeders or targets," Blair said softly, her eyes glued to the fire. "We're powerful, but mortal. If war breaks out again between the Allied Nations and the Magic Nations, everyone will be at the Demi-Gods' mercy. We'll either be pawns or collateral."

Dread settled in Aurora's stomach. They hadn't spoken this openly about war before, and hearing about its realities from Blair made her hair stand. What was it about the heist that had drawn this conversation out? Aurora stared at her feet. "Are. . .they really that strong?"

Blair tugged the collar of her jacket and shirt down, revealing a gnarly scar streaking down the right side of her neck to the center of her chest. "Got caught up in The Pearl Kingdom, and it only took one shot for their queen to give me this. I'm real damn lucky to be alive. Between Euryale and her sister, the Gorgons are the nastiest bitches I've ever faced. They have us at their mercy, as painful as it is to admit."

Aurora frowned. It couldn't be that hopeless, could it?

Blair's smile returned, along with that trademark dimple Aurora had grown to adore. Blair reached over and pinched Aurora's cheek. "Aye now. You too young to be frownin' like that, chile. Don't wanna end up stuck with that face like auntie, do ya?"

Aurora stifled a laugh, blots of red fueling her brown cheeks. Blair continued.

"They're strong or whatever, but not invincible," she said. "Knockin' them down a peg will be a hell of a lot easier if we get our hands on the Divine Sorcerer's Stones. With those jewels, I mean, we'd be untouchable. We'd have infinite magic."

"The jewels? Wait, I heard of those!" Aurora perked back up. "Are they really that powerful?"

"Infinite magic. Pay attention, kiddo."

"Ooo! Have you ever seen one? Are they pretty? Do they glow in the dark? Do they look like your amethyst, or are they more dull? What do they do?" Aurora swayed back and forth, unable to sit still. Her imagination danced with images of multi-colored gems.

"Kiddo!" Blair chuckled, holding her hand outward to gesture for the young witch to settle down. "One question at a time!"

She took a breath, as Aurora giggled to a pause.

"The stones are powerful, but guarded," Blair said with a gentle smile. "And usually, they're guarded by the exact people we want to defeat with their power."

Aurora's smile vanished. That definitely wasn't what she wanted to hear.

"As to your second question, I've come close to one. Found one guarded by that Euryale and, well. . ." Blair pointed back to her scar and laughed, high and pained.

Aurora's eyes twinkled with wonder. Her god-sister had gone through so much and lived a full and adventurous life. She was truly the most amazing person in the world.

"So cool," Aurora said before taking another bite of her meat. Aurora wanted nothing more than to be just like Blair one day.

Blair smiled gently, feeling the young girl's admiration fill her. "But maybe things would've gone differently if I had you with me. You're a one-of-a-kind witch."

"I . . . I am?" Aurora's eyes widened.

"Duh! You're the only witch I know who doesn't need to manipulate existing forces for your elemental magic," Blair shrugged as if it was entirely obvious. "Yours seem to just come from nothin'! Plus, you can use all of 'em! In a few years, you should be strong enough to handle your own without passing out. Once you do, we'll go after those stones together."

Aurora beamed at the sound of that. "You really think I can? I mean...you think I can help you with all of that?"

"I know you can, kiddo. With your badass elemental magic and my crystal magic? We'll steal one of those jewels of infinite magic and be at the top of the peckin' order forever."

Aurora nearly cheered, the excitement bubbling up through her whole body. "Why wait? I mean, I'm plenty strong now. We can take on anyone if I just–"

"Nah, kiddo." Blair held up one hand to stop her. "You still can't control your aura that well. You use way too much of it at once. I saw you grabbing at your chest again this last time."

Aurora bowed her head, ashamed at not having that all figured out yet. "But I can do it . . . you said I could."

"With trainin'. Just be patient. We'll get there. And we've been doing just fine in the meantime. I mean, ain't this great?"

Aurora nodded, but couldn't lift her gaze from her feet.

Blair's arm wrapped around Aurora and reeled her in. The young witch's honey-beige cheeks flushed red as she leaned into her god-sister's warmth. It felt good to have family to fight beside. It was a life Aurora wished would never end.

A faint rustling of leaves interrupted the calm, crackling of firewood. One of Aurora's pointy ears twitched, and she jerked her head around. "What was that?"

"Probably just a rabbit or a stray pixie," Blair said as she leaned slightly away from the younger girl. "Hurry and finish your dinner. Tomorrow, we're gonna work on your elements again. Speakin' of which, would you conjure up some water and put this fire out?"

Aurora nodded and then closed her eyes and focused on her aura. The energy quickly surrounded her body, appearing like a glowing emerald mist. A scorching heat radiated from the center of her chest, making her wince as her scorpion tattoo glowed. Energy flowed from the center of her chest, through her arms, to her hands. *Keep the aura flow steady, like water. Convert the aura into magic. Then release!*

The green aura circled her hands and then condensed into a sphere of water the size of a marble. Suddenly, a thin stream of water sprinkled from her hands, as if it were coming directly from a spigot. Aurora narrowed her eyes at the tiny water sprout. She was accustomed to her water magic being more like a fire hydrant than a water fountain.

Blair raised an eyebrow. "Are you slacking on me?"

"It's been a long day, okay?"

Blair laughed at her. However, the campfire wasn't dwindling from the water at all. Instead, the flame grew hotter, more intense. Blair stood and kicked dirt onto it. The fire expanded, flickering wildly, as though it were being fanned. Blair's eyes widened, and Aurora's did in turn.

"GET DOWN!" Blair leaped toward Aurora and tackled her, shielding the young half-witch with her whole body.

As if in response, the campfire quickly became a blue blaze and exploded. Aurora heard her godsister wince in pain. Blue flames danced on Blair's back, burning a huge hole into her jacket.

"Blair!" Aurora yipped. She scurried and quickly fired another water spigot to extinguish the flames.

Blair sprung to her feet and assumed a fighting stance, her fists raised high. Aurora quickly did the same.

Four men emerged from the bushes, each bearing large dragon wings, horns sprouting from their heads, and spotty scales upon their faces. The tallest of the group lashed his long orange tail and grinned, sporting jagged, pointy teeth. His orange, freckle-like scales gleamed from the dying flame's light. *Half-Dragons? Here?* Aurora swallowed, her pupils shrinking at the mere sight of them.

"Can I help you?" Blair asked in mock-friendliness.

The orange-scaled half-dragon pulled out a wanted poster with Blair's face on it from inside his black robe.

"Amethyst Witch," the creature declared. "Says here you're worth a small fortune. Thanks for the fire by the way. The smoke made you easy to track."

"Half-dragons, eh? Don't you reptiles belong on the other side of the Atalanta? What are you doing in Eden?" Blair asked.

"You could say we're running errands. The name's Shoto. We're here to offer you a job."

Blair folded her arms. "A job? What, you want me to be a Magic Nation slave like you? I'll pass."

Shoto slammed his heavy tail against the ground. "We don't serve the Magic Nations' Demi-Gods. We're more *freelance liberators,* and we would like for you to be one of us."

Blair wore a slight grin. "Liberators? What are you liberating people from exactly?"

Aurora struggled to quell her shiver. She had no idea how Blair stayed so cool in interactions like these.

Shoto and the other half-dragons laughed. "Isn't it obvious, Amethyst? The very people you *used* to serve."

Blair fell silent, and then narrowed her eyes. Aurora's own eyes flicked back and forth between the two parties.

"You've built quite the name for yourself over the years, Blair Salem," the creature continued. "A respected soldier of the United Military turned one of the world's most wanted, all for serving your country? Isn't fair, is it?"

Aurora tugged at Blair's jacket. "What's that ugly man talking about?"

"Not now, kiddo," Blair said sternly. Aurora's face colored with embarrassment, but Blair gently touched the younger girl's shoulder for comfort. Then, she redirected her attention to Shoto and his goons. "You want to challenge the Demi-Gods too then?"

"It's a little bit more complicated than that. But rest assured, our organization's goals and yours align."

"You don't know shit about me, fire-breather."

Shoto grew impatient. "Come on, Salem. Your talents shouldn't be wasted being on the run and sleeping on the streets. If you work for us, you can use your magic freely and never have to worry about the United Military hunting you down. Hell, with the work we do, you might be able to get payback on the Gorgon Queen one day. The entire Demi-God reign on the world could come crumbling down with your cooperation. This world order is much more tenuous than you might believe."

Blair was silent momentarily, and her eyes lowered to the ground. "An end to the Demi-God reign, eh? Sounds too good to be true."

"Don't do it, Blair! Forget these losers! Let's go back to fighting the police, c'mon!" Aurora pleaded.

Blair didn't respond. She didn't even look Aurora's way. The little half-witch frowned.

"If you're so confident in your organization's plan, what do you need me for?"

Shoto wore a frown of his own, as though stunned she would even ask. "Your talent would greatly expedite our plans. Your responsibilities wouldn't be too different from what you do already. The job may involve more…*blood* than you're used to. Given your crystal prowess, mercenary work should be easy."

Aurora's stomach turned. Despite not understanding much of this conversation, she understood that aspect very well. She stared up at her godsister, unable to get a read on her blank expression. Her hands had even started to shiver.

"What about my sister?" Blair asked, catching Aurora off guard. "Say I join your organization. Do your dirty work. What happens to her?"

Shoto shot his eyes at Aurora, making her flinch. A gnarly smile stretched on his face, showing rows of sharp, jagged fangs. "I've heard rumors of a little tyke of a witch being your accomplice. If her magic has even a slither of potential to become as potent as yours, she might be useful. We could always use another monster like you."

Heat shot through Aurora's bloodstream. Her shivering finally stopped, and her brows furrowed. Blair looked over to her, the pair meeting eyes briefly.

"A monster like me, eh?" Blair said, her eyes not leaving Aurora's.

Shoto offered his outstretched, scaly hand to Blair, reaching across the fire. "So, what will it be, Amethyst Witch? Will you join us in re-shaping this world or continue to be hunted by it?"

Blair gave her godsister a tender smile, the same one that never failed to wash Aurora's worries away. Aurora smiled back in kind, giving Blair a nod.

Blair set her sights back on Shoto, propping a hand on her right hip. "That's really tempting! But the life of a terrorist or a murderer is not a life I want to bring my sister into. Sorry, chief." She shrugged.

"Despite already being a domestic terrorist yourself and using that child as an accomplice?" Shoto pointed at Aurora, and Blair's lip quickly curled upward in anger.

"We fight, we commit crimes, but we don't *kill*." Blair fixed a hard glare at Shoto. "Besides, last time I was a part of a group that claimed to fight for peace, it didn't end too well, as you know. So you'll understand if I don't quite trust organizations like yours."

Shoto rested his scaly hand on the hilt of the sword tied to his waist. "Are you declining our offer? I'll have you know that you don't have the luxury of refusing now that you've seen our faces."

"Yup. But look on the bright side. None of ya will have to worry about recruiting anymore." She cracked her knuckles. "After I'm done with you peons, you'll have to retire early. Hope your organization has disability."

Shoto sucked on his teeth and tightened his grip on the hilt of his sword. "Fine. We can use the money for your head anyway."

Aurora threw up her dukes and jumped in front of Blair. This was her chance. "Blair, I've got your back!"

"Stay out of this one, kiddo," Blair whispered, grabbing the kid's shoulder. "You're too exhausted from earlier. I can handle it."

"What? I'm plenty strong too! It's four on two, and you need all the help you can get."

"You'd do best to listen to your sister, child," Shoto said with a grin and a step forward. "We have no real need for the kid, and I'm your only opponent. My boys are just here to watch. If she gets in the way though, I'll happily cut the tyke down!" Shoto whipped his katana from its sheath, then flew at the witches in a blur.

Blair immediately shoved Aurora out of the way and evaded Shoto's blinding strike.

"Kiddo, just sit tight!"

Blair dug her fists into the ground, and her aura–shimmering lavender–spiked around her. Soil and pebbles engulfed her fists and began hardening to solid rock. Aurora watched in awe as they liquified to appear magma-like and cooled again to form crystals. She ripped her hands from the dirt, and spiky amethyst crystal clusters surrounded them.

Aurora dusted herself off just in time to see her godsister blitz the half-dragon. She loved watching Blair use her crystal-style fists. It was mesmerizing every time she witnessed it. Blair dodged Shoto's swipes gracefully, moving like the wind but striking like lightning. Shoto put some distance between them and fired flames from his mouth, but Blair evaded the inferno with ease. She dove and dug her crystallized hands into the ground again. In mere moments, the ground beneath her caved in, this time around her entire body. Crystal shards extended up her arms and covered most of her body, appearing like sharp armor. Her aura flared as she jumped from the hole in the ground and raised her fists again.

Shoto scoffed. "The infamous crystal armor. They don't call you the Amethyst Witch for nothing."

Aurora's grin grew, and her eyes sparkled. She knew that no one could touch her once Blair surrounded herself in the crystal armor. As expected, she put the pounding on Shoto, tearing through his clothes and cutting him up with her crystal fists. Despite being dense and bulky, the armor didn't compromise her speed. She was still a blur as she rocked the dragon. Shoto couldn't keep up or land a blow.

Yet, something was off. Shoto's onlookers were still smiling, even though he was getting beaten to a pulp. A few of them even laughed. Aurora also noticed a weird, black snake-like tattoo that made itself visible on Shoto's chest, with his clothing being torn from the beatdown.

Blair decked him with a devastating left hook, making him stumble backward. Aurora pumped her fist. One more shot to the chin would be enough to put Shoto down, or so she thought. Shoto quickly regained his composure, wiping his blue-colored blood from his face. He flew a few feet backward, catching his breath and clutching the hilt of his sword tight. He was covered in deep gashes, blood streaming down his face, and yet he still wore that confident smirk. What was his deal? He should've been on the verge of passing out after a beating like that.

"You're as strong as your price implies." His voice was rugged, and he spat out blood. "That ability of yours, creating diamond-hard crystals from soil, must take a lot of aura. You'd have been better off not using it against me."

Blair caught her breath and wiped a coating of sweat from her forehead. Despite looking winded, she smiled and raised her fists once more. "Talk is cheap comin' from a half-dead lizard. Let's get this ova' with!"

Blair charged at full speed. Before anyone could understand what was happening, Shoto swiped his katana through Blair's armor and cut her in the shoulder.

A chill shot down Aurora's spine. Crimson blood dripped down the edge of Shoto's blade. The blade itself glowed, as though it had an aura of its own. *Swords can't do that, right?*

Her godsister stumbled backward, wincing from the cut and eyes wide. Shoto smirked at her as his scales spread out enough to cover his entire body but his neck and abdomen. His face stretched out into a beastly snout. His claws sharpened, and his wings extended, as his orange aura erupted around him like a raging flame. Shoto zipped at Blair like a bullet, slicing off another large chunk of Blair's armor, baring her shoulder to the air.

Aurora's jaw dropped. No sword, blade, or strong magic had ever been able to penetrate Blair's armor before, yet Shoto's sword cut through it as if it were paper. Blair lost ground quickly, only able to dodge and try to defend herself in the face of such surprising power. Each slash from Shoto left a bigger gash in Blair's armor. Even his punches left cracks in the amethyst. Blair flailed, her counters and strikes missing. She got sloppy, and it was clear she had no answers to Shoto's revitalized assault.

Soon, all of her armor was torn off. Before she came up with a new defense strategy, Shoto pierced Blair's shoulder, pinning the witch to a tree. Shoto slowly rotated the blade in her flesh. Blair staggered with teeth gritted against the pain, unable to move, as her jacket quickly dyed red.

"As I said, you'd have been better off without it. Tsk, tsk. To think Minerva hasn't caught you yet!" Shoto remarked.

Blair's aura dissipated, and Shoto's katana shone brighter red than before. Her face lost color. Her breaths shortened. Aurora quaked, her anger boiling at the sight of her godsister's blood.

Aurora charged at Shoto without a second thought.

One of Shoto's comrades jumped in her way, but Aurora quickly left the ground and slammed her foot into his jaw, knocking him out cold in a single shot.

"Strong for a child. What a waste . . ." Shoto mumbled.

"Aurora! Stay back!" Blair yelled, her eyes flicking quickly between her godsister and her enemy.

Aurora weaved through the other dragons before reaching Shoto himself. Just as she cocked back her fist, Shoto yanked the blade out of Blair's shoulder and drove it through Aurora's stomach. A searing pain permeated from her abdomen. Her jaw dropped, blood erupting from her throat. She watched her glistening blood seep down the sharp edge of the katana, which glowed once again. Just as her body temperature dropped like a stone in water, her aura drained, quickly.

"Masamune is a hell of a sword, isn't it, kid?" Shoto said, even though Aurora could hardly focus on his cruel smile. "You should take some pride in dying to a celestial weapon. Don't worry, your *sister* will be next."

Blair screamed out for her sister, but only white noise filled Aurora's ears. Gradually, her vision blurred, before all around her disappeared.

Aurora sat up and rubbed her eyes, groaning from delirium.

"Wh . . . what happened?" she mumbled to herself. The world around her was spinning rapidly. She couldn't figure out which way was up. "Blair, did I pass out again?"

It all came rushing back. Her stomach. The blood. The blade. She reached down to feel for her wound, but she was met with nothing. No wound. She looked down. It looked like she hadn't been stabbed at all, save for the fact that her hands were wet and red. Aurora flinched at the sight.

Who's...This isn't my blood, is it? Aurora struggled to stand, but her legs were so weak that it took her a few tries to find balance. Everything hurt, a dull ache. When she could finally stand and take in her surroundings, her eyes widened with terror.

The surrounding trees were ravaged, as though a tornado had torn through it. Small fires crackled through piles of fallen trees and severed wood. And there, amidst the destruction, Aurora spotted the half-dragons. All of them, including Shoto, were dead and bloody, scattered around the forest floor. Her stomach turned, as she approached their blue-blooded corpses.

"Blair. . .you couldn't have..." She took a closer look at the half-dragon's bodies. "Wait."

All of them shared wounds that looked to be a result of a mauling by a wild beast. Aurora shielded her mouth with her forearm and nearly fell to her knees at the sight. The torn skin. The massive gashes and bruises. Some of them even had their entrails ripped out. *Blair didn't do this! That's not her!* As she stood over Shoto's lifeless, bloody body, Aurora witnessed Shoto's snake tattoo in full, curling into an 'S' shape for just a moment before vanishing.

Aurora trembled even more. *Wait, where even is Blair?*

She didn't have to search very hard at all. Her heart sank within moments when she found Blair in the same bloody condition as the dragons, lying against the stump of a tree that had been snapped in half. Aurora cried out, all caution gone, and rushed to her godsister's side.

Blair's eyes had lost all their color and were halfway shut. Aurora tried to shake her awake.

"Blair, wake up! Please, Blair!" Aurora cried out.

Blair slowly turned her head towards Aurora. Despite her numerous deep wounds, she wore a small smile. "Y–you're okay? I'm . . . so glad. My Aurora."

"Wh-who did this to you, Blair? I fainted again, I didn't see anything after . . . after he stabbed me. Who did this?"

"You . . . don't remember? That . . . ma–makes me happy."

"Blair, what are you talking abou—" Aurora suddenly caught a glimpse of her hands, pressed against her godsister's face. Her bloody fingers featured the sharp claws of a feral beast, sharp enough to shatter flesh easily. It only took a moment for her to realize who the blood on her hands belonged to. As though afraid of her realization, those sharp claws slowly retracted back into normal fingernails. "What . . . what the–?"

"I couldn't stop you this time," Blair said gently, no malice or hurt in her voice. "I . . . wasn't strong enough. Aurora, please, don't die weak like . . . like I did. T–take care of Aunt Ria. Make sure everyone remembers the name I gave you. Never stop fighting . . ."

"But I . . . did I . . .?" Aurora's bloody hands quaked. Her scorpion tattoo glowed. Her head thumped, and her entire body felt as if it was scorching from the inside out. "No. *No!* You can't die! You're the strongest! Blair!"

Blair's head fell to the side, and her god-sister, now alone, wailed to the heavens.

1
Say My Name

The witch raised her hands to the sky, the steel barrels of many aimed rifles encircling her. Police cars filled the city block, and every officer fixed their gaze on the hooded witch. Her violet hoodie did well to mask her eyes, but not the cheeky, giddy smile she wore. Not that she cared at all. She wanted to ensure that every pig in the vicinity knew that she was having a good time. After all, blaring sirens and loaded rifles were a recipe for a wonderful Saturday afternoon for the now fifteen-year-old Aurora Salem.

"Slowly remove your hood! And keep your hands in the air!" The officer's voice boomed from the megaphone.

Sheesh. How can I take my hood off and keep my hands raised? Pick a lane. She slowly reached for her hood and pulled it down, revealing natural scarlet curls and emerald eyes.

The officer with the megaphone, boasting a head full of gray hair, looked to his armed subordinate once he got a clearer view of the girl.

"Bill. Did we find our little witch?" the elder officer asked.

"Short, scarlet hair. Green eyes. She has the maroon scorpion tattoo around her neck too. And that crescent moon charmed necklace she's wearing. She matches the description to the tee, sir," the younger officer confirmed.

"Crimson Witch! You're under arrest for illegal use of magic in a robbery and ensuing property damage!" the elder officer yelled into the megaphone again. "Lay down on the ground and put your hands behind your back!"

Aurora's eye twitched. *They're using that name again.* She glanced around at her one last time, counting in her head. *Ten, eleven, twelve . . . twenty-five punching bags.*

"Hurry it up, witch!"

Aurora scoffed and began to lower her hands.

"On the ground, now!" the officer barked again.

Aurora showed them all the gleam of her teeth from her wide smile. "Come on! You sure you don't want to talk this out? I mean, all this for one measly apple?"

"You cut an entire vendor stand in half! Not to mention, that truck!"

Aurora shrugged. "It shouldn't have honked at me! That's rude."

"You've been terrorizing not only Westtown but all of Verona for years! Your illegal use of magic has gotten so far out of hand that—"

Aurora released an exaggerated groan. "Fine, fine. I'll surrender. But *only* if you can say my name."

Rifles clicked in response.

Aurora snickered. "Fine then. Fireworks it is."

She swiftly put her hands into her hoodie pockets, and the city block blazed with gunfire. Bullets sprayed around her, yet Aurora remained spotless and still through them all. She stood calmly inside a small, translucent green dome formed from her own aura. Their bullets failed to penetrate her forcefield, as it often did. No matter what city in Verona she made into her playground, the police always resorted to those pathetic guns. Aurora wondered if any of the various precincts even shared information with each other. Despite her handy work the past several years, they always seemed so ill-prepared.

The elder officer signaled for his men to hold their fire. Once the dust settled, Aurora got the clearest view of their collective slack-jawed expressions. One of the many faces that gave her life.

She gazed down at the wasted bullet shells on the ground, giggling to her heart's content. "Look at all this wasted tax money!"

Swears and slurs echoed at her from every direction. Music to her ears.

Aurora pulled out a shiny red apple from her hoodie pocket and munched away. She made sure to chomp loudly as if she were eating it in their faces. "I don't know why Minerva keeps funding you guys. She may be better off having the U.M. deal with crime instead of you clowns, ya know?" she said with a full mouth.

"Damn," the old officer swore. "The rumors are true. She knows aura shaping and can create barriers."

"Rumors?" Her eyes lit up, and the corners of her mouth stretched upwards. "C'mon guys! You heard of me so you should've known better than to use bullets. There's gotta be a witch or two amongst you humans. Step up, will ya? Let's make this fun!"

Their groaning and complaining turned into bickering. Some argued that they needed more funding to deal with magical threats, while others cried about how they weren't getting paid enough for military-grade work. What started off amusing got dull rather quickly. They were supposed to be fighting her, not each other. It was time to change that. She finished her apple and tossed the core. *Blair always said to strike first and strike hard.*

Without warning, Aurora sprung through the police perimeter like she was being shot out of a cannon. Her fist rammed into the jaw of the elder policeman, launching him and his megaphone into the air before anyone could even register what happened.

Another officer flinched and stumbled to aim his rifle. Aurora kicked the weapon out of his grasp and fed him a volley of blinding punches. The poor man collapsed in a blink.

"Two down, twenty-three to go!" Aurora mumbled with a smile before they opened fire again.

She evaded the gunfire and knocked out cops one by one, keeping a mental count. Aurora tossed the officers around like ragdolls, each smack harder than the last. *Seventeen, eighteen, nineteen.*

Six officers remained, and they had all ditched their guns. Aurora noticed they all had ears with pointy tips, identical to her own. They weren't ordinary humans, who toted round ears and no affinity for magic or wielding aura.

Aurora's excitement only elevated at the sight of the bright blue auras that surrounded each of them.

"Finally, some sorcerers and witches! Capturing me would be a hell of a lot easier if there were more of you and less of those useless guns."

The magic-wielding officers drew their batons while forming a circle around the witch.

"Don't let her escape!" one of them shouted. The rest charged.

Aurora evaded their swings and fists with relative ease. Failing to land blows, the officers fired magical blasts. Flames and blasts of water zipped at her faster than the earlier gunfire, and she struggled to dodge them all. Perhaps she'd overestimated her ability to hold off so many magic wielders at once. Things worsened when they mixed martial arts with offensive magic.

A punch from the right. A kick from below. A blast of water from above. A fireball from the right. Aurora's dodging became sloppy. Their attacks became quicker and sharper, to the point that Aurora couldn't predict their movements. Then, *bang!*

Flames struck her in the abdomen and flung her backward. She tumbled on the rough concrete, tearing up her arms and legs. Aurora quickly hopped back up to her feet, though she quaked from the pain. Her heart beat like a drum. Her arms and legs throbbed from the freshly torn skin. Everything stung, but that rush. The thrill! Even the pain that came with it all! She yearned for more!

Alas, she had to focus. Her skin reformed over her scorched abdomen and scraped limbs. In mere seconds, all of her wounds were gone.

"She healed!" one of the officers noted.

"That rumor's true too then," another one said while fixing a nasty glare aimed Aurora's way. "She's one of *them*."

Aurora's body tensed upon hearing that. However, her attention snapped to the hole in her hoodie. *Oh fuck! Blair's hoodie!*

"No, no, no, no!" she cried.

The magic-wielding cops fired their elemental magic at Aurora again. Aurora put up another translucent bubble shielding her from all their attacks. Her face reddened the more she looked at the scorched, blackened fabric. All amusement left her psyche. She didn't want to drag this out a second longer. A green aura shrouded her body in a violent rush. *Only one shot at this, and it has to be quick. The fastest element should do.*

The tattoo on her chest lit up like a lamp, shining bright green. However, her chest felt as if it were burning from the inside. Again, she shook off the pain. She put her hands together before her, the influx of energy making her hair stand. The police ceased their fire. One of them stumbled backward, recognizing Aurora's stance, as well as the sparks popping around her.

"Don't let her use *that* element! Destroy that barrier!" One officer shouted as they sprinted towards her.

The street beneath them quaked and cracked, the splinters in the pavement growing out directly from where Aurora stood. Before the officers could reach her, Aurora released her dome barrier and fired streaks of lightning from her hands, so intense that they struck all six officers at once, and scorched the ground beneath them in the process. They all flew backward from the blast and crashed into parked cars, metal poles, and nearby buildings. Pieces of rubble rained from the sky like hail.

"Twenty-five," Aurora muttered with a slight grin. Now that the performance was over, her burst of strength quickly faded. Her arms vibrated from numbness, and her chest pain slowly subsided. She wiped the coating of sweat from her forehead with her forearm.

Aurora approached one of the unconscious policemen and pressed her fingers against his vein. She felt a steady pulse and sighed with relief.

Her mind began to rest easier, but only momentarily, as his eyes flashed open. He immediately started to squirm and hyperventilate, staring at her with bulgy eyes. He reached for the pistol on his hip, but Aurora struck him in the nose and pinned him, her foot on his wrist.

"Don't move. It's over."

The injured officer winced, a stream of blood flowing down his lips from his nose. "Is this all you ever do? Just ruin lives for fun? Why?"

"Why? Say my name."

He remained silent. Aurora shook her head. "If you or any of these clowns died, no one would remember you. No one important, anyway. Hell, I'm gonna forget your face tomorrow. I refuse to let anyone in this world say that about me."

He groaned. "What the hell do your parents think? You're just a kid."

"You think, after all this, I have parents? Come on, dude."

Even through his tremendous pain, he managed a chuckle. "Don't know why I bothered asking a *demon* like you."

Aurora hesitated, her stomach beginning to sink. She averted her eyes from him and frowned.

"When the United Military gets a hold of you, it's your ass, *you monster*."

Aurora kicked him in the face, knocking out a few teeth and putting him to sleep.

A sizzling heat permeated through her blood. She glanced at her hand and saw those familiar claws forming from her nails. Her crescent moon charm on her necklace flashed with bright purple light. Aurora closed her eyes and took deep breaths. *Five . . . four . . . three . . . two . . . one.* The glowing dwindled and eventually stopped. Her sharp claws dulled, turning back into her regular nails.

Once she could think straight again, she snatched the radio off the unconscious officer's chest.

"Attention, please send about uh . . . twenty-five ambulance units to Aries Street. Over and out," she said.

With that, she crushed the radio in her hand. Aurora blew a whistle through her fingers, and a broom materialized right before her. She hopped on and flew off into the clear blue sky.

Aurora made her way to a familiar alleyway with comfortingly thick walls littered with various posters. There were recruitment flyers for the United Military, mixed in with propaganda signs and wanted posters. The poster with a crystal cluster covered by an X, reading: '*A Magic Nation Is a Hellish Nation*' stood out the most. She could find at least one of those on every other block.

Aurora eventually stumbled upon an old wanted poster of Blair. A big stamp reading *DECEASED* covered her godsister's face, with her name scratched out entirely. *Bad enough they etched out her face, but her name too? Damn it all!* She fumed as she snatched the poster off the brick wall. When it was gone, crumpled in her hand, she realized all her energy had left her. She curled up into a ball with her back against the wall.

Helicopters circled high above the towering skyscrapers. They were likely looking for her, but Aurora didn't care. Her eyes remained buried in the hoodie she had in her lap. She fixated on the scorched hole.

"Sorry, I got your hoodie burned. Guess I got carried away again," she mumbled with a light, pained laugh. "Wish you could've been here to see it."

As Aurora fought back tears, cars zipped on nearby roads, blowing trash and debris into the narrow alley. Her face was met with a flyer, soaring from the street wind. She quickly snatched the paper off her face and wanted to incinerate it out of irritation. However, she halted upon registering the poster's content.

"No way," she uttered.

Aurora leaped with joy. "My own wanted poster! Yes, yes, yes, yes, YES!" she cheered. "It even has a good picture of me! I did it, Blair! I did it!"

She raised her fist to the sky.

When the initial thrill faded, she took another look at the poster, particularly the name and price on her head. She grumbled. Maybe it still deserved to be burned to ashes.

"They're still using this nickname and not my actual name, and this price is so damn low! This is half of what Blair had and not even an *eighth* of what Medusa had before she died!"

Surely, the poster would be much more to her liking if she had more strength and control of her various abilities. "It's a good first step, but if I genuinely want a place in this world, I need to get stronger. I need the whole world to know my name . . . and keep Blair's dream alive. At the very least, this bounty on my head will send some stronger fighters my way. Stronger than the cops at least. Real competition will up my stock and strengthen me. But first . . . let's get this hoodie patched up."

With the sun blazing overhead along with police choppers searching for her, Aurora discreetly made her way to the eastern part of Westtown. The avenues were bustling, full of mostly humans.

Aurora blended in with the crowd, keeping her head down as she sped-walked. When she reached eastern Westtown, everything around her looked as though it were from an entirely different region. The small part of the city was mostly residential, with small buildings covered with cracks and thick vines. Trash littered the streets, full of potholes devoid of vehicles.

There was also a distinct lack of humans as compared to the rest of the city. Dwarves scampered around. Giants sat near buildings they couldn't fit inside. Beastmen—people with animal appendages and features—ran from bar to bar. Despite it not being as clean as the inner city, Aurora felt more comfortable around other magic wielders. Here, she was likely to find a greater challenge, one she could use to sharpen her own skills. But for now, this trip was just to patch a fabric hole.

Aurora flew over to a small corner shop. Upon spotting the neon sign for *Salem's Needle*, she smirked.

She kicked open the door and marched straight in. The bright colors and sparkles nearly blinded her, all shining from different garments that hung in midair. There were suits, dresses, overalls, kimonos, robes, sets of battle armor, and gowns, all with gold, sparkling pixie dust falling from them. An elderly witch sat at a desk in the back of the store, with prune-like dark skin and long, straight silky hair the hue of a spider's web.

Aurora slammed the hoodie on the desk. "Ria, I need you to fix this hole in my hoodie, pronto!"

The witch blinked at Aurora before popping a cigarette into her mouth and shaking her head. "I'd call ya one of a kind if my niece wasn't the same way. Neitha' of ya take care of ya clothes. Always getting 'em torched or shredded."

"Yeah..." Aurora scratched her head and looked down bashfully. "You can fix it though, right?"

Ria held her hand out.

"Oh, come on, Ria! Don't I get a Salem family discount?" Aurora batted her eyes.

Ria stared at her blankly. "Family discounts are for *family*."

"Oh. Right." Of course, it was going to be another one of those times.

Aurora dug in her pockets and pulled out a small brown pouch tied together with black string. Turning the pouch upside down spilled a series of gold coins onto the table. Aurora counted them one by one, the pair of wings on one side of the coins facing up.

"Shit! Thirty coins is all I have!" Aurora cried.

Ria shook her head. "Ya act like you can't steal more. It's what ya do. Fork it."

Aurora handed the thirty coins and returned the empty sack to her pocket. Ria had always been able to see right through her.

For the next few minutes, purple threads spewed from Ria's long hair, changing colors as she moved. Her narrow, pointy nails were precise as they stitched and sewed the hoodie. The silence smothered Aurora, even though it was always this way.

"Kid, ya made the news again," Ria said, after a few minutes of silence.

Relief overtook Aurora. Finally, the silence was over. "You saw that? Ain't it great? Wish the cops weren't so weak—"

"How many corpses?"

Aurora rolled her eyes and took a deep breath. "None. I didn't . . . you know."

"Good. It's working."

Aurora tried her best to keep a straight face. "Yeah."

Ria shook her head. "Ya know, if those police-folk were anything like the United Military, you'd be dead by now. All these stunts you pull . . ."

"That's the challenge though. I do all this to send fighters my way to get stronger." She glanced around the shop as she considered the problem of her legacy once more. "I need my name out there, ya know?"

"Omni almighty, ya sound just like Blair." Ria shook her head. "I asked her this once, and it's high time I asked you. Why do you seek power?"

Aurora fiddled with her crescent necklace as she sat on the thought. The question reminded her of her talks with Blair after their raids. She clutched her charm firmly in her grasp.

~ Never Stop Fighting ~

Blair's last words rang fresh in her ear as if she just heard them. The thought alone tugged on her heartstrings. Truth was, aside from her hoodie, the promise of strength was all she had left of Blair. She couldn't afford to let Blair's name or dream of power die with her.

"Who wouldn't? The strongest make their place in the world. Euryale, Arthur, Icarus, Cleopatra, Minerva, and even Eira are all respected and feared. Why? Cuz they're Demi-Gods. The strongest. Their magic is second to none. Not that it matters, cuz imma surpass them all."

Ria didn't even raise an eyebrow. "Kid, that's a tall order."

"Is it?" Aurora twirled her finger, and a droplet of water appeared, along with a small flame, a spark of electricity, and a small pebble in rapid succession. They all danced around her finger swiftly before colliding and turning into a cluster of blue sparkles. "How many magic wielders do you know can use all the elements?"

Ria blew a puff of smoke from her mouth. "Most magicians are lucky to wield an element at all. You're wasting your unnatural talent, doing all this. You're a thug with no vision."

Aurora's eyebrow twitched. She hadn't expected validation from Ria, but the woman's directness was frustrating. "I got a vision, and I got a plan." Aurora reached into her pocket and pulled out her wanted poster. "I'm already halfway there!"

Ria stopped stitching. She squinted at Aurora's wanted poster for a long moment, too long, and then shook her head. "I don't know why Blair didn't just let me raise ya. Keep this up, and ya gonna end up like her."

Aurora's grip tightened on the edge of the poster. That incident was the last thing she wanted to be reminded of today. "Not like you didn't have a chance to."

Ria scoffed. "If ya insisted on bein' a fighter or street rat, there was no way you'd grow under my roof. Dealt with enough stuff like that in the war. Don't put up with it no more."

"Stuff like what, Ria?" Her heart rate picked up. That familiar burning feeling returned as well.

Ria blew out another dark puff of smoke. "Relax, kid. All the same, ya should hang the gloves. Bein' wanted with your abilities . . . and *that one* specifically, ya gonna end up hurt. Or worse, you gonna hurt someone else and have to live with it."

Aurora's hands quaked. Her impulses roared at her to swing on Ria, elderly or not. "So just because I'm different, I can't fight? That's bullshit, and you know it. You let Blair do all those things and didn't say a word. I want to be like her. No, *better* than her. But just because I wasn't born a Salem, you think I can't?"

"That ain't the point! We were soldiers in times of war. We had to fight. That damn war *forced* Blair on that path. But ya didn't grow up during the Great Wars. You weren't forced to fight. You chose to live that life, you chose to follow that girl, you chose to waste all that talent. And then it's even worse that you can't control that rancid—"

"OK, I get it!"

Ria stopped stitching. Aurora's eyes flickered red and her necklace glowed. She closed her eyes and counted backward from five once. Then, a second time. The glowing stopped. Her blood simmered down.

"My point." Ria slid the finished hoodie toward Aurora. She put out her cigarette and tossed the butt into a nearby bin. "Ya should cut it. Make some friends. Get a trade. Start over with a new identity and go to school. Do something productive with all that power. Anything is better than livin' on the streets or doing whatever the hell you've been doing."

Aurora's necklace glowed again. "But I can't live here though, right?"

Ria averted her gaze. "It wouldn't be right. Not after . . ." She drifted off, staring at the small, framed photo on her desk. The image displayed herself and a much younger Blair in United Military uniforms.

"Noted." Aurora bit down on her lip, her face burning. She stared at the hoodie with soft eyes, remembering when it was drenched in blood. Ria was wrong. Blair's greed didn't kill her. The truth was far more heartbreaking. Aurora shook her head and snatched the hoodie from the desk. "Thanks, Ria. I'm leaving. Bye."

Aurora turned toward her and pulled the hoodie back on. "By the way, I'm plenty strong, even without my curse. I can handle myself by myself. I don't need anyone, and I especially don't need you."

She stormed out of the shop and slammed the door behind her.

Aurora walked quickly through the streets with her head down and hood on, weaving as best she could through the thick crowds. She heard the whispers, which steadily grew louder all around, echoing over the honking cars and the footsteps of all the metropolitans. *Did you hear she was out again? The Crimson Witch hospitalized twenty-five people. She's a monster. When will Lady Minerva deal with her? Some say her eyes turn red and she grows fangs. She needs to go back to the Gates of Tartarus where she belongs. Monster. Monster. Monster! MONSTER!* Aurora covered her ears and was picking up the pace when she slammed into someone accidentally.

A young girl in a turquoise hoodie, her wired headphones hanging out, stared at her.

"Oh shit, sorry. You okay?" Aurora fumbled with her hood but quickly realized it was too late. The girl looked up at Aurora, and her face drained of color.

"You, you were on the . . . news. And in the ads . . ."

"I—"

The girl jumped up and ran, screaming to call the police. Everyone surrounding them jumped back at the sound and intensity of the situation, and when they all realized what was going on, they began to run as well. Aurora sucked on her teeth, summoned her broom, and flew away.

When the coast was clear enough that she wouldn't be followed, Aurora returned to the alley she'd rested in earlier, leaned against the side of a building next to a large dumpster, and buried her face in her knees. After a moment, she turned her gaze to the orange and blue sky. If only Blair were still around to train her. Her grip tightened on her kneecaps. She needed to get stronger, and she needed to do so quickly. The stronger she got, the closer to Blair she could be. Rather, the closer she could get to achieving the dream Blair fell short of, but what was the difference anyway?

Never stop fighting. She couldn't afford to forget those words.

As she watched the sky with dampened eyes, her god sister's memory vivid, Aurora spotted some strange creatures high above. Curious, she summoned her broom. Was this a bad idea? Perhaps, but regardless, she ascended to get a closer look.

As she drew closer, more details came into view. There were six of these winged creatures.

Are those . . . birds? No way. Too damn big.

Aurora flew in closer and saw them for what they were: large, scaly creatures with wings, spikes, and horns.

"Dragons? What the hell are dragons doing in Verona? They aren't allowed to fly here. . ."

They were wyverns: winged dragons with only two back legs. Aurora saw men riding the backs of the scaly creatures, and one wyvern even pulled a flying carriage, which she saw emerge from a nearby cloud. The burgundy carriage brimmed with gold spokes around its circular wheels and gold, sparkly dust falling from its underside, likely due to an aviation enchantment. *Red and gold. . .those colors are. . .*

Aurora gasped. A burgundy shield with a scorpion at its center, and a pair of golden swords in the shape of an "X" behind it.

"I know that crest anywhere. That has to be a royal from the Pearl Kingdom. A Gorgon! Either we're going to war again, or. . ." Aurora snickered. "It's time to blow off some steam. Maybe even increase my stock."

Aurora waited for them to cross the sky to see where they were going before following from a distance. *I'll show you, Ria. I'll keep Blair's name alive and become the baddest witch this planet has ever seen.*

2

Enter, Polaris!

Aurora tailed the flying carriage east of the main city to an under-developed section of Westtown. The neighborhood was devoid of both people and large infrastructure. Every other building was without electricity and, much like the roads, decorated with large cracks and invasive vines. Old cranes with shattered windows and rusty steel beams stood like metallic skeletons up and down the lifeless city block—a seemingly perfect location for foreign enemies to convene without drawing too much attention to themselves.

The wyvern-led carriage landed in the perimeter of a construction site with an unfinished steel-beam structure standing within it. Loose gravel was strewn everywhere, and some wide wooden planks were stacked into a pyramid on the left side of the perimeter. Much to Aurora's surprise, a police squad was already there, their blue and red lights flashing atop their vehicles. Aurora inched closer on her broom but with trepidation. There were so many eyes now. She hid behind the steel beams of the unfinished building, towering almost thirty feet above them.

The wyverns landed, and six men hopped off the saddles of their respective beasts. They all wore black and gold uniforms, with the emblem of an encircled crystal cluster embroidered on their backs, depicting the crest of the Magic Nations. Their white military caps featured the same Pearl Kingdom crest from the carriage.

"Magic Militia?" Aurora mumbled, practically salivating. She had never seen a soldier of the Magic Nations' Military in person before, and now she was blessed with six.

Each soldier was armed with a sword or halberd, which only made her crave combat even more, especially after she sized up the biggest man among them.

He was a stout beastman with bushy brown hair as thick as a lion's mane, a lion's tail, and a bulky, stout frame. The beastman wore several badges on the left side of his chest, including a chess piece of a knight. On the right side of his chest was his name patch, reading: "Knight Class: Reiya."

The Knight Class is one of the higher ranks of the Militia! He's gotta be strong! But even he doesn't compare to a Demi-God. She stared at the unopened carriage, struggling to contain her jitters. After all the stories she'd heard about Blair's encounter with Queen Euryale Gorgon, she was itching to see what the woman was made of. Itching to test her mettle against one of the strongest beings in the world.

The three Westtown police officers approached the Militia quickly. The soldiers aside from Reiya formed two parallel lines and knelt, creating a path in front of the carriage door. Reiya raised his hand, signaling for the three officers to stop advancing. Then, he walked over to the carriage and reached for the golden door handle. Aurora quaked with excitement.

"Introducing Her Grace, the illustrious heir to the Pearlian throne, Princess Polaris Gorgon," Reiya announced before opening the door.

All excitement died.

A young girl with midnight-blue hair tied up in a fishtail braid emerged. She wore a scarlet, royal combat-style dress with gold straps and buttons and bore the Pearl Kingdom sigil on her back. A sheathed sword rested on her right hip and a golden circlet shimmered on her head, with a radiant sapphire at its center. She approached the officers with a confident smirk.

Despite hoping for someone of royal blood to exit the carriage, Aurora couldn't help but suck on her teeth. *That's not Queen Euryale. Dammit! Should've known. She'd have probably drawn way more attention had she showed up herself.*

Upon closer inspection, Aurora noticed the princess carrying a thick binder as she stood before the officers. Her soldiers remained close with straightened postures and their hands hovering near their respective weapons.

"You three are representing the Metropolis of Westtown?" Polaris asked with a cocked brow.

One of the officers, a middle-aged woman with dark skin and short black hair, ground her teeth together but quickly took on an expression of neutrality. She wasn't being particularly subtle if Aurora could see that micro-expression from her vantage point.

"That's correct. I am the Chief of Police of the Westtown Sector, Clara Banks. It's an honor to meet you," she said with a bow.

"I would say the same if you were President Icarus. Is it not customary to meet a representative of another nation with someone greater than or equal to them in status?"

"Our sincere apologies, Princess Polaris. President Icarus departed Verona for Zerex on official business. We couldn't reach him in time for your arrival."

"Interesting. He didn't inform us that he'd miss our arranged meeting." The princess narrowed her eyes, failing to mask her irritation. "And I presume this concrete jungle is devoid of other government officials that are more qualified to meet us in his place?"

"Again, many apologies. Mayor Capulet has other priorities, as does our governor—"

Polaris huffed, rolling her eyes, and raising up a hand. "I should expect nothing less from you Allied Nation swine. Not a shred of respect for anyone who isn't already aligned with you. If Mother were here herself, she'd drown this entire city for greeting her with three measly pigs."

The officers scowled at Polaris, as did Aurora from afar. She clenched her fists. *The hell does she think she is? Waltzing in here with that attitude.*

"I apologize on behalf of Westtown." Chief Clara wore a strained grin to mask her annoyance. "But President Icarus informed us you're here searching for a runaway prisoner within our borders. Who in particular are you searching for?"

"Such informal proceedings. Very well." Polaris rolled her eyes again. She opened the binder and pulled out a flyer. Aurora couldn't see it from where she was watching, but she could see very much how pale Chief Banks's face got after looking at the flyer.

"We're after *her*," Polaris said. "The Crimson Witch is a wanted prisoner of the Magic Nations. We are aware that this city, as well as several others in the region, has had some . . . problems trying to corral her, no?"

Clara's face twisted into a contorted scowl. "Just today that *freak* hospitalized twenty-five of our officers and destroyed an entire city block. She's absolutely out of control. You'd be doing us a favor if you take the little bastard off our streets."

Polaris chuckled in delight. "Twenty-five of you couldn't take down a single girl? Let me guess, you resorted to ordinary gunfire?"

"Well—"

"Aren't the majority of your forces human, therefore lacking magical prowess? *Ha!* So your kind is both weak and incompetent."

The scarlet hue on the officers' faces was on full display and probably would've been visible from outer space. Clara especially looked as if she could pop a vein at any moment.

"In any case, just show us where to find this Crimson Witch," Polaris demanded.

"As far as we know, the girl is homeless," one of Clara's subordinates said. "We get reports of her raising hell all over Verona, yet she's caused the most damage here the past six years. So, you won't need to travel far."

Polaris folded her arms. "And are the rumors true concerning her abilities?"

The police officers shared a glance.

"Yes, she can use more than one kind of elemental magic," Clara said. "All these years and we still haven't been able to figure out how she does it. She's the only living being we ever heard of that can wield all elements, and as far as we can tell, she's no Demi-God. Even the best of them can wield no more than two. Unless you Magic Nation folk know something we don't."

Polaris laughed again. "So that rumor is true too! Excellent news!" She clapped in celebration, disregarding Clara's inquiry entirely.

Aurora couldn't fathom why Polaris didn't share the officers' anxiety about her magic. Usually, her abilities freaked out most. But not only was Polaris pleased to hear about it, but she was unbothered by the possibility. Why?

"Yes, we shall have her. However, I'm afraid you're all useless if you don't know where she is. You can all take your leave." Polaris waved the officers away as if they were troublesome gnats.

The officers remained frozen, eyes wide and mouths agape.

"Knight Reiya, grab my crystal ball and prepare to summon more of our forces to this city. We'll scour the entire continent of Verona if we must."

"May I take the binder into the carriage for you, miss?" Reiya asked.

Polaris's grip tightened on the binder. "Now, now, don't get ahead of your rank. This is for royal hands only. You know this."

The knight seemed to stutter towards a response, but he didn't have to stutter long.

"Hold it!" Clara shouted. "You can't bring more Militia here! It might have been before your time, but the Third Great War wasn't long ago for most! Seeing an unauthorized battalion of soldiers from an enemy nation will disturb the peace."

Polaris hurled into laughter. "Oh no, no, no, no Mrs. Banks. What disturbed your peace was your failure to capture a little girl on your own. Your people failed to acquire the necessary strength, power, and resources needed to carry out a trivial task. You saw the amount on the girl's bounty I presume. She's hardly worth the effort, yet you and your men have proven you're all worthless."

"Say what you want, girl. It doesn't matter. Lady Minerva won't allow any army to enter our borders, especially to capture one little witch," Clara said, her jaw set. "Are you trying to start another war?"

"A war in which you are destined to lose again?" Polaris shook her head with a smile. "As if this industrial forest could afford such resistance. Make no unnecessary moves, and there shan't be any conflict. If you insist on not letting us proceed as we please, we won't hesitate to turn this city into the next Anubian Desert."

"That's it, you rude little brat!" Clara marched over to her, rolling up her sleeves.

Reiya shielded Polaris, as did the other soldiers. "You will not get any closer to Princess Polaris. Stand down or any further signs of aggression will be treated as an act of war."

"You've made enough war threats!" Clara barked as her subordinates pulled her back, trying to convince her it wasn't her call to spark such political conflict.

Aurora's ears fumed. She had heard enough of Polaris's drivel. All this talk of war, all over her? If they wanted her so badly, why not confront her personally instead of threatening an entire city?

Aurora leapt off the steel foundation and over everyone's heads. She landed hard on the hood of one of the police cars, crushing it like a tin can and spraying glass shards in every direction.

Aurora cracked her knuckles with a grin. She basked in everyone's shocked expression. "Heard someone was looking for me. Said I wasn't worth the effort. Let's see who's worth what."

The three officers whipped out their pistols and aimed them at her. Aurora rolled her eyes, uninterested in them. The Militia, however, kept her attention, forming a small circle around her. Five of the soldiers also aimed their weapons. Knight Reiya, meanwhile, shielded the princess.

"Stand down, Crimson Witch! You're surrounded!" Clara Banks shouted.

Aurora cut her eyes to the police. "Come on, piggies. You ain't learn from your earlier ass-whoopin'? Though, cracking the skulls of these Westerners sounds way more fun. Especially the blue-headed bitch with the big ass mouth." She set her sights on Polaris.

"You dare speak of her that way?" one of the Militia shouted, fueling their sword with a coating of their own aura. The other Militia did the same, mounting Aurora's excitement.

Polaris emerged from behind the Knight, raising her hand to signal her men to yield. The soldiers hesitated but ultimately lowered their weapons.

Polaris approached the crushed car Aurora stood on. The pair locked gazes.

"Careful!" Clara yelled, still aiming her pistol at Aurora. "She's dangerous."

Polaris shot her a nasty glare. "While I appreciate the concern, I'll be the only present danger if you continue aiming those useless weapons at her. Lower them. Now."

Clara gritted her teeth. She and her fellow shared a glance before lowering their guns.

Aurora whistled and clapped. "You've got these piggies whipped, prissy. That last name of yours must be what has them pissing their pants."

"Come down this instant, Crimson Witch," Polaris demanded. "I'd like a word."

"I could give a damn what you like."

"I will not repeat. Either you come down, or I come up. You may find that second option hazardous to your health."

Aurora's eye twitched. Polaris had the nerve to command her? She wasn't even her ruler, not that Aurora listened to her region's rulers anyway. She couldn't wait to knock this girl's teeth in. She jumped down from the smashed metal of the vehicle and faced the princess.

"I hope you run as fast as your mouth," Aurora seethed, rotating her right shoulder. "You're gonna need to when we start swingin'. So, let's get this over with—"

Polaris got into her face with wide eyes, too wide. She was hardly inches from Aurora's face. Aurora instinctively jumped back. What was her deal, getting so close like that? Did she want a busted lip that badly?

"That scarlet hair. Those green eyes." Polaris chuckled softly and shook her head, as though entirely in disbelief. "Without question, you're her! I can't believe this. Mother didn't speak fallacy of you, Solaria. You're truly alive!"

Aurora tilted her head and furrowed her brow. "I'm sorry, who?"

"Oh, of course. You were likely raised under a different name. No worries. Mother and I will see that you get into proper royal form. The learning curve shouldn't be too steep."

Aurora looked towards the police, but they all looked just as confused as she was. "Look, prissy, I don't know who this 'Solaria' is, sounds like a disease, but I ain't her. The name's Aurora. It's gonna be a world-renowned one before you know it."

"Aurora? Oh, what a silly name. No. You're Solaria Gorgon, daughter of Euryale Gorgon, and my older sister," Polaris declared.

Aurora scrunched up her face once more. "OK, so you're crazy. You don't know what you're talking about. You're mistaking me for another witch."

Clara opened her mouth to add something, but Polaris raised her hand to silence her.

"My, my, you're such a delusional girl," Polaris said, swaying back and forth between her feet. "Take a look at your chest. Did you think that scorpion was just an ordinary tattoo?"

Aurora looked down at the scorpion tattoo on her chest. From what Blair had told her years ago, she'd had it ever since she was a child. The resemblance to the Pearl Kingdom's mark was uncanny. How hadn't she noticed that before?

"That's . . . just a coincidence," Aurora muttered.

Polaris shrugged, lifted the sleeve of her right arm, and pulled down the sleeve of her white glove. Upon seeing her skin, Aurora's jaw nearly dropped. Polaris had the same tattoo in the exact same color, coiling up her arm and shoulder. Aurora's stomach did a somersault.

"This is no mere tattoo. It's a brand, showing we're children of Queen Euryale Gorgon. Are you convinced now, sister?"

Aurora couldn't find a response right away. Even with all the dots connecting, a flood of questions raided her mind. Her head pounded at the mere thought of being a Gorgon. That was just an entirely unbelievable thing to consider.

"Shut up!" was the response she landed on. "I've had it with your dumb little story about us being siblings. You've got the wrong witch!"

"Why do you continue to deny fate? Goddess Echidna has brought us back together! We can return home! You can live a better life off these streets and free from thuggish behavior." Polaris extended a hand to Aurora. "Come, now. I'm sure once Mother sees you, she'll jump for joy."

"Stop!" Aurora snapped. "I ain't no prissy princess, and I ain't no Gorgon. The only time I'll ever go to that kingdom is to kick Euryale's ass on my quest to be the world's strongest witch! So take your little soldiers and overgrown flying lizards, and get the hell out of my city!"

"How dare you speak out against the royal Gorgon family and deny your heritage!" Reiya yelled.

Aurora turned to him, her anger boiling. The militia had grown restless watching this conversation, but Aurora didn't care. She glanced around, considering who in the crowd she would attack first.

"Hold on just a minute!" Clara barked. "If she is really one of you, the Gorgons are responsible for everything she's done!"

Polaris narrowed her eyes. "Knight Reiya, please escort these swine back to their pen. They've exhausted their usefulness."

Reiya grabbed Clara firmly by the arm, squeezing so she couldn't pull away. Clara hardly knew what was happening, and her gaze darted from side to side in anger. The other militia grabbed the other police officers and started to drag them away. They all fought and pleaded, trying to break away, but to no avail.

"Can't have this all being public news just yet," Polaris said. "This is a family-only matter, understand?"

"Yes, ma'am," Reiya responded, then set off toward the screaming officers.

Despite her dicey relationship with the police, what Polaris said raised Aurora's concern.

"Are they gonna kill them?" Aurora asked.

Polaris folded her arms and smirked. "With the amount of blood on your hands, what does it matter to you?"

Aurora felt that anger boiling even higher in her chest. She grabbed her shaky wrist to keep herself from knocking Polaris's perfect teeth out of her mouth. At least not before Aurora could get a proper challenge out of her, and potentially more answers.

"You look like you're going into cardiac arrest, dear sister," Polaris said and tilted her head to one side.

"Do not call me sister!" Aurora yelled out. Grabbing her wrist wasn't working. She truly was going to knock this girl's teeth in. "I already have one! Her name was Blair Salem, and she was one of the greatest witches ever."

"I'm sorry, Blair? Who is that?"

Aurora gritted her teeth, fuming even more.

"Hold on! Salem. That sounds oddly familiar . . . Would she happen to be the Amethyst Witch? A crystal specialist and former U.M. Colonel, was she not?"

"You . . . you've heard of her?" Aurora asked. She couldn't help the bit of excitement activated within her at this.

"Of course! I've researched a lot of notorious war criminals in our world's history, especially the ones who would dare try to take my mother's life. Or, our mother's life, that is. As concerning as it is that such a dastardly being raised you, it is fascinating." Polaris stroked her chin. "Tell me, how did she perish?"

Aurora's lips tightened, and her face darkened.

Polaris gasped before Aurora could say anything at all. "Oh, you took her life? Why, I knew you were a criminal, but I didn't know you were a *monster*. To kill the woman who raised you? Why, you're no different from our treacherous aunt, Medusa."

She rushed right at Polaris threw a fist

It didn't matter. Polaris caught her punch with minimal effort and nearly popped Aurora's knuckle with a squeeze. Aurora's jaw almost dropped from the shock. She exchanged glares with the golden-eyed princess.

"Are you done?" Polaris asked, irritation fueling her tone.

"Yeah. Done listening to your annoying ass voice," Aurora growled. "I'm not your sister. Even if I was, why come for me after fifteen years?"

Polaris tossed Aurora's fist aside and paced two steps back. "Sister, I found your confusion charming initially. I was genuinely glad to meet my older sister for the first time. You must know how lonely it is to grow up an only child. That being said, you're becoming quite a nuisance. I need you to come home with us, but your compliance isn't required." Polaris's hand hovered over the hilt of her sword.

She dodged my question. She's hiding something. Aurora cracked a grin. "The princess wants to fight, eh? You're finally speaking my language."

Polaris raised the binder she was holding, and suddenly, a water bubble formed over it. She tossed the object back behind her. The bubble holding the binder floated back into the carriage all on its own.

Aurora tilted her head. *Water magic user. Easy.*

"Once I've rendered you unconscious, I'll drag you back to Mother. We'll instill some manners into you."

"You talk big for someone who's supposed to be the younger one."

"You being a year older doesn't imply that you outrank me. Currently, you're just a peasant." Polaris drew her sword. The blade shimmered with a gold tint, reflecting the evening sun. She stood straight, put her left hand behind her back, and pointed the blade upward at a forty-five-degree angle. "Peasants obey the powerful. Or they get punished accordingly."

Aurora's eyebrow twitched at the sight of Polaris's stance. She straightened the fingers of her right hand, and a green aura formed around it. It extended until a glowing, translucent blade formed around her hand, almost the same length as Polaris's sword. Polaris tried her best not to react to the emergence of this aura blade, but Aurora knew it was quite a sight to see.

"I agree. Those with power call the shots. Which is why you'll leave after I pummel you."

Aurora charged. She ferociously swung her witch blade, and it clashed hard with Polaris's sword, lighting up the battlefield with glowing sparks. Aurora pushed her back, but she couldn't find an opening no matter how persistent she was with her swings. She tried dipping low and sweeping Polaris's feet, but was met with a heel to the face.

The shift in momentum sent Aurora tumbling. When she popped back up, she felt blood pouring from her nose. She grabbed at it, blood pooling in her hand. Polaris smiled as she reassumed her initial stance and beckoned Aurora with her finger.

Aurora rushed her again, as Polaris pointed her right hand at her. Aurora slid to stop her momentum but was met with a hydrant-like cannon of rushing water from Polaris's hand, which blasted the half-witch across the construction site. She crashed into a pile of wooden beams.

The force of her fall crushed the wood, sending splinters in every direction and pains shooting up Aurora's back.

Polaris snickered with delight. "I must say, you're not at all like what this town's news outlets describe. You're . . . what do urban folk of this land say? Trash?"

Aurora picked herself up again, grunting with irritation and pain. She wrung out her drenched hoodie before tying it back around her waist. "Don't mock me, princess. I was sizing you up. You're not bad for a prissy bitch, ya know?"

"Your profanity is quite unpleasant. We'll be sure to have the world's best soap clean that defiled tongue."

Polaris swung her sword, sending waves of water at Aurora. She evaded the rushing waves easily, and they merely swept away more wood and gravel. She sprinted toward the steel-beam structure. Aurora leaped from beam to beam, going higher and higher to get a better vantage and force Polaris into a chase. She then watched as Polaris entered the structure from below.

"Climbing won't aid you in this duel, Solaria."

Polaris placed her sword in the sheath and followed, leaping up the unfinished building and climbing it like a jungle gym. Aurora patiently waited for her to reach the same beam she was standing on. When Polaris finally reached her, Aurora created her witch-blade again. Polaris drew her sword but couldn't help but glance down. They were twenty stories high and on a narrow beam. Aurora grinned.

"What's wrong, Princess? Scared of heights?" she mocked.

"You're getting more irritating by the second." Without a warning, Polaris sprinted toward her.

She fell for it.

The two locked swords again, Aurora's ferocity growing. Polaris stood her ground, parrying and dodging every swift strike. Aurora kept her eye on Polaris's left hand, watching as she pointed her palm at her again. Aurora stopped and swung her witch-blade through the beam beneath them. The creak and screech of the sliding metal tore both their ears as the beam was severed. Aurora jumped up, and the beam dropped, just slightly. Polaris lost her footing, tripped over her heel, and fell.

Aurora summoned her broom and jetted toward the falling, screaming princess. Before she could reach her, Polaris aimed her hand at the ground and sprayed water once more. This time, the water froze, creating a slide of ice that coiled around the unfinished steel structure. Aurora immediately flew to the end of the ice slide.

Polaris landed and slid on the ice feet first. When she reached the ground—*smack!*—Aurora belted her in the face with a solid punch, flipping Polaris into the air. Her fist stung from the strike. Polaris lay on the ground, and Aurora blew the steam off her knuckles.

A wave of anxiety washed over Aurora when she realized Polaris wasn't moving. She approached cautiously.

"Hey," Aurora gulped. Her heart started to race. "You better not have died on me, Princess. I held back a little."

Blair flashed through her mind. Her hand trembled as she reached for Polaris.

Then, Polaris threw her arm up and blasted Aurora with icy water and white mist.

Aurora's entire body went completely numb. She was immediately submerged in a thick coating of ice. Polaris sprang right up and wiped the blood from her mouth.

The princess stumbled and grabbed her reddened nose and jaw. She pulled out a small mirror from her pocket and shrieked in terror. "You ruffian! You've tainted my image! If we weren't blood, I'd have you publicly executed for this transgression."

"Tr-tr-tr-tragic." Aurora's teeth chattered, but she still derived some joy, seeing Polaris's countenance ruined.

Polaris squinted her eyes and put away her mirror. "Nonetheless, I've won our duel. You're not completely without talent. Your punches don't rival Mother's, but they are more of a wallop than that of most of our royal guard. You may even fare against a few of our lower-ranking Militia with proper training. We'll be sure to provide that at the castle."

Aurora couldn't budge in the miniature glacier. "I-I-it's n-n-n-n-not over."

Aurora closed her eyes, concentrating once more. Her chest contracted and inflamed. *I need a different one this time. Think heat . . . think heat.* An orange light began to glow from the miniature glacier, and warm air formed around them.

Polaris felt the heat and reached for her sword. "What is this—"

Aurora's ice prison exploded into a wave of flickering fire. Polaris jumped back before the flames could reach her. She watched as Aurora stood amongst the fire emitted from her hands. Polaris's anxiety-ridden face was priceless. Aurora grinned through her exhaustion.

"Mother was right. She must have it. Which means . . ." Polaris ground her teeth and stood her ground, pointing her sword at Aurora. "If we must continue, then let's. So long as I draw breath, you're coming with me to the Pearl Kingdom!"

"You're going home alone!" Aurora fired blasts of flames toward Polaris.

Polaris countered Aurora's fire with blasts of water, creating a thick steam that engulfed the area. Polaris stopped and rammed her sword hard into the ground. Her blue aura stormed around her, and she raised her hands. An immense, tsunami-like wave swelled at her feet, expanding and stretching over Aurora's head.

"Oh Omni, where'd she learn that!?" Aurora shrieked.

"It's over!" Polaris threw down her arms, and the tsunami fell toward Aurora.

Aurora refused to concede.

She widened her stance and expanded her aura, making all of her muscles tense. The flames in her hands grew, turning from orange to a bright blue. She then twirled the flames around her in a circle and threw her arms high in the air. The flames formed a tornado-like wall around her, firing into the sky. The twisting flames collided with Polaris's tsunami, evaporating the waters and leaving thick steel-like steam in its wake. The mist spread over the entire city block, obscuring the witches' sight of each other.

"Incredible. She can use that much of it?" Polaris uttered.

Aurora panted, drenched in sweat. She remained focused despite the suffocating steam.

"Time to finish this, Princess." She aimed her hand in Polaris's direction.

Suddenly, the pain in her chest returned, and with a gruesome vengeance, as though it were tearing her apart. Her tattoo glowed and she fell to her knees, groaning and clawing at her chest. *No, no, no! I can't be this low on aura already! One more attack!*

Aurora's vision faded in and out as the pain permeated from her chest throughout her entire body. In seconds, Polaris stood before her, the tip of her sword pointed directly at Aurora.

"Changing the state doesn't change the fact that it's all water."

The thick steam around them twirled and converged around Polaris's sword as if it were wind. The steam turned into one giant water sphere at the end of her sword, twice Aurora's size. "It's over, Solaria. Surrender."

Aurora ground her teeth. She couldn't afford to lose to that snobby princess or be dragged to her castle. She just couldn't. Yet, no matter how she tried, her body wouldn't budge. Her head thumped, and her crescent charm shined purple. Finding all the strength possible, she funneled her aura to her right hand. Sparks crackled and popped around her fingers, with an intensity enough to make her hair stand.

"I refuse to surrender to you—"

Polaris swiped her sword and doused Aurora. In an instant, her entire body went numb. The water froze on impact, trapping her in a thick, crystal-like glacier. Her vision blurred from the ice, and her aura dropped like a weight. Her remaining strength dwindled. In the corner of her eye, she saw Reiya returning to Polaris's side. It was the last thing she saw before her consciousness slipped, and her eyes shut.

3

The Deal

Aurora's head spun. Just lifting it was like trying to lift tons. The soft chatter reverberating around her didn't help, sounding like she was underwater. She focused her ears to listen in, unable to open her eyes for the moment. It didn't take her long to pick up on Polaris and Reiya's voices.

"Whatever do you mean, Knight Reiya?" Polaris asked in that snobby, proper tone Aurora had already grown to detest.

"The storm will pass over the Atalanta Ocean tonight. It should miss this land, but taking the wyverns to travel back to Gennomy tonight would be foolish."

Reiya's rugged voice had more grit than Ria's own. If Aurora didn't know any better, she would've sworn they were smoking buddies in a past life. She couldn't help but wonder if was because he was part lion.

"Hogwash! Surely our wyvern can handle a little water. Also, aren't Private Victor and Corporal Xior capable of aura shaping? They can create a barrier of sorts."

"They could, but maintaining an aura barrier manually without energy from an airship for seven hours is almost impossible, even for those with their strength. We're talking a potential hurricane here. No matter your power, traveling through one unprepared is a recipe for death."

"Ugh, how utterly irksome! Mother expected me back tonight! I gave her my word!" Polaris complained, her voice shrill. "I suppose I should contact her and let her know we'll return tomorrow."

"Unnecessary, Princess. I've already taken the liberty to inform Queen Euryale of the situation. She's more than pleased to learn we successfully found and secured Solaria in a single day."

"Who gave you the liberty to contact Mother without—wait, she's pleased? Truly?" Polaris's voice heightened with delight. "Did she sing my praises?"

"Only the highest."

Polaris squealed like a preppy schoolgirl. "Oh, how wonderful! I cannot wait to see Mother's face when she sees Solaria! She's going to be absolutely delighted!"

"Right..." Reiya's voice was riddled with doubt. "Princess Polaris, what exactly is inside that binder? Why not share it with us if it was vital to our mission?"

"Knight Reiya, you are quite the careful, curious feline. Mind your place."

Aurora shivered profusely from her damp clothes, goosebumps forming all over her body. Reiya's persistence with the binder was odd and a bit suspicious, but that was the least of her concerns. She finally opened her eyes and found herself in a very unfavorable position.

Her wrists and ankles were tied up in cold chains with a hunter-green tint to their links. She was restrained as though she were a wild beast. She sat upright on the fuzzy, wet cushion of burgundy fur beneath her. She'd never laid atop anything so soft. Aurora could've lied on it all day, had it not been for her damp clothes and cold chains. She quickly scanned surroundings, realizing she was inside the carriage, as displayed by the scorpion insignia on the other side. Aurora peeked outside the door and felt immediate irritation upon meeting Polaris's eyes.

"You're finally awake! Rise and shine!" Polaris said with a smile.

Aurora tried to jump out of the carriage before falling face down into the gravel.

Polaris snickered. "Fool. You didn't think we'd allow you mobility, did you?"

Aurora's face burned from the impact with the ground. She squirmed to sit herself upward. "You're the fool if you think these chains will hold me."

Aurora's aura fueled her body as she tried to break through the chains with all her strength. The cold chain links pulled on her skin more than anything else. The half-witch squirmed and struggled, earning more laughs from the princess than anything else. The princess applauded the comical display.

"I must say, Solaria, you're up there with some of our best jesters back home!"

Aurora gawked at the princess. "Did you just compare me to a clown?"

"Sister, there's nothing to compare! You're one and the same! After all, only a clown would try to break chains forged with dragon scales. After all, they are the hardest natural substance on the planet. Outside of your head, of course."

Aurora stopped squirming and buried her face in the ground again.

Reiya lifted her and put her back on the carriage's seat. As he did, Aurora saw a familiar look in his eye, though she couldn't pinpoint where it was from.

"Miss Solaria. I'm curious as to how a single being like yourself has so many different magic affinities," Reiya stated, his voice level. "Using multiple elements should be impossible for mortals, let alone all of them."

Aurora wasn't a fan of his tone. He knew something she didn't. "Don't ask me like I know, creep."

"Don't pester her any further, Knight Reiya," Polaris commanded.

"But Princess, you inherited water magic from the Queen. It's not like she inherited her capabilities from your mother, father, or late aunts. Where could she have inherited these affinities?"

Polaris took a step back. It seemed the question caught her off-guard at first. "You forget that my grandmother was a goddess who ruled the entire planet. I think we can both agree she too was like no other."

Reiya stopped, and his eyes fell to the ground. "Of course. Excuse my foolishness, Princess Polaris."

Aurora rolled her eyes. She couldn't believe he bought that.

"Knight Reiya, what is taking those soldiers so long? It's already dusk. They should've taken those officers home and bought their silence by now."

"Probably taking their time," Reiya said, looking straight ahead, expressionless. "I can go check to see what's delaying them. It could be a currency transfer issue. I'll return shortly."

"Excellent."

Reiya returned to the outer city forests, leaving Aurora and Polaris alone.

Aurora didn't even want to look at Polaris's face. She frowned and stared away into the corner of the construction site. The two wyverns were parked there, humming gently to one another.

"For whatever could that glum face be for, Solaria? You're going to have a home and a real family finally. You'll no longer be hunted. You should be more excited!"

Aurora huffed in response.

"Oh, come now," Polaris said, leaning against one of her hips. The silent treatment is such a childish tactic."

"Piss off," Aurora muttered. "There, happy?"

Polaris shook her head. "Such a foul mouth. Sol—"

"Stop. Stop calling me Solaria. It's Aurora! Aurora Salem. Use it."

"Salem? That was the Amethyst Witch's surname, was it not?"

Aurora again said nothing.

Polaris shook her head. "You'll need a much better attitude when we get home. Mother will not be a fan."

"I. Do. Not. Care."

"You will once you two meet," Polaris squealed. "It's so exciting!"

"Would you cut it? You act like I want to meet your stupid royal family, live in your stupid castle, and learn your stupid customs. Well, guess what, *Polaris*, I don't! As I said before, I'll only ever come to that place to kick the queen's ass once I'm strong enough to do so. I don't want to play house with her or you. So cut the shit, and leave me the fuck alone. 'Cuz the first chance I get, I'm leaving and returning to what I do best."

Polaris folded her arms. "So, you're insistent on living the life of a wanted criminal?"

"I'm not a criminal, I'm a warrior. Fighting is how I train and survive."

"Warrior? Oh, come now, you're no warrior. Warriors have vision, ambition, and honor. What you have is simply greed based on what I've heard thus far."

Aurora fumed. Polaris sounded just like Ria. "Oh yeah? And what about you, you–you–puppet!"

"Pardon?"

"I know you're only here 'cuz the queen couldn't bother to come after me herself! You're just running an errand for her. I bet you didn't even know I existed before she told you to come get me."

For once, Polaris was speechless, her mouth hanging open.

"Bet you lived the perfect little life, huh?" Aurora continued, on a roll now. "Got everything you wanted from your mommy, so long as you did what you were told. You're just a pawn, Polaris. What are you without Gorgon in your name anyway?"

Aurora felt a splash of water hit her mouth before freezing her lips shut.

"Enough! Not another word of this insolent drivel!" Polaris's face was as red as Aurora's hair. The princess pointed a droplet of water at her. It looked like she was holding Aurora at gunpoint.

Aurora was taken aback. The princess was nearly in tears.

"I'll have you know that I'm doing my due diligence as the next heir to the Gorgon throne. My birthright! Coming after you is just a step towards my legacy as queen! You're in no position to question my worth."

Polaris snapped her fingers, and the ice around Aurora's mouth melted.

Aurora sucked on her numb lips in an attempt to warm them back up. "Whatever. Even if you're queen, your legend will pale in comparison to mine."

Polaris took a deep breath and wiped her eyes. "Ha. You talk as if I hadn't already bested you in combat."

"You got lucky," Aurora said with a shrug. "I've been fightin' all day, so my aura reserves were low. Catch me at full strength, and I'll bury you."

Polaris scoffed. "A brawler like yourself doesn't have the necessary training to defeat me."

Aurora was going to retort, but then she remembered something Reiya had said. Now was the best time to ask something she had wondered about herself for years. "How did I get these powers?"

"Pardon?"

"That lion dude had a point. Blair always told me that having all these affinities meant I was special. But you don't have them. I may not have gone to school, but even I know Echidna didn't pass all her godly powers to any of her children."

Polaris frowned and looked away from Aurora. Yet, Aurora remained persistent.

"Magic is a heredity thing, right? You're insistent we're related. Is our..." Aurora nearly gagged from the implication of admitting they might be sisters. "Is our father some super being or something? Does he have the same magic I do? And does he have . . ."

She shuddered, unable to even speak about *that other power.*

"We needn't discuss *that man* at all." Polaris bit down on her thumb to the point that it looked like she was choking on the answer. "To tell you the truth, Solaria, I wanted to save this until we were together with Mother."

Aurora narrowed her eyes. "Save what?"

"Well—"

"Princess Polaris!"

Aurora and Polaris turned to see Reiya running toward them, panting and hunched over.

"Knight Reiya? Where are the others?"

Reiya shivered, his eyes bulging as if he'd seen a ghost. "They were attacked, Princess. We underestimated the people of this land!"

"Excuse me? You mustn't be serious! At their rank?"

"Princess, use the Nevma Shards. You have to save them. We cannot allow the queen to learn of injuries to our soldiers in enemy territory! It will surely provoke war!"

Polaris matched Reiya's ghastly expression. "Right!"

She darted into the carriage, and then she returned with a small blue pouch that seemed to be filled with luminous pink crystal shards.

"I'll see to their injuries. Knight Reiya, you stay here and keep an eye on Solaria. And please get in touch with Rook Lazuli with the crystal ball."

"Right away, Princess," Reiya said with a salute.

Reiya pointed Polaris in the direction of the incident, then she took off.

Aurora watched as Reiya walked towards the carriage, no longer losing breath like he had been before. Her suspicions were confirmed.

"She's a gullible one, huh?"

"Oh, whatever could you mean, Miss Solaria?"

"Drop the act, jungle breath. I know you lied. I've been fighting these cops for years. There is no way in hell they even sniff Militia-level. There are very few witches and sorcerers among the police here in Westtown, and they don't include any of those three."

Reiya paid Aurora's comment no mind. He snatched purple crystal ball from inside the carriage and shattered it.

"Is your militia made up of traitors? Are you a United Military spy or something?" Aurora asked.

"Silence, freak."

Aurora wanted to drop-kick him. Reiya rummaged through Polaris's belongings in the carriage until he found the binder. Seeing it up close, she could finally read the label: *Project Solaria*. Aurora's blood froze.

"Let's see if it's true."

With a flourish, Reiya tried to open the binder. As soon as he made the move, he was immediately electrocuted. He crumpled and writhed on the ground. His hair puffed up high, and steam emitted from his body.

Aurora couldn't keep herself from laughing. "Serves you right!"

"Damn thing has an electric-based curse on it!" Reiya huffed when he finally found stillness again.

He opened it again, though a tad more gingerly this time. It didn't matter. He was met with the same fate, only more intense. Aurora's laughter intensified too.

Reiya slowly pushed himself off the ground, static sparking around his body. Aurora felt bad for him for half a second, but the feeling faded.

"The damn Queen must've put this on. I bet only Gorgons could open it."

Aurora stopped laughing. Now, that was interesting. "I can open it for you."

He stared at her blankly. "What was that?"

"I can open it. But only if you let me free."

Reiya continued his blank stare momentarily and then laughed in her face.

Aurora was not about to be deterred. "Whatever is in there has to be important, right? I don't know your reason, and honestly, I don't care. You could overthrow the Queen herself, it doesn't matter to me. I've no ties to these people. I just want my freedom. So I think this arrangement would work out well for the two of us."

Reiya squinted at her. "How can I be sure you won't flee when I set you free?"

"I'm a woman of my word," she said with a nonchalant shrug. "Like I said, I don't care about the Gorgons. After all, looks like you went through a lot of work to get Polaris away from this binder or whatever. You want all that to go to waste?"

Reiya stroked his chin in consideration, but Aurora knew she had him. There was no way he'd refuse at this point.

He reached into his pocket and pulled out a keyring. One of the colored keys shared the same green tint as her shackles. He unlocked the locks that bonded them together and set Aurora free. She immediately hopped to her feet and raised her hands into the sky.

"Oh, Omni! It feels good to be free!" She let out an exaggerated sigh, just for show.

Reiya's hand hovered over the hilt of his sword. "Our deal, Solaria."

She looked at him with a mock pout on her face. "I wouldn't call me a Solaria again if I were you. Unless you want this binder turned to ash."

Reiya straightened his back, a defeated look on his face. Aurora grinned. She loved the power she had over him. "This must be how the prissy bitch feels. Maybe bein' a royal wouldn't be so bad."

Aurora picked up the binder and opened it with ease. If it was true that the electric curse only shocked non-Gorgons, then Polaris was right. Any doubt of her being a Gorgon evaporated.

She tried not to dwell on the confirmation too much. Whose blood she had wouldn't matter soon enough anyway. She spread the contents of the binder out before her. She hardly took the time to read the headings of the pages. She left the components there in front of him and stepped back. "Have fun, lion man. I'm outta here."

"Your assistance is much appreciated, *Aurora*." He bowed with a smile.

"That's more like it." She blew a whistle into her fingers, calling for her broom.

Once she was far enough away not to worry about pursuit anymore, Aurora twirled through the sky, cackling joyously. She hadn't had a day like this one in quite a while. With her gaining the attention of the Demi-Gods, she figured things could get much more exciting going forward. Who would've thought?

Yet, even as she flew fast and celebrated loudly, she couldn't help but wonder more about her past. What was in that binder? What was Polaris going to tell her? This all had to do with her affinities, but did it matter as much as they were acting like it did? Was this just some elaborate control tactic to get her to question herself?

Aurora shook her head to silence the questions. She just had to focus on getting stronger and getting on top. Besides, her price would rise if word got out that she was a Gorgon. Honestly, this could turn out for the better in the grand scheme of things.

A pain-filled screech interrupted her daydreams of grandeur. She looked west toward the direction of the scream. That sounded like some-one she'd just come to know. Polaris.

Aurora tried her best to ignore it, continuing her flight in the oppo-site direction. It just wasn't her business anyway. If anything, whatever was happening to Polaris was probably her own fault. She was prissy, stuck-up, and Aurora didn't care if she lived or died.

Screams echoed again, this time louder and mixed with cries. Auro-ra's fingers twitched on her broom. Polaris's strife lingered in her mind. *Why?* She'd just met the girl, and she tried to kidnap her. Polaris had considerable combat prowess, as much as it pained Aurora to admit it, so she should be fine in whatever situation she got herself into. Aurora had no stake in the girl's life. She should just let it go.

Aurora turned around anyway. Maybe Polaris was in a battle with a stronger opponent. At the very least, Aurora could get a satisfying win after defeating them. *Yeah. A good fight. Who would turn that down?* She kept that mindset as she flew toward Polaris's screaming.

She flew closer to the forest outside the city as the sound of screaming grew louder and louder. A foul stench filled her nose, intensifying the more she descended. Aurora shivered, knowing that smell all too well—fresh blood.

She also noted the traces of destruction once she landed: raised ground, ruptured trees, crumbled stones.

"Earth Magic?" Aurora mumbled to herself. It sure did look like an earthquake.

It sure did sound like she was getting close. She hopped off her broom and began to slide quietly through the bushes. She didn't have to travel far on foot before she reached her destination.

Her face drained of color upon witnessing the scene. All four of the militia and two of the Westtown cops laid in pools of their own blood. Aurora figured one of the officers escaped, but that knowledge did little to soothe her horror. Almost none of the bodies were recognizable, decorated in deep wounds and their uniforms shredded. If there was a fight, it seemed pretty one-sided with the evidence of earth magic left behind. Craters, small rock formations, and tears in the ground decorated the area as much as the blood did.

Polaris was on her knees, hovering over one of the bodies. She had her hands on his chest and bright pink water twirled swiftly over him.

"Come on, please!" she cried out, her voice cracking. "Corporal Xior, wake up! That's an order, soldier!"

The scene brought back several familiar memories. She felt nauseous, and her heart ran a mile a minute. She turned around and blew chunks into the bushes behind her.

When she turned back around, she did her best to gather herself. She wiped off her face and then stood. Polaris was so distressed that she didn't even notice her. Aurora approached Polaris and put her hand on the princess's shoulder. Polaris ignored it and kept using her water magic.

"Don't die," Polaris whispered to the body. "Please, don't die."

"Polaris, stop. He's gone."

"I can save him! I can save all of them! I must! It can't happen again. Not again. Not again!"

"Polaris!" Aurora yelled. "They're *dead!* Give it a rest!"

Polaris's water dispersed. Her hands were dyed entirely with blood and shook uncontrollably. The princess slowly turned toward Aurora, finally registering her presence. She immediately went for her sword.

"S-Solaria?"

"Still Aurora."

Polaris released her grip on her hilt, turning back toward the bodies. "It's awful. They were all—"

She burst into another round of tears. Despite herself, Aurora's heart started to ache.

"Relax!" she said, trying to act as though she had some realm of wisdom on how to handle witnessing such horror. "It's . . . okay. Don't freak out."

"It's not okay! Do you know what will happen when Mother finds out the men who accompanied me on my mission perished without my knowing? No, no she mustn't find out, I won't–"

Polaris immediately reached for her neck.

Aurora grabbed Polaris's shoulders before the girl could spiral more. "Crying won't do anything right now! It won't bring them back. Trust me."

Polaris stared blankly into the distance, so Aurora checked out the corpses. She noticed that all the bodies wore deep claw marks as well as long horizontal lacerations as if they had been mauled by a beast or maimed with a weapon.

"They went down in a fight. Looks like with a sword." Aurora gritted her teeth. Only one man could have been responsible. The same one she'd just let into a top-secret document. "This is bad. Really bad."

"I'm not irresponsible," she mumbled to herself, still not even looking at Aurora. "I swear it . . . I swear, Mother."

Aurora raised an eyebrow at Polaris's incessant shivering and mumbling. She could tell Polaris was more afraid of her mother finding out than anything else. That dynamic she hadn't been honest about, not that it mattered now.

"Polaris, we gotta return to your camp," Aurora said. "We can come back and give them proper burials later."

Aurora helped Polaris to her feet, even though the girl resisted. Polaris turned towards her. "Hold on . . . how are you freed?"

"Can't you deduce it for yourself? Ugh, never mind! We have to go, now!" Aurora blew a whistle into her fingers and summoned her broom. She hopped on and extended her hand. Polaris didn't make any motion to begin their departure, and Aurora felt frustration bubbling once again. "Come on, let's go!"

Polaris hesitated once more. "Why are you . . . helping me? I tried to kidnap and freeze you—"

"We don't have time for this, Polaris! We can chit-chat later! Besides, part of this may be my fault."

4

The Crimson Witch

Aurora and Polaris flew back to the construction site through the starry night sky. When Polaris calmed down and stopped muttering, Aurora caught her up with everything that had happened between her and Reiya.

"You did *what*?" Polaris shouted. "How could you do something so foolish?"

"What did you expect?" Aurora said. "I told you I'd do whatever it took to escape! Not my fault your military is so unstable."

Polaris squeezed Aurora's shoulders tightly while riding behind her. Aurora turned back to her. "Yo? You OK?"

"Reiya was a fine Knight of the Magic Militia. One of the best soldiers stationed in the Pearl Kingdom. To think he'd go rogue is . . . unfathomable," Polaris mumbled. Her anger seemed to have faded into her familiar fear once more.

"I'm surprised this kind of thing doesn't happen more often. Especially with tensions between the Allied Nations and the Magic Nations. Always in and out of war, fighting over dumb rocks. But who cares? We'll just kick his ass next time we—"

"No! You don't understand. Why do you think a curse-enchantment was placed on those documents?"

Aurora remained silent.

"Did you ever stop to think about that?" Polaris pushed against her shoulders again.

"You're blaming me again? If whatever that's in there is so important, why bring it way out here anyway?"

Polaris paused, completely distraught. "No one would have seen the contents had you not opened it!"

"You *kidnapped* me!"

"You should've known it was important!" Polaris yelled. "It was made more than clear to you that the contents were for family only."

She's still not telling me something. "Ugh! Okay, whatever. I'm sorry for wanting freedom. We'll settle this after we take down the cowardly lion, alright?"

Polaris didn't respond in words, but Aurora took her silence as an affirmation that this was indeed the plan.

Soon enough, the witches hovered over the site, brightly lit from the street and work lights all around. Once they descended to take a better look, Polaris let out a bloodcurdling scream that nearly knocked Aurora off her broom.

The six wyverns all lay lifeless on the ground with perfect, clean slits in their necks. Their blue-colored blood seeped out slowly, forming puddles on the ground around them. Her royal carriage was crushed by some of the steel beams from the unfinished building. Polaris felt herself grow misty-eyed once more, and the pit of guilt in Aurora's stomach grew. She had seen a lot of blood, but this was a bit much, even for her.

"It's a nightmare." Polaris fell to her knees. "My men are gone. The documents are stolen. I have no means of getting back home. I'm stranded here with you and—"

"Would you get up and stop crying!" Aurora couldn't stand it. How could someone face this much carnage and start feeling sorry for themselves? "Don't you want to find that traitor and turn him into ice cubes?"

Polaris seemed not to hear her at all. Aurora just shook her head and scanned the area for Reiya. She called for him, wishing for the lion to show his face. The wyvern blood was fresh. He couldn't have gotten far.

Polaris wiped her tears and rose to her feet, sniffling. "Solaria . . . why do you insist on going after him? I dare say, now is as good a time as any to flee from me."

"Those people are dead, Polaris. Partly because of me. If what you said is true, who knows what will happen? I still don't want to go back with you. But I'll clean my mess before leaving."

Polaris did her best to regain her composure, but she was a bit shocked at that. "Well . . . fine, then we should search this city area. We may find him if we get movin'—"

A loud bang rattled their ears, and suddenly, all the lights in the city block shut off. Aurora and Polaris were submerged in total darkness.

"Perhaps a transformer exploded?" Polaris muttered.

"He set a damn trap, and we fell right into it." Aurora assumed her fighting position as a smile crept onto her face. "This should be fun."

Polaris pressed her back against Aurora's as she drew her sword. "We should remain close and fight him together. Even in the dark, our numbers strengthen our chances."

Despite her strong words, Aurora felt Polaris's trembling from her back. She could almost feel her heartbeat from how hard the princess breathed. Aurora wished Polaris could see the irritated scowl on her face.

"Fuck that. You just chill. I can corral him myself," Aurora declared. "Wouldn't want your nightmare to get any worse."

"Excuse you?" The trembling stopped. "Neither of us will fare well if we split! Solaria, this isn't your run-of-the-mill bandit. He's a seasoned soldier!"

Faint growling echoed around them, the sound bouncing off the desolate street. Aurora turned toward the direction of the sound. "Exactly. So stay out of my way."

Before Polaris could say anything more, Aurora drew her witch-blade and sprung toward the sound source. She swung her witch-blade violently but struck nothing but air. She tried again—the same result.

Her frustration grew. "Come out, Reiya! Don't be afraid now!"

His bellow filled the void, and she could hear the pleasure in it. "Be careful what you wish for, Solaria Gorgon."

Polaris whispered angrily. "Solaria, you simpleton! You threw away our only advantage!"

Though Polaris was reaching out, trying to locate Aurora's hand, Aurora paid her no mind. The sounds of loose gravel crunching from running crawled into Aurora's ears.

"Where are you?" Aurora asked the void, growing restless.

There was a loud *yip* from Polaris, along with the tearing of fabric. The clashing of metal rang through the silence, and sparks danced in the darkness. Aurora created her witch-blade and sprinted toward the light. Polaris screeched again, louder this time, and Aurora halted.

"Polaris!" Aurora yelled.

Aurora swung at nothing but air again. Her nose hair curled up from the aroma of fresh blood.

"Polaris, I can't see you. Say something!"

"Something," the ominous voice bellowed.

Aurora yanked her head around. She swung her blade behind her frantically but again was met with nothing. Then, she felt a blade cut into her ankle and slice her thigh.

The pain was immediate. She buckled to the ground, feeling her warm blood seep down her legs. After a moment, her wounds slowly healed.

"Coward! Fighting us while we're blind!" Aurora yelled.

"Blind? But the dark works fine for me! One of my many perks as a beastman," Reiya said, sounding nearby. "Of course, you have many perks too, Solaria. Not everyone can regenerate without the aid of nevma shards."

"Stop calling me that and fight me like a man!"

Reiya's fist eclipsed her vision just moments before crushing her nose. She fell to the ground, grabbing at her burning, aching face. She felt a familiar yet unpleasant feeling of her body heating and her muscles tensing. Her necklace's crescent charm flickered with purple light. *No! Not now, please not now!*

The ground beneath her began to shift once more. Gravel engulfed Aurora's hands and feet before spreading apart as if the ground were moving on its own. She faced upward in a star position. Her tattoo glowed a dim green light. Chills ran down her spine the moment Reiya came into view, and she was filled with the most ominous feeling of déjà vu. A sadistic grin stretched across his blood-splattered face.

"I must thank you," Reiya clapped his hands slowly, mocking her. "You've truly made my job easy, Solaria. I thought I'd have to sniff you out through this entire city, but you've returned to me all by yourself. Excellent work."

Aurora tried her hardest to break through the gravel that restricted her hands and feet, but to no avail.

"I believe you've suffered in the dark enough."

Reiya reached into his pocket and pulled out a shiny orange crystal. He tossed it toward the dead beasts and the steel structure. After it dinged off a steel beam, the entire ground burst into flames, illuminating the entire area. The flames engulfed the destroyed carriage and the drag-on corpses. It was hellish. It was like nothing she'd ever seen before.

Aurora frantically looked around before easily spotting Polaris on the ground. Her white gloves, clasped over her stomach, were covered with more and more red by the second.

"Polaris? Polaris! Wake up!"

Reiya shook his head solemnly. "She's not dead. But she's going to be down for a while." He wiped his sword out and dried the bloody blade with a handkerchief. "Good riddance too. Taking orders from her for the past two years was a pain in the ass. Though worth it for my prize, I must say."

"All this for some stupid documents? Hurting your princess? You're sick, Reiya!"

"The documents aren't my prize, Solaria. It's you."

"Wha—"

Reiya drove his sword deep into Aurora's chest. Blood spewed from her mouth.

Aurora's chest burned more than it ever had before, yet it wasn't coming from the wound. Her tattoo shined bright. "What are y-you—?"

"Aww, she didn't tell you?" His pursed his lips, as if feigning pity. "The whole reason she—no—we came out here wasn't just to bring Euryale's long-lost daughter home. You're precious cargo of the Pearl Kingdom. Or, at the very least, you are a vessel for its property."

Aurora's eyebrows furrowed. A vessel for what? She didn't want to stick around to find out. She tried to break free again, using all her strength to press against her confines. The only thing this motion did was spew more blood from the wound. Reiya drove the sword deeper into her, prompting more pain-induced wailing.

"Best I just show you what I'm talking about."

Before she could refuse, he yanked out his sword. Aurora bled for a moment before the wound sealed itself. Just when the pain began to subside and Aurora caught her breath, Reiya cut a slit down Aurora's sternum. He dug his beastly claws into the incision and pulled parted her flesh. Aurora screamed bloody murder as she watched his hand reach deep inside her chest.

She felt as though she was in the process of exploding. Her tattoo continued to shine, and the indescribable pain continued spreading throughout her entire body. The further he stuck his hand down her sternum, the more Aurora's muscles contracted. She felt as if her heart was being yanked back and forth. As if all her organs were pulling against each other. As if her flesh was tearing itself apart from the inside. Her eyes nearly rolled into the back of her head. She knew she had to stop him.

Her fingers had little movement underneath the crushing gravel, but she felt flame particles spark.

"No, you don't!" Reiya closed his free hand.

The gravel over Aurora's hands tightened until her fingers snapped and shattered. She screamed louder, though her throat didn't feel like it was producing sound anymore. Never had she been in so much pain. Aurora just wished she could pass out. For some reason, her body wouldn't let her.

Then, out of nowhere, she stopped screaming. An odd pulse was coming from inside her body, a surge of energy. Reiya had grabbed something within her, and his smile indicated that. It felt as if a bone was being pulled out of Aurora, though her bones had never been something she'd been able to feel before.

"Got it."

Reiya pulled his hand upward, nearly pulling Aurora's body up too. He struggled to pry something out of Aurora's chest. As he was more and more successful, Aurora saw the curved surface of what appeared to be some spherical crystal being pulled from her chest. The spherical emerald illuminated them both in green light.

The sphere emitted green sparks and scorched Reiya's palm at the touch. Steam rose from his fingers. He grunted, but his eyes bulged in awe. "How magnificent! It's potent power isn't just fallacy. It truly is a jewel of infinite magic!"

Screaming took its toll on Aurora's throat, so much so that she had to force the words out and bear the discomfort. "Infinite . . . magic?"

"Yes. That wench Euryale has some balls for a woman! Leave it to a Demi-God to put a Divine Sorcerer's Stone inside her child."

Did he just. . . No. A Divine Stone was inside me? One of the stones Blair tried to steal?

"It's still hard to believe such a stone is inside you. What a waste of power. Even with it, you stood no chance against me. Hell, you couldn't even defeat the brat! You're pathetic, absolutely pathetic!" Reiya reached for his sword and aimed the blade at the flesh that connected the stone to Aurora's body. "Either way, the boss is gonna love this."

A rushing stream of water grazed the top of his shoulder, the pressure and speed great enough to cut him. He tumbled over Aurora and dropped the stone. It quickly snapped back into her body like a magnet, and as soon as it did, her chest wound closed. The sphere sank back into its spot inside her. The otherworldly pain subsided. The witch remained still on the cold, hard ground, struggling to catch her breath while covered in sweat as well as her blood.

She looked up to see Polaris barely standing and holding her stomach. Her right hand had pink water levitating over her stomach before it dropped. Any signs of a wound were gone. The princess then dusted herself off and drew her sword.

"Reiya, do note that, after this severe punishment, you will be court-martialed! Your treason will result in execution," Polaris panted.

The princess wore a furious yet confident face, but Aurora could still see the shivers in her hands and knees.

Reiya jumped back to his feet and snarled. "Those nevma shards won't heal a severed head!"

Polaris aimed her sword at him. "Betraying a royal, no, a Gorgon, is one mistake too many. It will be your last."

Reiya howled with laughter. "You're one to talk! Don't act like you haven't betrayed anyone before."

For a moment, Polaris's eyes glossed over, and her mouth fell slightly open. Fury took over that solemn expression with a quickness. Water gathered in a sphere at the tip of her sword, but only enough to grow to the size of a marble. Her face loosened. "What?"

The air around them had become hazy, filled with so much smoke that Aurora began to cough. The surrounding flames were the clear culprit. The fire's strength made it hard for Polaris to pull moisture from the air. The moment Reiya noticed it, he attacked.

He punched the ground, and two thick earth walls sprang up and sandwiched Polaris in between them. He dashed toward the trapped princess with his sword. "You should've kept playing dead, Princess!"

"Polaris, get out of there!" Aurora screamed from where she remained trapped.

Polaris squeezed through the rocky walls just before Reiya could stab her. She rushed him with her sword and the two clashed blades. Reiya swung ferociously, parrying each of Polaris's strikes and nearly knocking the sword out of her hand. She jumped back toward Aurora to keep her distance.

"Polaris, free me!" Aurora asked.

Polaris panted. She reached for Aurora but was tackled by Reiya in the process and forced to drop her sword. He pinned her to the ground and dug his claws into her arms.

"Never take your eye off the enemy. Didn't your mother ever teach you that? Or was she too busy?" His fangs grew, and his mane grew frizzy.

Polaris grunted in pain, maintaining an icy glare. "Just as the fire aids you, it aids me!"

Aurora watched as small water droplets rose from the skin on Polaris's face. *Is she . . . she is! She's using her own sweat!*

The small water beads condensed into ice shards and shot right into Reiya's face. The beastman howled and stumbled backward, releasing Polaris just enough for her to escape. The ice shards looked like needles poking out of his face and his right eye. Polaris hopped to her feet and grabbed her sword. Then, she charged and pierced Reiya's ribcage with her sword whilst his defenses were down.

Aurora's eyes nearly popped out of her head. *Oh my Omni . . . she did it.* The gravel around Aurora's hands and ankles loosened. She was freed, but her body still wouldn't move. She had no strength left in her.

Reiya staggered, his blood dripping down the end of Polaris's sword. "You little shit."

"Reiya, didn't anyone ever teach you not to let your eyes off your opponent? Funny how things work out, is it not?" Polaris scowled at the beastman as she drove her blade deeper into him, making him grunt in pain. "I do admit, I'm not fond of this side of me. But even you must know that every Gorgon has a hint of bloodlust in them. You can consider your execution early."

Reiya snickered before bursting into a bloody cackle. "You take pride in being a Gorgon like I take pride in being a beastman. Even you know this isn't the peak of my strength."

Polaris's conniving, sadistic expression vanished. She swiftly yanked her sword out of him, and in that split second, Reiya belted her with a right hook. She flew up into the air and then collided into the dirt.

"Damn," Polaris cursed to herself before dusting off and running towards him.

Reiya punched the ground again, and the earth beneath Polaris wrapped around her legs and torso, keeping her in place. He placed his sword back in its sheath. His aura twirled wide around him. His muscles grew, and his mane grew frizzy once again, turning from brown to a wild orange. Deep brown fur grew on his arms and face, and he sprouted whiskers. The bulge of his pectorals, shoulders, and biceps tore through his militia uniform.

He was a nine-foot-tall, hulking lion man. The wound on his ribcage steadily bled until he pulled a pink crystal shard from his pocket and pressed it into his open wound. With a twinkle of pink light, the wound closed. Polaris shook her head slowly as if trying to assure herself that what she saw was fictional.

"Where's that bloodlust now, Gorgon?" his raspy voice deepened even more.

He dashed toward Polaris like he had been shot out of a cannon and slammed his giant arm through the rock formation that held her captive. He tossed her around like a rag doll, slamming her through the ground with every impact. She couldn't defend or attack. Aurora tried her best to move but couldn't find the strength. Polaris was turned into a bloody mess. After toying with her, he held her up by her skull, dangling her limp body in front of him.

"Why the face, Princess? Sad you'll never become queen?" Reiya asked with a beastly smile.

Polaris couldn't respond. She could hardly open her eyes.

"Don't worry. You'll live. Not for exceptionally long, but *I* won't be the one claiming your life today."

She noticed something on his fur as he approached Aurora, covering his abs and pecs. It appeared to be a tattoo. She squinted, trying to make it out amidst the flame-lights. Once Reiya was more clearly in the light, she registered it. It was the same snake tattoo she'd seen on Shoto's chest six years prior. Heat surged within her blood.

"Hold it!"

Reiya turned towards her.

"Do you know who Shoto is?"

The beastmen curled a brow, puzzled. "Shoto? How in Tartarus do you know Shoto?"

"You have the same tattoo he had! Shoto tried to hunt Blair. You're affiliated with each other, aren't you?"

He rubbed his chin in mock speculation, then smirked. "You were close with the Amethyst Witch. Of course, now it makes sense! It was you who laid them all to waste! It's hard to believe the poor bastard fell to someone as weak as you."

Polaris reached for his hand, barely able to raise her own, but Reiya tossed her aside like a bloody towel before she could move any further.

"You stay there and don't move. My partner will handle you when she gets here," he said.

Reiya then approached Aurora and stood over her. "To think a little lab rat like yourself killed a former member of the Shinobi Corps ..." Reiya pressed his foot into Aurora's cheek. "Shoto must've been even weaker than we gave him credit for. Him killing the Amethyst Witch may have been pure luck."

He rubbed his foot into her face as if she were dirt, wearing her skin against the rough bottom of his boot.

"He didn't kill Blair." Aurora could feel her body temperature spike at the thought.

"He didn't? Then who the hell did—wait. You? It was you? You're pulling my leg!" Reiya hunched over in laughter. "That's sad! A sorry excuse for a witch like you killed Shoto *and* Amethyst? I knew that crystal wielder was just an overrated slouch."

"Sh-shut up. Don't talk about her like that!"

"Why the hell not? What's a powerless, pathetic, weak *bastard* like you going to do about it?"

"I'm not weak! I'll make you *suffer.*" Her necklace went berserk, shining to the point of blindness.

Reiya shielded his eyes but then kicked Aurora in her face. Not seeing all that well didn't stop his overt dominance of this ordeal. "You Gorgon descendants are like little puppies. All that yapping with a weak pinch of a bite."

Reiya pulled Aurora through the gravel and to her feet. Her fingers remained broken. Her body felt wobbly. She could barely see straight.

"Come on. Make me suffer."

Five . . . four . . . three . . . two . . . one. Please. Please not now. "I don't want to kill you," Aurora muttered as her necklace's light darkened.

"First, you threaten me, and now you assume you can kill me whenever?"

Before she could raise her bloody, broken hand, he rocked her with a right hook. He treated her the same way he did Polaris, beating her down to the point of not being able to fight back. Polaris looked away, hearing the echoes of his fist smacking Aurora's face.

Once bored, he drew his sword and impaled Aurora again. He reached into her chest for the stone. "It's time I collect my prize and get back."

Aurora's head and body ached in a frenzy. Her blood felt like lava. The harder she fought to calm her nerves, the more her body thirsted for blood. She couldn't find the strength to hold it off anymore. Her control had vanished entirely, lost in the sea of pain.

She blacked out.

"Dead already? Figures."

Reiya grabbed the stone in her chest and began to pull as he had before, but a powerful shockwave zapped through him. He stumbled back and dropped her. A sudden cold overtook his face.

Aurora raised her head. Her once-green eyes were now a radiant scarlet. Her sclerae darkened from white to pitch black. Her teeth extended into sharp fangs, and her nails sharpened to claws, all black. Her biceps and thighs tensed. Her wounds vanished, and her fingers snapped back into their places. The ground beneath her shook, and a red aura swirled violently around her. She locked eyes with Reiya, barring her fangs like a feral beast.

In a blink, she lodged her fist into Reiya's face. He tumbled through the dirt and lay on the ground, writhing in agony as he grabbed his freshly broken nose. For the first time in this fight, the color drained from his face.

"What the hell is going on here? This wasn't in the schematic!" Reiya whimpered as he got back up. "She's–she's a **demon**?"

Aurora slowly marched toward Reiya, now shaking in his boots just looking at her. His eyes bulged, and the once roaring lion trembled like a wet kitten. Aurora clenched her fists as her aura illuminated the construction site in crimson light.

Polaris watched from afar, her eyes round and her bottom lip quivering. "Mother . . . you truly meant it when you said you infused her with demon blood. The air, it's bloodlust. It feels almost like the Furasakus'. No . . . it's denser than that. Colder."

Reiya quaked in the presence of the crimson aura. His eyebrows furrowed, and he jumped back. "So, this is where you get the title, Crimson Witch? It's no wonder you're able to regenerate on your own. Doesn't matter, though. Demon aura or not, you'll still fall here!"

He slammed his fist into the ground, and the flat surface split and rose on both sides, forming miniature plateaus. Aurora leaped over the change in terrain without any care before charging forward. Reiya slammed his fist down again, and the rising features split from the ground again, creating small tremors and craters. When Aurora was high in the air over him, he slammed his hands together. Pieces of the earth flew out of the ground and converged on Aurora, crushing her into a giant cluster of rocks and earth.

Reiya had just a moment to laugh at his accomplishment. Almost instantly, the cluster burst like a balloon in an explosion of dense red aura. Aurora emerged, falling from the miniature earth sphere along with raining debris. She drop-kicked Reiya on the way down, cracking his skull in a simple motion. Then, she attacked again, moving like a blur, and striking him with immense force. Her punches shattered his ribs with just two strikes. He hunched over and gasped for air. Aurora proceeded to drag her claws through him like a wild animal. She snarled and grunted ravenously the entire time, while Reiya howled.

"Stop! I give! You're not weak, I surrender!"

Aurora hesitated at the admittance, staring into his eyes which blended tears and blood.

"I promise, I'll leave you and your sister alone! I'll never harm you again, just please, let me g—"

Aurora rammed her clawed hand through Reiya's chest in one motion. Once his body fell limp, she yanked her arm out and tossed his body to the ground as if it were nothing to her. Reiya's wound oozing blood made the corners of Aurora's mouth curl upward. Her pitch-black, razor-sharp fangs felt satisfying against her bottom lip.

Reiya coughed as his dark blood oozed from his mouth. "Those eyes. That devilish smile. You look just like *her*."

Bright flames crackled in the palms of both Aurora's hands.

"This victory of yours . . . you'd better enjoy it . . . before the rest of the Vipers strike." His eyes lost their glisten, and the snake tattoo on his chest disappeared.

Her flames flickered from orange to blue, and she aimed her hand down, ready to decimate his corpse and anything else still in her sight.

"Solaria! Stop!" Polaris called out.

Aurora locked her sights on Polaris. She zipped to her in a flash and snatched Polaris by the neck, choking her. Polaris fought to break Aurora's grip but made no headway.

"Solaria . . . please," Polaris choked the words out.

Aurora cocked her hand back, prepping to ram her claws through yet another chest.

Suddenly, Aurora's grip loosened as she stared at Polaris's blood-stained face. Blair's face flashed through Aurora's mind, bringing her consciousness forward for just a brief moment. Her necklace's charm again shined, the intense purple light illuminating the burning construction site.

Aurora's demon aura dissipated, and her sharp claws and fangs dulled. She released the princess. Polaris's desperate gasps for air faded from her ears, and Aurora's vision darkened. She collapsed to the ground once again, all power draining from her.

5

Project Solaria

A urora awoke in a cold sweat to the softness of a fleece blanket and a stiff futon beneath her. Her entire body was sore, though none of her soreness compared to her ringing head. The bright lights and the soft noise of a playing television above her weren't helping.

"Ugh . . . what the hell—" her blood chilled before she could complete her thought. Aurora knew full and well what waking up in a random place and feeling physically drained meant. She swung up her hands before sighing in relief. *Clean. Good.*

Aurora scanned her surroundings: a television playing the evening news in the upper right-hand corner of the room framed photos hanging on the walls around her. She also spotted a round glass table in the center of the room, plastic chairs surrounding it. She realized exactly where she was: Ria's living room, a part of her small apartment in the back of her shop.

Aurora wanted to gripe about being back there, but her mind fixated on Polaris and her fate. The last thing she remembered was Reiya impaling her. Yet, albeit a bit fuzzy, she recalled Polaris crying, begging for her life and covered in blood. Her head pulsated while trying to piece things together.

The door under the corner TV swung open with a sharp creak, making her flinch.

"You're awake." Polaris stood in the doorway, putting Aurora's rampant heart at ease.

The princess, much to Aurora's surprise, was out of her royal garments and instead in shorts and a baggy blue T-shirt. She was also covered in bandages, from her face to her arms. The sight of those bandages connected too perfectly with the one thing Aurora could recall of the previous battle. It all but confirmed Aurora's fear on what happened. What she did. Her eye-lids lowered along with her head.

"The witch that owns this shop arrived moments after you lost consciousness. She flew us right over on her broom and agreed to keep us—or rather you–hidden from law enforcement," Polaris explained.

Aurora didn't want to give Ria credit or thank her for what she'd done. She didn't want to address the situation at all.

"Wearing that doesn't suit you. You almost look local," she shot at Polaris.

Polaris gave her a small smile. "It's not my taste, I assure you. But look at you. Even after all that, you're spotless. Not a scratch."

Aurora chuckled a bit but straightened her face immediately. "Where's Reiya?"

Polaris averted her gaze. Aurora knew that look all too well.

"He's . . . well he's—"

"Dead." Ria entered from behind Polaris. "And you know exactly how he died."

Aurora gripped the collar of her tattered shirt. Everything came back to her in droves. Images of their intense battle and Reiya's final plea flooded her mind, along with Polaris's cry. The half-witch leaned forward, burying her face as she let out a tearful sob. Aurora had claimed yet another soul, all against her will. She grew weary of this accursed, involuntary transformation.

"I did it again! When will this end!?" Aurora screamed into her wet palms.

Ria folded her arms. "Kid, we talked about this earlier. So long as you run around seekin' smoke, you'll always leave behind ashes. This girl may not be here if I didn't see the light from the fire from halfway across the city. And who knows what would've happened if the police arrived before I did."

Aurora wiped her face and sniffled. "Shut up. I don't need your shit right now."

"Oh no, I don't wanna hear that! If this life of yours doesn't change, who knows how many more people will die? Ya should drop this stupid run to the top while you ahead and live a normal li—"

"I said **shut up!**"

Aurora's necklace started glowing again, and Ria's brows drew together. Aurora took a few deep breaths and counted backward from five. She had to settle, or she would do something else she regretted.

"Lady Salem," Polaris interrupted. "With all due respect, Solaria cannot live a normal life, not after learning her heritage, and after Reiya learned her secret. Dead or not, if others were to find out she's connected to our family, she could endanger you as well. 'Tis true, her nefarious actions can do that on her own. But if the world found out she was a Gorgon, then she wouldn't just draw her enemies, but also enemies of the Pearl Kingdom."

A cord snapped in Aurora as she recalled something else from earlier. She looked back up to Polaris with furrowed brows. "I'm really sorry if I hurt you in my demon state. I've no control over it and I don't . . . ya know?"

Polaris sighed but smiled. "It's quite all right, Solaria. I should've recognized the aura-binding enchantment on your necklace."

Aurora stared down at her crescent charm.

"It wouldn't be the first time this happened," Ria said.

Aurora cut her eyes to Ria.

Ria paid no mind to Aurora's frustration. "That form of hers has a blood trail, startin' seven years ago with my niece. Blair even kept the kid's transformation a secret from us. She'd open her mouth soona' and she'd still be kickin—"

"Don't blame Blair!" Aurora shouted.

"I ain't."

Aurora's eyes flared with fury, but Ria wasn't swayed. Aurora found herself counting backward again, this time from ten.

"I got that Salem's necklace enchanted to suppress her demon aura. If that crimson aura gets too rampant, some will leak through, and shit will get nasty. But it at least keeps her from bein' a fiend all the time," Ria finished.

Aurora's gaze dropped to her lap as her face burned. Polaris's eyes shot her way.

"Lady Salem, again, with all due respect, you did adopt Solaria despite her demonic power. Must you be so harsh on her? I'm certain it's as hard on her as it is on you, given her transformation is involuntary," Polaris said, her voice calm and diplomatic.

Aurora's head sprung up in shock.

Ria whipped out a cigarette. "I didn't adopt her. Blair found her. If she's ya sister, it makes sense. She found the child at a research base in a Pearl Kingdom colony twelve years ago, after she fought that damn Euryale herself."

Hearing the queen's name triggered a vital memory.

"Polaris . . . I'm sorry for what I'm about to do."

"Pardon?"

Aurora approached the princess and fed her a vicious punch. Polaris collapsed in a heap. Ria quickly snatched Aurora by the arm and held her back before she could swing on her again. Polaris squealed, rubbing her reddened nose and teary eyes.

"How many times are you going to ruin my face, you unholy wretch!" Polaris cried.

"How long were you gonna wait to tell me what was inside me, huh?"

Polaris stumbled back to her feet. "Come again?"

"You knew from the beginning I had a Divine Sorcerer's Stone inside me, didn't you!?"

"A Divine *what*?" Ria screamed.

"Solaria, keep it down," Polaris whispered.

"I don't care! I don't care if everyone hears!" she cried out. "If that's why you were after me, you should've said that first! You lied to my face!"

"I did no such thing!"

"You did! You said Euryale wanted me there! That *you* wanted me there! That this was a family affair or whatever lies you told me. Instead, you just need me because I have a magic nuke in my chest! Isn't that right, *sister*?"

Aurora's eyes flashed red, and Polaris jumped back at the sight of it. After noticing her necklace glowing, Aurora yielded. "Reiya called me an experiment."

Polaris hesitated but nodded.

A broken smile formed on Aurora's face. At least she was getting something out of the girl. "The stone at least explains why my chest hurts whenever I use magic. I know exhausting your aura with magic can make your body sore and drain your stamina, but I'd never heard of anyone's magic causing themselves pain like mine." Aurora sighed. "But since you came all this way, at least you won't have to return empty-handed."

Aurora dug her nails in center of her chest, groaning in pain as she broke skin. Blood coated her fingertips.

"Girl, what are you doing?" Ria yelled, her expression fearful.

"Back off, Ria!" Aurora snapped. "It's my stone, my decision!"

She struggled to claw through the inside of her chest and reach between her ribs to find the Divine Stone inside. She eventually discovered its burning hot surface. Touching it sent surges and spasms throughout her entire body, causing her to fall to the ground. Her entire body went into the same frenzy of pain as before, forcing her to scream.

She cried out. "I don't want to stay a freak!"

"Solaria, stop! If you rip that out, you could perish!" Polaris yelled.

She stopped and glanced back up at Polaris, a pained expression etched on her face.

"The Divine Stones are very delicate and immensely powerful. Removing one could very well destroy you or drain your aura completely. We have no idea what could happen. Don't be rash."

Aurora gritted her teeth and pulled her hand out of her chest. Despite the immense pain, her wounds healed within moments. Once she could breathe again, Aurora pushed herself back up to her feet with bloody hands.

Polaris stroked her hair and put on a nervous smile. "Why don't we discuss it over a cup of tea? After you wash up, of course."

After Aurora showered and changed, she joined Polaris and Ria back in the living room. The three of them sat at the table, the old television playing in the high corner of the room. Ria never seemed to turn that thing off. She always needed her background noise. Aurora could hardly think as it was, but she had no desire to argue with Ria about this. She had other fights to win.

Aurora and Polaris were each given steaming cups of tea. Aurora had no interest in the beverage and just stared down into the cup, seeing the reflection of her bloody-faced, demon self looking back at her. Polaris on the other hand sipped away, her pinky slightly raised.

"Oh, dear me," she said, with a beaming grin. "For a commoner, you sure know how to prepare tea!"

Ria looked like she would bust a vein trying to hold her smile. "Why, thank you, 'Your Heinous.'"

"You mean 'Highness?'"

Ria acted as though she hadn't heard a thing.

Aurora finally ended her staring contest with her demonic reflection and set her sights on Polaris. "Well. You gonna explain, Prissy? About this stone shit?"

Polaris seemed far too into her tea to be bothered with such conversations. Aurora found herself surprised that the princess even looked up at all.

"Hm? Oh, yes sorry." She finally put her cup down.

Aurora and Ria exchanged glances and then set their sights on the girl.

"As I said earlier," Polaris started, "I wanted to save this conversation for us to have with Mother. She knows more about the Divine Stones and the nature of your experimentation than I do. She thus could provide a better explanation of your abilities. But alas, the circumstances are..."

Polaris searched for a word but gave up within seconds. Aurora nervously sipped at her tea. Learning so many new things about herself was almost as taxing as any dragged-out fight she'd been in. At this point, she wouldn't be surprised if Polaris told her she was an alien or from a different dimension.

"You are the eldest daughter of Queen Euryale Gorgon, and shortly after your birth, you were used as a vessel for an experiment. Your body houses the Divine Sorcerer's Stone of Elements, which is, as you now know, the source of your elemental magic. Mother claims she wanted a bioweapon in the event of a potential Fourth Great War with the Allied Nations. She believed, with her Demi-God genes, you'd be an ideal vessel for an otherwise unstable power source. Most mortals and even Demi-Gods are overwhelmed by exposure to any Divine Sorcerer's Stone. However, Mother hypothesized that housing such a jewel would be possible if a living being were to recover from potential injuries passively."

Aurora gritted her teeth. "Demon blood." The puzzle pieces fit perfectly in her mind.

"You're sharper than you look." Polaris smiled. "Yes, the innate regenerative abilities of demons were vital for this experiment's success. She went all the way to the Gates of Tartarus in Colona to obtain the blood of a very powerful pure demon. Infusing it with your own was risky but clearly worked out in the end. However, Mother ensured your demonic blood remained a secret, in the event. . .incidents ever occurred. She even went as far as to keep the details of your demon blood out of the schematics and documents kept for the experiment. If others started to practice what Mother did and succeeded with the other Divine Stones, we could see a war that could lead to the extinction of all races as we know them."

Aurora stared at the table, silent, trying to process the many bombshells Polaris had dropped on her. "I . . . I see." It was near-impossible to wrap her head around all this at once, but she stumbled into the questions she could articulate. "If I'm so valuable, why is she trying to find me after all this time? Why not earlier?"

"I wondered that myself, believe me." Polaris took another sip of her tea. "I threw quite a fit over it, in fact. As you know, most major nations, under both the Magic and Allied Powers, house one of the Divine Stones. However, there could be more we don't know about just floating around. Mother was the one who discovered the Elemental Stone and tested its immense offensive power. She wanted to keep it to herself. However, after she tangoed with a certain witch, you went missing."

Aurora's heart sank. "Blair."

"I'm assuming she gambled that the Amethyst Witch wouldn't discover the stone you possessed. Even when I asked, Mother wouldn't explain much about their encounter. Personally, it comes across as an unnecessary risk. However, once we heard she was dead and you became infamous, we couldn't risk you falling into the hands of the United Military, or people like Reiya. We'd be in quite the pickle if that happened." Polaris sipped on her tea again, this time sighing in delight. "My, that tea is almost as good as Lady Matilda's! May I ask what's in it, Lady Salem?"

"It's store-bought," Ria said plainly.

Polaris marveled at the cup. "Fascinating."

Aurora squeezed her fist. "So that's it, huh? Now that your superweapon has gone viral, you wanna bury the evidence."

"Solaria . . ." Polaris sighed, putting down her empty cup as gently and precisely as she could. "It's more complicated than that. I cannot speak on Mother's future intentions regarding you and your powers. She wouldn't even tell me that much. She just told me she wanted you back home and alive. I trust her judgment."

"This is about trust to you? Tsk, Blair always said the Demi-Gods liked to stack their power. This whole situation sounds no different!" Aurora slammed her fist on the table, and the cups rattled. "If Blair knew that a stone was in me, she wouldn't have considered stealing one! We could've even beaten Shoto handily! She would still be here and none of this . . ."

"Shoto?" Polaris asked, interrupting Aurora's descent into emotion.

Ria glanced up at the TV, as she always tended to do when nervous. Yet, this time, her eyes stuck. "Hold it. Y'all may want to listen to this."

She grabbed the remote and turned up the broadcast. It showed the construction site where they'd just been, mostly burned down, the carcasses of the dragons blurred out. The reporter stood in front of the scene, clearly rattled.

"Sources report that two unidentified Westtown Officers were found dead near this area. The police are labeling this a magic-related homicide. The terrain shows evidence of the illegal use of magic in combat. Sources are suspicious that the infamous Crimson Witch may be responsible but have no evidence pointing to this at the moment. Officials have tried to contact the Magic Nations regarding the five deceased Magic Militia but have gotten no response. There are no signs of others being involved in this scene, but we will update you as we gain more information. Back to you, Tom."

Polaris's eyes widened, her face losing color. "With the Militia involved, the news is surely to go global! If Mother finds out from anyone other than me, then– then–Wait . . . five? There were six militia, including Reiya. Surely, they miscounted."

"Wait!" Aurora stood from her seat abruptly, her mind spinning. "Ria, that Reiya guy had a snake tattoo on his body, the same one Shoto had."

"Snake tattoo? And that dragon boy from back then had one too?" Ria asked.

"The same exact one! I can remember much other than the tattoo but . . ." Aurora's mind went fuzzy. Reiya had mentioned something right before he died. What was it? "When . . . the Vipers . . . strike?"

Ria's face paled. "Vipers?"

"That's what Reiya said."

"Oh, Omni, I need anotha' cigarette," she said as she rubbed her head. "We're dealin' with *them*."

Polaris had been sitting stock still, taking in the intensity of this information. Now, she leaned forward against the table. "Hold on, you know who those people are, Lady Salem?"

"I didn't think they were legit," Ria said, shaking her head in disbelief. "There's been a bunch of rumors about some underground crime syndicate that goes around killin' and blowin' shit up, callin' themselves the Vipers. Come to think of it, the rumors started about seven years ago . . . around the same time—"

"Same time Blair died," Aurora said.

Ria rubbed her numbing head. "Great. Those heathens better not come lookin' for me while trynna find you."

Even though she knew Ria was only looking out for her safety, Aurora would be lying if she said hearing that didn't sting. That aside, If these 'Vipers' were real, there would probably be more people like Reiya and Shoto. More people who were as strong could come after her. On one hand, her stock and overall bounty could rise from fighting those thugs off. On the other, the chances of her entering a demonic state, and then waking up to corpses, would increase as well. With the Divine Stone inside her, this situation created one stressful migraine for the young half-witch. Fighting had been pretty simple just a day ago. Now, so many elements were at play that seemed completely out of her control.

That was until she remembered something crucial.

"Polaris, was Euryale able to use the Divine Stone? You know, to test its power?"

"I can only presume. How else could Mother determine the stone's function?"

"So, she knows how to use it?"

Polaris furrowed her brow. "What are you getting at?"

Aurora smiled, then stood up and extended her hand towards her sister. "Polaris, let's go to the Pearl Kingdom!"

Polaris was taken aback. "You literally fought me in order to resist going home."

Aurora did take a fair amount of pleasure in seeing Polaris's confusion about the whole situation. "That was before I knew all this! Think about it. Who else could teach me how to control the stone's power besides the one who put it inside me? There's literally no one else who can. Plus, we can wax these Viper dudes after. They'll be coming after me anyway."

Polaris squinted. Aurora could feel Polaris seeing straight through her smile.

"How do I know you won't use it against us as soon as you get the chance?" Polaris asked.

"You ran that risk when you pulled up! Besides, do you want to go home empty-handed? I can always fly away while you're asleep, and you'll never find me without your militia and those dragons."

Polaris immediately looked sick at the way this conversation was turning. "You are incredibly unpleasant. Did you inherit that from the Amethyst Witch?"

"Maybe."

Ria blew out a dense puff of smoke, and Aurora was surprised to see a slight smile on her face. "Goin' to the Pearl Kingdom to live with royals? Sounds too good for ya."

Aurora glared at the elderly witch.

Ria stood before Aurora could start some dialogue on the topic. "Make sure ya both gone by mornin'. Holding enemy royals and street thugs is bad for business."

With that, she left the room through the back door. Aurora huffed and downed her hot tea, which was not the best idea.

"She seems . . . pleasant," Polaris said.

Aurora coughed after downing the hot tea. Without a second thought, she tossed her mug against the wall and shattered it completely. "She's a bitch."

"I . . . understand that." Polaris cleared her throat. "All the same, we should leave first thing in the morning. I'll contact Mother first thing to send transportation. I would contact her now, but these hours are quite unprofessional."

"The sooner the better." Aurora popped up and marched back to her futon, not even sparing another glance for Polaris. "I'm heading to bed. Night, Princess."

With that, Aurora threw the blanket over her head.

"Hold on. Where shall I slumber? Where's my bed? Solaria? Stop!"

That night, the normally peaceful forests outside of Westtown roared with gunfire. A hoard of police officers ran through the woods, firing their guns wildly in an attempt to shoot an elusive target. Bullets pierced through tree trunks and whistled through leaves on bushes and canopies. The grass rustled with a blur of wind that zipped around the officers.

"How is she moving like that?" one of the officers cried out.

"Keep firing! The U.M. should be here soon and—" His head sprouted into the air and then spewed blood down onto the rest of the squad.

Not a single police officer could lay eyes on the fiend that zipped around them like a horrible twirling wind. Even with their pistols in hand, they were helpless. Limbs flew. Uniforms were torn. Throats were slit. The leafy greens of the forest were drenched with a deep scarlet that then dripped down the trees and leaves like the aftermath of summer rain.

Eventually, only one officer remained: a young man, covered in the warm blood of his fallen comrades. He slowly backpedaled with a tremendous tremble.

"Sh-sh-sh-show y-yo-yours-s-self! N-n-n-now!" His teeth chattered.

He felt a sharp prick on his back, and he screeched. He swiftly turned around and fired. Nothing was on the receiving end outside of bushes and trees.

"Boo," a voice crept into his ear.

He rapidly swung his arm around again, and a piercing *slash* tore through the air. His pistol-wielding arm fell to the ground before he could even feel the pain of the impact, and blood began to seep from his shoulder. He fell back.

There, before him, was a sight that made him quake in terror: a young woman in a pitch-black trench coat with long, black hair, skin as pale as snow, and irises pink like cherry blossoms. She leveled a bloody, black katana at his nose.

The girl shook her head the moment they made eye contact with one another. "No one had to die today. Your whole squad should've been better about minding their own damn business," she said, boasting fangs sharp enough to pierce steel.

The radio on his chest went off. *"Private, what's your 10-20?"*

"Don't," she threatened.

He trembled, staring at her, drenched in sweat. He reached for his radio. "I've got a 3–"

Without even a breath's worth of time, she thrust her sword through the center of his head. His blood dripped from the blade, down his face, a crimson river. She yanked it out and watched his body drown in a growing pool.

"They could've at least sent a witch or sorcerer. Much more fun to fight when I get something out of it." She grasped the silver pentagram pendant hanging from her beaded necklace before closing her eyes and bowing. She began to pray. "Lord Fraizen, I, your humble servant, ask you to grant these poor lost souls salvation in the afterlife. I am forever grateful to be the one to have ended the path you chose for them. May you show everlasting mercy. Amen."

She marched through the forest filled with police corpses, stepping over butchered, bloody bodies as she moved. Within moments, she reached a tree where Reiya's corpse was propped up. His fur had lost its brown shine, and a gaping hole in his chest was surrounded by dried blood. His body was brutally ripped up and bruised. She squinted with disgust.

"All that boasting of being a Magic Militia spy, and this is where it got you? You couldn't even bring me the Gorgon like I asked."

The girl pulled a small syringe from inside her trench coat and pierced his hide with a needle. After siphoning some of his blood, she placed the syringe in the inner pocket of her jacket.

"Least your blood will mean more than that of those humans."

The girl felt a buzzing in her pocket and pulled out a black crystal ball with a roll of her eyes. "Answer."

She saw a man who had the face and height of a young boy, but she knew he was well into his thirties. He had spiky white hair, scarlet eyes, and sharp teeth. A snake tattoo stretched across his nose. A sight she knew all too well, unfortunately. "Fangs! You picked up this time! Never been so glad to see that pale face."

She rolled her eyes. She felt the burning passion to kill again. "Hatake, for the last time, it's Serena."

"Fangs, we can see you're in Verona now. Any answers as to how curiosity killed our favorite cat?"

Still using our crystal balls to track us? Typical. Serena's eyebrows furrowed. "He was with the Gorgon. What else could've killed him?" Her lip curled with disgust.

Hatake poked out his lip. "Oh well, that's no good!"

"I doubt they learned much about us. If they did interrogate him and he squealed, the curse would've triggered."

"Really? Oh goody! The boss is going to love that!" he cheered.

"Yeah. Goody." Serena cringed at his attitude.

"Well, go ahead and clean up the little mess Reiya made. You still have those two major assassinations of those electees tonight in Eden. You can manage that, yes sweetie?"

"I just took out an entire precinct, and I would rather not be both-ered with more human fodder. Can't I handle that later? I'd rather focus on finding—"

Serena stopped, caught in his disturbing glare. His crimson eyes glowed on the other end of her crystal ball.

"This is a direct mission from the boss. You don't want to disappoint her, do you?" Hatake warned.

"Of course not. I'll handle it, right away."

"Good girl! Keep up the good work, my little orphan! Make the boss proud." Hatake winked.

The transmission ended. Serena nearly cracked the ball from how hard she squeezed it. She took a deep breath and put her ball back in her pocket.

Serena drew four black crystals from her pockets, but right before she chucked them at the forest ground, she saw a folded piece of paper sticking out of Reiya's own. She pulled it out and unfolded several doc-uments. She flipped through them and skimmed their contents. They were schematics with an toddler's body and a crystal on it, symbols littered throughout. The vampire squinted, unable to decipher any of the text aside from the top, which read "Project Solaria." *That name sounds familiar. Didn't he refer to that Crimson Witch girl by that name in his last report?*

She flipped over one of the documents, and her breath zapped out of her mouth. Reiya left a message on the back that read: "Crimson Witch is Euryale's daughter. Has a Divine Sorcerer's Stone inside of her."

She giggled at first before completely exploding with laughter. "That son of a bitch! That's why he was so adamant! If that's what this all means, then . . . then!" The girl couldn't stop grinning. She could practically dance. *A stone with infinite magic will be more than enough to handle her! I'll be free!*

Serena swiftly folded all the documents and put them in her trench coat. She flew into the sky and chucked the black crystals down at Reiya's corpse. His body and the surrounding trees were engulfed in black flames. Slowly, everything around began to wither away to ash, including the bodies and other remnants of her battle. Serena grabbed her necklace and bowed her head in prayer again.

"Lord Fraizen, I thank you for once more providing a clear path for me. I, your humble servant, shall see it through. Reiya's death will not have been in vain. Amen."

Serena pulled down the sleeve on her right arm to reveal her snake tattoo.

"Soon, Cassie."

6

Departure

Aurora tossed and turned in her sleep, her dreams plagued by disturbing images. Blood glistened from her hands and claws. Glowing pools of red rose to her knees. Bodies floated around her atop that sea of blood. Aurora saw her demonic features in the reflection of the crimson pool, right before chained links began to sprout from it. The chains wrapped around her and yanked her downward. She squirmed, trying to wrestle her way free before the strong chains pulled her under. *Don't break free. Don't break free!*

Eventually, the chains snapped, and Aurora leaped out of the red pool.

She jumped awake in a cold sweat. She hated that she frequently had these nightmares in the middle of the night. But at the very least, it was better to wake up on a futon than behind a dumpster.

Aurora wandered around the dark living room, nearly tripping over a table leg. She wiped her eyes as she left through the backdoor, entering the hall in search of the bathroom. However, when she stepped foot in the hall, she heard chatter. Aurora spotted a very dim light piercing from a crack in a door at the end of the corridor, emanating from the same source as the voices. She followed both sources and quickly realized the door led to Ria's main shop. *Polaris and Ria.* Aurora peeked through the open crack and neither of them noticed her. *Perfect.*

Polaris sat on the opposite side of Ria's desk, her legs crossed. She wore a face of disgust, which Aurora didn't find too abnormal. In the short time she knew her, Polaris was generally displeased with one thing or another.

"You let her keep your family name, yet refused to house her for six years? How dare you call yourself a guardian!" Polaris hissed.

Aurora's eyes widened. Was Polaris defending her?

Ria slammed her fist on the desk. "I ain't her damn guardian! She and Blair got in all types of trouble. Stealin', destroying landmarks, starting riots. Hell, they even pulled a stunt trying to steal from President Icarus once. When my niece died, the girl grew even more outta control. I tried once to open my home, but she insisted on bein' a thug, so I insisted she live out there. I can't afford other thugs and the military walking into my shop just to get a crack at her. I'm too old for that shit. Not worth my safety to take care of her."

"You say that, yet you openly criticize her for her lifestyle. If So-laria's words were true, she was only eight at the time of Blair Salem's death. You want to convince me you couldn't nip that attitude out of an eight-year-old?"

"The same eight-year-old that took my niece's life?"

Aurora grabbed her arm in shame. Her gaze fell.

"I'm the one who found them, ya know. After the incident. I saw her tiny little claws covered in my niece's blood. Those burning red eyes. The butchered bodies. That's all I see when I look at the girl. All she does now is fight, and for what? Power?" Ria choked up. "My niece is gone, so she could continue seeking power. Fuckin' rich, ain't it?"

"Lady Salem, I know you grieve her loss. So does Solaria. Just differently, it seems. I cannot speak for her, but she likely saw your niece as a mother."

Ria squinted at Polaris. "Monsters don't grieve. They fight and consume. You saw it for yourself. I was fortunate enough to find the right enchantment at the black market to keep her from one day snappin' and killin' me too. I *knew* she was trouble before she ever flashed those red eyes." Ria's glare hardened. "That damn scorpion mark. The girl bein' one of you was obvious."

Polaris crossed her arms tightly. "I beg your pardon? One of me?"

"That's right. You Gorgons have been up to no good for thousands of years! All ya do is flaunt your power by committing genocides and startin' wars!"

"Nonsense! We may not be saints, but not all of us are devils."

"I watched your Aunt Medusa kill my sister and her husband during the war. They weren't even soldiers like I was! She just slaughtered bystanders for the fun of it, as she's done countless times before. Hell, the woman even killed her own before my time."

Polaris sighed and brushed her long, blue hair to the side. "We don't claim that woman as one of our own. After all, she's deceased for a reason."

"Yeah? Then how about the Alucard incident? That wasn't forever ago."

Polaris's lips pressed together. Now, she was the one looking away.

"Your mother had just as much of a thirst for blood as your sister. That passed down to the gal. I hope, for Aurora's sake, she doesn't become *too* much like Medusa. But even if ya didn't come, she may have been on that path anyway—"

"Enough!" Polaris was the one slamming her hands on the table this time. "I won't sit here and listen to you slander your own. Luckily, she'll be in our care for the foreseeable future. You can rest your fear of her, as well as your resentment. I hope you'll learn not to bear such petty grudges for such accidents, you decrepit buzzard."

Aurora retreated to the living room and jumped into the futon, before throwing her blanket over her head. She listened to Polaris, who similarly marched through the hall and slammed a door, likely the one that led to the sole guest room.

As heated as Aurora was, Ria was right. Ria loved Blair, as much as she disagreed with her lifestyle. Aurora took her away. She wished she could go back and stop herself from attacking Shoto without a plan. She wished she had been strong enough to fight on her own. Better yet, she wished she wasn't cursed with demon blood. Cold tears ran down her face at the thought of it. Blair's smile, laughs, corny jokes, eating together, bathing together, their days sparring, everything.

Ria had every right to hate her. Even so, Aurora owed it to Blair to get stronger now, no matter what. It's the last thing she had promised her, after all.

Morning rolled around, and Aurora paced back and forth across Ria's living room, stuck in thought. On her hundredth pass through the space, she spotted a particular framed photo amongst many on the living room wall.

She took the frame off the wall and examined the photo. A younger Ria in a United Military uniform stood, Blair's parents next to her, and Blair herself as a young pre-teen. Seeing the bright smiles on their faces was almost enough to bring one to Aurora's own. Aurora wasn't featured in any of the photos on the wall, but that didn't surprise her. The only person she considered family was gone; now, a new family had sprung into her life. Yet, seeing these photos, she was glad Blair had a chance to have a family.

She ran her hand through her vibrant red curls and contemplated everything that happened. First, she found out she was a part of the royal Gorgon family, and then she was an experiment with a sphere of infinite magic inside of her. All of this was delivered by her "sister" who first tried to kidnap her and ended the night defending her. To say it was mind-numbing would be an understatement. At the very least, training with a Demi-God to master infinite magic sounded helpful in the grand scheme of things. She could still become the world's strongest.

That thought brought a genuine smile to her face.

Aurora darted toward the backdoor and made a beeline to the bathroom. When she swung open the door, her heart stopped. She caught

Polaris changing, her shirt lifted barely past her neck. The blue-haired witch turned around and shrieked. As much as Aurora wanted to scream "sorry" repeatedly for just barging in without thinking, her eyes couldn't look away from the deep, dark, red scars stretching down Polaris's back. They looked like lashings or carvings, even worse than the one Blair had on her neck years prior. Aurora wondered if it was hard for Polaris to walk or stand without feeling those scars.

Polaris slammed the door in her face, yelling at her to learn how to knock.

Aurora sat on the couch and waited for Polaris to finish dressing. Once she was done, the princess emerged and caught Aurora by surprise. Aurora expected her to be in that same red royal combat dress or something close to it. Instead, she wore a light blue shirt with a long navy skirt. Her hair was undone from its braid, which allowed her long, straight blue hair to hang freely past her shoulders. She looked normal but didn't appear particularly thrilled about it.

"I'm grateful to Lady Salem for lending this outfit for me, but this just . . . feels wrong. I look like . . . you." Polaris shuddered with disgust as if she couldn't bear to say it. "How can you commoners dress like this daily?"

Aurora wanted to make fun of her discomfort but couldn't shake the image of Polaris's back. She frowned.

"What is it?" Polaris asked.

"How did that happen? Those scars?"

Polaris retreated. Aurora thought she was looking in a mirror, but she wasn't. They shared the same frown. The princess seemed troubled that this was even being asked of her.

"That's all from training," Polaris finally answered.

"Training?"

"Of course, combat training. I may be a Gorgon, but I wasn't just born with such flawless talent. It was rigorous, and there were roadblocks. But you saw the results firsthand, did you not?" She winked at her.

Aurora grumbled. She didn't buy a word of it but decided not to push on it right now. "Don't go acting all high and mighty, Princess. Your win was a fluke. I want a rematch. But before we can get to that, we're gonna turn those Viper thugs black and blue."

Polaris rolled her eyes. "There won't be any unnecessary combat. We're enough of a bind as it is. We will wait for a rescue party and depart this country posthaste. Now, where is your household's crystal ball so I can call for our forces?"

Aurora tilted her head. "Hm?"

"What's with the confusion? How else are we to contact the castle other than using a crystal ball?"

"A phone . . . like a normal person."

"What? Those annoying industrial devices? You use those in this city?"

"Don't they use them everywhere?"

Polaris placed her hand against the side of her head, absolutely exasperated. "Good Echidna . . . don't tell me. This section of Verona doesn't utilize crystal balls at all?"

"Not like we have a lot of magic wielders around here anyway," Aurora said with a shrug. "I'm surprised you guys still use those crystal balls. Kinda archaic if you ask me." She pointed over to the white telephone hanging on the wall. "Go ahead. Call your mommy."

Polaris fell to her knees and rustled her hair. "No, no, no! This will not do! Contacting anyone in the Magic Nations without a crystal ball is impossible! Surely there's a store that sells them around here?"

"If there were, I'd probably have stolen a few by now."

Polaris's wail tore through Aurora's eardrums. Did she have to have a meltdown every time something didn't go her way?

"Damn that traitorous Reiya! My life is now over thanks to him!" Polaris buried her face in her hands.

"You're just a big ball of optimism, aren't ya?"

"Oh, spare me! We may as well swim across the Atalanta at this rate."

Polaris mumbled repeatedly about what she was going to do, about how unfit she was to be a princess. Just hearing Polaris stress out irritated Aurora. But she had an idea.

"Oh! The black market."

"Pardon?" Polaris whimpered.

"If you want to get anything magical from a foreign land, you can go to the black market. That's where we all got our brooms, where Ria got my necklace. It's in Moro Town. I'm sure we can get a crystal ball there."

"You're . . . you're certain?"

"Duh. Also, it's close to Verona's shores, so we'd have to go that way anyway. I know how you love efficiency."

Polaris got off the ground and regained her composure. "Well then, freshen up! Quick!"

Aurora dressed hurriedly, sporting her favorite black t-shirt and capris that reach halfway down her thigh, with Blair's hoodie wrapped around her waist. She saw Polaris wearing her sleeved, silk gloves and her shimmering golden circlet, with a blue sapphire in the center. Her shirt also changed, sporting golden trimming around the armholes of her sleeveless shirt and collar. Polaris tightened the straps of her black backpack, which held her belongings and a map.

"You look like a magical girl," Aurora sneered.

Polaris scoffed. "And you resemble a punk, per usual."

Ria entered the room from the door to the main shop. The atmosphere changed immediately upon her arrival. Polaris grimaced at this, while Aurora averted her eyes. Ria started past the two of them but stopped.

"Good luck," she said.

Before she continued, Aurora turned to her. "I just want you to know, I am a thug."

Ria stopped again. Polaris's jaw dropped.

"I am. I'm a bandit, a thief, a fighter, and a warrior. I am the Crimson Witch . . . but I'm not a killer. I never intended to or intend to kill anyone or rule over anyone. I just want ya to know that. The next time you hear my name, I'll be famous, but not for those reasons."

Ria turned to her. Her eyes were baggy and dark, and if Aurora thought too hard about it, she would wonder if Ria actually cared about her. Rather than stick around for a moment of vulnerability like this, Ria walked off, not saying another word. Just as Aurora had originally expected.

Aurora and Polaris took to the skies on Aurora's broom. They ascended past the tall, blue skyscrapers and into the puffy, bright white clouds. Aurora cheered as she rocketed into the sky, the wind blowing through her face and hair. She then felt Polaris squeezing her waist tightly.

Aurora expected the princess to start complaining that she was going too fast, but her lips seemed sealed. In fact, Polaris was the most silent she'd been since they'd met.

Once they were high enough above the clouds, they coasted.

"Oh, by the way, Polaris," Aurora started.

Polaris shuddered. "Yes?"

"Thanks." She paused for a long moment. "Ya know, for defending me?"

"Pardon? I did no such thing."

Aurora laughed. "Sure." She took in a deep breath of the fresh, moist air. "Alright, an adventure!" Aurora squealed. "Pull out the map. You're gonna navigate."

Polaris tightened the straps of her backpack to her shoulders. She held the map out in front of Aurora to show where they were going, all while fighting against the wind. "We're going due west near the coast. Should land here." She pointed to the map, though Aurora could hardly see it.

"Awesome! Been a while since I've been to Moro Town. Should be fun!"

"Fun? We aren't going for a joyride, Solaria. We're going to pick up a crystal ball and call for a rescue team."

"No joyride? You must not know how I roll!"

Aurora leaned forward, pulling Polaris along with her.

"Solaria, what are you doing?" the princess panicked.

Aurora chuckled, and the broom took off like a jet. The wind blew against their faces and through their hair. Polaris dug her nails into Aurora and screamed for dear life, while Aurora cheered into the sky. Neither could even keep their eyes open, as Aurora guided them through loops and zigzags in the sky.

After the roller-coaster ride, Aurora slowed down to coast once more. She laughed at Polaris's clear frustration before the princess could find the words.

Polaris had nearly busted a vein. "Solaria, enough games! You need to start taking this seriously."

"Oh, quit crying. This is what adventure is about! After all, the flight there will be at least two hours."

"Oh. Splendid. Two hours in the air with you. I couldn't think of anything better," Polaris muttered.

"Me neither!"

As they jetted through the clouds again, Aurora noticed the world below. She hadn't been this high up since she and Blair had traveled to Eden. The cities and towns looked like miniature doll sets, with people barely visible. The forests were the same way, the trees like tiny plants. Even the birds didn't fly as high as they flew now. Aurora was filled with joy, free, and ready for an extraordinary journey. Polaris, however, was filled with terror the entire time.

After two hours of soaring through the sky, they landed atop a tiled roof. Aurora immediately stepped down and stretched, feeling refreshed despite the long ride. On the other hand, Polaris had wobbly knees and was a second away from losing her lunch, based on her pale face.

"I'm never getting on a broom with you again. That was horrid," Polaris muttered before covering her mouth.

"Shut up, you loved it. Anyway, we're here. Welcome to Moro Town!"

The town was a complete one-eighty from the metropolis of West-town. White village-style houses filled the town, and the tallest building stood in the center of town: a church with a bell tower. They also noticed a white marble statue of a woman with an owl on her shoulder, her hands clasped in prayer. This statue depicted one of the Allied Nation's founding Demi-Gods and the current ruler of Zerex, Minerva Athens.

After jumping from the roof and entering the streets, the sisters walked through the brick roads before quickly stumbling into an out-door market and seeing several vendors with vibrant tents and banners running up and down the street. The various merchants—some human, some beastmen—were all dressed the same as the common folk they sold to. A merchant was selling steaming pink salmon from Serrenie, another selling shimmering gold necklaces and jewels from Ptolemy. There was even one with silk dresses from the Pearl Kingdom, which Polaris ran to like a kid visiting a toy store.

"How. Absolutely. Marvelous!" Polaris beamed. "It's a cultural won-derland, unlike the other Allied Nation towns! How is it that I haven't learned of this place sooner? Ugh, I'm sure there are some great pastries from around the globe!"

Polaris saw Aurora smirking at her and decided to fix her posture and clear her throat. She tried adjusting her tone to look like she'd never been excited. "But we mustn't dawdle. We need to head to this black market immediately."

"We have all day. Relax. Moro Town is fun, so we can look around and—"

Aurora gasped. There was something before her so holy she couldn't find the words to say what she was feeling. A bubbly, oozy, smooth orange texture. The steam slowly rose from its surface. The bright scarlet hue shone from the top, where a white stick pierced its center. Aurora salivated.

"Solaria? Are you brain-dead? What's the matter?" Polaris asked.

"Caramel apples!"

Aurora bolted to the vendor, where several apples freshly dipped in hot caramel were displayed. The merchant wore a hearty smile behind his thick, silvery mustache. He was a round man with a green apron, which sported an embroidered apple patch on its center. A steaming pot of caramel sat behind him on a burner, beside a sack of shiny, smooth red apples.

The merchant gave her an inviting smile. "What can I get for you, miss?"

"How much for these godly treats?" Aurora asked, her excitement peaking.

"Twelve gold coins!" the merchant said.

Aurora reached into her pockets and felt emptiness. She remembered spending the last of her money repairing Blair's hoodie with Ria. She hung her head in disappointment and didn't respond to the man before slowly walking away.

She saw Polaris, her arms folded. "Enough of this. Point us in the direction of this black market."

Aurora's eyes darted back to the caramel apple stand. She could practically taste its sweet, juicy goodness! She had to have it. Aurora scanned the area, noticing the surplus of people walking around. Their lack of visible auras, beastly features, and the fact most of them had rounded ears told her they were human. Moro Town police officers stood on each corner, with their pistols and batons visible on their waists. She spotted at least six in the immediate vicinity.

Polaris snapped her fingers in Aurora's face. "Earth to Solaria! You're like a zombie today."

"Oh, uhh. Sorry! Can you give me a sec? We'll go, I promise! Just . . . gotta make a trip to the ladies' room."

Polaris rolled her eyes and gestured for her to go.

Aurora started walking in the opposite direction, still favoring the stands. She kept her eyes peeled as she slowed down before passing the caramel apple stand. When the merchant noticed her, Aurora aimed her finger and zapped him with electricity. Just a shock. Not enough to permanently harm an adult, whether they had magic or not. She fully expected him to pass out harmlessly without anyone noticing.

However, after taking the electrical charge, he fell backward like a domino and knocked the pot of molten caramel onto himself. He screamed so loudly at the burn, that Aurora was certain Ria could hear it from all the way in Westtown. Everyone's head turned, and all eyes were on her within an instant.

Shit. Aurora snagged a caramel apple on a stick and jetted, pulling Polaris along with her.

Screams rang out in every direction. Two nearby policemen blew their whistles and began to run after them on foot, calling out, *"Thief! Thief!"*

Aurora sprinted as fast as she could on the brick roads, weaving and shoving through crowds. She dragged Polaris along, but the princess quickly dropped her hand as they cut into narrow alleyways, jumping and knocking over crates and boxes. Polaris kept up under her own power, increasingly distressed and frustrated as the cops drew closer.

"Stop! Stop, or we'll–"

Aurora halted and turned around, to both the cops' and Polaris's surprise. She snickered, as though this whole interaction held no tension or concern.

"What on earth are you doing?" Polaris shouted.

Aurora aimed her hand at their pursuers, and they immediately halted. They aimed their guns and approached slowly.

"Get down on your knees!" one of them demanded.

Aurora closed her eyes and concentrated her aura. Rushing water spewed from her hand and stretched over the police's heads. They fired their pistols, but the thick wave of water stopped the bullets. Aurora closed her fists and the water wall froze solid, emitting a cold mist through the alleyway. A tall, thick, sharp ice structure now separated the two groups.

"A young witch? And with that hair?" one of them yelled.

"No mistake," said the other. "That's the Crimson Witch! We need backup!"

Aurora panted but snickered once more before taking a bite out of her candy apple. "Dinner and a show? Hell yeah."

Polaris yanked her hand from behind. They didn't have a lot of time. "Idiot! Let's go!"

7

The Black Market

After a goose chase that lasted about half an hour, the two rested in an alley behind a run-down shop, miles from the outdoor market. The darkened alley space reminded Aurora a lot of the alleys back in Westtown, but with fewer newspapers and trash and many more anti-Magic Nation flyers. Aurora and Polaris caught their breaths there, even though sirens still echoed in the distance.

"What. In. Tartarus. Was that for?" Polaris huffed through her question. "The idea was to leave without drawing attention. What in Echidna's great name is the matter with you?"

Aurora chuckled through her panting, wiping the sweat off her forehead with her forearm. "Stop whining. It was so much fun! Wish we could've fought those pigs though. Oh well."

"Oh well? *Oh well?*" Polaris's face brightened with a reddish tint, an expression Aurora knew quite well. "Solaria, attacking an innocent man just for a treat and wanting to combat the authorities for no reason doesn't warrant an o*h well!*"

"Would you lighten up? I didn't kill him. That much electricity couldn't kill a cockroach. He'll be—" Aurora stopped, her gaze finding the posters on the building wall behind Polaris. She spotted a particularly "wanted" flyer, the photo obscured by a much larger anti-Magic Nation poster that read *"Death to the Scorpion*!" She expected to see her name as her eyes glided down to the title and price but was disappointed to see instead, *"The Last Alucard*." Aurora disregarded Polaris's lecture entirely. She snatched the anti-magic propaganda poster off the wall and revealed the poster underneath: a teenage vampire with silky black hair and pink eyes. Aurora also punched the wall when she saw the price for her capture—100 million gold coins.

"What the—? She's no older than us and already more than double Blair's worth. Dammit! This is so unfair . . . "

Polaris fell silent as she gazed at the poster, her mouth slightly open.

"Uhm . . . Princess?" Aurora snapped in her face.

"Oh." Polaris adjusted the circlet on her head. "Sorry, I . . . what were we talking about?"

"This shit." Aurora snatched the poster off the wall, balled it up, and chucked it away. "I still got a long way to go if I want to beat those numbers. Maybe we should hit Eden and rob President Icarus's Lab."

Polaris pinched the space between her eyes in frustration. "That right there is precisely the problem. That nonsensical desire to commit crimes for the sake of status. You cannot do that anymore, remember?"

Aurora rolled her eyes. Of course, she was wanted by almost everyone in the universe at this point, but wasn't that part of the fun? She leaned against the brick wall and slid to sit on the ground. She picked her teeth with the stick left from her caramel apple.

"Princess, you need to relax," she said with a shrug. "You don't wanna ruin your perfect skin by stressing. We're allowed to have a little fun, yeah? The black market ain't goin' nowhere."

Polaris groaned, practically pulling out her hair at the thought. "No, we don't have time for fun or any of that childish nonsense. We were supposed to have you within our borders yesterday. Mother's probably up a wall by now!"

"Like a spider? I thought scorpions were her thing." Aurora tossed the stick away with another shrug.

"Enough! We aren't traveling for you to have your cheap thrills!" Polaris reached into her bookbag and found a rubber band. "Now, tie your hair back and put on that hooded jacket. We need to find this black market. Thanks to that stunt, it's better you aren't recognized."

Aurora glared at Polaris as if she were speaking another language.

"What's the matter?" Polaris asked.

"Why should I hide my face and hair? I'm glad to let the entire world know I'm here."

Polaris batted her eyes. "Solaria, this isn't just about you anymore! If you get discovered here, with me, in this nation, you could put my whole kingdom in danger. I have a duty to get you home. As much as you don't care about anyone but yourself, I've risked everything."

Aurora averted her eyes. She released a sigh. "I know, I know. We have to get to the Pearl Kingdom. But—" Aurora got in Polaris's face. "—I'm coming for my own reasons. Not to uphold your stupid customs or preserve your stupid kingdom. So, don't tell me what to do. That's the only way this is going to work."

Aurora felt the heat radiating from Polaris's reddening face. She squeezed the rubber band. "Insolent, foolish, petulant child! I've heard about enough. Either you lead me to the black market and drop these endangering shenanigans or—"

"Or what?" Aurora's blood started to rush.

"You remember our last physical encounter, do you not? I have no problem transporting frozen Gorgon property."

"Property? I'm not your property."

Polaris poked the center of Aurora's chest, just over Aurora's scorpion tattoo. "Are you certain of that? Don't forget what you are. Unless you wish for the incident with your so-called idol to be commonplace."

Aurora lunged at the princess and lodged her forearm into her neck, pinning her against the wall. Aurora's scarlet eyes, claws, and fangs were on full display.

"I'll snatch your tongue right out of your throat!" She clenched the soft fabric of Polaris's shirt. Her necklace glowed, and her mind flashed back to when she'd held Polaris by her neck the other night.

She had to stop this. She could feel it in her mind, even as her gut bid her to keep fighting. Still, she counted backward from five and released the princess.

Aurora regained her composure with a few deep breaths. Her stomach immediately tightened with regret.

"I'm sorry. I didn't mean to," Aurora mumbled.

Polaris straightened her shirt and dusted herself off. "Save it. I mean only to stress the importance of the situation. My task is to bring you home and it's overdue enough."

Aurora felt a sense of urgency, given the power she had to fight off to calm herself. Polaris was right, even if it made Aurora want to punch her even more. She snatched the rubber band from Polaris's hand and tied her hair into a bun. She then pulled her hood over her head to hide her scarlet curls and pulled the strings of her hoodie to tighten it.

"Don't lecture me," she said as she walked off. "Come on. Let's go."

Aurora led Polaris toward a less populated part of town, all while sneaking around the police posted at every corner. She heard them talking into their radios about her, along with the mysterious blue-haired girl she allegedly had as a hostage. The whole situation felt hilariously ironic.

Eventually, they reached a large manhole with a single, deep claw mark stretching across it.

"All right, it's down there," Aurora said.

Polaris stared at her, completely dumbfounded. "Pardon?"

Aurora lifted the manhole, ignoring Polaris's pale expression.

"Absolutely not," Polaris protested.

Aurora snatched Polaris by her wrist and pulled her in. Then, she closed the manhole behind her before the pair jumped down.

Sewage seeped through their shoes and socks. The stench burned their nose hairs, and tears budded in Polaris's eyes.

"Ew, ew, ew! This cannot be happening! I can feel it between my toes!" Polaris squealed, an evident cringe on her face.

"Oh, how awful," Aurora said in a mocking tone, complete with an eye roll. As much as she'd usually get a kick out of the prissy princess suffering in the sewage, she still couldn't get the bitter taste out of her mouth from their previous conversation. She'd ditch Polaris altogether if she didn't need her.

Polaris jumped up and froze the water before her with a huff. She landed atop the ice path and marched on it like a solid walkway. "Not ideal, but much more tolerable."

"You just gotta be a classy bitch, even in a sewer? Do you even have friends?"

Polaris hesitated, her original answer hanging on her tongue. "Of course, I have friends. Some were even commoners." She bit down on her thumb again.

Were? Aurora raised her eyebrow.

"What about you, Ms. Criminal? Do you have friends?"

"Ha! You think a girl like me has friends? I barely have an aunt, as you saw."

Polaris stopped. Even though it had been a pointed question, she was surprised by Aurora's transparency. "Hold on, no one?"

Aurora kept walking. "Blair was the only friend I needed. I don't need anyone else trying to slow me down anyway. So please, try to keep up."

Her face warmed and her throat closed. Aurora wasn't interested in having this conversation right now. She lit a flame in her hand as they walked through the dark sewer tunnels, surrounded by smudgy, rusting walls. A distinct blend of voices grew louder by the second. Eventually, they saw an orange light in the distance.

"We're just about there," Aurora announced.

The two entered through a tunnel and spotted the market below on a series of spacious metal platforms, sewage and water separating them like a river. The Black Market was exactly how Aurora remembered it, only bustling with many more people. The volume of attendees took Aurora by surprise since most people couldn't handle the foul stench. The patrons were mostly magic users, wearing either dirty rags or spiffy, sharp suits, nothing in between. Some were large and beastly, while some had clean, gelled hair. Orange and yellow lanterns lit up the market. Rather than having exotic food and materials from different nations, the stands and tents held mercenary blades, military rifles, wands, brooms, and various enchanted cloaks. The more Aurora looked around, the more amped she got.

Polaris was just the opposite, practically cringing. "This is it? Seems . . . appropriate."

"Come on!" Aurora happily leaped out of the tunnel opening and down to the metal platform. Polaris shook her head and jumped after her.

Aurora wandered around without aim, all of her interest in efficiency entirely lost. She was absolutely in awe of all the weapons and gear in the tents. Yet, despite her excitement, she also felt the wandering eyes of everyone on her and Polaris. The pair hardly blended in, regardless of being amongst such a diverse crowd. Polaris even pinched Aurora's sleeve out of nerves.

Aurora wasn't worried, though. She was used to seeing thugs and businessmen alike on the black market. Plus, she was itching for some real action anyway. She wouldn't be upset by any means if it came to her.

She stopped in her tracks after a few minutes, as something caught her eye: a salesman, showing off a tiny, sleeping humanoid creature with small horns, red skin, and a thin, wispy tail inside a tiny cage with luminous turquoise bars. Aurora's heart dropped when the creature opened its eyes, revealing scarlet hue and thin irises.

That's . . . a demon.

Aurora walked toward them without thinking.

"Solaria? Where are you going?" Polaris called out.

She didn't receive an answer. Crowds began to form around the tiny demon in the cage, Aurora among them. Most gatherers were either men in black suits or run-of-the-mill street teens in hoodies. The salesman looked like a circus ringmaster, sporting a black top hat, a blue bowtie and suit, and a monocle.

"Behold the fierce, the ferocious, the savage Imp Demon!" he announced. "Only a few sightings of these beasts happen every few years. This particular one was captured near the Gates of Tartarus!"

Polaris scoffed and folded her arms. "Preposterous. The Gates are in Colona, with natural conditions far too harsh for any commoner. Come, this man is a fraud. Let's go."

Polaris tried to tug Aurora away, but she wouldn't budge.

"No way," a young man commented in the crowd. "Imps are small, but not *that* small. There's no way you survived down there and got close enough to the gates to get one."

Aurora was entranced. The man had asked the same question Polaris had just raised. The salesmen snickered. "I'll be happy to let you know the Gates loosen every solstice, allowing these tiny devils to crawl through. But you wouldn't mind touching it if you think it's so fake."

The teen looked around, confused. "Touch it?"

"Why not, kid? It won't hurt you if it's fake, yeah? Come on up!"

Frigid air overtook Aurora. She watched the teen, no older than her, approach the cage of the tiny demon. Its eyes opened fully before meeting Aurora's. Goosebumps grew all over her. Something that felt like icy water slid down her back. She saw herself in that cage, with long, black fangs and razor-sharp claws, glistening with scarlet blood. Her heart sank, and her chest beat like a drum. In her mind, her demon self sprang up and swiped at the metal bars. The teen yipped and pulled his arm back. A thick red aura swirled around her as she gnawed on the bars and tried to claw at them. Its hands and mouth steamed on contact, forcing it to jump back and squeal.

Aurora felt sick. She didn't know what to think, or which pain to focus on.

The salesman slapped his knee in laughter. "Don't worry, kid! It can't hurt you! This cage is forged with anti-magic metal."

"Dude, that thing's a freak!" the teen panicked.

"This little freak can be yours with the starting bid of let's say . . . six thousand gold coins!"

Aurora heard whispering and chatter around her. People called it a freak, a heathen, scum of the earth, a monster. A dangerous monster that could kill everyone. Something that shouldn't exist. All of it was true, to an extent, but when they said those words, she felt they were calling her that. Her chest contracted. Her breathing picked up. Aurora was stuck in the cage and trying to claw her way out. Her head thumped harder and faster. *Don't break free. Don't break free. Don't break free!*

Polaris yanked her by the shoulder, and she snapped out of it. "Solaria, are you alive?"

Aurora glanced back to see the tiny demon behind the bars once more. She wasn't trapped. She wasn't in a cage. "Sorry. I . . . did you say something?"

Polaris shook her head. "I was explaining the Gates of Tartarus and the origins of the Furasaku demon clan to you. But you clearly weren't interested in the history lesson."

"N–not really. We should keep looking," Aurora said. She took a final look at her demonic counterpart and turned away for good.

Polaris shook her head. "Ugh. You're the worst."

The two walked through the market, fighting through the crowds. They didn't see a single crystal ball. At one point, they came across a vendor selling other variations of crystal shards. Polaris motioned toward it, stating she had to purchase some nevma shards. Aurora didn't pay her any mind. Her mind was still stuck on that demon.

Polaris approached the elderly merchant with a smile, but it wasn't returned. Instead, he offered a grimace and a glare.

"One pound of your finest nevma shards, please," Polaris said.

The merchant reached into a pile of magenta crystal shards and put them into a velvet pouch. "Nine hundred gold coins."

"For a single pound? That's absurd! They are less than a quarter of that value in the Magic Nations!"

"You're not in the Magic Nations, kid. You aren't going to find these anywhere else around here. So nine hundred. Take it or leave it."

Polaris fumed, but the man had a point. There was little chance they'd find a Magic Nation-produced product anywhere else in the Allied Nations.

Polaris pulled a small purse from her backpack and then pulled out nine rolls of gold coins. After the exchange, she reluctantly put the bag of nevma shards in her backpack.

Aurora shook her head when Polaris returned to her side. "You could've haggled him."

"As in talk him down to a lower price?" Polaris laughed in her face. "I don't have to resort to commoner tactics to get what I desire. If I wanted, I could purchase this entire market—" Polaris stopped, staring at the inside of her purse in pure bewilderment. "This cannot be real."

Aurora peeked in, spotting only three gold coins remaining. "Damn, for a princess, you're broke as shit."

Polaris hung her head as Aurora's face brightened into a snicker.

"How could I be so careless not to bring more funds? Wonderful. Just wonderful."

Aurora rubbed her chin, searching for an out. It didn't take long. A devilish grin grew on her face.

Polaris quickly recognized that smile. "No. No Solaria we aren't—"

"You're out of options, Princess. We're doing things my way now."

She scanned the area. There wasn't a single vendor dedicated to crystal balls. However, there was one with a random assortment of jewels, weapons, and—as if Omni himself blessed them—a sole sapphire crystal ball. Without another moment of hesitation, Aurora dragged Polaris there.

Shimmering necklaces made of pure gold, rubies, and sapphires dazzled the countertop. Several weapons were littered amongst them: photon firearms exclusive to the United Military, halberds with golden spears from Neo-Camelot, red-tinted long-swords from The Pearl Kingdom, and even harpoon guns from Atlantis. However, seeing the blue crystal ball sitting alone in the center was enough to distract Aurora from the hideous display. She couldn't contain her smile.

"Shut up and follow," Aurora whispered in Polaris's ear.

This merchant was slightly taller than the last, and much younger, probably in his twenties. He wore a sleeveless, black button-down shirt and boasted scruffy neon-green hair. Several piercings decorated his face and an anchor pendant hung from his neck. His scowl showed his shark-like teeth, and he reeked of seaweed. He'd be a tough cookie to crack for almost anyone except Aurora. She'd seen Blair succeed at this challenge more than enough times.

Aurora leaned on the counter and boasted a sly grin. "Hello there, mister . . . uh . . ." She hesitated at the lack of a name tag.

"Vakari," he replied.

"Vakari! Is this the only crystal ball you have?"

"Ain't it the only one ya see, chump? Seventy thousand gold coins."

Aurora patted her own pockets. "Oh. Ugh. You see, man, we're just broke students. From Westtown High. We don't have that kind of cash." She poked out her lip. "But . . . we can make an exchange."

"High school students, huh?" Vakari raised an eyebrow, staring the girls up and down. "Sure, kid, but I doubt ya got anything worth what I got."

"That's where you're wrong!" Aurora's mind spun as she yanked Polaris forward and pointed to her circlet. "I present to you, a crown. This baby right here is worth twice as much as your whole stand! Pure gold imported straight from Neo-Camelot and a perfectly-cut sapphire."

"P-p-p-p-pardon?" Polaris panicked.

Vakari leaned closer and squinted his eyes at the golden headpiece. Its radiant glow reflected off his face. "I'll be honest, that does look like some good shit! We may be able to cook up a trade."

Polaris shoved Aurora off her. "We absolutely will not make that trade! This *circlet* is worth more than both of your lives."

"Stop being a little bitch!" Aurora snapped. "You're the one who said we need to get a crystal ball, right? Well, this is the only one we'll find in Verona. So, give up the crown."

"No, you filthy ninny!"

"But we need the ball!"

"Not at this cost!"

Aurora reached for it, only for Polaris to catch her wrist and hold her back.

"You're the one saying you're in a rush to get us home. Give it. I know you can get a new one." Aurora continued to reach for it, but her sister wasn't letting up.

Polaris palmed Aurora's face, struggling to push her away. "She entrusted the title to me! I refuse to just hand it over."

"You don't care that you're already a day late? You don't care if she's angry at you? Then what was all that bitchin' for?"

Polaris slowly started to push her back.

"Of course, I need to get you home, but I refuse to forsake the only gift Mother ever gave me!" Polaris's voice cracked as she spoke.

Aurora couldn't keep her confusion contained anymore. "Only?"

Polaris looked away. "I'd rather be stranded than hand it over."

"Take your fight outta here. Bad for business," Vakari grumbled.

Just as the pair moved further away, his eyebrow curled up. He eyed Polaris. Aurora almost stepped in, but she was a second too late. His mouth fell open.

"Hold on," he said. "I thought you looked familiar!"

Polaris pulled her arms up in a defensive position. "I'm sorry?"

"Yeah, yeah!" He snapped his fingers twice. "You're the Gorgon's daughter! You got the scorpion tat' and everything!"

"Shoot," Polaris whispered as she grabbed her shoulder tattoo.

Aurora palmed her face. *Why didn't Ria give her a damn shirt with sleeves? That withered old bitch!*

"I . . . I believe there's been some mistake. I'm not affiliated with the Gorgon family name at all." Polaris's pitch skyrocketed as she spoke.

Aurora shook her head. She was an awful liar.

Vakari clapped his hands. "I think we got a deal, kid. You can have everything you see on display. In exchange, I get her."

8
Mayhem

Polaris's face drained of color upon hearing the merchant's offer. Aurora reached over and shielded Polaris with her arm.

"Forget it, shark bait," she said.

"Shark bait?" Vakari's eyebrows elevated, and he was clearly offended.

"I'm not trading her or anyone else's life for an item. How could you even ask me something like that?"

Polaris was taken aback. "Y–yes. She's right! Very rude of you."

"Tsk, tsk, tsk . . ." Vakari shook his head. A forest green aura surfaced from his skin. "You see, I wasn't asking."

Aurora smelled a fight. She raised her guard and watched as he reached underneath his table and pulled out a megaphone.

"Lemme guess, sound magic?" Aurora put up her fists, though she couldn't deny how confused she was at the move.

145

"Guess again, chump." Vakari leaped to the top of his tent and turned on his megaphone. "Everyone, may I have your attention, please?"

Everyone at the market stopped, turning in their direction.

"The daughter of Queen Euryale is here and threatens not only my business but the livelihood of all of us here in Moro Town! She plans to cut off our imports for the sake of killing the United Military's access to magic weapons."

"What?" Polaris screamed.

Witnesses fixated their glare on the two witches. They cried out, cursing Euryale's name, calling her a ruthless tyrant. They called the Magic Nations a 'magic wielder's hell'. Polaris was trying to act unaffected by the madness, but she looked as though her hair would start falling out. Slowly, people pulled away from the various stands to crowd around the two witches.

"Holy shit," Aurora mumbled.

"This is an absolute nightmare." Polaris looked white with shock.

"Those hellish Gorgons!" Vakari yelled into his megaphone. "First, their false goddess Echidna subjected our human brethren to slavery. Then, her children ravaged our lands. Murdered thousands and took more than just the lives of soldiers, all on her own! Now they want to destroy small businesses for the sake of their own agendas! Are we going to stand for that?"

"No!" the citizens surrounding yelled.

Aurora thought Polaris's eyes were going to pop out of her head. Her lips quivered.

"Stand with me to bring her down! Sell her back to her damn mother, and her friend, too! Those able, grab your weapons! Fight with me to prevent a Fourth Great War and protect our home!"

Cheers roared once again.

One by one, shady characters emerged from the crowds. A handful of thugs whipped out previously concealed knives. Some punk teens drew heavy swords tied to their backs. The men in suits pulled out brass knuckles. Beastmen bared their fangs and claws. Sorcerers flared their auras. There were even a few elves and dwarves that waddled up with sledgehammers. There had to have been one hundred angry magic users surrounding them, and the merchant was now grinning at them from above. Those who didn't emerge to fight cheered loudly from nearby tents.

Aurora and Polaris stood back-to-back, surrounded.

"Your ignorant words can be ignored if you retract this slander," Polaris called out to him. "Surely, there's another way to deal with this."

"Another way, eh? You give the Alucards that option?" Vakari fired back.

As the crowd slowly inched closer, Polaris's aura bubbled around her.

"You don't know anything about that," Polaris hissed.

"The universe knows by now! Erasing whole cultures and families seems to be a Gorgon tradition, doesn't it? Seven hundred years and your kind hasn't changed a bit."

The crowd roared in agreement. Aurora felt her sister's back steaming like a stovetop. Polaris bit down on her lip as her blue aura exploded around her, pushing the crowd back with a powerful gust.

"I refuse to listen to any more of your drivel!" Polaris whipped out her sword and pointed it at the merchant. She turned back to look at her sister. "Solaria, you can handle the crowd. This lowly cockroach belongs to me."

Aurora couldn't hold back her smile. "Hell, yeah! Look at you, bein' all badass! You'd better not get in my way, though." She took off her hoodie and tied it around her waist.

She was ready to crack some heads after forming her witch-blade.

Vakari leaped into the crowd as everyone converged to attack. Aurora dodged and parried each blade thrown her way. However, she quickly lost the offensive edge she'd started with. She dodged a jab from behind. Blocked the swing of a hammer from below. Sidestepped metallic projectiles zipping from all directions. Amidst her frantic dodging, an orange light shined in her peripheral. When she turned, a blazing sphere of flames struck her on her right side, melting part of her skin. She tumbled to the ground.

She pushed herself to her feet as her burned skin regenerated. She could feel the impacts of the pain in her body. The vibrations in her knuckles. The pounding in her chest. The blood rushing to her head. The glorious sensations of true battle! She loved nothing more! She grinned as she re-assumed her fighting stance.

A soft drizzle hit her skin, and she heard screaming from voices she didn't recognize. People were being rocketed into the air on her left, thanks to Polaris's water waves.

Aurora huffed. She refused to let Polaris outshine her. She formed a barrier-dome as blasts of fire and lasers fired at her. Then, she concentrated her aura, pulling energy from the core of her chest, and feeling it surge through her arms. She released her barrier and shot streaks of lightning into the mob. Bodies jerked violently from the electric shock, their expressions dazed. Aurora bolted forward and smacked her opponents down one by one with hard strikes.

The cheering was quickly reduced to a few whispers. Just when Aurora assumed she'd reached victory, a blur zipped down and sliced her cheek, forcing her to leap away. She saw the merchant, Vakari, standing across her with a pocketknife.

"Show me whatcha got, chump," he said, waving the pocketknife around.

Aurora cracked her neck and then drew her witch-blade. The combatants clashed, and it wasn't long before Aurora's ferocity pushed back the merchant. His parries were soft, and his strikes were slow. One violent swing from Aurora sliced the blade right off his knife handle. As she whipped her blade at his torso, his arm coiled around her own as if it were a snake with no bones whatsoever. It squeezed until her blade dissipated.

"What the hell?" Aurora panicked.

"You're strong, kid. But you ain't me."

Vakari swung her upward before slamming her down into the metal platform. Her bones rattled from the shock. He yanked her forward and struck her in the face with a solid punch.

Then, the merchant coiled his arm around her neck and lifted her again. His arm tightened around her neck and vocal cords. Her eyes watered. She clawed away at his arm and tried blasting fire at him, but he just slammed her into the ground again and again. Her head throbbed from the beating, and her blood simmered at her helplessness. For a moment, she almost wished for her demon aura to emerge. She would overpower him easily and heal her minor injuries to boot. Her necklace shined, keeping her demon aura bottled. She counted backward over and over.

Abruptly, he stopped, then screamed. His grip loosened enough for Aurora to breathe and open her eyes.

Ice shards poked out of his bleeding back. Polaris held her hand outstretched, and the mob of fighters behind her lay on the ground, either drenched or frozen solid. Polaris was spotless, coming out of the brawl with nothing but frazzled hair.

"You. Me. Now," Polaris hissed.

"Damn. You're good." Vakari grunted as he picked the bloody ice shards from his back. "But you aren't a threat. Call her my hostage."

Aurora had her opening. She swiftly created a witch-blade and sliced right through his stretchy arm. He shrieked at the top of his lungs and held his fresh wound, while Aurora rubbed her throbbing neck. She also had a nasty cough but was thrilled to breathe again.

"You BITCH!" Vakari snapped with bloodshot eyes. "How dare—"

A stream of rushing water circled him like a whirlpool, before lifting him into the air. Polaris opened her hand, and the water burst into dense, hot steam. Vakari screamed in agony. As he fell, Polaris smacked him with another geyser, flinging him across the sewer and into a tent.

Part of Aurora was relieved, but another part of her felt even more infuriated. "I didn't ask you to save me! I had it under control."

Polaris rolled her eyes. "Sorry, it was hard to understand you amidst your choking. But you're very welcome."

Aurora tightened her fists.

"Had you used that demonic aura of yours, you might have disposed of him without my assistance," Polaris continued, unfazed. "If anything, blame your trepidation."

Aurora loosened her grip. She scoffed and looked away.

Polaris pulled out her sword and marched toward the tent where Vakari had crashed. "Speaking of disposal."

Aurora ran towards her then and yanked Polaris by the shoulder. "Whoa! You won, alright? What are you doing?"

"His disrespect of my family and attempt to sully my name won't be ignored. He shall get what he truly deserves. Now, out of my way."

Aurora stood in her path. "No way. He got what he deserved already."

"No," she continued, her eyes clouded with anger. "He deserves a true Gorgon's punishment. Step aside, Solaria. That's an order."

Aurora grabbed her fuming sister by the collar. "What did I tell you about telling me what to do? Plus, if you kill him, won't you just be proving him right?"

Polaris bit down on her lip and then smacked away Aurora's hand. "You don't know what you're talking about. You don't know anything about our heritage!"

"Okay, are you gonna kill me too?"

Polaris's tight face loosened.

"Or how 'bout all those people behind you?" Aurora continued, her gaze straightforward. "They don't know Gorgon history. You wanna kill all of them too?"

Polaris turned to see the fallen men and women in the aftermath of their heated battle. Most were unconscious, drenched in slush water. Others had a few bad lumps on their faces and struggled to get up. Not one had a lethal wound.

"Polaris, you're a princess. You're not a killer," Aurora said with a finality that Polaris knew she couldn't argue with.

Polaris dropped her sword and slowly fell to her knees. "What in Goddess Echidna's name am I doing? I've resorted to thuggish behavior."

Aurora snickered at the dramatic response. "Nah. You just lost your cool. It's okay. I do it all the time."

Polaris rubbed her temples, breathing deeply, and then readjusted her circlet. "Thank you. And not just that, but for, you know, not selling me."

"Come on. I wouldn't trade ya for that," Aurora said with a shrug. "Though, if he was selling a few caramel apples, you might be in trouble."

Polaris huffed. "Swine."

"Bitch."

The two of them locked into a stare before laughing. Aurora pulled Polaris up.

"Not gonna lie, you looked pretty badass out th—"

A hard metal had dinged her in the head, making Aurora stumble. She looked down to see a crushed soda can.

Polaris caught a stone that had been chucked at her with minimal effort. The onlookers began to converge on the two witches, the most recent in a string of swarms. The angry mob carried miscellaneous weapons like stones, shuriken, and bats.

"The Gorgons are at it again!" one of them shouted.

"Magic Nations trying to cause trouble on our soil," yelled another.

"Will they ever stop? It's the Alucard Incident all over again."

"Kill the witches! Burn them alive if we have to!"

Aurora and Polaris eluded everything being chucked at them.

"Solaria!" Polaris yelled after what felt like a minute too long of evading projectiles.

"Yeah, yeah."

Aurora whistled into her fingers and summoned her broom. The two hopped on, scooped up the lone crystal ball from Vakari's tent, and then blasted off.

Hundreds of people pursued them towards the wide sewer tunnels. They had no choice but to duck in for hiding. Sewage water splashed in the girls' faces as they zoomed through the wet tunnels. Three beastmen with fluffy birdwings were the closest pursuers, which led Polaris to look back in panic.

"Lose them! Faster!" Polaris yelled.

"I'm going as fast as I can!" Aurora barked back.

"Drat!"

Polaris peeked down and found her solution. She aimed her hand and closed her eyes, focusing her aura. The water swirled up, forming a tidal wave that engulfed everyone still chasing them. Then, she closed her fist and the water solidified into a giant, black and green glacier.

Aurora turned back with a wide smile. "Holy hell! You're on fire today!"

The two sisters found refuge in a dark alley once again, before catching their breath and wiping the remaining sweat off their faces. Moro Town's streets were filled with more policemen and sniffing hounds, clearly seeking them out. Helicopters circled overhead. The two kept their heads down, but Aurora was still ecstatic after the rush at the Black Market.

"That was fun! And you got on me for being a troublemaker. Guess we're related after all." Aurora laughed.

Polaris didn't share her enthusiasm for troublemaking. Again, she sat there quietly, staring at the ground in deep thought, but to Aurora's annoyance.

"What's up with you?" Aurora asked.

Polaris sighed and rubbed her temple. "It's nothing."

"Looks like something."

Polaris leaned back against the wall. "It should've never come to this, you know? Starting public brawls? Stealing? One of my officers going rogue? A terrorist group on our heels? Not to mention that all this horrible news must be delivered to my mother!"

"Wow," Aurora said with a mock sigh of relief. "You made me think something was actually wrong."

Polaris glared at her.

"C'mon, who cares, right? You're about to bring me back, so it's whatever."

Polaris sighed once more. "You can maybe afford to say that, but I can't. I'm the heir. It's my responsibility to keep things like this in order. How can I ever uphold the throne when I'm literally stuck next to a dumpster after a simple mission?"

"Forget about it," Aurora said, throwing her arms in the air. "We have the ball now. Make that call, and we can get home."

"I envy your simple-mindedness," she said, staring at the ball. "But I guess, in some way, you are correct."

Her hands shook like she was out in a winter storm.

"Why are you shivering?" Aurora asked.

"It's . . . nothing, nothing." Polaris shook her head with a forced smile. "She could be busy, and I don't want to disturb her."

"That's the lamest excuse. Quit stallin', prissy."

Polaris rested her head against the wall and took in a deep breath. "All right."

Each time they circled back to this kind of conversation, Aurora pondered just what kind of woman Euryale was. She heard stories of her fight with Blair and the gloating from Polaris. As infamous as a Demi-God she was, Aurora had never even seen a photo of her or any of the Magic Nation's Demi-Gods. She couldn't help but think the woman was a decrepit prune since she was hundreds of years older than Ria. Wondering aside, Aurora handed the blue sphere to Polaris.

"Solaria." Polaris's voice was shaky. "I'll speak to Mother alone for now. Stay on standby unless she requests to speak to you."

Aurora shook her head. "Still trying to order me around. Yeah, yeah. Got it."

Polaris swallowed and regained her composure. "Dial Nation 7, District 1, Pearl Kingdom, Gorgon Castle."

The alley lit up with a bright blue light.

Aurora marveled. The ball clouded for a moment, before revealing a clear picture. Aurora expected her birth mother to appear but was met by a young man with skin as blue as Polaris's hair. He had long, floppy, pointy ears pointing east and west, scruffy green hair, sharp teeth, and a scar stretching from his jaw to his right eye. His eyes, specifically his sclerae, were all yellow, with thin reptilian pupils. He was a goblin, a race Aurora rarely saw, let alone one so young. Usually, they were feral creatures with more wrinkles. She tried her best to act as though this occurrence was normal for her.

"State your name and reason for . . . Princess Polaris?" he shrieked.

"Bishop Norman Agura? What an unexpected surprise!" Polaris smiled.

"M'lady has been trying desperately to reach you. Why are you calling from a district-less ball? Where are you?"

"A lot has transpired," she said, skipping through her words with an all-business attitude. "I'll give a full report upon my arrival. Wherever is my mother? How come she didn't pick up?"

Norman sighed. "M'lady is in Neo-Camelot. An important council meeting is taking place. Unfortunately, one even I couldn't accompany her to. The session is set to last a week and some change."

"Council meeting? Now, of all times?" Polaris bit her lip in frustration.

"Princess, you were to arrive last night. We also haven't received the status of the mission from Knight Reiya."

Polaris quaked, her eyes darting in every direction. From her vantage point, concern decorated the goblin's face.

"Please, don't tell me. Was Solaria more formidable than we anticipated? Or. . .were you attacked by the United Military?"

"Bishop, wait—"

"Give the order. I'll dispatch Rook Lazuli, no, the entire Big Three Rooks to retrieve you and combat the enemy."

"No!" Polaris panicked, catching both Aurora and Norman by surprise. "That won't be necessary. Erm. There were some minor complications, but everything is going as planned! We will capture Solaria and return before Mother emerges from the Council meeting."

Norman curled a brow.

"Please, Bishop Agura, keep word of our call from Mother's ear. She should focus all of her attention on whatever Magic Council affairs concern her at the moment. I will return with Solaria within the week and give a full report. All is well."

Norman sighed. "If you insist, Princess." The goblin bowed. "*Chaíre sti vasílissa tou skorpioú*." *Hail to the Scorpion Queen.* He continued, "I devote my undying loyalty to the Magic Nations."

"Loyal til death," Polaris replied before swiftly ending the transmission.

Aurora stared at her, her jaw agape. "What. The fuck. WAS THAT!?"

"What?"

"Did you *choke*, Polaris? Why didn't ya tell him what happened? Hell, why didn't you tell him we needed a FUCKING RIDE!? Isn't that the whole reason we bussed our asses in the Black Market in the first place?"

Polaris shushed her. "Keep your voice down!" She urged in a whispered tone. "Listen. . .Knight Reiya was one of those Vipers, yes?"

"Okay. So? Wouldn't that be important for your royal crew to know?"

"Precisely. But, what if Reiya wasn't the only Viper within our military?"

Aurora hesitated to respond, considering the possibility.

"Solaria, it took us all we had and an involuntary transformation of yours to best him." Polaris's gaze fell to her lap. "If the Militia is informed of such events, it could bring to light more traitors. Traitors that could pursue us directly, masqueraded as allies."

"And we could kick their asses—"

"That's not the entire point, moron! This situation could incite a civil war if we don't proceed cautiously!" Polaris snatched Aurora by her shoulders. "Solaria, this has to be discussed with Mother and Mother alone first. The situation must be dealt with delicately, to prevent other lives lost." Polaris tightened her grip on Aurora's shirt. "Xior, Victor, Clegard, Ian, Montague. Those men died in foreign land, and such news is already public. I imagine that's what the Council convened for. If we inform them now that we're stranded and that terrorists from within our military are responsible, we could trigger a fallout that'll be responsible for much more bloodshed. Do you want that?"

Aurora smacked Polaris's hands from her shoulders. "Of course not. But the Queen ain't home? Fine. She has a personal crystal ball, right? Call that number."

"Are you hard at hearing? She's in a Council Meeting. Interrupting her own official business with such news would be. . . hazardous."

Aurora raised an eyebrow. "Just what kind of woman is Euryale anyway? Sounds like a total bitch."

"How dare you!" Polaris hissed. "That's our mother. She's the absolute perfect queen. The type of queen I shall succeed."

Even though Aurora should've been the one upset by this, Polaris was the one to bury her face in her hands. Polaris's relationship with her mother made no sense to Aurora. One minute, Polaris spoke highly of her, the next she wanted to avoid her altogether. All the same, the geopolitics of the situation at hand made her head hurt. How difficult was requesting a ride home without potentially sparking an international conflict?

Before Aurora could reflect on their current situation any longer, Polaris lifted her head and boasted a dorky smile.

"Found a loophole?" Aurora said with a tilt of her head.

Polaris palmed her head. "Why hadn't I considered that first? There's someone else I can call! We won't have to remain stranded here any longer. . . but . . ." Polaris turned her back towards her. "You'll stay out of this call as well. I don't want to hear a peep. Understand?"

Aurora scoffed. She made a mental note to never get into politics. It all sounded overly complicated. "Whatever."

"Good." Polaris glanced at Aurora once more. "Dial Nation 7, District 0, Kingdom Forest, Furasaku Village, Ball 9."

"Sheesh," Aurora muttered.

"Silence!" Polaris's ears reddened.

"Mephion down below! Blue? That you?" a boyish voice answered.

"Sir Jason! It's been oh too long! How are things?"

"You don't have to call me sir, your Highness. We've been over this." He chuckled.

Her voice got all squeaky and high. Aurora had never heard Polaris reach a pitch like that, so something was definitely up. Something real. She crept closer to her to see who it was but was met with a water blast to the face.

"Asshole!" Aurora screamed.

"Whoa," Jason said. "What was that?"

"Oh, just a pesky pixie," Polaris said without missing a beat. Aurora wiped her drenched hair from her forehead with a grumble, and Polaris couldn't keep from smiling. "You were saying?"

"Okay, but, um, things are good. About to prepare for a raid. Why are you calling from this unknown ball?"

"It's a long story," she said, still keeping her vocal tone expertly level. "But I'm in desperate need of your assistance! A . . . friend and I are stuck here in Verona. Is it possible for you to use one of your dragons and pick us up?"

"Verona? Did you go to an Allied Nation willingly? Is this some type of war espionage I'm not supposed to know about?" He paused momentarily, and when Polaris didn't answer, he continued. "Wait. Please don't say you're with Princess Camella."

"Oh heavens no! Thank Echidna for that." Polaris rolled her eyes. "She's . . . a new friend. This is a special situation, and it's . . . it's an emergency. I must be back in the kingdom immediately."

"Immediately, huh? Euryale must be *pissed*."

"Not yet, but she will be," she said through her teeth.

"Well, trust me, I'd love to, but I don't know if Alicia would let me take the wyverns for free."

Her squeaky tone shifted to one of frustration. "Must you consult her for everything?"

"She's our leader, Blue. I can't just take our resources whenever I want."

"Fine. Tell her money is no object. This is an emergency."

"Really? Is it that bad?"

Polaris nodded.

"Umm . . . alright, let me check the map. I mean, a trip over the Atalanta Ocean could take seven hours. And I'm in a bit of a bind already, so I don't know if—"

"Jason, please. These are desperate times. I'm . . . I'm begging."

"Begging? Okay, so this is *actually* bad. I mean, I should be able to convince her. But can you meet me at Cyclops Island eight hours from now? Landing inland can be an issue and for many reasons."

"Perfect! That sounds wonderful. Thank you, thank you, thank you—"

A bright white light beamed down from above, and twirling propellers tore the air. The witches looked up to see a helicopter shining a bright light on them.

"Crimson Witch! Remain where you stand! Any retaliation will be met with brute force!" The words echoed down from a megaphone.

"Blue? What's that?" Jason asked.

"Oh, look at the time. Must be going, see you soon!" Polaris quickly hung up again.

"Feds are here," Aurora said, deadpan.

"Really? I didn't notice!"

9
Control

Aurora summoned her broom again, and they zoomed through the streets before ascending into the sky. Their hair flickered in their faces as they blazed through the harsh wind.

Aurora turned back to see three choppers hot on her tail, each with a turret gun underneath pointed at them. She formed her aura barrier dome around them to deflect the raging gunfire.

"They're shooting at us over some damn apples?" Aurora yelled.

"You're the one who built a criminal reputation!" Polaris snapped back, exasperated. "Just fly faster. We'll outrun them."

"That didn't work at the Black Market," Aurora said, more to herself than anyone else. "You know what I gotta do."

Aurora turned the broom to face the assault copters, and Polaris immediately squeezed both of Aurora's shoulders.

"Wait, Solaria, consider what may happen, I—"

Aurora aimed her hand at the chopper. She focused her aura on her stone and power surged through her veins. Almost immediately, the stone's potency got the best of her. The immense rush of power seared at her chest like flames. She gasped for air and clawed at her glowing chest. *Damn! Right now? I didn't even use the elements much today!*

"Solaria! Pull away!" Polaris screeched.

Gunfire tore into the air. Aurora raised her head, but it was too late. Gunfire struck, leaving holes all over her chest and torso, while a stray bullet grazed Polaris's arm. Aurora jerked backward, and she and Polaris fell off the broom.

Polaris screamed as they plummeted toward the ground. Aurora's head spun, and the flame within her began to spread throughout her entire body, bringing her running blood to a boil. Her necklace glowed momentarily but fizzled out as soon as it started. Her bullet wounds closed. Her claws and fangs grew, and her aura erupted into a crimson flare.

This was it. She whistled for her broom, which came immediately, and scooped the pair up before they hit the ground.

"Solaria, it's happening again! You need to relax!" Polaris grabbed her shoulder, but Aurora could hardly hear her. It didn't matter.

"Shut the fuck up or you'll join them!" Aurora yelled, her voice horse and distorted.

"Don't! I've already—"

Aurora aimed her hand at them again. This time, she could draw upon her stone's immense power and fire streaks of lightning out from her hand. All three copters were zapped by the same bolt, tearing through them like a hot knife through butter. Aurora smirked, watching the explosions born from her handy-work. That felt good–no–great! Her elation quickly fizzled out however, as her demon aura suppressor activated with a purple glow. Her crimson glow faded as quickly as it had arrived, along with its associated bloodlust.

Just as the heat within her cooled, she noticed it. The helicopters' turret guns were all submerged in thick ice, courtesy of Polaris. The vehicles were engulfed in flames as they fell to the ground. More explosions roared from the crash, igniting nearby villas into a bright orange blaze. Her bloodlust completely dissipated. Shrieks of terror came from everywhere, but Aurora couldn't bring herself to make a sound. It was too late. She'd done this. She hadn't been able to stop herself.

"Solaria . . . what on earth did you do?" Polaris mumbled.

Aurora's hair stood and her entire world spun like a globe. "I—I didn't mean—"

"Kalville Beach! Verona's continental border. Head there, now. We're done here."

Tears threatened to fall down Aurora's face. Her broom shot through the sky with as much speed as she could put into it. Though she couldn't help but look around her shoulder to the orange flowers dancing in the middle of Moro Town, with nothing but screams sprouting from its bud. The image was etched into her mind, a common practice whenever her demonic aura emerged.

Serena walked through the messy, oddly busy streets of eastern West-town with her umbrella shielding her from the evening sun. She yawned and rubbed her bloodshot eyes, ignoring the wandering eyes of the civilians. She passed a much taller beastman with the ears and fluffy tail of a wolf, wearing a black leather jacket. Said beastman yanked her toward him by the shoulder.

"Hey, cutie, you from around here?"

Just a crumb of sunlight from her umbrella being slightly moved was enough to sear a small burn mark on her cheek. Serena grunted, shielding her cheek which emitted steam. Bloodlust took over, and her cheery blossom irises were daggers aimed right at the beastman. He recoiled upon seeing her colorless face.

The wolfman flinched. "Oh, shit you're a vampire! No wonder your scent was off." His eyes wavered with fright as he initiated a retreat.

Serena grumbled as she reached into one of her pockets and pulled out a nevma shard, pressing it against her burned cheek. The shard glowed before her skin reformed on her face, making her cheek as good as new. Despite the brief irritation, Serena figured the beastman could be useful. She didn't want to let this prime opportunity pass.

"Hey, hold on!"

The wolfman turned back to her in hesitation.

"You heard of The Crimson Witch?" Serena asked.

His scoff came with a beastly growl. "That damn half-demon, half-witch, half-bitch? Yeah, yeah, real popular 'round here."

"Know where she lives?"

"Nah. But I heard that she frequents The Salem's Needle, though. Some tailor's joint."

"Where's that?"

"Right at the corner of Williams Street just four miles south. It has a big purple sign up front, can't miss it." The wolf eyed Serena up and down. "You look kinda familiar. Were you on TV or sum?"

"What, do all vampires look the same—" Serena paused, then smirked, getting an idea. "Sorry, never was a star. But I like your jacket."

"For real?"

"Mind if I get a closer look?" Her sword loosened from its sheath slightly, unbeknownst to the wolfman.

Serena tugged the wolfman by his sleeve and led him into a shady alley where no one could see them. The wolfman's blush pierced the thickness of his furry beard. Serena could feel his excitement peaking from his prickly fur coat. She also had goosebumps but craved something entirely different from the wolfman.

"So, like, what are we doing—"

Her fangs pierced his throat before he could blink. The wolfman snatched the shorter vampire by the shoulders and dug his claws into her. He didn't even have the strength to pierce her skin with his claws, let alone wrestle her off him. Within seconds, she drained most of his blood through his neck, bringing his now withered body to its knees. She snatched his jacket off of him before releasing him from the grip of her jaws. The wolfman fell face flat and bled out from his neck.

The wolfman gasped for air as his beastly features vanished, leaving the beastman to appear more human. He stared at Serena with beady eyes as fur emerged on her face and arms. Her face also morphed into a wolf's snout and her pink irises turned orange, matching his former features. Terror filled his eyes.

"I knew I—" he choked on the blood spewing from his mouth. "See-en you! Al-u-card."

Serena smirked, throwing his jacket over her shoulder. "Your genes will ensure that you're the only man who will recognize me today. For that, you have my gratitude."

The wolfman reached out to her, his hand shaking. Serena's eyes widened for a moment, catching a glimpse of a memory she wished she could forget. She'd seen such desperate eyes before, paired with a helplessness she would've given anything erase back then. The mere thought of that pain provoked a sharp pain in Serena's chest, one in which Serena already knew the remedy for.

Serena unsheathed her blade and raised it over his head. For a split second, she envisioned the face of the one that possesses her cure. The face of the same girl who caused her such pain in the first place. How she yearned to have her at the end of her blade. But alas, this wolfman didn't deserve that same vitriol. He deserved nothing but eternal peace for aiding Serena on her path.

"May Lord Fraizen have mercy on your soul. Amen." She drove her blade through his skull, silencing him permanently.

Serena marched down Williams Street with the leather jacket in her hand. She licked the excess blood from the corner of her mouth. "Salty."

Serena walked into Salem's Needle, which had customers walking in and out with suits or dresses in bags. A television played in the high corner of the room as she approached Ria at the counter. A puff of smoke left Ria's mouth, with a lit cigarette hanging in the corner of it. Serena didn't even get close before the aroma of cigarette ash hit her like a runaway train, likely made even more intense thanks to the beastman blood she ingested. She did her best to mask her disgust. Serena let down her umbrella and tossed the jacket onto the counter.

"This jacket isn't in my size. Can you fix that, ma'am?" Serena asked, forming one of her signature fake smiles.

Ria blinked at her. "Odd to buy sum' that don't fit ya."

"It was my father's."

"Whatever, kid, I can. Step ova' here and let me get ya measurements."

Serena placed her sheathed sword next to a chair beside the right wall underneath hovering green dresses. While Ria grabbed a measuring tape from under her counter, Serena scanned the store, ensuring it was vacant. She scratched behind her ear and felt a wave of different smells invade her nostrils simultaneously. She wondered how canines could function with so many scents going up their noses. It vexed her, but she had to deal with it for now.

"Ya not gonna take off the trench coat?" Ria asked.

"Sorry. The bright lights can harm my skin. It's already killer on my face."

"You beastmen are so damn needy."

Serena maintained her smile but desperately wanted to split Ria's head open. She calmed herself and just let Ria measure her waist.

"I heard some crazy things have been happening in this city," Serena said as Ria measured the length of her arms.

"Crazy things been happenin' 'round here for years, chile," Ria responded.

"Have you ever witnessed any of it?"

"Believe you me, crazy blows down these doors every damn day."

Serena tilted her head slightly. "Oh?" Her sword vibrated on the wall, the sheath loosening. "I heard there was a half-demon in this city. I wanted to see if the rumors were true. Never seen one in person. They're a rare find in the Allied Nations."

Ria stopped measuring Serena's waist and gawked at her. "Demon? Ha. Chile, ya gotta better chance snoopin' 'round Colona near the gates to see one of those."

The corner of Serena's mouth twitched. Was Ria playing coy?

Ria returned to the counter and black thread spewed from her long hair as she used her long nails to direct the thread. The jacket gradually got thinner around the waist. Serena folded her arms and tapped her leather-gloved finger steadily.

"I saw on the news a bunch of police died. And that the Magic Militia were in our borders," Serena said, shifting her strategy.

"A whole bunch of mess. Probably a setup. Those Demi-Gods love war, I'll tell ya."

"You lived through a few, didn't you, granny?"

Ria stopped stitching for a moment. Her eyes narrowed as if she were reliving a painful memory. "Served in the Third." She sighed, lowering the jacket to the counter. "Never seen so much senseless bloodshed. The bodies. Soldiers and civilians on both sides dyin' over a petty Demi-God squabble!" She slammed her fist on the counter. "Even lost my sister and brother-in-law to that snake Medusa, and they were just bystanders."

Serena was taken aback. Chills slithered down her spine. "The. . .Snake Witch?"

"Of all the Demi-Gods in both Magic and Allied Nations, very few were as frightening as her. She turned entire battlefields into her concrete garden. Even Lady Minerva was powerless against her. Glad she's gone now but pray we don't have another war like that. Children like ya don't need to grow to fight in no war like my niece did."

The mention of Medusa's name alone made Serena's stomach bottom out. She struggled to mask her scowl. In the end, she opted to sigh and bury her discontent.

"Of course." The runaround grew tiresome. She eyed the old witch as her sword slowly levitated. She surveyed the area again, seeing no one about to enter the store. "Granny, have you ever heard of Lord Fraizen?"

"What's that, a character off some show?"

"Lord Fraizen is our gracious god who determines the paths of fate before us. Everything that happened and ever will happen is by design. Whether we like it or not, everything has a purpose that he bestows on us. It's through recognizing Fraizen's path that we mortals discover meaning in our lives, especially when considering how abruptly that path can end."

Ria's eyebrows furrowed and she stopped stitching. "They teach that bullshit in school?"

A devilish smirk smeared on her face, but just then, a familiar name echoed from the television set: "Polaris Gorgon." The pit returned to her stomach. She whipped her head to face the television, seeing the reporter standing in front of blazing fires being put out by firemen.

"Sources say that the girl that was with The Crimson Witch here in Moro Town was none other than the princess of the Pearl Kingdom, Polaris Gorgon. Both witches were seen in Owl Circle where The Crimson Witch allegedly attacked a man working at a vendor. The two were spotted again later flying on a broom when The Crimson Witch took down three United Military helicopters. Local firefighters are still struggling to get the flames behind me under control. Sources confirm at least twenty-five casualties so

far, and twelve more in critical condition. Sources also say President Icarus has contacted Queen Euryale of the Pearl Kingdom and King Arthur of Neo-Camelot. He hasn't gotten a response back from either."

Serena maintained her stoicism, masking the joy of a child tasting candy for the first time. Ria on the other hand facepalmed herself as she shook her head. "Damn, again? Knew that kid couldn't keep it together," she mumbled.

"On second thought, granny, I never liked the jacket. Keep it." Serena went to grab her sword and zoomed out of the store.

"Wait, chile! Ya still owe me a service fee!"

ઠ

Serena stood behind the store with her umbrella shielding her. She reached into her coat's inner pocket and pulled out a black crystal ball. "Dial V-ball 12." The ball lit up before revealing the image of a man covered in sweat with scruffy, messy neon hair. His skin had deep red blemishes all over.

"You look a mess," Serena jeered.

"And you look like a dog," he jabbed back.

Serena forgot about the blood she had just consumed. "Ugh, don't remind me. Anyway, heard Moro Town's gone to shit."

He grunted in pain. "You can say that. It ain't my fault though, I swear, so don't go snitchin' to the boss!"

"Whatever. You seen The Crimson Witch?"

"Seen her? The bitch cut off my hand! Even with the nevma, that shit fuckin' hurts!"

"Quit being a baby, Vakari. And you saw Polaris, too, then?"

"Yeah. Fuck! Can't believe I let so much money slip away!"

Serena wore the biggest smile. "Vakari, listen to me. I need you to find and corral them. I'll fly over to retrieve The Crimson Witch when the sun sets."

"Why her? Is this about that thing Reiya boasted about last week? Where is that damn tomcat anyway?" Vakari asked.

So, he doesn't know about the stone? Good. This should be simple. "Those witches killed Reiya. They may have Viper intel and I'm tasked with dealing with them."

"Really? Oh, this is soundin' fun!" Vakari grinned, his shark-like teeth gleaming.

"Hold them and I'll zero in on your location with the tracker. Whatever you do, don't kill either of them. Boss's orders."

"I get the princess, right? The boys in South Serrenie will bid fortunes for a live Gorgon! I think it'll do the organization some good, and stuff my pockets simultaneously."

"Listen to me, squid." Serena narrowed her eyes. "The bitch is mine and mine alone."

"What? You listening? She can be worth—"

"Losing every drop of blood in your body?"

Anxiety swept over his sweaty face. "Whateva', chump. Don't be late, I got an important shipment to catch at eight to bring to HQ."

"Of course."

The transmission ended. Serena couldn't help but giggle. She grabbed her pentagram pendant and closed her eyes. "Lord Fraizen, thank you for shining on me once again. I will not fail you with this task. Please, take mercy on the innocent soul I had to deliver earlier. Amen." Police sirens rang in the distance. Serena kept walking, hiding her furry face under her umbrella. *Cassie, justice will be served.*

The two witches zoomed through a sky mixed with thick purple clouds with beams of bright orange piercing through from the setting sun. While the brisk air would be enough to give most people a cold, all Aurora could feel was immense heat behind her face and warm tears dripping down her face. She fought with every fiber of her being to keep herself from wailing to the heavens.

Her hands twitched as if they were still drenched in cold blood. The only thing on her mind amidst the silence was: how long until this ends?

While soaring through the darkening sky, Polaris decided to break the silence. "You are aware that what you did wasn't all bad. You aren't required to shoulder the burden of that."

Aurora bit down on her lip. She didn't want to hear a word of it. She felt Polaris's hand grab her shoulder. It felt like water trickling down her back.

"I know you're frustrated, but it will be quite all right. We will be home soon, and all of this can be put behind us." Polaris offered her a small smile.

Aurora didn't even bother turning around. "No. You *don't* know," she grumbled as the broom picked up speed.

After an hour of flying in silence just below the black clouds, they reached the beach town of Kalville. The lights from the streets and buildings twinkled like stars. The ocean was just up ahead, dark and vast. Sea breeze struck Aurora's face. The air warmed, and became noticeably humid, so much so that Aurora's curls frizzed up. For a second, she swore she felt a raindrop.

The vast ocean and shoreline were well within their sights. Several boats were lined up near the docks up and down the coastline.

"We need to find a cruise or ferry headed toward Cyclops Island. Get closer so we can ascertain what's going where," Polaris said.

"Whatever." Aurora descended slightly.

They found a cargo ferry set to go directly to Cyclops Island. The vast and long boat occupied nearly a quarter of the length of the pier by itself. Multi-colored metal shipment cubes were stacked up and down the ferry, leaving few narrow spaces to walk outside the huge main deck near the front. They saw several crewmen walking up and down the brightly lit boat. Aurora and Polaris hovered high above and waited for the ship to depart from the dock. Once it was far enough from shore, they flew discreetly onto it.

They tiptoed around, ducking around the corners of shipment cubes to keep out of sight. Aurora peeked around one of the metal shipping cubes to count the number of crewmen further down the railing and onto the deck. There were six total, not counting the captain in the navigation room on the upper deck. Aurora figured if it came down to it, she could handle them all easily, especially if they were human. Still, she couldn't clear her head of those screams.

After sneaking around more, Aurora spotted a latch and metal door on the deck.

"We can go under until the ship stops. Come on," Aurora whispered.

Polaris stood starstruck, staring at the doors of one of the shipment cubes behind them. She swallowed her saliva and slowly pointed at the door. "Does . . . that look at all familiar to you?"

Aurora squinted her eyes, and her heart sank. She saw a black logo resembling a squiggly letter "s." It was a snake, the mark of the Vipers, the same one featured on Reiya and Shoto.

"What the hell is one of those . . ." Aurora muttered.

A flash of light followed by a clap of thunder caused them both to flinch. The downpour began, drenching them both. Aurora and Polaris rushed to pry open the hatch. They hurried down the metal ladder and into a vast engine room. It was a metallic jungle with metal bars, clocks, and switches. Aurora and Polaris rushed to hide in a small corner between a pair of metal pipes. They both panted and shook from the frigid air, which matched their being soaked.

Polaris slammed her fist against the pipe next to her in frustration. "Impossible. Are these Vipers traveling and transporting goods in Allied Nation waters? Just what in Echidna's good name is going on around here?"

"Are you that surprised? One of your soldiers was a Viper. Figures these thugs would be everywhere, ya know?" Aurora said.

Polaris released a deep breath. "So long as we get to Cyclops Island safely, we can have Mother and the Magic Council handle this ordeal. They're more than equipped to deal with those monsters."

Aurora cut her eyes toward Polaris.

"What is it now?" Polaris asked.

Monsters. That was the last word Aurora wanted to hear. "It's nothing."

"You're still thinking about that incident earlier?"

Aurora stared into her lap, not uttering a response.

Polaris straightened the circlet on her head. "Solaria, there's no need to worry about it anymore. Forget it ever even happened."

"Yeah. Let me just forget about the people I just killed. I'll get right on that."

"You'd rather just cry and whine about it all the way home? That does you no good." Polaris stood up, casting a shadow over her. "I thought you were a warrior. Whatever happened to that attitude?"

Aurora fumed at the ears. "I don't need your lip service, princess."

Polaris folded her arms. "Come now, Solaria. There are a few silver linings in this. For starters, we're alive—"

"I said I don't need your lip service!"

Polaris batted her eyes, her lips curled downward in a frown.

Aurora averted her gaze from the princess. "I get it. We're gonna get to the Pearl Kingdom and Euryale will fix everything. Cool. Just leave me alone." She fought back the heated tears.

Polaris huffed. "If that's what you wish, fine. I could do with some quiet." She got up and marched to the opposite side of the engine room. She squatted and pulled a book out of her backpack.

Aurora dwelled on the last two days. She had never lost control of her power so frequently. She wondered if it had more to do with the strength of her power or her weakness. The thought of the latter made her quake, and her wet skin wasn't helping. Who knew what would've happened in her last few encounters if it had not been for Polaris?

Just staring at the girl calmly flipping through pages made her fume. Aurora felt she didn't need her help or her strength. She could win those battles outright without her and despite her curse. She just wanted another opportunity to prove that point and get that nasty taste out of her mouth.

"Solaria," Polaris said, breaking the silence.

"What?"

"You aren't alone in this. I just . . . hope you're aware of that."

Aurora and Polaris met eyes. Her tight face loosened. She didn't expect to see Polaris looking as down as she did. She was compelled to ask why, but a loud *clack* echoed through the engine room. Both the witches crawled into a tighter spot between the pipes to hide. The clanking of boots and dripping of water got louder, as did Aurora's heartbeat. A shadow of a man overtook her, and she covered her mouth to conceal her breathing.

10
Wrath of the Vipers

"Stowaways on my ship? Best come out. Don't make this harder on yourselves," a familiar masculine voice called out. "Gorgon, Crimson Witch. Come out. No sense in hidin'."

"Drats. He knows we're here," Polaris whispered.

"Oh!" Aurora realized who it was. She vacated her hiding spot to face him.

"What are you doing!" Polaris shouted.

Aurora raised her chin, exuding confidence through her smirk. "Came back for more, huh Vakari? How are those third-degree burns?"

Vakari's reddened, bubbly skin was drenched in water. The nub left behind by Aurora cutting off his hand was wrapped in a thick black cast. His shark-like teeth were ever apparent in his scowl. "Confident for a chick I had gasping for air. Don't act like that can't happen again."

"Don't act like I can't cut off your other hand. Give you some symmetry and all."

Vakari's eyebrow twitched. "Snarky little bitch, ain't ya?"

Polaris also hopped out of hiding, throwing her backpack straps back around her shoulders. "Echidna on earth, how did you find us?"

He pointed to his eyes. "Hide all you want, you can't hide your heat signatures. Findin' y'all under the deck of my ship was a surprise, but it's a welcome one."

"Your ship, eh? You're a Viper, aren't ya?" Aurora asked.

Vakari smirked. "A birdie told me you killed Reiya. Can't believe he got done in by some high-school punks."

The corners of Aurora's mouth pointed north, and excitement bubbled in her chest. "I'm glad you're here, and a Viper on top of that! I've been meaning to vent some frustration and you're the perfect stress reliever."

Polaris threw her arm in front of Aurora, stopping her in her tracks. "Hold it. There shall be no physical altercation if he's willing to talk. His salamander skin and missing appendage should be enough of a reminder that we aren't to be trifled with, 'high schoolers' or otherwise."

Vakari's eyebrows, or what was left of them, furrowed.

Polaris folded her arms. "This room may be small, but it'll suffice as a grave if you don't comply. Best you start talking, or face the execution you were so graciously spared from."

Vakari snickered through his crooked smile. "One stroke of luck and y'all both think y'all hot shit?"

The surrounding air thickened. Vakari's growing laughter didn't sit well with Aurora. Vakari exuded the same foreboding presence Reiya did during their fight.

"You lil' chumps ain't in no position to threaten me, especially since you cost me a shit ton of money! You got lucky when cutting off my hand, but I doubt ya'll can handle the other eight." Vakari ripped off his shirt, revealing the snake tattoo coiling around his chiseled abs and pecs. His green aura erupted, pushing Aurora and Polaris back with massive force. Hunter-green scales covered his skin, while his elbows grew small fins.

"He really is a merman!" Aurora shouted.

"Wrong!" Vakari snarled.

"Enough of this!" Rather than allow his transformation to continue, Polaris drew her sword and bolted toward him.

A dark blur whipped from his back and smacked Polaris upward through the ceiling of the engine room.

"Polaris!" Aurora screamed.

She saw a weird, appendage resembling a tail come back down the hole he made after throwing Polaris through the roof, said hole leaking with the heavy rain. However, upon closer inspection, the suction cups on the giant extra appendage spoke for itself. *Is that a fucking octopus tentacle?*

"Hey! Are you alright, Princess?" Aurora called out.

Polaris groaned.

"She'll be 'aight. You won't, though." Vakari's shark-like teeth formed an unsightly sneer akin to a demon's.

Aurora instinctively backpedaled as seven more tentacles sprouted from his back and filled the engine room. Aurora leaped with all her strength through the hole in the ceiling just as the tentacles lashed at her. She was out of the engine room onto the lower deck and immediately rushed to Polaris's aid through the pouring rain. Aurora found the princess crouched next to a shipment cube, healing her bleeding cuts and dark bruises with her nevma shards mixed with water. Polaris especially favored her back, wincing. Luckily her wounds didn't take long to heal with the nevma. She was back on her feet in seconds.

"That was certainly new. These freaks are certainly one of a kind, aren't they?" Polaris lamented, her legs shaking as she stood.

Vakari leaped through the hole and onto the deck. His tentacles lashed around the wet deck as both parties stood against each other, surrounded by shipment cubes. Thunder rumbled and lightning lit up the sky.

"Sorry you just now seein' this. Can't have the public knowin' what I'm really about. Bad for business." He winked at them, his smoky aura emerging around him.

"And who are you exactly?" Polaris asked.

"Call me The Kraken."

"Kraken?" Aurora's excitement escalated. "No way, you're like, famous!"

"I–I am? Really?" Vakari appeared merry.

"Yeah! You were on the wanted list for like seventy million! But . . . you look a lot smaller. Actually, wasn't the Kraken killed by Neptune ages ago?"

His happiness washed away with the rain. "That was my grandaddy!"

"Huh? And you're just out here using his name? Ain't that identity theft?"

"Shut the hell up! The Kraken is just a title, one passed to me!"

"Really?" Aurora frowned. "I don't know. I never heard of a 'Vakari' on the wanted list or a resurgence of the Kraken. You must be kind of lame if you're supposed to be this generation's 'Terror of the Atalantic'."

Vakari's face turned bright red. "You shut your mouth! I'm gonna run this whole ocean one day and be a household name! Get me? You ain't got a clue of what I can do!"

Polaris looked back and forth between the two of them. "Did—did you just embarrass him?" She regained her composure. "In any case, you'd do best to surrender. Eight arms, one hundred arms, doesn't change how this will end."

Vakari took a breath, calming himself down. "You're like a broken record. I'm just itchin' to snap your neck. You lucky someone has it out for you."

"I beg your pardon—"

Aurora heard a shriek from above. She looked up to the upper deck and spotted crewmen staring down at them, appearing startled.

"Vakari! Should we phone in reinforcements or notify the boss?" one of them yelled.

"No way! Another one of our own is already en route. Just sit tight while I handle our intruders." Vakari redirected his menacing glare to the Gorgon siblings.

"He has an assailant en route? All the reason to deal with him quickly." Polaris drew her sword and Aurora created her witch blade. "Solaria, we need a plan."

"I got one. Stay out of my way!" Aurora darted toward him, determined to take him alone.

"We are not repeating the Reiya incident! I'll freeze him and you—"

Immediately, his tentacles lashed at them. The two witches eluded the tentacles flying at them from all directions. Aurora clashed her blade against one of the tentacles but couldn't pierce their scaly surface. It was like trying to cut through concrete. Another tentacle struck her back and slammed her into the ground.

Polaris didn't fare any better. Each time she tried to freeze him, a tentacle rushed her and knocked her off balance. She was reduced to defending and dodging, unable to even raise her sword.

Vakari laughed at their misfortune. "Dance, witches. Dance!"

His tentacles swooped in and smacked the two witches together, back-to-back. Aurora felt a shockwave pulsate through her body. Her back throbbed with an intense striking pain. They both plopped to the ground. Again, Polaris screeched, clawing at her back as she writhed in pain.

"This isn't working. He's keeping us at bay, and we can hardly get close," Polaris muttered in a croaky tone.

Aurora knew Polaris's scarred back was bothering her. "Just go and hide. One bolt of lightning is all I need to fry this clown."

"You can't fire lightning in this rain, you ninny! You'll only hurt us both—"

The two sisters were whipped off the ground by their ankles and dangled above Vakari with his tentacles.

"Trying to scheme against me in the middle of a fight? Rude as hell." He slammed them back into the ground.

He kept yanking them up and slamming them as if a rope lassoed them. The floorboards cracked with each slam, ringing Aurora's head and stinging Polaris's back with throbbing pain. Aurora's blood bubbled like carbon in soda. How easy it would be for her to yank his tentacles straight out of his back, and strangle him with it. She envisioned it so clearly. However, like always, her necklace's charm suppressed that bloodlust.

"Solaria!" Polaris yelled as she was whipped around. "Your demon aura. Take off the necklace and use it. You know it's our best chance!"

"No! How can you even suggest that?" Aurora yelled back before eating the wet floorboards while being slammed face-first.

"He isn't an officer or civilian, Solaria. He's a Viper. We're in survival mode now, and he's just toying with us," Polaris barked.

"Will you shut up? I don't need it!" Aurora got yanked and slammed into the side of a metal shipment cube, ringing her bones.

"Prioritize for once! Do you want these heathens to get your Divine Stone?"

Vakari stopped swinging the girls around. He pulled them back toward him, dangling their brutalized, scarred bodies above him. "Did you just say Divine Stone?"

The blood rushed to Aurora's head and leaked out her nose. "Yeah . . . and? Isn't that why you and your little club are after me? For the stone inside me."

Vakari's eyes opened wide. "You're bluffin'. Is that why . . ." Vakari rubbed the back of his neck. "Oh, that sly son of a bitch! That's why Reiya was so interested in you. I figured it wasn't your cheap ass bounty. He ain't a useless spy after all!"

"Hold on a moment. . . you didn't know?" Polaris asked.

"I would've if you two didn't kill 'em."

Aurora looked away in shame.

"It's all good now. A Divine Stone will make us millions more than you would have, Princess. Maybe even more."

His tentacles coiled around their bodies. He pulled them both in closer, especially Aurora. She was just inches from his scaly face. "So, where is this bad boy stone? In ya skull?" Vakari pulled out his pocket knife.

Aurora didn't know what she feared more: him cutting into her body, or her ripping through his. Although, if she did allow that power to leak through, she'd be free. And she'd crush him without a second thought.

No! She shook her head to fight off its influence. Even if it meant getting free, was it worth killing for? Worth reliving every instance she dragged her claws through someone's flesh? Worth risking Polaris's life? All the same, if she didn't do something, they were both dead anyway.

Just when things couldn't get any worse, the scorpion tattoo on her chest glowed again. Aurora couldn't infuse magic with her hands being restrained. So, Aurora used her head for once. She cocked her head back and bashed her skull into Vakari's. Her ears rang and blood seeped from her forehead and nose.

Vakari screeched, stumbling backward and gripping his bruised skull. "Bitch!"

His grip loosened on the girls, dropping them both.

"Genius move, Solaria! Blitz him!" Polaris commanded.

The sisters charged, but his enormous tentacles swatted them both into shipment cubes. They struggled to stand as the tentacles lashed at them again. They managed to scurry to their feet and fled in opposite directions into the expansive cargo maze.

Aurora sprinted and weaved around the metal shipment cubes as the giant tentacles rushed around them in pursuit of her. She zigzagged around the maze, tentacles just inches from coiling around her.

"Runnin' and hidin' won't save you from these eyes!" Vakari yelled.

Right, he can see heat signatures. Wait, that's it! Aurora deflected the tentacles with her witch-blade. She leaped on top of the stacked cubicles to stand above the maze. She watched Polaris running around and trying to freeze the tentacles as they missed her. Just when she thought she had a break, more tentacles swung her way. Aurora created a small barrier-dome around herself to deflect them. She took a deep breath. *I really hope this works.* She expanded the barrier. The dome grew, expanding fifty feet around her and deflecting both the tentacles and the rushing rain.

"The hell?" Vakari barked.

Her chest glowed as she concentrated as much of her aura as possible to her hands. They erupted with blue flames and she formed a tornado of flames around her. Aurora put everything she had in it, making her flames larger and brighter. The heat smothered her, the witch practically baking in an oven of her own creation. Still, Vakari's painful screeching made it all worth it. She smiled. Her plan worked.

She released the flames along with her barrier, panting and blinded by steam. Once it cleared, she saw Vakari's tentacles wrapped around himself, no longer chasing her sister. He vigorously rubbed his eyes and cried, "It burns!"

Aurora zipped toward him and gave him the pummeling of a lifetime. She belted him with a barrage of rapid fists, lumping his face and knocking the scales off him. Her knuckles tore and bled with each strike but rattling someone never felt so good. One last uppercut tossed him in the air, finishing him.

Polaris swooped in and blasted him with rushing water. He crashed into a shipment cube, leaving a dent. She closed her fists, freezing him solidly against the wet metal and forming a miniature white glacier on the ship. His teeth chattered and his head shivered as cold blood leaked down his forehead.

Aurora panted rigorously, stumbling to a knee. She hadn't realized she was still disoriented from her earlier headbutt. Despite her headache, relief washed over her, seeing Vakari frozen in place. She collapsed to the ground, her chest pulsating and her arms losing all feeling. Polaris knelt over Aurora and smiled at her, giving her a rare high-five. Her exhaustion didn't even allow her to laugh, but it at least couldn't extinguish her enormous smile.

Polaris redirected her attention to their frozen captive. "Not quite the powerhouse. I assume you weren't built for the Arctic, Sir Kraken." Polaris sheathed her sword.

Vakari's teeth chattered. "I-if-if-if you gonna' interrogate me f-f-f-f-f-forget it! I-I-I-I ain't s-s-sayin' n-n-nothin'!"

"Your resilience is astonishing. Most don't retain consciousness after such a pummeling. You can remain silent, and I can wait for your body to fail from hypothermia. Or you can be compliant and start talking. Maybe then I shall consider giving you aid."

Aurora stared up at the rainy sky, listening to Polaris trying to interrogate the octopus. She smiled, pointing her fist at the sky. *Beat another one, Blair.* She squinted, seeing something floating high above. The figure grew closer and closer, resembling a person.

"Hey . . . Polaris. The hell is that?" Aurora pointed to the sky.

"What?" Polaris looked up.

"B-b-b-bout t-ti-time she showed up!" Vakari smiled. "St-st-st-stalled 'em long en-enough."

In a flash, the sky dot zipped like lightning and crashed onto the top of the shipment cube. Aurora jumped up in reaction to her speed.

The mysterious figure wore a black trench coat and had straight, silky jet-black hair, both drenched from the rain. Her pink eyes, appearing almost luminous, narrowed with fury. Her presence was much more daunting than that of Vakari and Reiya. It practically choked Aurora. The newcomer carried a black crystal ball, squeezing it in her grasp and scowling with her long, pointy fangs. With her paper-white skin, Aurora quickly recognized her species.

Aurora had never seen a vampire before and never imagined seeing one around her age. She also never expected to see Polaris so shaken. The princess backpedaled so much that she slipped and fell on the wet deck.

"It . . . you . . . no," Polaris stammered. "You're . . . you. I—" she covered her mouth.

Serena hissed through her teeth. "You're all grown up. I guess seven years will do that to you. Right, sis?"

"The fuck she say?" Aurora felt thrown for a loop but stayed on her guard. However, Polaris was frozen stiff. Her mouth hung open and her bottom lip quivered. Even when facing death at both Reiya and Aurora's own hand, Polaris never looked this pale.

Aurora grabbed Polaris's shoulder. "Hey, earth to princess! Who the hell is that sparkly vampire up there? And why did she call you sis? Don't tell me . . . we have another sister?"

Polaris swallowed her saliva. She slipped trying to get back on her feet. "We. Need. To go. Now."

Serena shifted her gaze to Aurora. "So, you're The Crimson Witch. Not so intimidating up close."

Aurora balled up her fist, focusing on Serena again. She didn't care how imposing her presence was, she was gonna cram those words back down her throat. "Wanna say that to my face, blood-breath?"

Polaris screamed, "Solaria, shut u—"

In a blink, Serena stood inches before Aurora. Aurora batted her eyes just to make sure her eyes weren't playing trips on her. She hardly saw Serena move, and only felt the blowback of misty wind hit her face. Now Aurora understood Polaris's panic. She had never seen anything move that fast. However, her fear was swiftly displaced with fury. Speed wasn't everything, and Aurora was ready to show this newcomer what she was about.

Aurora jumped back and whipped out her witch-blade. A second later, she couldn't feel her arm anymore. Her body stiffened before being overcome with a streaming pain. Her right arm flopped on the deck, and her blood splattered all around her, blending into the flooded deck.

Aurora's bottom lip quivered, not a sound escaping her breath. *When? How?* Aurora's eyes glided toward Serena's black katana, covered in a striking red aura. A stream of Aurora's blood trickled down the sharp edge of the blade.

"Slow, too? For a Gorgon, you're disappointing," Serena said.

As her arm regenerated, Aurora swung her other fist. She struck a blur before having her face smashed into the wooden deck from behind. Serena sliced off Aurora's left leg, prompting her painful screams. She writhed on the ground in pain, tearing up. Serena then drove her sword through Aurora's back, pinning her down. Aurora's throat strained with how loud she screamed in agony.

Serena knelt and whispered in her ear. "Try not to bleed out and die. I have questions later, Solaria Gorgon."

Polaris remained a petrified statue up until Serena approached her. She started to retreat until they were shoulder to shoulder.

"Go ahead. Pull the blade out and save your sister. Do what I couldn't," Serena said.

Polaris swallowed her saliva. "Don't tell me you're one of them. You're a Viper?"

"You can say that. But you know who to blame, right?" Serena walked off toward Vakari, still frozen against the shipment cube.

Aurora struggled to reach the sword sticking out of her back, blood dripping down her shaky fingers. Her necklace flickered with a purple light as she grunted in pain and her eyes teared up. An immense heat swelled within her, and she tried to fight it off. Her dismembered arm had re-formed skin to seal the wound and stop the bleeding, along with her leg. However, the appendages didn't regenerate fully. Her suppressor likely was withholding the necessary demonic aura she needed to restore her limbs. Worse than that, she felt her energy being drained from her. It gave her intense déjà vu. It didn't help that Polaris stood still, seemingly staring off into space.

"Hey! A little help would be nice!" Aurora screeched to Polaris.

Polaris snapped out of her trance and rushed over to Aurora.

Aurora winced. "My body. It— it feels like it's getting weaker. Get this thing out."

"If you had used your demon aura to regenerate properly, this wouldn't have happened!" Polaris grabbed the handle, but it scorched her white gloves, leaving them singed with blackened holes surrounding her reddened palms. The Princess winced. "What on earth?"

"You won't be able to wield that blade. It'll never choose you," Serena shouted back at her.

"Then . . . is this a Celestial Weapon? But how?" Polaris mumbled.

Aurora's eyes nearly popped out of her head. She knew she recognized this draining feeling, along with the last time she heard mentions of a celestial weapon. "I know this weapon. That bastard Shoto had it!"

Polaris raised an eyebrow. "Shoto?"

All the while, Serena had pulled out a small syringe of blood from the inside of her trench coat pockets. She stuck the needle into her mouth and ejected all of the blood. A pink aura surrounded her and, for a moment, her eyes turned a bright orange. Serena placed her hand on the ice and steam surrounded them. A dense heat smothered him as the ice melted into a thick mist, freeing Vakari from his ice prison.

"What took ya so long? They nearly killed me!" Vakari griped.

"And yet you're alive. Count yourself lucky. Not many people live after dealing with Gorgons," Serena hissed.

"Gorgons? The Crimson brat is a Gorgon too?"

"Yeah. Did you not notice the scorpion on her chest?"

Vakari scoffed. "Least now I can deliver the goods back to Dr. Fekoku. Any more of a fight with these two little shits and all the goods are resting at the bottom of the Atalanta."

Serena and Vakari approached them as Polaris struggled to take the sword out of Aurora, burning her hands each time.

"Vakari, do me a favor and make sure Crimson doesn't go anywhere, okay? My old friend and I are going to catch up." Serena stared ice-cold daggers at Polaris.

Even at a shorter stature, Serena's presence was smothering. Seeing Polaris so petrified wasn't helping Aurora's morale or will to free herself and fight. Even Vakari seemed off-put by Serena's demeanor.

"Ah, right! You Alucards and Gorgons have bad blood," Vakari said.

Serena shot a glare his way, which made him recoil slightly.

"Chill! Sheesh. You mercenaries are all terrifying."

"Just do what I say and stay out of it."

"Yeah, yeah; have fun. But I'm not gonna lie, Serena, this is one hell of a haul for the Vipers." Vakari rubbed his chin and smiled. "The Divine Sorcerer's Stone will make a fortune for us. Or be a helluva bargaining chip for the boss," Vakari laughed.

Serena was taken aback. "What?"

"The Divine Sorcerer's Stone. It's inside the Crimson girl, right?"

Serena bit her bottom lip. She grasped her pentagram pendant hanging on her neck. She closed her eyes, and bowed her head, mumbling under her breath.

"Oh!" Vakari grinned "I know that ritual of yours. You're praying for a future body. Which chump are you about to put in a body bag?"

Serena's sword levitated out of Aurora's back and zipped at the two Vipers, flickering their hair. Serena caught her blade's hilt in mid-air. Vakari tensed up. Blood spewed through his shark teeth and his tentacles plopped to the ground like weights. His head slowly slid off his neck.

The bleeding and wounds aside, Aurora felt like spiders were crawling up and down her body. She'd witnessed mutilation before, but that left her speechless. Polaris mimicked her sister, unable to utter a single word.

Serena bowed her head in prayer. "May Lord Fraizen seek mercy on your soul. Amen."

11
To Be a Princess

Those rose quartz eyes once filled Polaris with immeasurable joy. Now, in the dead of night, amid a raging storm, it instilled her with a terror far greater than any beast or dragon could inflict. Serena's once friendly face became more alien with each passing second. Long ago, Polaris couldn't fathom the one she adored exuding such malice and hatred through her grimace. If only things could've turned out differently. Maybe Serena wouldn't be standing before her with blood splattered on her face. Perhaps she wouldn't have just beheaded her own partner. Then again, Polaris couldn't blame her. After all, seven years prior, Polaris's actions weren't too different.

Normally, young girls in The Pearl Kingdom headed indoors around sunset, especially during the snowy winter. However, for seven-year-old Polaris Gorgon, dusk was her favorite time of the day. When her royal studies, magic combat training, or trips to neighboring Magic Nations to participate in play sessions with the other royal children weren't filling her schedule, she would leave the castle and venture into the forests just outside the inner Kingdom.

She did the same that winter evening, trotting through the thick snow with a vibrant smile plastered on her face. She headed for the dark caves at the western edge of the Pearlian Forests, where a younger vampire stood in wait. The vampire's face mimicked the snow, and her short, black bangs hid her glowing pink eyes. Despite that, she saw Polaris right away. Polaris grinned upon seeing her but was put off by the pair of armed Magic Militia standing on opposite ends of the cave entry, armed with halberds.

Polaris had no time to address the soldiers directly as the young vampire trotted to her and leaped into her arms. "Big sis!" the child exclaimed with the purest of smiles.

Polaris stumbled back, slipping and falling on the compact, cold snow. "Hold it! You're much too heavy, Cassie!"

The soldiers were startled, readying their weapons. "Unhand the heiress at once!" one of them yelled.

Polaris raised her hand, ordering the soldiers to hold their weapons and tongues. The Militia obeyed, lowering their halberds. Just then, another vampire emerged from the darkness behind them. Polaris beamed upon seeing her, but the vampire was initially preoccupied with her impromptu staring contest with the soldiers she marched past.

"No funny business. You'd better not even dream of escaping!" one of the militia warned.

Ten-year-old Serena Alucard scoffed at them before fully emerging from the cave. Polaris couldn't help but curl her nose at the sight of her friend, who wore nothing but a white tank-top and black shorts. Meanwhile, she had to wear several layers, topped off with a vibrant red trench coat and a yellow scarf. Despite all that, Polaris still shivered. How she envied the vampires' collective natural resistance to the cold.

Serena folded her arms and poked out her lips in disapproval. "You're late, sis. What's your excuse now? Polishing your glass slippers?"

"I beg your pardon? Don't be unfair, Serena. I was merely finishing my duties for the day."

Serena narrowed her eyes. "You're seven. What 'duties' could you possibly have?"

"I had a formal tea party scheduled with Princess Camella. Mother said it was mandatory."

"Ugh. The annoying blonde?"

"You referring to her or her father?"

They both shared a chuckle. There it was, the smile of her best friend. A smile that, at the time, Polaris wanted to cherish forever.

"Oooh, princess stuff!" Cassie cheered. "Can I be a princess like you when I grow up?"

Polaris couldn't just ignore the twinkle in those hopeful eyes. "Well, why ever wait?" Polaris set her down and aimed her hands at the snow. The soft snow clumped together before forming a pile. Her aura shimmered a soft blue around her body as the snow became two snowmen. The snowmen bowed in front of Cassie. One of them extended a hand to her, forming a tiny tiara made of hardened snow. Polaris walked over and placed it on Cassie's head. The younger vampire radiated with a grin, showing off her tiny fangs.

Serena couldn't help but snicker. "You're such a showoff."

"I present the first Queen of the Alucard Caves, Cassie Alucard." Polaris bowed.

Serena played along, bowing as well. Cassie cheered and gave Polaris and Serena a huge hug. Serena gave Polaris a thumbs-up behind Cassie's back.

The three played together in the snow before heading inside the caves. The trio walked toward soft emerald lights, casted from bulky crystals emerging from the crevasse of the cave walls. They soon arrived at a cluster of tents, all with the embroidery of a double pentagram, signifying their worship to Fraizen, God of Fated Paths. Polaris witnessed the same marking on the other Alucard Clansmen, whether it be stitched on their clothing, or dangling from their necks. While Cassie ran deeper inside to the other Alucards, Polaris and Serena took their time to stroll and chat rather than rush.

"She's quite chipper today," Polaris commented.

"She's always chipper. Especially when it comes to you. All she ever talks about is being a princess. Tea parties, coronations, all that." Serena stopped in her tracks, apparently coming to a realization. "Now that I think about it, someone's coronation is coming up in a week."

Polaris stroked her blue braid, unable to impede her forming grin. "You remembered?"

"How could I forget?" Serena rustled the top of Polaris's hair, prompting Polaris to fight her off. "You're going to be all official now! Do we have to bow every time we see you, *heiress*?"

Polaris hid her face with the collar of her jacket. "Please don't! It would be quite embarrassing. I implore you to treat me the same as always."

"So, still a tiny, helpless squirt? You don't have to tell me twice." Serena wrestled Polaris's hair again. Again, Polaris fought her off, nearly pushing Serena off her feet. "Whoa, someone got stronger!"

"Of course. Combat is a major part of my training. That and all those rigorous sparring matches with Princess Camella and Princess Kiko. I can never best them, but I have improved significantly."

Serena rolled her eyes. "I wish you'd talk your age for once."

"What's wrong with my dialect?"

"You use the word *dialect*."

Polaris pouted. "Why must you insist on poking fun at me?"

Serena pinched Polaris's red cheeks. "Because you're so easy, rosy!"

Polaris smacked her hands away, poking her lips out in a pout. Still, she couldn't help but be swayed by Serena's laugh and smile.

"For my coronation, I wish you and your family could attend."

Serena stopped again. Her smile vanished, catching Polaris off guard. "I don't see that ever happening." Serena put her index finger in her mouth and lifted her lip, showing off her long fangs. "Not so long as we have these. Besides, you know they won't let us leave unless it's to hunt for food, with supervision of course."

Polaris scanned the surrounding cave. She caught the eyes of several Magic Militia soldiers, most of whom sat or rested on the edge of the cave walls. While initially believing their gaze was fixated on her, she soon realized they were studying Serena's movements, which was made more evident by their hands resting on their respective weapons. Polaris couldn't have been more disgusted by her own men.

"Must they show such fear over an event Count Dracula was responsible for? He was punished for his crimes long before even the Militia's establishment!"

"I agree, sis, but it doesn't change anything. So long as we look like demons, we'll be treated like them. That's just our fate."

Polaris didn't take Serena's defeatist attitude kindly. There had to be another way, and Polaris soon found it. "I can ask Mother to give a decree to allow you, no, all the Alucards to attend! There needn't be such tension. You are all Pearlians as much as I am."

Serena couldn't even meet her gaze. For Polaris, that was a first. Her friend fiddled with her pentagram necklace.

"Lord Fraizen saw to it that we all lived separately for a reason. It's not a good idea. Sorry, sis."

Polaris bowed her head. "I understand."

"Don't be too glum. When you come over with your little crown, we'll have a huge tea party in your honor!" Serena smacked Polaris on the back.

Immediately, Polaris yipped in pain. The surrounding militia perked up, their hands hovering over their weapons.

Serena backed away instinctively. "What's wrong?"

Polaris's legs shivered. She fell to her knees and rubbed her stinging, burning back. She winced and her eyes watered. *No, I mustn't. A true princess doesn't show weakness, even in the presence of insatiable pain.* The young girl wiped her eyes and stood up straight, bearing a fake smile. "Nothing at all. 'Tis a cramp, nothing more."

Serena curled her eyebrows. "A cramp? In your back?"

"Yes, yes, never mind me. You caused no harm. But thank you. For the offer . . . it means a lot." Polaris's voice strained to maintain her façade.

Serena had inquisitive eyes but seemingly took her word for it. "You can thank me by staying overnight. It's been a while since we had a sleepover."

"Oh?" Polaris curled a brow.

Serena's white cheeks became a soft rose. "Uh, yeah! Erm, Cassie really wants you to! Yeah, that's it! She practically begged for it!"

Polaris saw right through her. "Well, I'll have to tell 'Cassie' that I'll be unable to tonight. I have important duties to attend to in the morning."

Serena pouted. "What is it this time?"

Polaris sighed. "I must attend a Council meeting at my mother's side. She wants me to observe the proceedings with the other Magic Nations and engage with the other royal children again."

Serena rolled her eyes. "You always have an excuse. You can't just tell her that you want to pass? I can tell you don't want to go."

Polaris's eyes fell to her boots. "I don't have a choice, Serena."

"Sure you d—"

"I don't." Polaris fiddled with her fingers. "Mother's decree is law. It would be . . . unwise to disobey."

Serena made no effort to hide the discontent on her face. Yet, she didn't argue any further. Guilt gnawed at the princess during their silence. Polaris knew well that Serena's disappointment was a small price to avoid everything that came with her mother's own.

As they continued their walk, Polaris took in the Alucard lifestyle, as she often did, marveling at how different it was from life inside the Kingdom. All the tents were embroidered with a pentagram on their sides. Some of the vampires were moving crates of food. Others were joined in a circle of prayer. There were even elder vampires reading books to some of the children. Polaris found their lifestyle primitive, but very charming.

She quite enjoyed the consistent peace, or at least she would have enjoyed it more had it not been for the Magic Militia standing on every corner. They stood at the cave walls and the entrance to the tents. It seemed there would be more and more soldiers dedicated to the caves each day. The other thing that cramped her enjoyment of the peace: the eyes glued to her. Stares from the militia were expected, but the native Alucards had their eyes fixed like daggers, especially that evening. She grew accustomed to being the center of attention wherever she went, but these stares were quite different from what she was used to. Before Polaris could comment, Serena snatched her wrist and yanked her toward her family's tent.

The expansive quilt tint was as dim as the rest of the cave, with only two candles providing visibility. The vampires didn't need much if any, with their natural night-vision, another perk Polaris was envious of. Serena's mother, Madeline Alucard, sat in an old chair made of sticks and twine, reading a book with the same pentagram symbol on its cover. Her black hair had silver streaks and her glasses barely hid the wrinkles near her eyes. She gave them both a warm, welcoming smile as she always did.

"Welcome home, girls," Madeline said with a hearty, gentle voice.

Polaris wanted to return the welcome but was distracted by Cassie wrestling down her father playfully. The tiny vampire stood on his back and laughed, claiming victory, while still wearing the ice tiara Polaris had given her earlier. She was surprised it hadn't melted.

"You two are so slow!" Cassie griped. "I already had enough time to beat Daddy and claim supremacy."

Polaris's face burned with embarrassment. She didn't unintentionally teach her that, did she?

Serena giggled. "Queen Euryale better watch out. With that attitude, she may see you as a threat to the throne."

Polaris started bowing over and over. "Please forgive me if she exhibits any unruly behavior! It wasn't my intention to make her a bother."

Serena's father, Bradley Alucard, also extended a warm welcome, despite Cassie still dancing on his back. "It's okay, no need to bow or apologize!"

After watching Cassie play-fight with her father some more, Polaris joined the small Alucard family at their dinner table. She declined the option to eat with them. She ate before coming to the caves, weary of the raw meats the vampires always ate. That night was no exception, with raw rabbit on the menu.

Seeing the vampires tear away at the red, bloody meat always made her stomach turn. Yet another thing she thought she would've grown accustomed to. Just when she was getting over the sight of blood dripping down from the corners of Serena's pale mouth, Serena's father broke the ice.

"Polaris, what's the inner kingdom like nowadays?" Bradley asked.

"It's wonderful!" Polaris replied cheerfully. "Still the best kingdom in all the Magic Nations."

He eyed the opening of the tent before lowering his head and voice. "I wonder, is it overrun with militia?"

The random question surprised the young heiress, but she didn't think too much of it. "Not at all. Mother sees no need to bolster military defense in the inner kingdom, given we are no longer in a warring period. She would rather delegate our branch of the Magic Militia to deal with potential foreign threats that may come from our eastern and southern coasts."

"Even with the demon problem?" Serena's mother intervened.

"Demon?" Cassie asked.

Serena shoved her sister lightly on the shoulder, indicating that she should stay quiet.

"Demons? Oh, you're referring to the Skewer Bandits? King Arthur dealt with that lot recently. I doubt they'll be making their presence known again for a long time. You all have nothing to fear. Mother will see to it that you all are protected."

Serena's parents stared at her blankly. For a moment, it was the same stares she was met with when she arrived earlier in the cave. Why was everyone giving her those eyes? Polaris turned to see the militia soldiers peeking through the opening in the tent. They swiftly turned away. Polaris sat at the edge of her seat. She never felt such discomfort in Alucard Caves.

Serena, reading the room, broke the thick ice. "My vampire speed came in today!" she blurted out.

Everyone turned to her. Her parents smiled.

"Really, sis?" Cassie asked gleefully.

Serena backed up from the table. "Uh-huh. Watch."

In a gust of wind, she vanished. Polaris felt a brisk breeze smack her neck. Her hair flipped up on her head. Before she knew it, her hair was tied up in pigtails. She turned to see Serena snickering behind her. Cassie and her parents clapped.

"Wonderful! Lord Fraizen has blessed you, and at so young an age!" Madeline exclaimed.

"Some wonderful things lie ahead in your path. I can see it! Even Brother Reginald didn't achieve his until he turned fifteen. You're going to do remarkable things for our people, Serena," her father added.

Serena undid Polaris's pigtails. "I should. With Polaris leading the country soon, who knows? Maybe a lot more can change with the both of us working together."

Serena's friendly wink and affirmation made Polaris smile. Just when she was about to congratulate her, Polaris felt a buzzing in her pockets. She pulled out her purple crystal ball and saw a call incoming from Nation 7, District 1. Serena frowned knowingly at the sight. It was the Queen, meaning her time was up.

As Polaris said her abrupt goodbyes, Serena followed her on the way out of the tent. When Polaris crossed the opening, the militia that stood there crossed their halberds to keep Serena from doing the same. Serena scowled at them.

"Do you have to go now? It hasn't even been an hour yet," Serena called out to her.

"I know it bothers you, but you know when Mother calls, I must heed to it."

"C'mon, don't you want to stay? Just a little longer?"

Polaris noticed Serena's face reddening. "Why is it you want me to stay so badly today?"

Serena stared at her feet. "Well . . . I—I know you're always sparring with the blonde and the Queen. I learned some speed magic and I . . . I, I wanted to . . . test it against you," she mumbled, scratching her cheek and avoiding eye contact. "We never sparred before. Thought it would be fun."

Polaris blushed. Never did she imagine Serena of all people asking to be her sparring partner. She grinned from ear to ear. "Tomorrow we shall spar. Don't expect me to go easy. My mastery of water improves each day. I care not that you're older, I shall claim victory."

Serena's face lit up. "Don't get a big head, sis. You won't even touch me when we fight!"

"I'm sorry I must depart early again, but I shall see you tomorrow."

The next day came as quickly as it went. Polaris returned to the cave that evening, eager to spend more time with Serena and Cassie. She took her usual route through the forest but came across a strange aroma the closer she got to her destination. Her nose curled at the rancid, burning smell of. . .rotten beef? Pork? Polaris couldn't fully make it out, but the smell was far from pleasant. Whatever was cooking, it couldn't have been good. She pushed forward regardless, struggling to ignore it with each step. However, she could not ignore the vibrant orange light shining in the distance, also coming from the direction of the cave. First, a bad smell, now an ominous orange light came from her friends' home. Polaris swallowed at the thought. Her stomach turned and her mouth dried. Polaris advanced, and soon arrived within mere feet of the cave entrance when she heard a blend of voices. She quickly hid behind the closest oak, so as to not be seen by the massive crowd gathered outside of the cave. What she saw made her want to vomit.

The crowd consisted of the adult vampires from Alucard Caves, surrounding a massive, raging fire. Fifteen burning wooden stakes were lined up just before the cave. The young girl's eyes bulged in terror at the sight of mutilated faces within the flames. Finding the source of the bad meat smell only made the heiress sicker. The absence of any militia gave away the identity of those burning. Polaris covered her mouth and squeezed the tree bark as hard as she could. To make matters worse, the vampires surrounding the fire were cheering and chanting while the bodies burned.

One bearded vampire stood before his brethren as he raised his blood-stained hands and rejoiced to the heavens. "Lord Fraizen! We send you fifteen sacrifices to buy our freedom! No longer will we be caged! You've set our new paths, and we shall walk them willingly!"

"Amen!" the other vampires cheered.

Polaris didn't want to believe what she thought but couldn't ignore the blood stains on the faces and hands of the vampires. Panic consumed the young witch. Why did they just kill all the militia? They had never acted violently before, as far as she knew. Nothing made sense.

"We're free. We're finally going to be free!" another one cheered.

"Indeed. For too long we've been caged like dogs, all because our grandfather Dracula dared to challenge the might of our oppressors. Because he dared to think differently and speak against the Demi-Gods. We shall honor him by taking the head of his assassin, Euryale Gorgon! Our comrades will join us tomorrow, and we will attack as a unit!"

The other vampires cheered. Polaris shuddered at the thought.

"Brother Bradley, remind everyone of the intel you received last night."

One of the middle-aged vampires joined his side. Polaris recognized him immediately. *Serena's father?*

"The young princess spoke of the militia's forces being minimal. According to my daughter, the girl is no liar. She finds every opportunity to boast about her kingdom and her disgusting mother. With assistance from our new comrades, our combined forces should be enough. We'll take the queen out, and after, we'll take the entire Pearl Kingdom."

Polaris backpedaled, fear strangling her tight. She slipped while backing away on the snow, falling back first. Pain permeated from her backside, making her yip. One of the vampires in the crowd turned in her direction.

"Who's there?" he said.

Polaris shrugged off the immense pain and sprinted off without a second thought. She ran back to the kingdom as fast as she could, ignoring the stinging cold wind.

Upon making it back to Gorgon castle, Polaris rammed through the doors to the throne room. She stumbled onto the velvet carpet, clutching her chest and waiting for her jackhammer of a heart to slow down. She struggled to regulate her breathing and cease her shaking. The sub-artic air didn't help, and the hell she witnessed certainly didn't either.

"Child!" a stern voice boomed through the room.

Polaris shot up and stood straight. She witnessed her mother, Queen Euryale Gorgon, sitting on her red and gold throne at the end of the long velvet carpet. Polaris marched down the extensive walkway, wishing she could marvel at the bright, sparkly glass chandeliers that hung overhead. She wished she could marvel more at the smooth, reflective marble floors or the white columns to the edge of the glistening red and gold walls. But the closer she got to her mother and the throne, the more she felt her entire body being pulled toward the ground. The weight of Euryale's aura suffocated the child as always. She could barely hold her head up to see her mother's face, or the burgundy banner with the family crest that hung above her.

The queen crossed her legs and her red, scaly scorpion tail hung on the edge of her throne. She wore a scarlet robe but still had her golden tiara sitting neatly on her crimson bun. She swished around the wine in her glass as she stared down at her daughter with irises made of gold.

"You nearly blow down my doors and enter hyperventilating? What's the meaning of this nonsensical behavior of yours?" she asked, her tone sharp.

Polaris shuddered at her mother's golden glare. "Mother . . . the Alucards. They've . . . they've—" Just thinking about it collapsed her throat.

"Spit it out, child. What about those ruffians has you so shaken?"

Tears welled in the girl's eyes. "They're planning a coup. They're planning to storm the kingdom and claim your life!"

The Queen narrowed her eyes at her momentarily. She then chuckled before taking a sip of her wine. "That all? If that's the case, the Militia should handle the lot. They'll be fine after a talking to. Nothing to fear, my dear."

Polaris's lip quivered. "The Militia . . . the Alucards already claimed their lives. When I arrived, they were . . . they were. They were all burning at the stake."

Euryale leaned forward on her throne. "Oh. That is troublesome." She downed the rest of her wine before placing it on the arm of her throne. "Aren't you friends with one of those creatures?"

Polaris nodded, her tears streaming down her face.

Euryale sighed. She brushed aside the hanging red curls of her hair and approached her daughter. She knelt to meet her daughter's eyes and placed her hand on Polaris's shoulder. "You're absolutely sure they are planning a coup? It would be unwise with their current numbers. Do you know of any assailants?"

Polaris wiped her tears and sniffed. "Well . . . they mentioned having outside help. I fear it may be the United Military. That only makes sense."

Euryale's grip tightened on Polaris's shoulder. The young girl retreated, feeling her heart sink. The fear she felt when seeing the militia's bodies was nothing compared to her mother's calm grin.

"Polaris, my dear girl. Thank you," Euryale said.

"P-Pardon?"

"You did well to report this. You're certainly more useful to me than the lot of those Militia. With this news, we can successfully prevent unnecessary bloodshed amongst our people. That is the work of a true princess."

Polaris's face brightened. "Truly? You believe I am useful?"

"You are *my* daughter. In fact—" Euryale snapped her fingers.

One of the maids scurried from the other room. She came in and knelt. "My queen?"

"Matilda, bring me the headgear we received from Neo-Camelot the other day."

"Wait, now? But it isn't—"

Euryale glared at her. The maid's face drained of color. "Right away my queen!" The maid scampered out of the throne room.

Polaris was confused. Shortly after, the maid returned carrying a velvet pillow with a golden circlet on top. Joy swelled within the girl. The headpiece was almost blinding, with a glistening sapphire in the center that mimicked the vast Atalanta Ocean. She loved it.

"I was going to save it for your coronation, but you can consider it a gift," Euryale said.

Polaris put on the golden circlet. It was cold to the touch on her forehead, but she was filled with so much joy that she didn't care. "Thank you, Mother! Thank you so much!"

"Now, we should go over to the Alucard Caves. Some negotiations should cool their frustrations, don't you think?"

Polaris beamed. "Absolutely! That's a wonderful idea!"

"Come with me, child. I'll teach you some more about diplomacy."

Polaris and Queen Euryale left the inner kingdom and went to the Alucard Caves. They soon stood before the burned corpses. Polaris turned from seeing their burned, black, melted skin, the red meat falling off the black bones.

Euryale's lip curled up in disgust. "First lesson as Princess, never stock up on dull blades." Euryale walked past the burned stakes and headed into the cave.

Polaris reluctantly followed, feeling a cold chill crawl down her back.

As they walked deeper into the cave, Polaris couldn't shake that daunting dread. She convinced herself all would be well in these negotiations. They were just going to discuss terms and possibly her mother would offer them a new place to live. So long as she could see Serena and Cassie, it didn't matter where. Her mother seemed to be in a much better mood than she anticipated, so anything was possible.

Upon their arrival to the village, the vampires whipped their heads to the pair of them in shock. All of them ceased movement, holding spears covered in blood. Some of the women and children were led into tents. One of the Alucards, the same bearded one leading the ritual from earlier, approached the queen. He got on his knees and bowed.

His voice was shaky. "My queen . . . what brings you to our home?"

Polaris stood close to her mother. She scanned the area but could not spot either Serena or Cassie.

Euryale's scorpion stinger lashed around. "Reginald Alucard. Perhaps you can explain why fifteen of the finest men in the Magic Nations were all burned at the stake?"

He shivered, slowly raising his head. The air thinned.

Polaris felt as if she was being pulled toward the ground, a feeling not at all unfamiliar.

"M'lady . . . the militia were insubordinate! They all attacked us of their own accord. We just defended ourselves!"

Euryale chuckled. "If they were weak enough to be killed with such little resistance, then you did me a favor. Fret not, I come to thank you for the service."

Polaris's eyes widened. What was her mother talking about?

Reginald smiled. "Of course, my queen. Anything for you!"

"Reginald, riddle me this. If they threatened your life, you all clearly find it natural to take theirs. It's all a means to protect your kind. Your women and children. Correct?" Euryale asked.

"Of course. No question, my queen."

"Then, it's only natural for me to slaughter you all for threatening the safety of my kingdom, correct?"

"Wait, what—"

Reginald's head rolled to the ground. His blood rained down around them and dripped from his mother's scorpion stinger. For Polaris, she felt as if time stopped.

She had to have imagined it. The subsequent screaming confirmed her reality, along with that disturbing image of her mother's sinister grin, with blood splattered on her face. Polaris backpedaled before falling on her butt.

"Alucards, due to your plans for a coup d'état, your entire clan has been sentenced to a swift, violent execution by decree of me, your queen."

Several vampires surrounded them in the blink of an eye. They bared their fangs and manifested their pink auras. The cave shook from their collective power. Their rage radiated through their aura.

"You are no queen to us!" one of them shouted.

Euryale folded her arms and shook her head. "You're correct. I'm your god. Warning, I'm far less merciful than the false god you've all followed for so long."

"You will not speak ill of Lord Fraize—"

Euryale's scorpion tail pierced straight through the vampire's chest. He fell to the ground and bled out.

Polaris crawled away as the carnage ensued. The vampires were all blurs, swooping in to take their shots. Euryale matched the blinding speed of the Alucards, tearing them apart with her bare hands and her tail. Blood rained through the caves, filling with the echo of screams. However, one of the vampires managed to sink their fangs into Euryale's neck.

Polaris knew of the Alucards' ability and her heart sank. Not thinking further, the young princess struck the vampire with a cannon of rushing water, blasting the vampire off her mother's back.

Euryale rubbed the specs of blood off her creamy skin. "Not necessary, child, but appreciated."

Polaris's hands shook. Even with the compliment, she wanted to beg her mother to stop. But the words couldn't escape her lips.

The vampire hopped back to his feet, laughing maniacally as his muscles bulked. His eyes turned gold, mimicking the hue of his swelling aura. Polaris grew worried her mother's powers would be used against her. But the vampire staggered, his aura dissipating in a flash. He fell to his knees and clawed at his neck until his fingernails became bloody. His skin bubbled and melted. He screamed as steam rose from his burning skin.

Euryale giggled at his misery with such delight. Never has her mother looked so joyous, even when celebrating with a fresh bottle of wine.

Although it was hard to tell, Polaris could've sworn she even saw her mother blush. She loved the bloodshed, and was far from finished.

She blasted through the tents with water and ice shards. Her attackers tried biting into her as well, and quickly met the same fate as the first to attempt it. Even their mightiest couldn't so much as scratch her. Their super speed meant nothing. Massive icicles and streams of water shot attempted escapees down with enough pressure to carve through stone.

Stop. Stop. Mother . . . please. Tears burned Polaris's eyes.

Men, women, children, elderly, none were spared in the slaughter. Euryale laughed as she ran around and picked them apart one by one. How long until she killed them all? How long until she killed Serena? Polaris couldn't even entertain the thought!

"Mother! Stop this at once, please!" Polaris shouted.

Euryale stopped. She turned back to her daughter, her face covered in red splatter. Her sadistic face froze Polaris in place. She wished she had kept her mouth shut.

"Daughter, you know it's unwise to interrupt me during one of my duties. You know the punishment for it."

Polaris backed away, clutching her collar. She struggled trying to force her breath. Her eyes glided to her right, seeing something moving underneath a fallen tent. A young girl popped up. Polaris's heart stopped, meeting eyes with Cassie. A glimmer of hope washed over Cassie's wet face, crushing Polaris's heart. She ran up to and embraced Polaris, clutching her as tight as she could.

"Sis! I can't find Mommy, or Serena, or Daddy! I'm scared!" Cassie whimpered.

Polaris met her mother's gaze, and she wished she hadn't. The Queen's devilish grin pierced right through her. Polaris shook her head. *No. Please, please, please!*

"On second thought, you can forget your punishment. Instead, I'll give you your first duty as Princess of The Pearl Kingdom. Execute that Alucard underling."

A storm raged within Polaris, tearing her apart from the inside.

Cassie looked up at Polaris with soft, glossy eyes. "Sis?" she mumbled.

"Do not hesitate. Kill her now, or I'll seek a more suitable heir!" Euryale's tail smacked the ground, and Polaris flinched.

Polaris backed away from Cassie, her heartstrings in a knot. She mouthed to her to run as she shakily aimed her hands at her. Euryale stood in wait, rather than tending to the escaping Alucards. Why wouldn't she just focus on them? Why won't Cassie run away? Why did she stare at her with those round, teary eyes that broke heart?

Polaris's face was as wet as Cassie's. Her hands lowered slightly. "Mother. Please! Not her. Please, she's a child!"

Euryale aimed her finger at Polaris, a bead of water forming at her fingertip. "So are you. Keep up your defiance, and I'll see to it that you never see the throne. Do you genuinely want to disappoint your mother?"

Cassie now shivered as much as Polaris did. She backed away until she tripped under her own feet. A ball of water formed at the palms of Polaris's hands, aimed at the young vampire. The ball stretched, forming a thick sickle before freezing to ice.

The young vampire crawled backward. "Sis, no. Please don't," Cassie begged.

Polaris couldn't stop the rain from pouring down her hot face. She gritted her teeth as her aura sputtered around her. "I'm sorry . . . Cassie. I'm . . . not your sister."

Time stopped again. All the sound around her drowned out, as if she were deep underwater. Her eyes dilated. Her head spun. Her heart thumped a million miles a second. She suddenly couldn't breathe. She snatched her chest, knowing full well the pain there paled in comparison to that of the young vampire. Cassie bled out, with Polaris's icicle piercing her through the sternum. Polaris couldn't bear the sight. Her eyes circled to the back of her head as she fell to the ground.

12

Friend

Polaris couldn't shake Cassie's horror-struck face from her mind, especially while facing her older sister all these years later. Serena herself was unrecognizable, going from a cheeky friend she once called sister to a Viper who wiped her partner's blood off of her blade. Polaris long knew of Serena being a wanted woman, hearing various reports of her crimes even on news outlets in the Magic Nations. Still, seeing her up-close, with specs of blood on her face, was something else entirely. It made her stomach even sicker than what transpired that day. Polaris trembled, knowing that this day would come eventually, ever since she first learned that Serena survived. She just never knew it would be today, and that she would drag Aurora into the middle of it.

The sound of raindrops pelting metal shipment cubes and railings blended into the rocking waves. Serena pulled an empty syringe from her one of her coat pockets and stuck the needle into Vakari's limp, headless body. The syringe quickly filled with the beastman's blood, and Serena pocketed her syringe once full. Finishing her work, she descended back to the deck, approaching the Gorgon sisters with a grimace.

"Why?" Aurora muttered, breaking their collective silence. "Why would you kill him? You're both Vipers, right?"

"Us being 'work partners' doesn't imply loyalty or friendship. He was unfortunate enough to know something he shouldn't have. If you want to ask anyone about betrayal, ask your sister. She specializes in backstabbing."

Polaris couldn't find a retort.

Footsteps echoed from the upper deck of the ship. "Captain Vakari!" someone screamed from above.

The four crewmen from earlier had their binoculars set on them. "Call the boss! She needs to hear this. We have a rogue!" another said.

"Shit," Serena sighed. "Hold tight, sis. I gotta take this."

She vanished from sight again in a gust of wind. Screams echoed from the upper deck before silence took over once more.

Aurora's injuries still weren't fully healed, and her necklace kept flashing. Her aura still phased between green and red like a light switch, and she tightened her jaw. She was fighting tooth and nail to keep her demonic aura restrained, but was in no condition for a physical fight of any kind. Polaris knew she couldn't rely on her the same way she did against Reiya.

Polaris pulled Aurora's arm over her shoulder. "Call for your broom at once! We need to flee before—"

Serena flashed into her vision and knocked them both to the ground with a powerful kick. She hissed at Polaris, as vampires often did to intimidate their prey.

"You never did listen to me. I said to hold tight. It would be rude to leave during our big reunion."

Polaris slipped on the wet floorboards, trying to stand but unable to quell her shiver. Serena was much too fast. Fleeing was no longer an option.

"Look at you. You used to be a swan. The most elegant creature atop a clear lake, the way you carried yourself. Now you're more like a rugged stray mutt in the rain." Serena folded her arms. "Why so shaken? Is it all the bloodshed?"

"Serena . . . please," Polaris said, her voice creaking. "Cease this!"

"It's so funny. My family's blood didn't have you all petrified like that."

"Polaris, what is she talking about?" Aurora asked.

"She's spouting n-n-nonsense," Polaris stammered, "You're mistaken, Serena! That wasn't what it was like at all!"

Serena's face scrunched up like a fist. "You say that. You say a lot." The vampire took a deep breath. "Normally, by now you'd have ended up like the squid. But it's your lucky day, sis. That annoying voice of yours can save you. All you have to do is tell me how to use that Divine Stone after I rip it from your sister's chest. After that, I'll let you both go."

"The stone?" Polaris mumbled. "You think I'd endanger my people by handing over the stone to a murderer like you?"

"The pot calling the kettle black. Don't make me reconsider my offer. It's the only way you walk away from this alive. My sword has had your name written on it for years."

Polaris's heart threatened to burst out of her chest. "I beg you to drop this grudge! What happened with your family was an unintended consequence, but I didn't have a choice—"

Serena punched her square in the mouth. The princess slid across the flooded floorboards, cupping her hand over her busted lip. Aurora screamed out for her, but still couldn't move.

"Tell that to Cassie! I'm sure she'd love to hear that!" Serena roared.

Polaris wiped her stinging, bloody lip. She couldn't bear to lift her head and see the hurt in her former friend's eyes. Her own eyes watered.

"All for your kingdom, right? To walk in the shoes of that devil you call *mother* and *Queen*? To put on that crown which you forged from my clan's blood. You're damn lucky I'm even offering you the chance to live at all. Every inch of my body wants to split your skull open," Serena hissed, her grip tightening on the hilt of her sword. "I want to savor this, so I'll be nice and let you draw your sword. Not like my prize is going anywhere."

Polaris got to her feet. She struggled to stop the trembling in her hand as she tried to reach for the hilt of her sword. All the memories of Serena's beautiful smile flooded her mind, along with the day it was displaced by Cassie's utter terror.

How could things have gone so wrong? Why couldn't they just go back to playing together in Alucard Caves?

Polaris took one last good look at Serena, staring into her murderous eyes. She looked no different than Aurora did in her demonic state. Only difference was that this was permanent. Aurora usually came to after succumbing to her demonic urges. Serena, or at least the one she once knew, was gone forever.

"Solaria, would you be so kind as to enter your demon state now?" Polaris squealed, hoping to get any kind of assistance. Even her fighting like a wild beast was preferable than facing one on her own.

"No!" Aurora shouted. She aimed her good hand at Serena, forming sparks of electricity. Her red aura flared around her before immediately dissipating. She curled right up and screamed in pain. Glowing, green streaks stretched across her body, starting from her chest. The Divine Stone was taking its toll. "It hurts, it hurts, it hurts!" she cried.

Polaris lost her patience. "Take the damn necklace off and use your demonic power. You cannot keep this up! Why are you avoiding using your strongest weapon at a time like this?"

"Because I don't know what I'd do if I accidentally killed someone again, especially if it's you!"

Polaris was taken aback. She watched her sister writhe in pain, struggling to move. She couldn't fathom why she would risk not using that power. Seeing how much Aurora squirmed and struggled rang a bell in the princess's mind. Despite Aurora's shortcomings and loathing for that part of herself, she was still willing to fight. Yet, it was Polaris's job to protect her, not the other way around. Aurora was struggling and could be torn apart by Serena at a moment's notice, and all Polaris could do was watch? All Polaris did was beg for her help, when Aurora was the one that really needed her?

What am I doing? I'm Princess of the Pearl Kingdom, and I have a duty! A mission I must see to the end! No Viper, thief, or monster shall lay their hands on that stone! Lay their hands on my sister. . . Polaris remembered the militia that fell to the hands of Reiya, and of her own loss to the beastman, that almost led to her losing everything. She grew tired of the losses. Tired of her mistakes. If anyone had to combat this ghost of her past, it had to be her, alone. *I refuse to fail again! To fail Mother again!*

Polaris unsheathed her sword with a swiftness, steeling her resolve. "Solaria, rest for now. I shall take her down alone." Her knees weren't fully cured of wobbliness, but she returned Serena's death glare.

Serena aimed her sword at her former friend, giving her a smirk. "Good, you look less like a frightened child now."

"I least of all want to hurt you, but I won't allow a homicidal maniac like yourself to bring danger to my kingdom." Polaris assumed her royal sword stance, raising her sword at a forty-five-degree angle. Her determination finally outweighed her fear. "Surrender or suffer a Gorgon's wrath."

Serena chuckled under her breath before erupting into a maniacal cackle. "You're threatening me? You. Have the nerve. To threaten *me?*" Her laughter ceased. Serena assumed her sword stance, scowling at her former friend. "You want to be a Gorgon so bad? Fine. I'll make sure you die like one."

Polaris and Serena locked swords. Their auras flared in a colorful blue and pink swarm illuminating the otherwise dark ship. Despite the light show, Serena overpowered the princess, pushing her back with heavy slashes. Serena shed Polaris's sword thrust and swiped at Polaris's stomach, barely slicing open her shirt as Polaris leaped backward. Serena swiftly closed the distance between them and kicked Polaris in the jaw, tossing her across the flooding deck. The princess crashed into a shipment cube.

The princess struggled to get up, having suffered a shallow yet stinging cut to her abdomen. She winced from the wound's burn, and the rain only worsened it. Though the cut wasn't deep enough to be fatal, the pain was far too great to leave untreated. She quickly created a dome of solid ice around herself to buy her at least a few seconds. She pulled a few nevma shards from her backpack and mixed them with her water magic. She sprayed the water onto her stomach, healing the cut entirely. She sighed with relief, but couldn't help but wonder why Serena didn't take advantage and attack her while she was in a vulnerable state.

Polaris undid her ice dome, surprised to see Serena still in the same spot, waiting patiently.

"You're done healing? Good. I want to make this as long and painful as possible."

Polaris huffed. "Arrogant enough to give your opponent a reprieve?"

"It can only be considered arrogance if I talk down to my equal. You are my *prey*. And I won't stop until I've dyed the entire Atalanta red with your filthy Gorgon blood."

The statement was enough to stir Polaris's blood. She stood back up and dusted herself off. Though the exchange was brief, Polaris felt she had used more aura than she actually did. *Though I hate to admit it, her words aren't entirely fiction. She's on an entirely different level. I shudder to think if all the Alucards had these reserves of strength. And that blade. Just what in Echidna's name is that? No matter. Provoking her could provide me with an opening.* "If you chose to live your life in revenge, so be it. Come, and I'll send you to the family you desperately miss."

The vein in Serena's forehead looked like it could pop. "Who knew those pearly-clean teeth could spout so much shit?"

Serena's sword darted at Polaris like a speeding bullet. She evaded it only to eat Serena's fist. The princess tried to shake off her bloody nose and stinging face as she retreated to put distance between them. Polaris threw up her hands and droplets of water rose off the ground, forming icicles that pointed dangerously at Serena. They flew and left cuts on the vampire's arms, cheeks, and legs. Having her opening, she shot a highly pressurized, thin stream of water directly at her. The laser-like stream of water cut through two shipment cubes, but the Alucard was out of her sight.

Polaris panicked. She quickly turned around and leaped backward, barely evading Serena's slash as it sliced into her left arm. Polaris tumbled onto the wet deck, shaking as she held her arm. She quaked, feeling winded as if her very aura was drained from her. *What is this? What's going on?*

Serena kicked Polaris in her bleeding arm, making her roll again. "Seven years. Seven long years of unfathomable torment. And every miserable second is worth seeing your royal blood flood this deck."

"Serena . . . sis. Please." Polaris huffed. "I . . . I couldn't stop her. I, I tried to stop her—"

"We aren't sisters!" Serena stomped on her arm, making Polaris scream and bleed even more. "You didn't try shit! You're always full of excuses! You haven't changed at all! Part of me is glad Cassie isn't here to see the piece of shit you've become!"

One of the many memories Polaris wanted to repress. Especially Cassie's soft, large pink eyes. Her tears and her final plea. The teary, plump face of Cassie's splattered with blood was an image she couldn't shake.

"Y-You saw that?" Polaris muttered.

"I watched you and that scorpion devil slaughter my entire family! And I know you're the reason Euryale came to begin with." Serena aimed her blade between Polaris's eyes. "I want to split your head open so badly. . . but, I want you alive to watch me rip the Divine Stone out of your sister's chest and use it to turn that woman you worship to dust. Or better yet, turn the kingdom you raved about ruling into an ashtray! If you lose everything, maybe you can understand what it's like to have nothing!"

A knot grew in the princess's throat. Polaris quickly aimed her good hand at Serena and blasted her with raging hot steam. Serena shrieked, her skin sizzling like hot grease.

Serena stumbled backward, rubbing her burning face and freeing Polaris in the process. She cursed over and over, writhing and falling to her knees. Polaris jumped and quickly shot Serena with a geyser from her palm, blasting her across the deck and off the boat. Serena splashed into the ocean.

Polaris swiftly rummaged through her bag and pulled out her nevma shards. She limped away, healing her wounded right arm as she ran to her sister's side. Her body spasmed as her wounds disappeared. Still, it didn't save her from the onset of soreness, nor exhaustion. She panted heavily, kneeling next to her sister.

"Solaria, can you move?" Polaris asked with a rugged pant.

"No." she moaned. Her aura still flickered between red and green.

"Your demon aura. It can heal you. Use just a bit at least." Polaris said.

"No! I can't risk losing it and hurting you!" she snapped.

Polaris was taken aback by the Aurora's watery eyes. Before she could respond, her head pulsated. Her breaths got even heavier, as if her exhaustion ramped up. "Am I out of shape? Even after these wounds, my magic shouldn't feel so drained." She gasped for air and hunched over.

"Masam . . . mune," Aurora muttered.

"Come again?"

"That Viper, Shoto, used that same sword when he fought Blair," she groaned as she reached for her chest, "I think it drains aura when the blade pierces or cuts your skin."

Polaris scoffed. "So that's its gimmick? I never heard of a celestial weapon that could do that. It's the most dangerous thing in the world with someone of her speed, though."

"Is it over? Did you . . . beat her?" Aurora asked.

"Hardly. It'll take more than that to put her down. But I refuse to falter here."

Polaris closed her eyes, focusing on what aura she still had left. She knew she didn't have enough to summon a tsunami, but she did for one last attack. She sheathed her sword and extended both her arms apart from her. She just hoped she could time it just right. The raindrops falling around them stopped, suspended in the air. The drops froze and formed long icicles.

As she expected, Serena flew out of the ocean and shot at Polaris like a missile. The ice sickles fired at Serena as her blade was inches before Polaris's neck. Serena resembled a porcupine, with hundreds of ice sickles sticking out of her back, arms, legs, and face. Her eyes bulged with utter shock.

Polaris knocked the blade out of Serena's hand and tackled her into a shipment cube. She rammed her forearm into Serena's neck to pin her, then re-drew her sword, aiming the tip of the blade at Serena's heart.

"It's over. If you have any information on the Vipers, speak it forthwith. If you choose to remain silent, I'll see to its permanence," Polaris threatened.

Serena gasped with trickles of blood spewing out the corners of her mouth. "Then go ahead. End my path."

Polaris's sword vibrated. She stared into her pink eyes through her melted white skin. She couldn't help but think of all the good times. The times they played in the Alucard caves together. The times she ate dinner with Serena's family. The nights staring at the beautiful, twinkling stars. All those years, she saw Serena as her older sister and best friend. But it had all ended in bloodshed.

Polaris could shatter her teeth with how hard she clenched her jaw. Tears rolled down her wet face. She never got to spar with Serena like she wanted, and their battle was far from what she ever wanted in a physical encounter.

Serena was a maddened killer, but the thought of killing her tore Polaris inside. Serena had every right to be angry. Yet, the same choice Polaris made back then was in front of her now. Protect one friend or potentially the kingdom she swore to lead one day? The choice was clear.

Polaris wept. "Forgive me . . ."

"Don't forgive me."

"Polaris, get down!" Aurora screamed from afar.

Polaris stumbled forward, feeling something pierce her from behind. A burning, pulsating pain emitted from her stomach. She slowly looked down and saw Masamune impaling her abdomen, with her blood dripping down the tip of the black katana. A red aura emerged from the blade as Polaris's energy dropped like a weight. Polaris stumbled backward and dropped her sword.

The icicles piercing Serena melted into water. The vampire straightened her posture and smirked. She grabbed Polaris's cheeks with her wet, black leather gloves.

"Just like old times, right, rosy? Normally, I'd ask Lord Fraizen to seek mercy on your soul. But for you, Gorgon, I hope you suffer in

Tartarus, being tortured by demons for eternity. It still wouldn't come close to the seven years of hell I've endured because of you."

Blood seeped through Polaris's clothes. Her wound burned and the pain spread through her entire body. Her head throbbed and her throat collapsed. "Serena . . . I beg of you."

"Sorry." Serena took Polaris's circlet off her head. "I don't have a choice."

Aurora screamed out for Polaris, desperately crawling her way toward them. Polaris couldn't hear her though. Her eyes glazed over, and her entire body went cold. She couldn't muster up the aura to resist or attempt to flee. Serena flew up into the sky, holding Polaris by the end of the sword. They hovered off the boat and over the ocean.

"A fitting grave. The source of your magic affinity. Goodbye, Polaris Gorgon." Serena tossed Polaris's limp body into the Atalanta.

As she plummeted into the cold ocean, Polaris didn't think of her good times with Serena or the fate of her people. The only thing in her mind was the result of it all: failure. Years of training, perfecting water magic to an elite level, mastering sword-wielding, and royal practices were wasted. After all that happened, she still couldn't do something as simple as bring Aurora home. Euryale's voice rang in her head, as it had been ringing in her ears for years. *Nose up straight! Too high! Too low. You failed. Do it again! Swing your sword faster! Don't talk to commoners if they have nothing to offer. You failed. Worthless. Pathetic. You're too soft. That barbaric anger is unfit for a future queen. You won't become an heir with those soft feelings. Bury that fragile heart! You failed. You failed. You failed. You're a failure. How can you call yourself my daughter?*

All those years and she couldn't fulfill her life mission. She sank into the cold depths, unable to hear her sister's painful wail.

13
Fury

The vampire hugged herself, laughing in euphoric glee. "Yes. YES! Lord Fraizen, her soul has finally been delivered to you! I praise you for providing me with this opportunity! I, your humble servant, shall see this path to the very end." Serena set her eyes on Aurora, "And now, the next step."

Aurora's throat stung from screaming out her sister's name. Her chest felt like it was being ripped apart from the inside. The beast known as fury made her body it's home, and was now desperate to claw itself out. She tried her hardest to restrain her tears, and withstand the radiating heat within. Her necklace's crescent moon charm beamed, almost blinding her from seeing the girl responsible for taking Polaris away from her.

Serena descended to the deck, approaching Aurora. The rainfall finally calmed, enough for her black utility boots to leave an echo with every step. "Solaria, right? Where were we?"

"FUCK YOU!" Aurora screamed.

"Angry? Seriously? I know you half-demons can regenerate. Don't blame me because you just sat there and watched."

Aurora's breath sucked right out of her.

"I don't know why you're sad though. Trust me when I say I did you a favor by killing that monster."

Her necklace charm dimmed. Aurora's claws and fangs finally made an appearance. Her bones pulsated and hardened as her missing limbs finally regenerated fully, bone, flesh, and skin. As red mist engulfed her body, Polaris's face appeared in her mind one last time. *We barely even knew each other. You fought so hard for me. So hard to get me back. And after all the things I said to you? I . . . I. Monster? You weren't that. Far from it. You're nothing like me . . . and paid for it anyway.*

Serena took Polaris's circlet and placed it on her head. "Perfect fit. Nice trophy, I'll say. Now, forget about her and start telling me about your stone."

"That circlet . . . doesn't ***fucking*** belong to you! It belongs to my sister!"

Everything stood still around them. An intense white noise filled Aurora's ears. Her vision darkened. She only felt heat. Rage. Hate. Bloodlust. Her throat tightened. Her chest glowed. Her hair stood and goosebumps formed all over her body. Her hands vibrated. Her mind vacated. The beating of her chest slowed but grew louder with every step. *Thump! Thump! Thump!* She had to kill her. Cut her open! Grind her to pieces! Tear her apart! Anything to make her feel pain.

Her red aura darkened in hue, twirling around her with the ferocity of a cyclone. The waves below violently crashed against the ferry, cracking the floorboard even more. Gales of wind tore through Serena's clothes and hair. She blocked the wind from her eyes as the deck crumbled beneath Aurora's feet. Her claws and teeth blackened, as did the white in her eyes. She bared her fangs, foaming spewing form the corners of her mouth. The tornado of dark red aura and the gales of frigid wind ceased.

Fury was free, and ready to spill blood.

Serena readied her sword. "This is the demon power I heard so much about! You Gorgons never fail to disgust me."

Aurora vanished in a blur and sank her claws into Serena's face, knocking her through the rails and off the boat. The vampire stopped her fall, hovering over the ocean, clutching her bleeding face. Serena hissed but noticed Aurora holding Polaris's circlet, covered in Serena's blood. Aurora placed it in the pockets of the hoodie tied around her waist.

"Guess you won't cooperate. Fine. I'm going to carve that stone right out of you!"

Serena flew right back at her. The two clashed repeatedly, bouncing all over the ship at blinding speed. Aurora's claws met Serena's katana with every swing, creating hot sparks that flickered around them. Despite Serena's vampiric speed, Aurora matched her step for step, and began to overpower her. Aurora knocked away her sword and ripped through Serena's chest, making her scream. The vampire stumbled back, grabbing her chest in pain, but receiving no reprieve. Aurora battered her with blinding punches and kicks, giving Serena no time to defend. The vampire was but a mere ragdoll to the demon. Aurora slammed repeatedly into shipment containers, leaving body-sized dents. She then launched her across the ship and through the captain's cabin with a herculean kick.

The way Serena screamed. How easily she bruised and bled. It was magnificent! But it wasn't enough. She needed her to suffer more.

Serena landed back-first on the opposite end of the ship, covered in gashes and lumps. Aurora leaped right on top of her in a hurry. She then wrapped her hands around the brutalized vampire's neck before giving it a tight squeeze.

Serena managed to kick Aurora off before she could choke the life out of her. The witch landed flat on her back on the main deck.

Serena coughed up blood and jumped up. Her knees buckled. Despite the black-and-blue state she was in, she forced a laugh. "I see how you killed Reiya! Your strength and speed are probably beyond most of our vanguard! Doesn't matter though. Your lust for blood doesn't outweigh my ambition!" She summoned Masamune and darted towards her again.

Serena thrust her sword at Aurora, but the half-demon took to the air with a leap, avoiding the attack. Aurora lifted her foot, and smashed Serena's head in with an axe-kick, knocking her straight to the floor. Aurora kicked Serena onto her back before lodging her foot into Serena's chest, where she maimed her earlier. The vampire hissed, grabbing Aurora's ankle in protest.

"Damn you!" Serena's aura swelled, and she sliced through Aurora's leg with Masamune, separating it from her body.

Serena rolled backward before jumping to her feet, while Aurora collapsed. She stumbled, gasping for air and heaving. Once again, Aurora wouldn't give her the satisfaction of a breather. Her leg grew back in an instant and she tackled her to the ground, separating Serena from her sword. She pinned Serena's right arm down with her left hand and pummeled her with her right, coloring the floorboards red. She cackled with each spray of blood. This was exactly what she needed. What she demanded! But, it was time to finally put the vampire to rest. Aurora raised her hand, sparks of embers giving birth to a flame. That flame swelled, shifting from a vibrant orange to a brilliant blue, and expanding until it was three times Aurora's size.

"Fire magic? This close?" Serena shrieked, eyes wide with terror.

Aurora's smile waned, her consciousness peaking through the bloodlust. She was about to do it again. Murder someone without control of her demon aura. How many times would this happen? How many people begged for their lives as Serena was doing? How long was she going to remain a monster?

Her necklace charm shined brightly, and her demonic aura dissipated like mist clearing.

Serena grunted as she struggled against Aurora's weakening grip. "Shrew demon! I refuse to have my clan end at the hands of a nobody like you! I'll bury you right next to your bitch of a sister!"

That's right. Serena killed Polaris. Serena took her away. She was an evil Viper just thirsting for power. No one would care if she so happened to vanish. Besides, beating her bloody felt. So. *Good!* Aurora's mind blanked again. She didn't feel Serena punching her in the ribs in an attempt to free herself. She didn't hear her curses and threats. She only felt the heat in her bloodstream, the tearing inside her chest, and the flame she held swell until it became a minature sun, blinding them with its vibrance. In return, her crescent moon charm lost its own light once again.

Tears rushed down Aurora's face, and her fangs pierced into her bottom lip. She squeezed Serena's wrist until she heard a *crunch*. The vampire shrieked.

"Die," Aurora whispered, her voice distorted.

Aurora blasted her with blue flames, causing a loud and bright explosion. The impact lifted the witch off her feet. Flames incinerated the deck, sinking through the ship and into the ocean. She was left with a giant, brightly lit, gaping hole in the middle of the ship that filled with rushing, boiling water. The vessel tilted, water spewing onto the deck.

Aurora fell to her knees. Her necklace shined and her demon aura completely dissipated. Her claws and fangs vanished. She fought hard to stay awake, grabbing her throbbing head. Her mind was a mess, unable to decipher what had just happened.

She gazed around the desolate ship, spotting Vakari's beheaded body, along with the butchered crewmen on the other deck. Then, Aurora noticed the gaping hole in the ship's center and the flames surrounding it. Her flames. With Serena out of sight, she realized she had done it again. She lost control, and just like years ago, was too weak to prevent other lives from being taken. Even if she only killed Serena, everyone else lost their life because of her. Even her own sister died just to protect her.

Waters rose to her thighs, and regret clutched Aurora's soul.

She looked up to the black sky. "Blair . . . I just wish all of this would stop. I'm tired of always waking up in a graveyard. Ria was right about me."

Aurora buried her face in her hands until a *splash* cut through the silence. She looked up and immediately wished she hadn't. Her blood froze, staring at the disgusting figure hovering in the sky.

"That was some attack! That mercilessness must be hereditary!" Serena's demonic cackle filled the air.

Half of the vampire's hair was scorched away, along with part of her clothes. Half of her face melted, exposing part of her skull and making her left eye bulge out of its socket. Her fangs pierced through stretchy molds of molten skin. Aurora saw a gleam in Serena's eye and a smile stretch under her liquified cheek.

Before Aurora could so much as blink, Serena closed the distance between them and sank her fangs into Aurora's neck.

Aurora quaked, unable to move. She could feel her blood and aura draining from her. Fortunately, conjured up enough strength to punch the vampire off of her. She stumbled backward and grabbed her bloody neck as it healed.

All the while, Serena's skin and body were completely restored. Her pink irises became a striking scarlet. Her fangs turned black, as did her fingernails as they sharpened into claws.

"Gorgon blood is so filthy, but this demonic aura has its uses. " Serena lifted her hands, which emitted sparks and flames and were surrounded by tiny pebbles and water. "Wait. . . is this? This must be the Divine Stone's power. To think I can draw on its power through your blood! Yes . . . YES! This is exactly what I need to kill her! The power surging through me is amazing!"

Aurora jumped to her feet and got in her fighting stance, despite her entire body feeling like jelly. Even with a majority of her strength having faded, her battle was far from over.

The two clashed again, trading blow for blow as the ship slowly sank. This time, Serena completely overwhelmed Aurora. The vampire effortlessly dodged Aurora's attacks and sliced her repeatedly with her katana. With each cut, Aurora lost steam, not that she had much to begin with.

"Where's all that bloodlust, Gorgon?" Serena laughed sadistically.

Serena's ferocity and strength had the once superior half-demon on her heels, striking her with a barrage of cuts and scratches. Aurora was pushed backward, and the water rose to her knees. She blasted fire at Serena, which she just cut through with Masamune. Serena blasted her with a fireball two times bigger and faster, launching Aurora across the deck and into a stray, floating shipment container.

Aurora pushed herself out of the dent of the container. She remerged into the water, now up to her hip, as her scorched skin reformed on her face.

Serena levitated before aiming her hand down at Aurora. The temperature around her dropped, coldness overtaking her in an instant. Aurora found herself submerged in thick ice, keeping her in place and her arms pinned to her sides. She could only watch as Serena flew high overhead.

"Your magic and aura are second to none! No wonder Euryale wanted you so bad. But you're done." Serena aimed her hand down at Aurora again.

Aurora's heart jumped when she saw a red aura rush around Serena. Massive appeared around her in droves, born from Serena's aura. The boulders became engrossed in various elements. Flames engulfed some, ice coated others, and even electricity engulfed some. *You're kidding me! Even I don't have that much mastery to create something like that! Just what the hell is she!?*

The barrage of elemental boulders rained down on the ship like a meteor shower. Aurora closed her eyes and formed a barrier dome over herself, but it meant nothing. The meteors destroyed her barrier on impact, burying her into the wreckage of the ship. The element meteors decimated the rest of the vessel before what remained erupted into a violent explosion. The blast scorched her, the ocean doing very little to sooth the impact. Shrapnel born of wood and metal cut her up as she sank. Her body was put through the ringer, and her consciousness threatened to escape her. Her head spun and her and though her body regenerated, no demon aura gave her any fighting strength. She spent everything she had, and didn't even have enough to hold her breath for much longer. Just before shutting her eyes, she thought she had caught a glimpse of a body floating amongst the ship's wreckage. *Polaris?* She wanted to reach out to it but couldn't hold her breath any longer. She inhaled water, then lost consciousness.

Aurora's head throbbed, numbness and exhaustion conquering her. She couldn't even lift a finger. She could only shiver, her body cold and her clothes damp. Streams of water trickled down her forehead from her drenched curls. Along with that, she could feel cold metal chains wrapped around her wrists, tying her hands behind her. Aurora struggled to open her eyes.

She felt the hard, sharp, wet gravel beneath her as she shifted into a sitting position. Her surroundings were mostly dark, with beams of moonlight piercing through holes above her. Rocky, cone-like stalagmites sprouting from the ground surrounded her, and sickle-shaped stalactites descended from the ceiling. Specs of light from above danced on the shallow pool of water before her.

A faint voice invaded the otherwise silent air. She shuffled to peek around a stalagmite, doing her best to stay quiet in her metal chains. She spotted Serena holding the silver pentagram pendant on her necklace. Most of her trench coat was scorched and tattered, along with the grey top beneath it. Her hair was mussed as if she had just woken up, but her skin was spotless. Aurora immediately put her guard up, until she realized Serena was praying.

"Lord Fraizen, I praise you for making the path clear. Thank you for allowing me to continue my journey and keep my bloodline going. For blessing me with this opportunity to grant my freedom. I pray that all the souls lost find salvation in death. Even . . . even Polaris. Their sacrifice provided light for my path, and I thank you again for the blessings. Amen."

Aurora frowned, having remembered what Serena had done. If she didn't know any better, she would've sworn Serena was on the verge of tears.

Serena stared at the snake tattoo on her arm. Her eyebrows furrowed and her teeth clenched. "All the years I've endured are about to pay off. I'll finally be rid of you, my greatest curse. There will be no salvation for you. Only damnation."

Wait, what? She couldn't be talking about me or Polaris. So then . . . who?

Serena flinched, her hand flying to her sword hilt. Upon noticing Aurora, she relaxed her posture. At first glance, Serena appeared to be drenched in sweat.

"You're awake. About time," Serena huffed. "Hope you're ready to talk."

Aurora fidgeted and rustled on the ground, attempting to break the chains to no avail.

"With the Princess gone, your loyalties to the kingdom have been severed." Serena drew Masamune and pricked Aurora's neck with the tip of the blade.

Aurora stopped her struggle. There was no way out of this. "What the hell do you even want to know?"

"I need to know how to draw the stone's power." Serena rummaged through her pocket and pulled out a few folded documents. She unfolded them all and showed Aurora. "Can you read these?"

Aurora squinted her eyes, seeing blueprints of herself and the Divine Stone. The text surrounding it looked like a bunch of small, random symbols. All five documents shared the strange language. "I don't . . . I don't understand this."

"Lying to me won't help you."

"I'm not lying! I've never seen that language in my life. Besides, it's just magic, right? I just, I don't know . . . how to call on its power. Wouldn't anyone be able to just use it?"

Serena sighed, folding the documents, and putting them back in her coat pocket. "No mortal can just use the jewels of infinite magic by ordinary means. Those who try normally get incinerated in the process. The various stones' powers are normally harnessed by mechanical means.

They're even dangerous for the Demi-Gods to use manually. Yet you use its magic as if it's your own."

Aurora sat on the thought. She remembered her conversation with Polaris just the other day. About her experiment involving the demon blood and her chest being in pain whenever she tried to draw too much power. After all, it's why she sought Euryale in the first place.

"Sorry, I don't know shit. I've had these powers for as long as I can remember, and I only just learned about the damn stone myself," Aurora explained.

"Fantastic," Serena snorted.

Aurora boasted a nervous grin. "You know, I bet Polaris could read that gibberish. Reiya got those from her. But you killed her, so blame yourself."

Serena huffed and chucked a fireball at a nearby stalagmite in frustration. The vampire yanked Aurora by her hair to pull her to eye level. "I'll do what I must to have access to its power. No matter how much I have to torture you, or how many people have to be slaughtered. Lord Fraizen demands it."

"Lemme guess, you just want the stone to kill Euryale?"

Serena raised an eyebrow. She dropped Aurora and brushed her bangs aside. "Don't mistake that I will cut Euryale to pieces. She slaughtered my entire clan and will pay dearly for it! But even with all my power, I won't be able to take her down right now. She's without question one of the most terrifying Demi-Gods." Serena bit down on her lip. "But what I must . . . who I must destroy is infinitely worse than even her. And I won't rest until she takes her final breath. To destroy them, the Divine Stone is necessary."

Aurora squirmed to sit upright against a rocky formation. With as much as she had heard about Euryale and the Demi-Gods, she couldn't even fathom there being someone stronger than them. If it weren't for everything happening, Aurora would be stoked about such a possibility. Despite that, she wasn't just willing to lie down and be used as a weapon. She continued fidgeting and squirming, anything to break her chains.

"You can't break those, even if you use your demon state. Dragon scales are—"

"Yeah, yeah. Polaris told me already. I don't care. I won't just let you go around and slaughter people for revenge's sake," Aurora declared.

Serena sighed again, this time with a heavier breath. She sweated even more, and her colorless face flushed red. "Gorgons love pointing the finger but never being accountable."

"What do you mean?"

"I did some research before taking my time to hunt you down. Your bounty may be on the lower end, but you've killed left and right just as I have. Just ask Reiya," Serena paused, seemingly to catch her breath.

Aurora bit her tongue. "I . . . I don't mean to kill. It's not like I asked for this demon power! Hell, I don't even want to use it. We are nothing alike."

"I don't care for your morals. You use your demon power to survive, just as I draw Masamune to survive in this hellish world. It's fate. Lord Fraizen's will. So, tell me again, from one monster to another, how different are we?"

Aurora faced the ground, her face warming and her head pounding. Serena was right. Regardless of the reasons, bloodshed is bloodshed. And maybe, if Aurora ran and never got involved, would Polaris still be alive? If she had run away years ago, would Blair still be here? The questions were numbing and almost meaningless. Aurora leaned her head back against the rock. Everything felt like a testament to her weakness.

Serena fell to a knee and started huffing. She looked as if she ran a marathon, and her scarlet eyes were glowing brighter.

"What's wrong with you?" Aurora asked.

"Shut up!" She rummaged through her pockets in the remnants of her trench coat and pulled out some pink nevma shards. She threw them in her mouth and swallowed. She took a deep breath before aiming her blade at Aurora's sternum.

"Enough chit-chat. Let's see this thing."

A sharp whistle in the wind and a *splat* followed by Serena's shriek pierced Aurora's ears. The vampire stumbled back and bled with a black skewer the size and length of Aurora's forearm piercing her left shoulder. The vampire looked completely bewildered and panicked.

"What, what, what in Fraizen's name? What is this magic?" she shrieked as she yanked the spear out and her shoulder wound regenerated.

Aurora's head jerked toward the light beyond the cave. She saw a candlelight grow brighter in the distance and heard echoes of water splashing from footsteps. When they were close enough, she saw a taller girl, six feet tall, and a boy almost a foot shorter than her, dressed in all black, walking through the clear shallow water.

The shorter, spiky-haired boy aimed at Serena, and his palm had a gaping hole that instantly closed. He wore a black, skin-tight shirt that tugged on his well-toned muscles. The girl held the lantern and had long, brown hair in a ponytail. She sported a black crop top and skirt, with a mole under her left eye, and abs and muscles even more defined than the boy's. She also had a sheathed dagger on her right hip. Both wore white fingerless gloves and white scarves over their mouths and noses. Aurora's heart sank when she saw they both sported crimson eyes with thin pupils, the same as hers in her demon form. For a moment, Aurora thought she was seeing things.

"Who the hell are you two?" Serena asked.

The girl giggled. "That's the Alucard? I was expecting her to be scarier. You know, more teeth? Probably buff muscles?"

The boy folded his arms. "She literally has a wanted poster of her. Where in Tartarus did you get 'buff muscles' from?"

"I dunno, that's what everyone acts like when they talk about her."

"Don't ignore me!" Serena barked.

"Sorry, Batsy. You don't demand our immediate attention," the girl winked.

"W-what!?"

The girl whipped out her black dagger from its sheath and swiped it in Aurora's direction. Black flames spewed and engulfed the chains. They withered into dust and the flames dispersed. Aurora pushed herself off the ground.

Serena's jaw dropped to the floor. "You . . . you!"

"V!" The red-eyed girl joked.

"Ugh! My business is with The Crimson Witch, not you. Turn back and I'll ignore your transgression against Fraizen's messenger."

The girl burst out loud with laughter. "Hear that? She says that as if she can kill us any time she wanted."

The boy pointed at Serena. "Not happening, vampire! The moment you hurt our friend is the moment you became our target."

Hold on . . . friend? What is he talking about? Aurora pondered.

Serena disappeared in a gust of wind, as she often did when she used her vampiric speed. In a blink, the boy caught Serena's wrist and stopped her in mid-air, with water splashing underneath them. The tip of Serena's blade was just inches before the girl's face, but she didn't flinch. In fact, Aurora could see her smile underneath her white bandana. All the while, Serena couldn't free herself from the boy's grip.

The boy dug his sharp claws into her wrist, making her grunt in pain. He yanked her forward and struck her with an uppercut that threw her into the cave ceiling. Aurora's jaw dropped. The strike was so swift, yet so powerful. He reacted to her speed and countered like it was nothing.

Serena fell to the ground amongst cave debris. She held her reddened jaw and glared at the pair from underneath the rubble.

"Nice shot, JayJay! Someone's coming into his own," The older girl chimed.

He sighed, palming his face. "It's Jason! Don't call me that in front of the enemy, Alicia."

"Hey, this is a mission. It's Captain, ya hear?"

"Those uniforms . . ." Serena mumbled, picking herself up. "You two. You're both Skewer Bandits, right? And he called you Alicia." Serena gritted her teeth and took a step back. "As in Alicia Furasaku?"

"So cute. She's heard of us!" Alicia boasted.

"She's heard of *you*." He sighed. "I'm a Furasaku, too."

"Don't cry about it. That at least means we don't need these masks anymore."

The pair pulled down their masks, revealing their sharp teeth as they were both consumed by red aura. Alicia appeared a bit older, probably in her mid-twenties. Jason on the other hand seemed a lot closer to Aurora in age. Aurora knew they were half-demons like her, given they shared similar sharp teeth, claws, scarlet irises, and crimson aura. They had all of the features that tormented Aurora her entire life. And yet, they weren't feral or driven by bloodlust. They were in control, and powerful if that punch was anything to go by. *Wait. Furasaku? I heard that name before!*

"Now, let's have some fun, shall we?" Alicia wore a confident smirk while tossing the lantern aside.

14
Claws and Blades

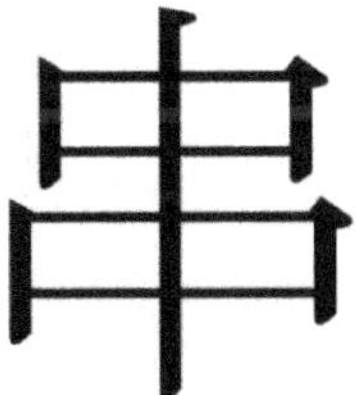

"You're free, Solaria. Best you go on and head out," Jason suggested. "We can handle this. Besides, someone is waiting for you." He grinned and winked at her.

Aurora was taken aback. He seemed so friendly, yet his and Alicia's auras felt unlike anything she had ever encountered. The red aura flow was so dense and fierce, but it didn't feel bloodthirsty or frigid like her own demon aura. Their auras were hot, imposing like a dragon's flame, and calm and steady like an evening river flow. Furthermore, they were. . . normal. They weren't driven mad or acting on animalistic impulses. They were nothing like she was with her demon aura, and nothing like what she heard about other demons. Was it some kind of trick? How could they exist in their demonic state without going insane?

Serena, on the other hand, cared not about their aura flow. She amplified her own and readied her sword for battle.

"Guess the stories about the Alucard's magic are true. She must've sucked the blood of a powerful demon," Jason said.

"It's funny how a vampire like her has scarlet eyes like she's one of us." Alicia's smile quickly disappeared, and she glared at Serena. "It's aggravating."

Jason sighed. "Don't forget, we're fighting together, Captain. I want to get some action myself, too."

"If you want it so bad then take it. It's what you trained for, right?"

Serena interrupted them with an array of fireballs, firing at them like bullets. The pair of half-demons evaded the rapid-fire with ease.

Both sides vanished, flickering water around them with the sheer force of their speed. Clashes of metal rang all over the cave, accompanied by hot sparks flickering wherever Aurora looked. She couldn't keep up with them until she saw Serena being slammed into the shallow water. Jason and Alicia reappeared and charged the vampire together. Both repeatedly countered Serena's katana with their own claws. The siblings fought as one, syncing their attacks. When Serena swiped at Jason, he dodged while Alicia landed a solid kick in her ribs. Jason punished her with swift jabs if Serena focused too much on Alicia. They dodged with a jaguar's gracefulness but struck with a python's potency and accuracy. And on occasion, they would outright strike her down together. The vampire that dominated Aurora and Polaris was completely sloppy against these demonic siblings. Aurora's jaw was agape, amazed by their ability. All the same, she couldn't help but be infuriated.

She had fought so hard all her life just to keep that side of her reeled in, just to keep her from losing herself. Yet, here came these two not only wielding demonic aura as if it were normal, but absolutely dominating the vampire that defeated her so easily. Just watching them made her blood simmer all over again, as amazing as their showcase was.

The vampire emerged from the shallow pool after being bludgeoned with a flurry of heavy blows. Her hair was drenched and her face reddened with bruises. She hissed with fury as her wounds regenerated, thanks to the demon blood she stole.

"Round one is ours!" Alicia cheered. "You kinda suck. Guess you're a vampire after all."

Jason shook his head. "Do you have to aggravate everyone we fight?"

"Ugh!" Serena reached into a pocket in her trench coat and pulled out a syringe of blood. She quickly ejected the blood into her mouth before tossing the syringe aside. Her demonic aura erupted once more, violently spinning and splashing the surrounding water.

Aurora's hair stood on her back. From the ferocity and coldness of Serena's aura, Aurora could tell Serena had just drank more of her blood. *She must've stolen more while I was unconscious! Dammit!*

Serena levitated and froze the shallow pool where the Furasaku Siblings stood, trapping their feet and ankles in thick ice.

"Dammit!" Alicia barked.

Serena dove at Jason and drove Masamune through the center of his chest. Blood oozed from his wound as his aura sputtered before dissipating completely. Serena chuckled maniacally through her pitch-black fangs.

"Jason!" Alicia yelled.

Serena aimed her hand at Alicia, blasting her point blank with water before freezing her entirely in a thick coating of ice.

"A memento from Polaris. Now, for you," Serena redirected her glare to Jason, who staggered as his aura drained from him.

Jason grabbed Serena's arm and threw a swift punch, only for her to electrocute him. Electricity engulfed the boy, making him groan and singing his skin. His aura slowly diminished, and he panicked.

"I don't need your blood, but neither do you." Serena leaned in to bite his neck.

Jason winced, clenching his jaw tight. Aurora feared the worst for the boy, and yet, he smirked all the same. Serena and her sword vanished in a split second, and blood splattered into the ice pool. The vampire hovered several feet away from the demon siblings, with cuts scattered all over her and blood dripping from them. Aurora's eyes darted back to Jason, seeing sharp black spikes poking out from all over his body. He pulled himself out of the thick ice and the skewers retracted back into his body.

Aurora cringed, rubbing her arms. *Never seen magic like that. That hurt or what?*

Even if Jason narrowly escaped Serena's crushing jaws, his exhaustion was ever apparent. Despite his injuries vanishing, he drew heavy breaths, and he stumbled, almost falling to a knee.

"Damn. That sword. It felt like it took all of my strength. The hell is that thing?" Jason complained, ripping the center of his chest where he was stabbed.

Fortunately, Alicia didn't share Jason's fatigue, or lack of aura. Hers exploded in a violent red rush, freeing her from her ice prison entirely and spreading a dense heat. The cave practically became an oven. Even Aurora started to sweat, and she hadn't even joined the fight. But even she wasn't sweating as much as Serena. She was even more tired than Jason from the looks of it.

Alicia stared Serena down. "That was a clever trick, Batsy. I guess your clan is as dangerous as rumors say. It's almost hard to believe you were all wiped out."

Serena hissed in frustration. Her face was bright red, but Aurora knew that wasn't from frustration alone. Her eyes even threatened to close. Was she going to pass out?

"JayJay, you okay?" Alicia asked.

"Yeah, I'm good." He put his fists back up, despite clearly being out of breath. "Let's keep going and put her down."

"No. I've got this. You take five."

"What? But I'm all warmed up now! Come on, Alicia!"

Alicia gave her brother a judgmental glare. She pointed at the small fresh cut on his cheek. "I can tell your aura is exhausted. You'll be weak, ineffective, and vulnerable even if we worked together. So, step aside."

Jason's gaze fell to the ground, and he tightened his fist. Aurora could see the bitterness written all over his face.

"Hey!" Serena barked with a huff. "Don't. Disregard. Me."

Alicia redirected her attention to Serena. "Batsy, didn't you hear me earlier? You don't require my full attention. Besides, it looks like you'll have a heat stroke before I even get the chance to put you down."

"You're just begging for me to rip that tongue out. I haven't even begun to tap into this power—" Serena stopped, dropping to a knee. Something was seriously wrong with her.

"Poor baby. You wanna take a wittle nap?" Alicia sneered.

"Die!" A raging blue flame erupted from Serena's hands and fired at them. Jason and Alicia evaded, and the flame struck the ice pool, creating a thick, warm mist. Serena nearly blew a gasket when she saw the siblings still upright.

Jason panted, grabbing his chest. Alicia appeared just as shaken, drenched in sweat from the steam. The oven of a cave quickly turned into a sauna.

"Interesting trick. You're full of surprises," Alicia muttered.

"No! No more of this shit! I'll incinerate you!" Serena fired sharp stones, water bullets, flames, streaks of lightning, and gusts of wind at Alicia over and over. Alicia evaded it all, irritating Serena more. However, Serena set her eyes on Jason, who stood off to the side. She grinned and began firing elemental blasts at him. He stumbled, caught off guard, and Aurora was sure Serena had him. However, Alicia dashed to her brother in a blink and shielded him just as the elemental blast struck, engulfing them both in a fiery blaze.

"Stupid girl! You fell for it!" Serena cackled.

The cave quaked and dust rained down upon them. Aurora shielded her eyes from the onset of dust and debris. At this rate, as strong as the newcomers were, they wouldn't last long. *I must help them! Serena's just too strong . . . but.* Aurora thought back to her previous encounter with Serena and where she was as a result. Even with the Furasakus' painful grunts that rang in her ears, what could she actually do?

She no longer had time to ponder. Serena already had her eyes on her. "Sorry to keep you out of the action, Solaria! Why don't you join us?" Serena aimed her hand at her.

A stone engulfed in blue flames formed in the Alucard's hand. Aurora just stood there. Her knees shook and her heart rate skyrocketed. Even if she dodged or fought back, what would change? The body count, or another defeat? Her throat dried and her hands sweated.

What did it matter?

Either Serena would kill them all, or Aurora would.

As Serena fired the blast, time seemingly froze.

A wall of water rose before her and froze solid, shielding Aurora from the blast. The ice wall crumbled, and Aurora stumbled backward, wide-eyed. *Water magic? But who could've. . .*

Aurora looked to her left for the source but refused to believe her eyes. For a moment, she thought she was staring at a ghost. She blinked continuously, just to ensure her eyes weren't deceiving her. But she was real. Alive. Aurora couldn't help but get misty-eyed, with such relief and joy overwhelming her. Never in a million years would she have thought that seeing Polaris again would get her so emotional. Yet, there she stood, in the water with shaky hands pointed at Serena. She was out of breath and had stringy wet hair. Her eyes had black bags under them, and her clothes were torn and drenched. But Aurora didn't care what poor condition she was in. She was alive. Her sister was alive!

The two half-demons lay in a large, fiery crater created from the blasts. Alicia appeared burnt to the bone before regenerating completely. But even suffering such a devastating attack didn't shock her nearly as much as seeing Polaris. Based on Jason's agape jaw, he shares similar sentiments.

"We told you to wait outside. It's not safe for you here!" Jason shouted.

"The heiress still doesn't listen," Alicia groaned, panting.

Polaris could barely talk with how hard she was huffing. "You expect me to remain still with all of that noise? You all said five minutes. Your tardiness raised concern."

Serena looked as if she had seen a ghost. Given she was a vampire, it would've been impossible for her to look paler, but somehow she did. "That's . . . impossible. You can't . . . you should be dead," she mumbled.

Polaris spared a glance at Serena but didn't respond. She instead marched right toward Aurora. Aurora froze, afraid to even blink. Unsure what to say. What to do.

Her sister didn't share her indecisiveness. She punched Aurora in the face, knocking her to the ground, much to everyone's shock.

Polaris yanked Aurora back up by her collar. "What in Echidna's name are you thinking? Were you just going to let Serena kill you just now?"

Aurora choked on her words and just looked away.

"Answer me when I speak to you!" Polaris threw another punch, though Aurora caught Polaris's fist this time.

"Get the fuck off me!"

"Then answer me!"

"There wasn't a reason to dodge, okay!"

"No reason to dodge? That's absurd! You're a brawler, are you not? What happened to your drive? Your will?"

Aurora avoided eye-contact with her.

"Do you have any idea what your death would mean?"

Aurora's anger crept right back up. "Sorry if I still don't care about your damn politics!"

Aurora stopped. She felt tears dropping onto her face.

"That's no reason to throw away your life! I've lost enough already!" Polaris sobbed.

Aurora's heart thumped. "But I thought . . . I thought you were . . ."

"And what if I was? Would that warrant suicide, Solaria? You're not the type of witch to give up over things like that! It's not the move of a Gorgon, nor a Salem!"

Aurora's eyes glossed over. She never would've thought Polaris of all people would say that. It brought her warmth to the otherwise cold cave. That fuzzy feeling was short-lived, as Serena fired a ball of flames at them.

Jason swooped in and knocked the fire blast away.

"Could you two maybe not do this right now?" Jason asked in a polite tone.

Alicia sighed, cracking her neck, and dusting herself off. She tore away some of the burned fabric off her shirt sleeve. "Way to kill the buzz as always, Princess."

Polaris sniffled, wiping her tears. "The girl needed scolding."

She got up and offered her hand to Aurora. Aurora's stinging cheek and the iron taste in her mouth bothered her, but she was glad Polaris did it. She needed that punch. She took her hand and thanked her sister.

"Touching." Serena's eye twitched. "Just another reminder of my failures. I'll be sure to kill you properly this time."

A black tendril wrapped around Serena's wrist and yanked her to the ground. The tendril came from Alicia's palm, retracting back into it like a rope. "Hey, Batsy, I wanted to have fun in our little fight. Not every day you get to tango with someone worth one hundred million." Her vein made itself visible on her forehead. "But you attacked my defenseless brother. That's not something I can overlook. So, congrats. You have my full, undivided attention."

Serena picked herself up and dusted herself off. "I'm tired of hearing your voice."

Alicia's aura flared around her again. "I'm tired of hearing you breathe. Let's fix that."

Serena drew her sword and prepared to lunge forward. However, she stumbled, dropping her sword and staring at the ground. Her breaths grew quicker and shorter.

"What's going on with her?" Aurora asked. "She looks sick."

Polaris's face broadened and paled with fear. "Those red eyes. Solaria, she ingested your blood, didn't she?"

"Yeah, so?"

Steam rose from Serena's skin and she howled in misery. She scratched and clawed at her neck. The vampire hunched over and violently vomited blackened blood. Her red aura dispersed along with the blackness of her claws and fangs. Her irises also returned to their normal pink hue.

Alicia whistled. "Someone bit off more than they could chew."

Serena set her glare on Aurora. "I should've known. You would have *that* blood. You're a Gorgon, that's for sure."

Aurora didn't know what she was talking about, but Alicia stepped before them. "No, no, Batsy. I'm your opponent."

"You mean *prey*!" Serena whipped out her sword and charged.

Alicia snatched the vampire by the neck and slammed her into the ground, creating a large crater, and clearing the shallow pool of water. Aurora and the others blocked their eyes from the mini hurricane the impact created. From that point on, Aurora's mouth hung open from Alicia's ferocity. She brutalized Serena with a volley of ferocious strikes. The Alucard had no answers to Alicia's violent lashes from her tendrils and claws. Serena couldn't even draw her sword. Even as she tried to fly away, she was just reeled back in by Alicia's tendril. Serena was but a domestic pet being mauled by a wild beast. Aurora never looked away from a fight, but this one was hard to watch.

Dust obscured everyone's vision, filling the air from Serena's constant crashing into walls and stalagmites. The cave was on the verge of collapsing. Yet, Alicia's aura just grew more. Serena ingested more nevma shards, but her wounds healed slower than before. She panted and her face washed over with blood and terror. Alicia approached her slowly, prompting Serena to tremble and back away.

"That pentagram on your neck. You must believe in Fraizen. Want to pray to him?" Alicia asked.

Serena's face cringed with a seething rage, terror having vanished. She pointed her blade at her. "I'll send you straight to him!"

Masamune glowed red, and a white sphere appeared at the end of the blade, slowly growing. Aurora and the others felt the gravitational pull of the sword, as debris and water sucked toward it.

Jason called out to his sister, "Alicia get out of there—"

Before Alicia could move, the blast went off, tearing through the cave and causing a rattling earthquake. Everyone else took cover. Aurora peeked up at the expansive, blinding white beam. Never had she seen that much magic fired at one time.

When the dust cleared, there was a shallow crevasse in the ground and a large hole at the end of the cave. Aurora covered her mouth when she saw what was left behind. Alicia was brought to her knees, most of her body charred and bloody from the powerful blast. She was even missing a few limbs, but nonetheless stared at Serena with a fiery glare, panting heavily and shaking.

Serena was brought to tears of laughter. "Where's all that bravado now, demon? What were you saying about ceasing my breathing?"

Jason scoffed. "Dammit! Alicia's aura must be running low. Another shot like that and she won't be able to regenerate! Can either of you still fight?" he asked Aurora and Polaris. "We gotta save—"

"Stay out of it, Jason! That's an order!" Alicia yelled, barely able to catch her breath. Her right arm, leg, and all major wounds regenerated. Her legs wobbled as she stood. "I got careless. You do live up to your bounty, Alucard."

Serena grinned. "You demons are the blight of the gods. All the power to recover from almost any injury to continue spreading ruin in the world. But you're far from immortal, aren't you? The more you heal, the more aura you spend, and from where I stand, you appear to be going broke. So, heal as much as you want, death is inevitable." She rubbed her chin. "Or I can end you quickly. The head or heart will do. Can't come back from that, can you, demon?"

"You know a lot about our bodies. Good for you. It won't save you though." Alicia drew her dagger, its short blade a matte black, with even darker, wispy smoke twirling around it. "You've got a neat katana there. That sword's beam is strong, but it's no Excalibur. Besides, you're not the only one with a Celestial Weapon."

"What?"

She swiped the dagger in the air and a wave of black flames flew at Serena. As Serena flew upward to flee, the wave of flames struck her left arm. She screeched and plummeted back to the ground, writhing in agony. Her hand crumbled to ash within the flickering black flames, and the flames quickly consumed more of her arm. Serena quickly took Masamune and cut cleanly through her shoulder, severing her burning arm before the flames could spread and consume her whole. Blood spewed from her wound, and her painful wails echoed through the cavern. Her severed arm turned to dust within seconds.

"Woah," Aurora said, swallowing.

Alicia was about to swing her blade again but paused as rocks crashed near her. The cave was collapsing.

Alicia sucked on her teeth. "Damn it all. Everyone, let's bounce."

"Wait, but the bounty, Alicia! We should grab her." Jason started running toward where Serena landed, but Alicia grabbed his wrist and yanked him toward her.

"Forget her. This place is coming down. Lives come first, so let's go!"

"But—"

"Now!"

Everyone ran for the exit, doing their best to avoid the raining stones. Sharp rocks barely managed to graze them as they all moved with unbelievable speed. The dirt and dust filled their noses and mouths, giving them a rough cough and watery eyes.

"We won't make it!" Polaris panicked while trying to clear her throat.

Polaris's earlier words echoed in Aurora's mind. Being buried wasn't an option. She gathered her remaining strength and created an aura barrier, protecting them from the stone shower as they bolted out of the cave. They all fell onto the soft, cold sand of the beach, panting as the cave came down behind them. Aurora exhaled with relief as she faced the dark ocean and starlit horizon.

15
Secrecy

After escaping the collapsed cave, Aurora and Polaris were guided by the Furasaku siblings to a thirty-foot-tall wyvern on the beachside. Aurora, Polaris, and Alicia got on the saddles strapped to its scaly back. Jason sat up front near its serpent-like neck, taking the reins of its harness.

"Everyone, hold on tight," Jason announced to the group. "All right, Zeta, bring us home!"

The dragon responded with a screech and took flight.

Aurora wanted to marvel at the beauty of the ocean and the small island that grew smaller in the distance. She wanted to enjoy the crisp ocean breeze blowing on her face and flowing through her hair. But she couldn't find the strength. The young witch's head throbbed, and her body had never been so sore. Her heisting days with Blair paled in comparison to the action she saw in just the last two days. It was a never-ending rollercoaster, and she expected to crash. She felt lucky to come out of it and even luckier that Polaris survived, too. If it weren't for the millions of questions she had, she would pass out right then.

"Polaris, you asshole." Aurora started off hot. "I watched her toss you over. How'd you survive?"

Polaris hung her head. She seemed to share her sister's exhaustion. She also was in poor shape, from her torn-up clothes to her disheveled hair.

"To be quite honest, I didn't expect to. I nearly lost consciousness until I was struck by some debris underwater. I had just enough aura to form an air bubble around myself. I floated to the surface to heal my wounds using most of the remaining nevma shards. I passed out again before awakening to Sir Jason and Miss Alicia atop this dragon, and the worst chest pain of my life," Polaris brushed away her stringy, damp hair from her eye.

"Yeah!" Jason confirmed. "We were waiting for you guys on Cyclops Island, and you weren't answering our calls on the crystal ball. Then we saw an explosion on the horizon. You guys got super lucky that we came to check it out."

Alicia chuckled. "Lucky? It was more like a miracle. Even when we found you, we thought you were pushin' up daisies."

"I'm truly grateful for the both of you. Your efforts saved both of our lives," Polaris said.

Alicia's eyes narrowed at Polaris. "You can thank us when we get to Gennomy. Don't forget our deal, Ice-Devil."

Friction permeated in the air from the brief silence that followed with those two glaring at each other. Aurora cleared her throat, trying to cut through the awkwardness. "So, you all know each other well? You must live in the Pearl Kingdom, right?"

Jason and Alicia stared blankly at her.

"Uh . . . did I say something wrong?"

"What did they teach you in Verona?" Jason asked.

Polaris placed her hand on Aurora's shoulder. "Solaria, it's . . . a bit more complicated—"

"Not at all, Ari! Nothing complicated about it. We may live in country borders, but not in the inner kingdom. I don't know what Allied Nation life is like, but being a half-demon in the Magic Nations doesn't make you . . . what do you call it, Polly, a citizen?"

"Miss Alicia, please it's not—"

"Don't hold your breath. I've been around long enough to know what it's like. It is what it is, though." Alicia stared at Aurora, paying particular attention to the tattoo on her chest and the necklace dangling from her neck. "That looks like . . . an aura suppressor."

Aurora fiddled with the crescent moon charm of her necklace. "Oh, yeah. It keeps my, um . . . demon aura from running amok."

"Demon aura?" Alicia's expression lit up. "So, the princess wasn't lying, you are a half-demon like us. Only difference is you have a collar."

Aurora fondled the crescent moon charm on her necklace. "Collar?"

"Here we go." Jason lamented.

"Let me guess, someone, probably close to you, gave you that because they thought one day you'd turn tail and tear out their entrails, right?"

She couldn't have been more right. Just thinking about Ria made Aurora's stomach sour. "Yeah . . ."

"Thought so. People say that about half-demons all the time. Love to compare us to the real thing. Bet whoever gave that to you said it'd be better for everyone if you wore it so you could fit in and all that."

"No. I was given this because I've done it already."

Alicia tensed up, and Jason's head quickly whipped back toward Aurora.

Aurora stared intimately at the charm. "Even with it, sometimes I . . . I, I'd rather not talk about it. I want to be able to win my fights without being taken over by it."

Alicia scoffed. "Taken over? Sheesh, kid, you're a Gorgon, right? You can't be that pathetic to let your own power control you."

"Alicia!" Jason barked.

"Okay, okay, sheesh."

Aurora stared down at the oscillating waves of the dark ocean. Alicia's words were like a blade to an open wound. Watching Alicia throttle Serena only poured salt down that wound. As grateful as she was for their help, both Alicia and Jason exhibited the very thing she lacked and never knew was even possible: control over immense power. Especially Alicia. Sure, she had maybe ten years on Aurora, given her age. But she remained in the driver's seat against Serena, even when her back was against the wall. Not to mention, without Alicia, Polaris would be dead. Aurora would be dead. Just thinking about the situation made her headache even worse.

She had desperately wanted to fight like the Furasaku siblings. She even wished she could've aided them against Serena. But Alicia was right. Having and relying on the necklace was proof of her weakness. Her fists shivered at the reality of it all.

"Solaria is a very capable fighter," Polaris argued, surprising Aurora. "Without question, she's one of the strongest I know. I fought against and alongside her, and she saved my life on multiple occasions. Serena provided complications, yes, but Solaria being alive is proof enough of her capabilities as a warrior, is it not?"

Polaris smiled at her, which Aurora returned in kind. Blair was the last person who had praised her combat ability. The warmth it brought was as welcomed as it was missed.

"Oh, shit, I almost forgot. I figured you may want this back." Aurora reached into the pockets of Blair's hoodie, still tied around her waist. She pulled out Polaris's circlet and saw Polaris's expression soften upon seeing it. Upon further inspection, the headpiece was now dingy, with dry blood stains obscuring its former golden shine and a crack streaking down the sapphire in its center. Aurora's smile morphed into a frown at the sight of Polaris's tears.

"Sorry . . . uh. I didn't expect it to get so banged up after I fought Serena—"

Polaris turned her around and embraced her. Her body stiffened. Aurora felt like she was having an out-of-body experience. Such physical affections were foreign to Aurora. It had been so long, she wasn't entirely sure how to react.

"What . . . what are you doing?"

"Thank you so much, Solaria. It means everything," she cried into her shoulder.

Aurora could've sworn she was being hugged by someone else. Aurora assumed that hugging Polaris would feel like hugging a rigid, frosty lamppost in the dead of winter. Yet, she found herself back in the forests of Eden, beside the campfire, in the loving arms of the woman she missed most. She'd nearly forgotten what a hug even felt like. She was compelled to hug her back, not even realizing she was crying, too.

"Yeah, yeah. Don't die on me again," Aurora muttered.

Alicia groaned. "Jason, can I fly Zeta the rest of the way? They're too cute and it's smothering. They may as well make out at this point."

"How are you the older one? Seriously?" Jason complained.

The two sisters separated, and Polaris put her circlet back on her head, beaming with pride.

They continued their flight through the calm, cool night sky. To pass the time, they discussed some of Aurora's upbringing, including stories of her past adventures with Blair. Polaris wasn't too fond of talking about Aurora's past crimes, but the Furasaku siblings got a kick out of their stories, especially Alicia.

"No kidding? That Amethyst sounds badass! Wish we could've worked together." Alicia said.

"She was! She taught me everything I know. She's the reason I'm a warrior. I just wish I could've learned more, ya know?" Aurora responded.

"I understand that," Jason said. "You know our dad taught us how to fight and—"

"Seriously? JayJay, don't bring up that clown," Alicia spat, venom coating her tongue.

Jason turned around. "He's not a clown. He was a respected warrior and leader."

"Respected? That shouldn't even be uttered in the same sentence as him. He was barely a warrior and look where his leadership got him. Hell, look where it got us!"

"You take that back!" Jason yanked the reins of the wyvern out of impulse. The dragon squirmed and squealed, nearly throwing them off. Aurora held on for dear life.

"I won't take back the truth, JayJay. Now shut up and focus on the skies."

Jason growled, turning back around.

Alicia shook her head. "Anyway, what's it like, having all that power?"

"What do you mean?" Aurora asked.

Alicia leaned back and folded her hands behind her head. "Ole Batsy had a lot of elemental powers but also had demon aura. Once she started to heave, she looked directly at you and pretty much admitted it was your blood making her sick."

Aurora's heart sank.

"From what I remember about Alucards, they inherit the magical and sometimes physical prowess of other people by sucking their blood. And having more than one element, let alone all five, is strange, wouldn't ya say? So . . ." Alicia sat up, staring daggers into Aurora. "What's your secret, Gorgon?"

Aurora's hair stood. Given Polaris's dilated eyes, she was freaking out too. "Well, yeah . . . uhm."

"Serena's an interesting case," Polaris started, trying her best not to sound panicky. "That girl apparently can use more than one magic affinity and inject more than one user's blood, or so I theorize. Solaria's only elemental affinity is lightning, inherited from our father. Isn't that right, Solaria?"

Aurora stared at her blankly for a second before she picked up what her sister put down. "Oh, yeah. Yeah, lightning."

Aurora was on edge from how skeptical Alicia looked, her eyes narrowed.

"*That* man. I suppose that makes sense." Alicia backed off. "Guess Batsy gets her talents straight from the Count himself. To bad she's a total bitch."

Aurora was relieved that Polaris was more prepared for that question. Aurora didn't know what she would've said but understood why she'd keep the stone a secret, given all they'd dealt with.

Alicia took a deep breath. "That doesn't explain why Batsy looked so ill when we fought her. It was almost as if your blood was poison to her, Ari."

Aurora was just as curious about that as Alicia was. Polaris's bowed head and lowered eyes didn't inspire confidence.

"That could be what Solaria inherited from our mother," Polaris sighed. "During the . . . Alucard incident, most of their warriors attempted to ingest Mother's blood and use her Demi-God abilities against her. Mother is part-scorpion, and her blood contains natural toxins and poison. Just a single drop can kill a rhinoceros in a few minutes once in the bloodstream. That's what made the massacre so . . . quick." Polaris hugged herself, discomfort evident in her lowered eyes.

"That's scary, holy hell. Wouldn't ever wanna fight Euryale," Jason said.

"Damn Demi-Gods," Alicia grumbled. "But nice one, Princess. Must be fun wearing that little crown forged in their blood."

"It wasn't like that!" Polaris snapped.

Everyone fell silent.

The princess bit down on her lip before taking a deep breath. "Don't think for a second I intended to hurt Serena, Cassie, or any of her kin. They were like sisters to me!"

"Then . . . what happened?" Aurora asked.

Polaris lowered her head. "Before the incident itself, I overheard some elder vampires planning a coup in the kingdom. They targeted mother's life and threatened the lives of many."

"And then she went running home to Mommy so that she could get rid of all the big bad vampires. That about sums it up, Gorgon?" Alicia jeered.

"I'd have you know that had I not, the fallout could've been detrimental! We all witnessed Serena's potential firsthand. Had the Alucards banded together, or worse conspired with our enemies and been equipped with the right weapons, we may not have been able to defeat them! They'd execute everyone in the kingdom! Could've even bested Mother." Polaris took a deep breath. "But I never intended a massacre. There had to have been another means to resolve that, but when mother tastes blood . . . it's impossible to reason with her."

Aurora remembered Serena mentioning something about Cassie. Right when she was going to bring it up, she remembered what she did to Blair. She also remembered her earlier conversation in the boat with Polaris. Perhaps the princess understood her more than she thought. Her lips pursed. Rather than prying about Cassie and the extent of their relationship, she grabbed Polaris's shoulder.

"It's okay. Regardless of what happened, you didn't intend for any of that to happen. Just lookin' out for your people. It doesn't justify what Serena is doing, so it's all good, yeah?" Aurora gave her a comforting shoulder massage.

Polaris stared at her with soft eyes. "I don't know. Perhaps I could've consulted Rook Lazuli first or Bishop Agura? I just . . ."

Alicia scoffed, clearly over Polaris's whining. "It's whatever. Spilled milk and all, no need to cry about it."

"Alicia's right for once. What happened in the past stays there," Jason intervened.

"Yeah, what he said. Hold on . . . for once? The hell does that mean?" Alicia barked.

"What do you think?" Jason laughed.

"Don't make me come down there, Tiny!"

"Short jokes aren't cute."

Aurora giggled, relieved the thick air was finally lifted.

"Sorry, Blue, my sister's a complete douche," Jason said.

"Dick!"

"But you and Solaria are welcome to stay at our village for the night."

"Still Aurora, but thanks. That would be nice. Should be fun, right Polaris?" Aurora turned to her sister.

Polaris was already fast asleep behind her. Her own eyes grew heavy and burned. Her mind started to drift as her eyes were shutting. After two long days of battle, bloodshed, and pain, she was ready to follow in Polaris's footsteps. She fondled the crescent moon charm as she drifted. Her mind lingered on Jason and Alicia, seeing how powerful they were and how none of them lost it and became murderous monsters. *What have I been doing wrong this whole time?*

Back on that small island, Serena emerged from the heavy boulders and stones she was buried under. Her right shoulder bled, and her entire body throbbed in unfathomable pain. She drew short breaths and her head spun. Serena reached into her pocket from what was left of her pants and pulled out a few nevma shards, shoving them up the wound left from her missing arm, nearly passing out from the pain. She bit down into her bottom lip, breaking skin and drawing blood. Her skin sealed over the arm wound, leaving it as a stub, but not regenerating it fully. She punched the ground over and over with her right hand.

"How does an insignificant creature like her wield the flames of Algieri? How did she even get her hands on a Celestial Weapon like that?" She griped. "Cassie . . . mother, father. Everyone. Justice and freedom were right in my grasp and I let it slip again! Is this the path Lord Fraizen has for me?" Serena cursed the fact those half-demons threw a curveball into her plans. The last thing she wanted was more obstacles. More people standing between her and salvation. She fumed at the ears.

"Gorgon trash, demon filth, it just keeps getting worse! Damn it all! They will suffer for this, I swear it!"

Serena felt a buzzing on her right hip. She pulled out her crystal ball, surprised to only see it cracked. Her heart sank, as she had a feeling who it could be. "Shit. I was sloppy!" she said, scolding herself. "Answer!"

She saw Hatake on the screen of her ball. "Fangs! A pleasure to see you again. You look like absolute roadkill!"

She exhaled, glad to see it wasn't who she initially thought. "What is it, sir?"

"I just called because I was worried when you didn't give your report," he poked out his lips in a pout. "The one due at midnight. Eden time every night."

Shit! That report completely slipped my mind! "Eden and the rest of Verona were quiet. Nothing out of the ordinary. Yeah. Goodbye."

"Not so fast, my little orphan."

Serena wished she could reach through the ball and strangle Hatake's neck. He was one of the few people she wanted to kill that wasn't a Gorgon.

"Vakari's curse is gone and his crystal ball is offline, along with several of our cargo squads at the Atalanta ports. Our maps indicate you were in their area when their signals vanished. Happen to know anything?"

Serena felt cornered, but she needed something to divert his attention. "Demons. The Skewer Bandits raided the ship. Vakari called me over, but I arrived too late. They killed him and the other men during battle. As you can see, I barely made it out alive."

"Very interesting! Shiro cultivated that gang years ago. I didn't know there were a lot left after the Neo-Camelot incident. Is the shipment of anti-magic weapons at least intact?"

"The ship was destroyed and sunk in the battle."

Hatake grabbed his forehead. "You know the boss doesn't like when Vipers die and people get away with it. Especially if one of our own comes back without a body, demon, or otherwise."

"Which is exactly why I'm going to find the Skewer Bandits base and eradicate the lot! I'll have it done before the week and return to base."

"Do you need backup?"

"No!" Serena stopped, realizing how panicked she sounded. She cleared her throat. "I can manage this alone. You can call it 'gaining the boss's respect.' But, I will need the coordinates to their little village. Shiro used to live there, so I know we have tabs on it."

"Look at you, taking the initiative! I'll send over the exact coordinates to your crystal ball."

Serena smirked. "Good. I'll have the rats smoked out soon. You'll get my report as soon as it's done."

Hatake clapped his hands. "Goody! The boss loves that kind of stuff. She'll be incredibly pleased! We'll check back with you within the week. If you aren't back by then, we'll send Shiro and Mordred to come and retrieve you."

Air escaped her throat. "Hold on, sir, that isn't necessary—"

"Keep us updated! Bye-bye now!" The transmission ended.

Serena stared up at the dark sky. She contemplated her new dilemma. It had slipped her mind that her location could be tracked. She had to find that witch and rip that stone from her chest before the Vipers sent two of their heaviest hitters her way.

She stared at the snake tattoo on her right arm. Her face cringed with fury. *Those demons are a huge problem. Even at 100%, I can't fight them and the Gorgons head-on. I'll have to get them another way, or just get Solaria alone. Either way, I have to move quickly. The longer I bear this mark, the longer I remain tethered to that monster.* Serena thought to herself, then got an idea—a way to eliminate all her blockades without even having to dirty her own hand.

16

Home to the Half-Demons

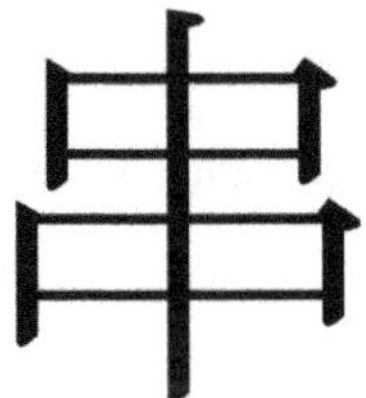

Frigid waters splashed onto Aurora's legs and ankles as she ran, her legs feeling heavier with each step. She panicked, looking around frantically. All she could see were the dark waters and the moon in which it reflected. She didn't know where she was, only to keep running. The further she ran, the water thickened, and the air became ripe with a tangy, coppery scent. She looked down, and her suspicions became true. The water became blood, stretching as far as she could see. Her stomach spiraled. *I have to stop it! I have to stop it! I have to stop it!*

Orange light beamed in the distance. She treaded forward through the ocean of blood, and though only her ankles were submerged, she felt as if she were running underwater. Her thighs tightened, and she treaded forward with all her strength. Instantly, several buildings appeared around her, causing her to halt her advance. She observed them, noticing none of them belonged together. Corporate skyscrapers, suburban homes, and village-style buildings all encircling her, and arranged at random. *What the hell?* She blinked, and those buildings erupted in flames.

She panted and took a step back. *Am I too late?* She flinched as someone appeared from thin air, standing just a few feet away from her. The newcomer was the spitting image of Aurora, even down to her scorpion tattoo. However, she didn't sport the same emerald irises. Hers were the burning crimson that she'd grown to despise. Her arms hung to her sides, claws dripping with glistening blood that reflected the fire. That same blood leaked out her eye sockets like the tears of the devil.

"You. You did this, didn't you? You destroyed this place!" Aurora yelled at the bloody demon.

Both of their scorpion tattoos lit up like lamps with green bulbs. The demon showed off her sharp, black fangs with a gnarly smile. She taunted Aurora by raising a glowing crescent-moon-charmed necklace. Aurora felt her chest, noticing her necklace was missing.

"That's mine! Give it back!" She didn't waste another second and charged at the demon.

The demon punished her with a fierce open-palmed smack that sent her tumbling across the bloody waters. She shrieked, the sharp edge of a claw puncturing her right eye. She held her burning face as warm blood seeped through her fingers. However, she caught something in the corner of her eye to her left. Upon looking at it, she wished both of her eyes were cut. Blair's colorless corpse floated next to her. Aurora screamed and leaped, nearly tripping on something behind her. She turned and saw Polaris with her chest ripped open and her circlet lodged inside of the wound. *No, Polaris, no! No!* Aurora covered her mouth, unable to calm her hurried breath.

Reiya, Shoto, and Vakari floated up above the blood, lifeless. Aurora quaked, slowly backing away. More bodies floated. Ria, Jason, and Alicia. Even the police officers from Westtown and Moro Town She held her stomach, quaking uncontrollably while cold tears ran down her face.

The demon witch approached her, cackling.

"How dare you? *How dare you!*" Aurora screamed.

"No. How dare *you?*" The demon echoed, pointing to Aurora's hands.

Her hands were seeped in blood, and the blunt edges of her nails narrowed and sharpened. She looked back up and the demon mirrored her, having the same wound on her left eye. She reached for the wound, peeling the skin from her eyelid down and tearing away like a candy wrapper. What lie beneath was white as snow, and that eye with a glowing, pink iris. Pointy fangs grew from her mouth.

"I told you, we aren't that different." She spoke with a monstrous blend Serena's voice and her own.

"No—I didn't. I'm not you. I'm nothing like you! I didn't do all this!"

"You did. You know it. The entire world knows it. Your weakness. Your shame." Masamune appeared in her grasp as she slowly approached Aurora.

Aurora raised her fist, despite her tremble. In an instant, Blair and Polaris sprang up behind her and grabbed each of Aurora's arms. They both wore Aurora's face like a mask. They even laughed in her voice.

"Break away. You should be able to," Her impostors all spoke in unison.

But she couldn't budge no matter how hard she tried to force her arms loose. She tried to infuse her magic but couldn't, furthering her panic.

The demon pointed Masamune directly at Aurora's chest. "Sloth is as much of a sin as wrath. Lord Fraizen will claim your divided, monstrous soul."

"I'm not a monster!" Aurora proclaimed. "I'm . . . I'm not. I'm not evil. I'm not!" she wept softly, lowering her gaze.

The demon smiled, swinging back her blade at Aurora's neck.

Aurora jumped awake in a cold sweat, shivering profusely. No nightmare ever shook her that much. She heaved with relief and rubbed her aching temple. The young half-witch sat upright on a strangely stiff mattress wrapped in a thick, black blanket. Now she really didn't know where she was. Thin rays of sunlight pierced through the shoddy roof above, composed of sticks and logs. She jumped off the brick of a mattress on the floor, which pricked against Aurora's bare feet and creaked with every step. The last thing she wanted was a splinter, so she reached for her sneakers, which rested on the bedside.

The rest of the room appeared like a small cabin but looked vastly different from the bedroom. The small kitchen area had an octagonal dinner table made of shiny mahogany, with chairs made of the same wood. There was also a countertop behind it, but no stove or sink was to be found. She walked to the far corner of the room where she found a tall metal can. It was filled with coal and had a charred grill over the top of it.

Aurora scratched her head, completely bewildered. *Where the fuck am I?*

There was a soft knock on the door. Like a light switch flickering, she remembered the previous night. She rushed toward the door. "Polaris!"

Her smile disappeared upon opening the door, and for a moment her heart dropped. Rather than her sister's golden eyes, she was met with scarlet. Her mind flashed images of her bizarre nightmare. She flinched before realizing who it was. Jason stood at the door with two steaming mugs, one in each hand.

"Good morning!" he said with a smile, offering her a mug. "Coffee?"

The pair sat on the wooden porch and Aurora basked in the scenery. The sun bathed the land in vibrancy, giving the surrounding grassy fields and forestry an evergreen shine that put Verona and even Eden to shame. Although the surrounding land was beautiful, the same couldn't be said about the village itself. She was surrounded by brown, leaning houses made of logs and sticks and walking pathways made of sandy dirt. Aurora had seen poor, run-down areas before, but nothing like this.

Despite the less than stellar architecture, the small village was busy with people, who roamed the walking paths or sat in front of their homes. Some were jogging. Others were hanging their clothes on clotheslines. There were even kids playing with a small red ball.

Something else caught her eye the more she studied the people. Despite interacting with Ria often while growing up, who was a resident tailor, she knew nothing about fashion or clothing. But even she knew something was off with how everyone in the village dressed. Everyone wore odd, mismatched outfits. Some wore old dresses straight out of the Gorgon Empire Era; others wore urban baggy T-shirts that didn't fit them. There were some dragon-style kimonos on some of the young girls, with some teens wearing button-down shirts with ripped jeans. The range of styles reminded her of the black market, but much weirder. Despite the odd clothing and everything reeking of poverty, the atmosphere and serenity gave a feeling of peace.

"This . . . isn't the Pearl Kingdom, is it?" Aurora asked.

Jason laughed, a reaction confirming that the answer was a big fat 'no'. "Not quite what you were expecting? We're in the Pearl Kingdom's outer forests, far south of that luxurious wonderland. But you are in the continent of Gennomy, though. This your first time being west?" Jason asked before taking a sip from his steaming mug.

Aurora stared into her coffee. "Apparently, I was born here. But of course, I remember nothing about it. Everything is so . . . I don't know, greener here? Is that weird?"

Jason stifled a second chuckle. "If you think this is nice, wait until you see the rest of this land. But I'd like to welcome you to Furasaku Village, named after the greatest half-demons in existence!"

Aurora tilted her head. She never heard of them until Polaris mentioned them the other day. "Neat." Aurora took a sip of her coffee before spitting it out. She couldn't get the bitter, burnt taste out of her mouth.

Jason gave her the side eye. "Please don't tell me. You expected some fancy tea."

"No."

Jason cocked a brow.

"Maybe."

He shook his head. "You really are her sister."

It struck her that Polaris was AWOL. She sprang up in a hurry. "Where is she?"

"Whoa, whoa, relax there, Little Red. She's fine, she's just resting at the medical cabin. Nearly drowning and exhausting her aura has her out of it, so she may sleep all day. But we're taking good care of her."

"OK, good." Aurora paused, narrowing her eyes at the boy. "Hold on . . . Little Red? I wouldn't make short jokes at your stature."

The corner of Jason's mouth twitched. "It wasn't a short joke," he said through his teeth.

"Whatev—" A fast-flying object struck Aurora in the back of her head, knocking her and her coffee mug to the ground.

Jason snorted into an ugly cackle. Aurora rubbed her burning ear, seeing a big red ball eclipsing her vision while on the ground. She jumped up, palming the red ball. She could pop it with a squeeze with how much she fumed. "Who the hell threw that?"

Two young girls and a young boy came running up to her. They looked no older than five years old and were all covered with brown dirt and black scuffs.

"Sorry about that, lady!" one of the little girls said.

Aurora simmered down, and gave a smile. "It's okay. It's—"

The witch froze as she looked into the little girl's eyes. They were scarlet with thin pupils, as were those of the other kids with her. They all had tiny sharp teeth and tiny little claws. She took another glance at her surroundings and found the same features on everyone else.

"Lady! Ball!" the girl pouted.

"Oh, sorry!" she said as she handed it over.

Aurora sat down, dumbfounded. Jason was still giggling next to her.

"You okay?" he asked, clearing his throat to stop his laughter.

"I'm fine . . . but," she struggled to find the right way to ask. "Is everyone here your family?"

Jason gave her a blank stare. Aurora wished she had just stayed silent.

"Everyone here is a half-demon, so they're like family to me in that way." Jason started. "Furasaku Village was founded to give half-demons a home. Alicia and I are the only actual Furasakus left, though."

She saw Jason staring down into his coffee mug. Now she really wished she hadn't said anything. "Sorry. I know what having few family is like."

"It's all good. We take pride in upholding the family name! Someone's gotta keep this place together, right?" He downed his steaming coffee as if it were water, making Aurora cock a brow out of concern. "You're a half-demon too, though, right? Where are your red eyes and claws? Looks like you were . . . neutered."

Aurora didn't know whether to be offended or not. But the question reminded her of that horrific nightmare, along with the actual horrors she lived through. "They only come in when I use its power."

"Really? That's weird. It's like your demon-ness has an off switch. Probably because you're a Gorgon, no offense by the way. I just have never seen anything like that."

Aurora scratched the back of her head.

"Even if you weren't a Gorgon, you could live a normal life without scorn, huh?" Jason questioned.

"Ha! Yeah right. I'm sure you've heard of The Crimson Witch by now. Not exactly a friendly face of the public, especially because I'm half-demon."

"Crimson Witch? Never heard of her."

Now Aurora was offended.

"But I guess you can kind of understand what we deal with then. That's reassuring." Jason smirked. "You called yourself a warrior last night. I take it you can fight? Blue vouched for you, and she never vouches for anyone."

Blue? He must mean Polaris. "You bet your ass I can. But you and your sister were amazing! I never seen magic like that, how do you guys do it?"

"You've never heard of anatomical magic?" Jason asked.

"Anatomical, like enhanced body features? I mean, yeah, from beastmen. But you guys aren't beastmen though, right?" Aurora stroked her chin. "How do spikes and thorns come from the body?"

"Man, not only do you not look like us, but you know nothing about us either," Jason said, provoking Aurora and making her narrow her eyes at him. "My sister and I, our demon anatomy allows us to create thorns and tendrils from the cells in our body and release them from any part of our body. Most half and full demons have some sort of anatomical mutation outside of our advanced regeneration. Please tell me you at least know we can regenerate, 'Red'."

"Yeah, I know about that, obviously. But that's so cool, I didn't know demon magic worked like that! That means no one else in the world has the magic you do. You guys are so awesome!" That twinkle returned to Aurora's green eyes as she geeked out.

"Oh?" Jason blushed. "You think so?"

"Yeah! I can't wait to beat you both down! It'll be great."

Jason was taken aback. Aurora could tell that wasn't the response he expected, but she didn't care.

Jason folded his arms, putting on a confident smirk. "Getting ahead of yourself. But if you're as strong as you say, maybe you can join our raid. We can see what you got."

"Raid?"

BOOM! The echo of an explosion made Aurora jump like a frightened alley cat. She looked in the distance and saw a large mass of red aura rising into the sky, more than any she had ever seen in one place. Her anxiety shot through the roof.

"Seriously? This early in the morning?" Jason palmed his face.

Aurora couldn't shake the memories of the aftermath of all the times she lost control. If someone else had the same problem she did . . .people could get hurt. She tightened her fists and took off without warning.

"Whoa! Where are you going?" Jason called out to her.

It didn't matter if it was someone as beloved as Blair or someone as nasty as Reiya, no one deserved the fate of being torn apart by a monster. Aurora never even considered that there were other people like her, and the idea of them losing control wasn't something she was willing just to sit by and entertain.

The ground vibrated beneath her feet as she sped through the dirt roads, zooming past the villagers. She ran toward the aura until she reached the source in an open grass field in the heart of the village. However, she didn't arrive to witness a senseless slaughter. Instead, she arrived at a sparring match with kids cheering from the sidelines. Her sense of panic flew out the back door.

On one side stood a bulky, bald, man with umber skin and biceps larger than Aurora's head. His massive build made him look more imposing than Reiya in his transformed state. He looked like he could crush a tree trunk in his palm. However, he glistened with sweat and appeared out of breath. Alicia stood across from him, boasting a smug grin, despite being in a similar condition. Her apparent fatigue aside, she hopped in place with glee.

"Let's go, Greg. We ain't done 'til one of us is on the ground," Alicia panted.

Greg bared his sharp fangs. He bellowed, charging at her like a mad bull, rattling the ground with each step. He swung his huge fists with enough force to blow the grass out of the ground, but Alicia dodged it effortlessly. She swept his feet and slammed him into the ground.

"Man, you're even slower than my little brother. Age must be catching up to you, huh?" Alicia sneered.

Greg leaped back to his feet. He reached in to grab her, but she zipped right through his defenses and jabbed him in the gut. His body shuttered from the devastating blow, hard enough to temporarily lift him from his feet. He crumbled, falling to his knees and wheezing. Alicia's name roared from the spectators' chants.

Aurora's jaw hung open. *She made that look so easy. So strong, and so much demon aura. Alicia's in control of it all.* Aurora's fists shivered to the side, and her upper lip twitched ever so slightly. *Come to think of it, everyone here is in this state and they're all normal.*

Alicia offered Greg a hand and a smile, helping the much larger man to his feet. "Remember, when facing a smaller, faster opponent, beware of attacks to your core and legs. Body shots to your solar plexus can paralyze even the toughest giants."

"I don't need a lecture from a brat."

"This brat just lifted your big ass off the ground!"

Aurora figured an argument would grow out of control, but much to her surprise, they both shared a big laugh.

"Thanks for the spar, captain. Good shit as always," he said with a slight bow.

She patted his shoulder. "Keep it up, old-timer. You're an excellent addition to our squad."

The kids who watched ran up to Greg and Alicia, giving them water bottles. Seemed Alicia as she was popular as she was strong.

Jason caught up with her, panting. "Why'd you storm off like that? The hell?"

"Oh." Aurora forgot she had left him. "Sorry. Just got nosey is all."

Jason noticed Aurora watching Alicia being fawned over by the others. "Lemme guess, Greg couldn't touch her."

"Not once."

Jason palmed his face. "She's so annoying. Ugh, can't wait until I catch up to her."

Aurora's eyes fell to her feet. She wondered just how well she could've performed in the ring against Greg. Her love for battle has been insatiable her entire life. Yet, she couldn't for the life of her envision a scenario that didn't end in disaster.

Alicia noticed them and waved them over.

"Look at you, Little Red! Unlike your sister, you're spotless. Not as beat up as when we found you," Alicia snickered.

"I— ugh. You too?" Aurora pouted.

One of Alicia's little fans was a young half-demon girl with blonde pigtails, appearing no older than eleven years old. She approached Aurora as soon as she noticed her.

"You're the half-demon from Verona? Will you be living with us, miss?" She asked.

Aurora was thrown for a loop. "Living?"

"Whoa there, Zena," Alicia interrupted. She pointed at Aurora's chest. "See that tat? She's a Royal Gorgon. She'll be living with the queen in that nice-ass white castle. She ain't one of us."

Zena lowered her head. "Aww, that's too bad."

Aurora didn't know how to respond, being so caught off guard.

Greg stared down at her. Up close, Greg looked like an actual giant, towering her at almost seven feet. His height alone made Aurora nervous; not many people could do that.

"You fought the Alucard and you're Princess Polaris's sister," he said in a deep, rugged voice.

"Uhh . . . yeah," she nervously extended her hand. "Call me Aurora. Nice to meet you . . . all of you guys."

Greg squinted his red eyes before shaking her hand and giving her a grin brighter than she expected. "Well, I'll be damned! You really do look like the queen. I never would've expected that! Greg Fulcon. A pleasure to meet you, *Your Highness*."

Aurora twirled her finger in her curls bashfully. "Oh no! Please I'm not a royal snob or nothin'. I'm just a regular gal, ya know?"

"So modest. You're nothing like your sister. Welcome to our village, Aurora," he laughed cheerfully.

"I know, right?" Alicia added. "I swear they can't be related, but it is what it is."

Aurora forced herself to laugh with them. Despite the slight toward Polaris, she felt welcomed by everyone. It was a new feeling. She would've never expected such jovial kindness from a group, especially other half-demons.

"So, Alicia," Jason interjected. "Are we doing a raid today?"

Alicia stroked her chin. "I dunno. I think we're good for at least a week."

"Seriously? Come on, I need to show my stuff," Jason pleaded.

"We fought a whole Alucard last night."

"Alucard? For real?" Greg asked.

"Long story."

"That was mainly you!" Jason argued back.

Alicia rolled her eyes. "JayJay, don't be impatient. Focus on why we do raids other than the fighting. Like I said, we have what we need for right now."

"Um, Miss Alicia," another one of the onlookers started, this time a six-year-old boy, "Grandpa said we're going to run out of food soon. We haven't gotten new stuff in four days and the last box was small." The boy gave her puppy-dog eyes.

Alicia knelt to meet the boy on his level and patted his head. "It's okay, Tommy. Big sis Fasha and big bro' Zai are actually bringin' in more food right now."

The boy brightened up immediately. "Really?"

"Yup! Should be here any minute."

Aurora couldn't figure Alicia out. Alicia was surprisingly pleasant when she wasn't punching someone or being rude as hell. Warm. Almost motherly. Yet, she and everyone else were not only half-demons but remained in that state constantly. Even the children. They seemed like ordinary people. Far from monstrous. So, why was she whenever she used that power?

Dragon screeching pierced into everyone's ears, turning all heads upwards. Everyone cheered as two wyverns landed in the thick grass across from them, carrying loaded brown crates. Two people hopped off, sporting the same black and white uniforms Jason and Alicia wore the previous night. One of them was a tall girl wearing thin eyeliner with short hair and a tattoo of a yin-yang symbol on her arm. Her caramel skin glowed like gold in the sun. The other was a pale man with prickly chin hair. He stood only a few inches taller than Jason and had hair so long that it reached his ankles.

The tall girl saluted with a grin. "Yo! Cap'."

"We have arrived," the young man said.

"Fasha, Zai, report," Alicia said.

Zai, the long-haired boy, slurred his voice in a monotone. "Seventeen crates total from Kysmiriga's factories and farms. We obtained boar, chicken, various fruits, veggies, and—"

"She means run-ins with authorities, Zee," Fasha said.

"Zai," he sighed.

"We were out of there before any Magic Militia could get a lock on us. We did tussle with the local police, but they're police." Fasha cracked the knuckle in her left hand.

Alicia gave her a high-five. "My gal! Excellent work too, Zai. Glad you're both on our team."

Aurora saw Jason frowning and staring off to the side.

"Okay, we should get these bad boys unloaded, but first—" Alicia redirected her attention to Aurora. "Go ahead and wake up sleeping beauty. We're taking you two princesses home."

It was almost as if time stopped. After everything, she was finally going to her true birthplace. The Pearl Kingdom. Finally, she could start her training to master the Divine Stone and become the strongest.

Jason pointed her in the direction of the cabin Polaris was resting in. As Aurora walked off, she overheard Alicia's conversation with Fasha.

"Aye, Cap'n, who's the redhead?" Fasha asked.

"Solar-something-whatever. She's the princess's sister I told you about. They say she's the Ice-Devil's older sister but she seems like a total weakling."

Aurora stopped and turned slowly toward them. "What?"

Alicia had a slight chuckle. "C'mon, Little Red, don't take it personally. Not everyone's got it like that, and that's okay. You're a royal so you don't gotta worry about it."

Aurora marched right back to her. "Listen here. I'm a warrior. Not some prissy princess waiting for someone to rescue her."

"Really? Because that's exactly what happened last night. You're welcome, by the way."

Aurora's ears burned red. She stared daggers into Alicia, who just laughed in response and waved Aurora off as if to disregard her. Aurora wouldn't take this lying down. She marched right up to Alicia and got in her face, her fists tight. She may have lacked the same control over her demon aura, but she didn't care. She was strong in her own right and had a Divine Stone to lean on. Alicia didn't have *all* the advantages, and it was high time Aurora showed her.

"Whoa there, you trynna buck up to your savior? Ungrateful, aren't you?" Alicia spoke low enough to where only Aurora could hear.

"I don't owe you a damn thing. But call me weak again and I'll have you on your knees."

Jason got between them. "Whoa there, guys, let's chill. Alicia, just apologize. It was uncalled for anyway."

Alicia shoved him out of the way. "Apologize for what? That Batsy upstart captured her. Nothing wrong with calling a spade a spade."

Aurora scoffed. "I was weakened from earlier battles leading up to that. Polaris and I both were!"

"Oh, I'm so sorry." Alicia cleared her throat. "A spade with excuses."

Aurora felt remarkably similar to how she did when she met Polaris. Much like her sister, Alicia exuded arrogance. It didn't take much for Aurora to tell when someone thought they were above her. Even if she saved her and Polaris's lives, her attitude was too smug to ignore. And her little grin was just the cherry on top. She wanted to wipe that smile right off her face.

The charm on Aurora's necklace started glowing again, catching everyone's eye. "This spade wants a fade!"

Everyone gasped, backing away. Jason, however, grabbed Aurora's shoulder to whisper in her ear. "Red, shut up. You do not want to do this."

Aurora huffed. "There's nothing I wanna do more."

Alicia shook her head. "You should listen to my baby brother. If the queen finds out I'm the one who sent you home black and blue, you could put my people in danger. Sorry. Can't have another Alucard incident on my hands, especially with your snitch of a sister around."

"And that's another thing! I'm all down for making fun of Polaris now and then, but you always cut deep, and it pisses me off!" Aurora barked.

"Oh, come on, you have known her long enough to know she deserves it. She doesn't care about anyone but herself. Hell, she doesn't even care about you. She's just following mommy's orders. Soon as you're home, you'll be nothing but a tool at best."

Steam flowed out of Aurora's nostrils. A raging flame expanded in her chest. However, the more she saw Alicia's crimson glare, the more it reminded her of that horrific nightmare. She counted backward from five and the light on her necklace charm dwindled. Aurora turned around and started to walk away.

Alicia smirked. "You're leaving? Come on, it was just about to get fun. I thought you were a warrior?"

Ignore her. Keep it together, Aurora. She picked up the pace.

"Guess my assumption was right. Without Gorgon in your name, you're a nobody. If Blair raised you, she must've been an even bigger pushover than you."

A chord snapped, stopping Aurora dead in her tracks. She turned around and shot a lightning strike directly at Alicia. In a flash, the strike zipped past the other half-demons and struck the crates by the wyverns. They exploded and ignited into flames, but that didn't catch Aurora's attention. What was at the forefront of her mind was the pair of crimson eyes inches away from her face. The leather grip on her wrist and the sharp claws digging into it. The tip of Alicia's dagger pointed at her neck. Aurora held her breath and stood as still as she could. She felt like she was staring into the eyes of the devil himself.

17
Pendragon

"Oh no! All the food!" Tommy cried as the flames raged on.

The dragons screeched and slammed their tails on the fire to put it out. Jason, Fasha, Zai, and Greg stared back at Aurora and Alicia with distraught expressions.

"Did . . . did you guys even . . .?" Jason mumbled.

"Nope. Too fast even for me," Fasha scoffed. "And 'Cap didn't just see it, she dodged and countered. Your sis' is a genuine demon."

"That's the captain for you. Are any of you genuinely surprised? Not that it matters." Zai sighed, hanging his head in defeat. "All that work for nothing. It may as well rain with my luck."

Aurora swallowed, her eyes locked on Alicia's fierce red glare. The tip of the black dagger poked into Aurora's neck, making her eyes bulge. Much like the spectators, Aurora couldn't track Alicia's movements. Even her fastest, deadliest magical element couldn't so much as touch her. Aurora's suspicions were confirmed. Alicia was just on a whole other level. And much like Serena the night before, Aurora just sparked the demon's ire.

"That stunt you pulled just scorched all our food." Alicia bared her teeth but then burst into joyous laughter. "That was some fucking attack! You got some balls on you!"

"I—what?"

Alicia gave Aurora a friendly slap on the back and put away her dagger. "I didn't think you'd actually attack me, and with lightning magic no less! Maybe you do have some demon in you."

"Um . . . thanks?" Aurora didn't know how to feel but staring at their food supply literally going up in smoke didn't exude anything positive. "How aren't you mad? I attacked you and burned your food."

"Cuz I would've tried a stunt like that if put in a corner. You're not a punk, and I like that. So—" She lightly punched Aurora's shoulder and smiled. "You got my respect, Ari."

Aurora was taken aback. That was the last thing she expected to hear. All the same, relief washed over the half-witch. "Thanks? But sorry about . . . ya know."

Alicia turned, watching the flames consume their food supply. "Eh. It's cool. Besides, you can help us get more with firepower like that."

Aurora cocked a brow.

"Hey, JayJay!" she called out to Jason and the others. "Go get Jack! Looks like we're going on a raid as a full team after all."

Jason pumped his fist in excitement. "YES! I'll go get my scarf and gloves!" He ran off toward the cabins.

Greg pulled a white bandana from his baggy pockets and tied it around his neck. "Captain loves spontaneous missions."

"We just came back though," Zai whined, hanging his head.

"Don't stain your uniform with your tears." Fasha rustled Zai's spiky hair, prompting him to smack her hand away. "Where are we headed this time, Cap?"

Alicia stroked her chin, pondering the situation. "Any farm or factory is off the table, so we'll just shop for something to hold us for a week. A short trip to Merlinia wouldn't hurt."

"Bad idea," Zai said. "Between Lady Eira and her Rook, we'll get buried if we even cross those mountains."

"Not Rhongomyniad, Zee—"

"Zai," he corrected her.

"Anyways, not their capital nation. I was thinking about the rural southeast. I heard the Pendragon family have a nice summer house out there." Alicia looked to Aurora. "Well, how 'bout it, Ari? You game?"

A wide smile crept onto Aurora's face. Not only was this a chance to dispel the bad taste in her mouth from previous battles, but it could be an opportunity to see if there was some secret to controlling demon aura. Or potentially show the likes of Alicia and the others that she was plenty strong, even without it. After all, she made it so far, so she had to be. Right?

"Hell yeah!" Aurora agreed.

Aurora soared on her broom, clearing clouds alongside the two wyverns that transported the others. Alicia piloted one of the beasts, riding with Jason and Fasha behind her. Greg flew another, riding with Zai and Jack, a skinny young man in his early twenties with short, scruffy brown hair and freckles. Jack tinkered with a blue crystal ball in his hand, which displayed a hologram. All of them wore the same black uniform with white gloves, a white bandana around their necks, and the character ▢ embroidered on their backs.

"I didn't know you guys did raids all the time!" Aurora jittered with excitement. She itched for the next opportunity to show what she was made of, especially around the other half-demons in Alicia's group.

"That's right, Ari. Around these parts, we're known as the Skewer Bandits, and I'm their beautiful, powerful leader," Alicia boasted, tilting her nose upward and placing a hand on her chest.

Jason shook his head. "Here she goes, stroking her own ego."

"Hey!" Alicia snapped. "Don't mock your captain unless you can survive an eight-thousand-foot drop."

Jason flipped her off, and Aurora laughed..

"Man, this sounds so fun!" Aurora grinned from ear to ear. "Feels like forever since I've raided with . . . another person." Memories of Blair made her bright smile dissipate.

"Don't get too amped," Fasha cut in. "We operate as a team. Just follow Cap's commands. We may be going to the countryside, but we'll still likely have to deal with Magic Militia if it's Pendragon property. If any one of us gets caught by those cretins, our whole village will be put in danger."

"Your whole village? I understand the risk of, like, jail or whatever, but how would that endanger everyone?" Aurora asked.

"Ari, as a half-demon you know what we're capable of. Well, so does the Magic Council. And if they ever found a reason to get rid of us, they would. Just ask Batsy," Alicia said.

The puzzle started to come together. But if they were anything like her and lost control like her, would the Magic Council be wrong? Aurora dispelled the thought faster than it arrived.

The wyverns stopped, hovering high above a dense cloud. Aurora wondered as to why.

"We should be right above Pendragon Manor. Jack, do your X-ray thing," Alicia said.

"It's *clairvoyance.*" Jack shook his head. His crimson eyes shifted hue into a luminous aquamarine, with white hypocycloid stars for pupils. Aurora gasped upon seeing it. The eye-pattern looked familiar, but she wasn't entirely sure where she saw it before.

He peeked over the side and stared down into the clouds. "The property is about 50,000 square feet in total with six floors, and–" He paused and bit down on one of his claws. "They're prepared. There's seven Magic Militia spread all around the perimeter."

Aurora was impressed he could see through a mansion from so high up. *So that's clairvoyance? Handy.*

"Armed security at an empty vacation home?" Alicia's eyebrows furrowed. "Don't tell me. . . Is that blonde bastard here, too?"

"I don't detect King Arthur's presence. I don't imagine him stepping foot outside of Neo-Camelot. There does appear to be another person there, but it's unclear who. They're surrounded by steam."

"Steam? Are they taking a shower?" Greg asked.

"Don't be a peeping Tom, Jack." Fasha giggled.

"Shut up," Jack fired back. "But, it is a vacation home. Could be Guinevere on a holiday."

Alicia tied her long hair into a ponytail. "No king, but seven Militia and one guest? They're either protecting something valuable or the king's wife as Jack suggested. That or they must've got wind of the job you did in Kysmiriga, Fasha. Either way, our work is cut out for us."

Fasha cracked her knuckles. "Bet! I've been waiting to break some militia skulls."

Aurora salivated at the idea. After dealing with regular police and humans for years, fighting the elite Magic Militia would be a nice change of pace and a wonderful challenge. However, she couldn't suspend the idea of her losing control or being too weak from the back of her mind.

"Jack, any update on that food supply locale?" Alicia asked.

"There are large pallets of packaged food located in a refrigeration unit in the east wing. There are some militia there, but if we can draw them away, we can grab what we need and go."

"You read my mind, bud!" Alicia clapped her hands. "All right, here's the plan. Fasha, Greg, Zai, the four of us are going to attack the front of the manor and break as many bodies as it takes to force every ounce of security toward us. Jack, you're our eye in the sky. Let me know if there are any incoming militia on the crystal ball. JayJay, Ari, you two will take Zeta to the back, load her with as many food pallets as possible, and then fly back to the village. We won't be too far behind."

Jason's jaw hung. "Wait! We aren't fighting at all? Come on, at least leave us a few soldiers, Alicia. There's one for each of us!"

Alicia glared at her younger brother. "It's 'Captain.' And no, we can't risk anything happening to that food because you want a skirmish."

"I can handle it though. And Red . . . I'm sure she could help, too."
He couldn't hide the doubt in his voice.

Aurora folded her arms. "Wow. Thanks."

His comment aside, she cosigned on Jason's sentiment. She wanted
to test her mettle against legitimate soldiers. Yet, if they were anything
like Reiya or Serena, would the result be anything outside of disastrous?

"Just do what you're told! This ain't open for discussion," Alicia
declared.

"At least switch me for someone else maybe? We've been working on
our combos longer than anyone. Let me fight with you!"

"I can't have you risking our diversion either. This is our best course
of action, so cut it."

"But—"

"Don't ever forget we have a responsibility to uphold to our people.
We are not doing this to have fun, so quit complaining. The only thing
I want to hear from you is 'Yes, Captain.' Got it?"

Jason grimaced and turned away from his sister. "Yes, Captain," he
mumbled.

Alicia stood up, the wind whipping her hair as she put her scarf over
her mouth. "All right, everyone has their orders. Oh, and Ari, put the
hoodie on. Don't want anyone seeing that special tattoo of yours," she
winked. "Fasha, Greg, Zai, let's dive!"

She tilted forward, diving toward the ground.

Zai sighed, "She always does this." He jumped off after her.

Greg saluted, "Good luck guys."

"She's lucky if I even catch her ass this time." Fasha sprouted large,
red dragon wings from her back and grabbed Greg's hand as they dove
off.

Aurora, Jason, and Jack sat in the sky watching the others dive through the clouds. Explosions echoed from below soon after. Jack kept his eyes glued down below, while Jason stewed in frustration.

"Uhh, you okay, dude?" Aurora asked.

"Fantastic."

Jack placed a hand on Jason's shoulder. "If it makes you feel any better, the captain doesn't let me fight either." Based on Jason's bitter frown, the statement didn't ease his irritation. Jack cleared his throat. "But it's best for the mission. We're all contributing. That should be enough, right Jason?"

"Sure."

Aurora understood where Jason was coming from. Blair would sometimes have her sit on the sidelines during big fights. But now Aurora knew why. She wondered if Alicia had similar reasons for sitting Jason out of the brawl.

"Hmmm. If it's a fight you want, maybe we can spar when we get back. Before I head to the Pearl Kingdom."

Jason sighed. "It's not just about that it's—"

"Guys," Jack interrupted. "All seven militia are engaging with the others. You guys should fly eight kilometers east before heading in through the back. If you're detected, their efforts are pointless."

That fast? Damn. Alicia is probably driving most of their attention by herself. Fuckin' showoff. Aurora put on her purple hoodie. "You ready, Jason?"

"I guess. Let's go."

After taking Jack's advice and flying further east, they circled down to the back of the mansion and approached the large gates in the back of the manor. The pair saw the mixture of light from dancing auras and dense smoke from the front. Aurora wanted to be on the front lines just as bad as Jason, but she didn't wish to burden them with her antics.

Aurora tried to bury the thought, and focus more on the task at hand. The pair cleared the gates with a leap, and sped to the back entrance. They entered the mansion and walked into a living room the size of an auditorium. Various framed photos decorated the walls, along with the mounted heads of unicorns and dragons with onyx scales. The mounted heads in particular chilled Aurora's blood. *Ain't dragons held in high-regard in the Magic Nations? Weird.* Aurora wasted no more time, tailing Jason as they sped into the nearest hallway.

Jack guided the pair verbally through Jason's blue crystal ball. "Make a right at the end of the hall then take another left at the end. You'll go through a door that leads to a vacant room. The entrance to the storage unit is through that door."

"Got it. Thanks, man," Jason said.

As they hit a right corner and sprinted, something caught Aurora's eye when they crossed a hall intersection. She saw a pale girl in all black, carrying a katana and sporting a sadistic grin. Her sneakers screeched against the marble floor as she halted and turned around in a hurry.

"Hey, what gives, Red?" Jason asked.

Aurora sped back to the intersection. "Serena!" Aurora stumbled backward. There was no one there.

"Did you just say 'Serena?'" Jason caught up with her.

"I . . . I could've sworn I saw her," Aurora mumbled.

"If someone else were near us then Jack would've told us. Serena's probably dead after that cave collapsed. Forget it. Let's get going."

Aurora tried to shake the thought of seeing her. They ran down the hall and went to the east wing. They opened a pair of double doors made of gleaming wood with an emblem carved into it: a sun containing a sword pointing north in its center. Jason kicked open the doors and they walked into an empty room bigger than the living room. The marble floor shined beneath their feet, boasting a mural of a knight wearing golden armor dueling with a black dragon. Looking past that, they both spotted the metal door at the back of the room.

"There it is!" Aurora exclaimed.

Jack screamed through Jason's crystal ball. "Hold on! Someone's coming to your location and they're moving incredibly fast!"

"Wait, what?" *Could it be her?* Aurora's hands quaked and grew sweaty.

Jason shook his head. "Alicia let someone break away?"

"He did say earlier there was a guest in the shower," Aurora mumbled. "Guinevere? King Arthur's wife, right?"

"No. This is. . .oh Mephion, it's her!" Jack yelled. "Don't dawdle! Just hide, she's almost there! Take cover so I can—"

"No! Furasakus don't hide and don't run—"

A bright light zipped between them, bringing a strong breeze nearly knocking them down. Aurora shielded her eyes from the shimmering gold light that stood across them. The light faded out, revealing a girl who stumbled and lightly panted. Her blonde, wavy hair just reached her shoulders, glowing under the light. Her sapphire irises matched her royal blue dress, and her golden heels were almost as shiny as the flashing light she arrived in. This five-foot-eleven, well-dressed witch took Aurora aback, yet her stomach turned when she saw her long blue gloves stretching to her elbows and a tiara on top of her head. The blonde pulled out a pocket mirror from inside her corset and checked out her milky face. Aurora stared at her in confusion, while Jason seethed through his teeth.

"Y-You! Should've known you'd be here!" Jason spat.

"You know her?" Aurora asked.

The girl raised her index finger, signaling for them to pause.

"Perfect." The well-dressed girl spoke in a silvery voice with a tone and accent similar to Polaris's. She put away her mirror. "Not a speck of dirt on my beautiful, clear face."

"You're always worrying about your damn face. I can't wait to sink my claws into them!" Jason roared.

Aurora widened her eyes in shock. Sure, Jason was a half-demon, but she never expected him to sound so violent. He reminded her of, well, herself.

The girl finally acknowledged them. "I . . . have we met before, little boy?"

"L-Little boy?"

"Oh wait! You're Baby Polaris's friend! I remember now." She placed her hands on her hips.

"Baby Polaris?" Aurora couldn't help but snicker.

"You two broke free of my militia defenses. You must've gotten stronger then, uhm. . ." She tapped her finger against her lip.

"Jason!" He shouted.

"Sure! For the sake of your health, I hope you're at least stronger than the last time." She pulled her royal blue gloves tighter.

Aurora looked between them. Yet, something about this over dressed teen put Aurora off. Sure, she was tall, but it felt as if she casting an even bigger shadow over them. Only Alicia and Serena put off such a vibe.

Jason's eyebrow twitched. "You have no clue how much stronger I am. This won't go like the last time!"

"Whoa, whoa, stop." Aurora heard enough of their banter. "Jason, who is this chick, anyway? And how does she know you and Polaris?"

The girl gasped, throwing a palm above her mouth in dramatic flare. "How . . . how dare—you don't know who I am? Your rudeness is so distasteful! Why, I'm none other than—"

Jack chimed back in. "Flee now! Do not engage with her! That's the heiress to the Neo-Camelot throne . . . it's—"

A laser shot straight through the crystal ball, the sphere exploding into little clusters. Aurora and Jason jumped back, both shaken by the swift attack.

Steam swirled from the tip of the blonde's finger, her smirk prominent on her face. "The rudeness you exhibit when interrupting a princess won't be tolerated. I am Princess Camella Pendragon, first daughter of the Pendragon royal family."

So fast! I could barely react to it. She could be a problem. And that name of her's. "Pendragon? I thought Arthur's only kid was that United Military dickhead, General Mordred," Aurora said.

"Ew! Don't speak of that traitor. How do you know of him but not *moi?* The finest princess and pop star in all of the Magic Nations? Do you live under a rock?"

Camella reminded Aurora so much of Polaris that it hurt. Aurora eyed the princess up and down, realizing the girl was unarmed. "Aren't the Pendragons famous sword wielders? Where's yours?"

Camella's smile vanished momentarily, and a death glare took its place. "Worry you not. I don't use a sword. I won't need it for what I'm about to do."

Jason's face tensed up and his aura spiked. "Red, this chick is no joke. You should step aside. I'll take her on by myself. I owe her a beating anyway."

"Hey now, I wanna fight, too! Besides, she sure seems overconfident. It'll be fun to humble her."

"Sorry, Red, but this is personal. You can focus on getting the food out of here. But she's mine and mine alone."

"You both can fight me at once," Camella announced. "Especially for the Furasaku's sake. He may need a partner. Their kind should be used to dying in mass numbers to Pendragons anyway—"

"Shut up!"

"Don't interrupt me, trash!" Camella snapped. "Ugh, how silly of me. You nearly broke my composure. In any regard, I'm glad I caught you two on camera. I'm enthralled that someone is here to finally provide me with legitimate entertainment. The result is clear, yes. However, I didn't rush out of the shower and lightspeed my way all the way here for nothing. Do your best to last at least five seconds."

Aurora leered at the princess. "I can see why you don't like her."

Camella flipped her wavy blonde hair. "He's just mad that my daddy killed his. Oh, and several of their annoying friends."

Jason's red aura flared around him. "Would you stop bringing that up?"

Camella snickered. "Is that resentment? Oh, excuse me. I wasn't aware monsters had feelings."

A spear grew out of Jason's hand. "I'll show you—"

Camella fired a laser from her index finger that pierced Jason's shoulder. He stumbled back, staring at the burn mark on his shoulder, at a loss for words.

"What's wrong, Tiny? Déjà vu?" She fired finger lasers from her fingers as if they were bullets. Jason's body shuddered with each strike and was left with steaming, reddened burn marks and holes littering his shirt. He shuttered, falling to a knee and shaking.

"Jason!" Aurora cried.

"How are you a demon and weak? Pick a struggle," Camella said.

His aura surfaced and his burns vanished. He slowly rose to his feet. "Damn you!" he seethed, baring his fangs.

Aurora thought Polaris was bad when they met, but Camella was much worse. She wanted to beat her bloody. She threw her hood off and stretched. "That's it. Jason, I'm dusting this bitch."

"Not you, too! I already missed out against the Alucard and I'm not missing out here! She's mine!"

"Again, you both can take me at once," Camella repeated. "That way you have a chance of seeing me sweat. Most would kill for that opportunity."

Aurora had heard enough. She dashed at Camella without another word. She went for the knockout punch right away and Camella dodged it easily. Aurora violently punched and kicked, and Camella danced around each strike. Her moves were akin to a ballerina or a graceful swan; she was as light on her feet as she was fast. When Jason jumped in himself, it was more of the same. Neither of them could land a strike. Right when they had her cornered, she leaped above them both, causing them to punch each other in the face.

Aurora rubbed her burning cheek. "Stay out of my way, man!"

"Your way? You were in *my* way!" Jason barked back.

Camella shot them both with lasers to their chest, following up with an obnoxious cackle "Your lack of technique is baffling! How did you ever break through the Militia? I suppose this what I get for utilizing Merlinia's forces instead of bringing my own from home. Ugh, having Lancelot here would've been more fun anyway."

Aurora's frustration rose. Her burn mark vanished and she popped back up.

Camella tilted her head. "I understand the tiny one healing, but you? You're no half-demon. You don't even have the same ugly rags. Yours are way uglier. Who are you?"

Aurora wished Camella was right about her not being a half-demon. "Aurora Salem. Etch it in your brain, Goldilocks."

"Salem? Haven't quite heard that name before."

Aurora was taken aback. "W-what? You haven't heard of The Amethyst Witch before?"

"Not really." Camella shrugged. "Whoever that is doesn't sound as interesting as a witch with the passive regeneration of a demon. I can dance with you a bit longer if you're suita—"

"Don't you dare forget about me! I'm your opponent!" Jason sprang back up and charged at Camella.

"Jason, wait!" Aurora yelled.

Camella slapped his jab away and kicked him in the throat with her heel. He choked, grabbing his neck as he stumbled back. She blew him away with just the force of her aura, which wrapped around her like a blue rose. A bright, red ball of light swelled at the tip of the princess's finger, emitting a dense heat that turned the room into an oven. Before Jason could recover, Camella fired the blast right through his abdomen, leaving a massive, gaping hole. The half-demon gasped for air, reaching at the hole.

"Jason? Jason!" Aurora yelled.

He fell backward, losing consciousness as a pool of blood grew around him.

Camella brushed strands of blonde from before her eyes cracking a grin. "I told him not to interrupt me."

18
Need for Strength

Aurora's heart pounded at the sight of the growing pool of blood underneath Jason. Similar images of Blair and Polaris from her nightmare flashed through her mind. Her charmed necklace shone through her shirt.

Initially, it looked as if the strange light caught Camella's attention, but the blonde princess quickly dismissed it, placing her hands on her hips and showing off a pearly white smile. "That's one victory. Time for my next. Come and dance with me, Salem."

Aurora exhaled. At the very least, she was relieved Jason's wound was closing thanks to his regeneration. However, his wound was closing slower than normal regeneration would warrant. He was alive, but clearly out for the count. She figured now was a good a time as ever to take Camella on one on one, and give Jason time to recover.

Aurora set her glare on the blonde princess. "You're gonna pay for hurting him like that! Ya hear me?"

Camella scoffed. "I don't understand why you're so upset. He's a demon. A *monster*. If I put enough in that blast to kill him, I'd be doing the whole world a favor."

Aurora could fracture her teeth from how hard she clenched her jaw. Monster? Him? Aurora hadn't known Jason for very long, but in the short time she'd known him he was nothing but sweet. Kind. Strong-willed. And most of all, he was in control of his power, and confident in it. He was nothing like a typical monster. Nothing like her.

Aurora's stomach turned again at the thought. Demons weren't monstrous. It was just her. And here was this snobby, princess girl, putting that label onto Jason, and for what?

Aurora couldn't let that stand. She at least owed it to Jason to beat Camella to a pulp. She beckoned for Camella to come to her, catching the princess by surprise.

"Want me to attack first? Such an unusual, and reckless request."

Camella, as expected, fired lasers from her fingertips, prompting Aurora to shield herself with her barrier dome. The lasers deflected off its glowing green surface.

"Aura shaping? So you *do* have some skill. But if that's all you can do, you're in trouble!"

Aurora smirked. She knew the advantage just shifted to her. *She doesn't know my magic. Just like everyone else. You're in for it now, Goldilocks.* She concentrated her aura to her left hand, her palm tingling from an influx of electricity. The moment Camella stopped firing her lasers, Aurora released her barrier and struck Camella with a powerful lightning strike. The princess rolled backward and crashed into the wall, covered in static.

"That was for Jason!" Elation took over. It felt like forever since she delivered a solid strike on an opponent without the aid of her undesired demon aura.

Princess Camella, however, stood and scowled in fury. She pulled her pocket mirror from her bodice and noticed her wild, frizzy blonde hair. "Hussy! Not only do you cheat and use such a cheap trick, but you ruined my beautiful hair, too?"

"Cheat? What are you talking about—that's my magic, goldilocks." Aurora folded her arms.

"No! Aura shaping is difficult enough for someone your age, but for you to have lightning mastery too? There is no way a rugged, lowly pest like you can master magics so difficult! Your regeneration is weird enough!" She stomped her heel on the ground in a tantrum.

Aurora cracked a grin. "Maybe I'm just better than you, Goldilocks. Ever consider that?"

The princess quaked with fury, her upper lip and eyebrow twitching. "Better than me? Than *me*?" Her aura stormed around her, illuminating the entire room with a sapphire glow. "I was going to be courteous and dance with you for a while, but instead, I'll ensure you never dance again!"

Aurora scoffed at her. *She wants to complain after what she did to Jason? Whatever. Let's keep the bitch on the move.* She fired more lightning strikes, however, Camella was prepared, weaving around the blasts like a leaf floating in the wind. Aurora did more damage to the room than the princess, carving through the walls and ground. As Camella evaded, a bright golden light enveloped her, differing from her ordinary blue aura.

Her shine intensified to near whiteness, just as her speed increased. *Shit!* Aurora was blinded by Camella's light, shielding her eyes just as the light flashed by her like a speeding car.

The blow black of the wind made Aurora stumble. Camella was no longer in her field of vision. Aurora couldn't figure out why her body suddenly burned all over until she looked down. Holes littered her entire body. Aurora's hair stood up when she heard a heel click on the ground behind her. She turned to see Camella standing with the diminishing light and steam coming from her fingertips.

"What's wrong? Out of tricks, Salem?" Camella asked.

Aurora staggered, her necklace charm shining once again. Her breathing picked up and her throat burned, along with other disturbingly familiar sensations she wished to avoid. *Five . . . four . . . three . . . two . . . one. No. I don't need it. I can beat her. I can beat her!*

"You can just give up. I can let you live and hire you as a maid. You can rebuild what you just destroyed before Daddy finds out. Plus, I'd love to have a personal punching bag," Camella said.

Aurora's burns healed, and she did her best to keep herself under control. She turned right to Camella and created her witch-blade.

Camella scoffed, wiping the sweat from her brow. "Raising a blade to a Pendragon? Where are your manners?"

Aurora swung her blade, to which Camella evaded effortlessly again. However, Aurora began to chip away at her dress, leaving small cuts and tears. She could tell Camella was slowing down. *That last move she did must've took a lot of aura! She's spent!* Aurora was one misstep away from victory. So, she took advantage. At short range, she doused Camella with a blast of water fired from her palms like a fire hydrant, launching her across the room. The princess slipped and slid along the ground.

"Water too? Impossible!" Camella freaked.

While the princess struggled to stand from the wet floor, Aurora struck her with lightning, this time intensified by the water.

Aurora's chest burned and glowed, the intensity of her Divine Stone being too much to bear, even to the point of making both her hands cramp. She couldn't fire another element. *Seriously? Right now, of all times?* Green streaks of light stretched across her body from her scorpion tattoo, and her skin was covered in static of the same hue. Her chest pain intensified, as did the glowing of stone and necklace.

While Aurora was in excruciating pain, Camella's head bobbed up, despite her struggling to move at all. Camella's aura flared again, and she created a white ball of light in the palm of her hand. She smiled as she squeezed it, creating a blinding flash and a loud *POP*.

Aurora's eyes burned from the sight, and her head spun. Then, Camella launched her fist into Aurora's abdomen, bending her forward, stealing all the air from her. Blood spewed from her mouth. The young witch stumbled backward, still only able to see white. Once her vision cleared, a heavy kick hammered the back of her head, slamming her with enough strength to create large cracks in the white marble.

As the defeated witch writhed in absolute agony on the ground, she saw those blue and gold heels eclipse her vision with specs of her own blood on them. She looked up as her pupils shrank. At first sight, she saw Serena. Upon blinking, she witnessed Camella's smug grin.

The princess placed her hands on her hips and put her heel on Aurora's head triumphantly. "Second victory. There was no other outcome, cheating or not." Camella pressed her heel into Aurora's skull. "Etch *this* into your brain: There's *nobody* better than me."

Aurora's necklace shined again. The undesired heat and tingling returned. It was happening again. Her ominous demon aura surfaced.

She tried her best to calm herself. She attempted counting backward, but she couldn't fight the urge to ram her fist through Camella's chest. Her fury only fueled that rancid aura. That's when it hit her.

As bad as she wanted to beat Camella bloody, she knew that as she was, she couldn't do it without the demon aura. Even with her fighting freely, she still lost a one-on-one fight. She was still underneath the heel of a royal. To make matters worse, if Aurora were stronger, maybe Jason wouldn't have gotten hurt. Perhaps she could've put Camella down faster. If Polaris was here in Jason's place and fell victim to the same attack, this would've been much worse.

These thoughts just fueled Aurora's frustration. She still didn't want to surrender control and kill just for the sake of satisfaction. Yet her own will weakened by the second. Sanity slipped, inch by inch. Camella boasting and trying to crush her skull only worsened it.

"I was taught the mark of a true princess is to extend gratitude at least twice. So I say to you, Salem, you can still return to Neo-Camelot with me. Become my personal attendant. Beats living with those filthy demons, I say," Camella offered.

Aurora dug her hands under her and pushed off the ground against Camella's pressure, now being fueled by her demonic blood. Camella stomped her back down.

"Fine, fine. I'll just put you down then." She pointed her glowing finger at Aurora's head but recoiled at the sight of Aurora's scarlet eyes. "What in the blazes? That's . . . you're half-demon, too?"

A black spear zipped past Camella's face, grazing her cheek. She leaped back, freeing Aurora from her heel. Aurora found the strength to sit upright and saw Jason back on his feet, with another spear in his palm aimed at Camella. He panted and was drenched in sweat but glared the princess down with an unrivaled intensity. Despite this reinvigoration present in his gaze, his minimal aura flow indicated his remaining strength only derived from will alone.

"You've had enough fun. This game is over," Jason boasted, despite his apparent fatigue.

Camella wiped blood from her cheek. "You've defiled my face. You must really miss your daddy, huh?"

Jason's interference gave Aurora time to calm down. Her necklace aided in suppressing that surge in demon aura, prompting the return of her emerald irises.

Jason dashed at Camella, wielding a javelin-sized spear. As fatigued as Camella was, Jason still couldn't touch her. She schooled the boy, shedding and parrying his strikes with her hands and lighting him up with lasers again.

"You should've stayed down, Tiny. You can't afford to keep regenerating. You'll burn out of aura eventually." Camella decked him with a swift punch in the nose.

Jason appeared just as winded as he was frustrated. Camella was right. Aurora could tell his regeneration and aura were wearing thin. He grew weaker and slower by the second. If this kept up, he'd be dead in mere minutes.

Just as Camella was about to deal another devastating blow, the metal door to the fridge flew off the hinges. A dense mist entered the room, and Alicia emerged from it, her uniform torn and covered in soot, sweat, and dirt. Everyone was surprised, but Camella especially went blue in the face.

"Y-y-you?" Camella stuttered.

"I get that a lot." Alicia smiled at her. "JayJay, you okay little bro?"

Jason fell to his knees and groaned. His wounds barely healed, but he managed to give a thumbs up.

"And you, Ari?"

"I'm alright . . ." Aurora scratched the back of her head.

Alicia redirected her glare to Camella. She slowly approached the princess, who backed away with each step the demon took.

"Camella Pendragon! Damn, you've grown, girl! What's up?" Alicia still issued a polite smile.

"Alicia Furasaku." Camella swallowed, most of the color drained from her face. "I should've known you'd be involved in all this. What is it you desire?"

"Oh, I got what I want. I'm just here for my brother and the newbie. I'm glad you gave them some exercise; they needed it."

Camella flinched upon seeing Alicia reach for her dagger. "You didn't kill my men, did you? Heathenish wretch."

"First, I don't kill unless it's necessary. Can't have your Magic Council terrorizing my people further. They are alive. All beat to shit, but alive. Second, I wouldn't be calling grown women 'wretches' unless I'm certain I will come out of it without a busted lip. Follow me?"

Camella scoffed at her. "You're just fortunate to have that pesky Celestial Weapon. Even more so, I'm low on aura thanks to toying with your underlings. Otherwise, I'd—"

Alicia appeared before Camella in seconds, getting within inches of her face. "You'd what? Use your little beams on me? Go ahead. You may get lucky, I'm exhausted, too. You're the best after all, right, popstar?"

Camella backpedaled with weak knees. "D-don't interrupt me!"

Alicia rolled her eyes. She ran over to her brother to help him off the ground. "Ari, you can stand, yeah?"

Aurora's knees were shaky as well, but she managed to stand under her own strength. She went over to Alicia's side.

"Hold it! You can't just leave! Who's going to clean this place?" Camella pouted.

"Figure it out, boo." Alicia started for the fridge.

Camella stomped her heel on the ground in frustration. "Now hold it just a minute. If you walk out that door, I'll ensure Daddy finishes you monsters off this time. I swear it!"

Alicia's aura swirled around her, a sea of red washing over the entire room. The heat smothered Aurora, much more intense than the first time she felt Alicia's aura.

"Listen, little girl. I'm not willing to deal with your father or any of the Demi-Gods. But if you're so willing to be turned to ashes, sweetheart, I may just risk that. I'll show you a real monster if you want to see one so bad."

Aurora wished she could be happier to see Camella's smug attitude overtaken by dread. Yet, she wished she were the one to inflict it. Instead, she was saved by Alicia, again. Gratitude aside, she couldn't help but glare at the girl.

Aurora, Jason, and Alicia escaped to the wyverns where they met with the other Skewer Bandits. To Aurora's surprise, one of the wyverns was loaded with multiple crates and pallets loaded with food. Once fully prepared, they all took to the skies and flew back to the village. While ascending, Aurora looked back at the manor and saw someone standing at the peak of the mansion. Again, she saw Serena underneath a big black umbrella, staring up at her and grinning. But when Aurora blinked, she was gone.

Aurora flew on her broom beside the others on the dragons once again, this time with Jason with her. Fasha, Greg, and Zai were all in just as tough shape as Aurora and Jason were, with their clothes torn and covered in scuff marks and dried blood. Despite everyone's fatigue, the bandits—apart from Jason–cheered, led by Alicia in chant.

"Good job, guys! We got what we came for and we all got out alive!" Alicia redirected her attention to Aurora and Jason. "More importantly, I'm glad Nightlight didn't off you two morons. At her level, neither of you would've made it."

Aurora looked away. Jason grumbled, hanging his head.

"Though, I'll admit, Ari. You put up a helluva fight against the bitch."

"Hold on . . . you saw that?"

"Yeah, I was watching from the crack of the fridge door. I thought I'd have to save you a lot sooner. But you did way better than I thought."

Aurora gripped her broomstick tight. "I still lost. I don't deserve congrats of any kind. I couldn't even land a solid punch on the girl!"

Alicia snickered. "True. But hey, she's just stronger than you. That's how it is. Food chain and all."

Aurora bit her bottom lip. Alicia couldn't have been more right in her assessment, but it couldn't have been more frustrating! She couldn't compete without her demon aura, whether it had been Serena or Camella, or even back when she fought Polaris and Reiya. They were above her, and it was clear that Alicia was also. However, she handled Reiya with her demon power, and handily at that. She even had Serena on the verge of death. She knew she had unimaginable power. But what is power without control?

"Ya know. . ." Aurora started. "My demon aura . . . If I could use it properly, I'd have Camella begging for mercy."

She drew every pair of eyes to her. There was a brief silence before Alicia undercut it with laughter. "You're funny, Ari. But no. I don't know what your 'demon aura' is like but, even with it, I doubt you'd keep up with someone like her. She's her father's kid and almost on my level, even at her age. And, well, you remember what happened earlier, I'm sure."

"You haven't seen it, and for good reason. Whenever I enter that state someone usually dies."

The other Skewer Bandits wore puzzled expressions.

"Woah. What is she talking about, 'Cap?" Fasha asked.

Alicia waved Fasha off as if to tell her, 'Don't worry about it'. "You mentioned that last night, Ari. But it's your power, and you couldn't even beat Batsy with it. You don't have to deny not being that strong. It's OK."

Aurora shot a glare at her.

"Sheesh, kid. Do you care that much? Why are you so obsessed with strength anyway?" Alicia asked.

"It's . . . it's what I live for. All Blair wanted for me was to be strong. I want to surpass the Demi-Gods and make good on her wish. Keep her legacy alive that way, ya know? To show the whole world that I'm not. . . That Blair didn't die for. . ." Aurora exhaled. Even all these years, she couldn't speak on the reality of what she did to Blair. "Point is, I can't do anything by remaining where I am. I'm talented, sure. But if I can control all that demon aura I have, and use it with my other techniques, then I'd be unstoppable."

Alicia chuckled at her again. "You sure sound your age. Even if you did master this mystery demon aura, I don't see you being any stronger than my brother."

"Hey!" Jason barked.

Aurora's ears burned. "Alicia, I mean no disrespect to you, or anyone else here. But with control of my demon aura, I'd destroy you."

Everyone else looked at Alicia, grinning.

"Whoa there! Hear that, Cap? I think Gorgon is challenging you!" Fasha teased.

"She surely seems confident in herself. She did attack you earlier," Greg added.

Jason kept his lips zipped.

Alicia brushed her hair waving in her face from the wind. "Ari, you're talking recklessly. I may just take you up on that bet."

"Try me," Aurora doubled down. "With proper training, I could master my demon aura, and control it in a week. You, Serena, Camella, none of you could so much as touch me."

Alicia beamed from ear to ear. "I like you! Okay, let's say it's possible you could master this. Who would teach you? I sure can't. I have a whole village to take care of."

Aurora looked at Jason, taking him by surprise. "Whaddya say? Up to teach this witch?"

Jason was so shocked he couldn't even respond before everyone cut him off with laughter.

"That's cute, kid, but I wouldn't say he's cut out to train you," Fasha said dismissively.

"What?" Jason shrieked.

"Yes. You can stand to work on your own combat training. You don't have the time or skill to train the girl," Zai added.

"But she doesn't need combat training! She needs aura training, specifically aura control, which by the way I'm really good at!" Jason whined.

Greg stroked his chin. "The kid may be onto something. For Jason's young age, he's exceptional and can even fight alongside the captain. Training a half-witch in aura usage shouldn't be that tall a task for him."

"I agree," Jack finally spoke. "They're both young and from what I saw of their fight, though they were bested, they both have potential. Training her could be an opportunity for growth for both of them."

Alicia shook her head. "Jack, Greg, I'd normally agree with you both. They have promise as combatants, sure, especially Ari. But Jason can hardly even follow orders. He nearly got himself and Ari killed by Camella for simply not fleeing when you told him to, Jack. He just isn't disciplined. He's too reckless and impatient to train anyone, let alone you, Ari."

Jason didn't even try to hide his frustration. He huffed from his nose and gritted his teeth. "Know what, Red? I'll train you. You'll be the strongest half-demon in Gennomy in one week. A fight between you and Alicia should seal the deal, right?"

Aurora grinned. "Wouldn't want it any other way."

Alicia shook her head again. "Man oh man, you're really doin' this. Fine. Ari wins, she gets that satisfaction. I'll even personally admit to her she's stronger. But, when I win, what do I get?"

"You've always treated me like a liability so I won't be anymore. If I can't have her master her powers and surpass you, I'll resign from the bandits and just look after the village," Jason mumbled.

"Bluff!" Alicia blurted out.

"Whoa! Jason, hold on, are you sure?" Aurora asked.

"Never been so sure. Do you accept, Captain? Worst-case scenario, I can stop bringing the team down."

The siblings locked eyes, Jason not wavering for even a second. Alicia slowly clapped in acknowledgment. "You're definitely my brother, that's for sure. After she loses, she can return to the castle and you'll be confined to the village. Hope you learn how to farm in the meantime."

"Deal."

After a few hours of flight, the team arrived at the village and distributed food to the joyful villagers. After Aurora was finished helping with distribution, she sat underneath a small tree near one of the cabins, contemplating the deal she just made. She had to master the very thing that she had worked so hard to avoid the most. The thing that's tormented her for years, taking so many people away and forcing her into isolation. Mid-thought, Jason joined her.

"Hey, uh." He rubbed the back of his neck. "Thanks for earlier."

Aurora fiddled with her necklace. "Thanks? I dragged you into my mess. The last thing I expect you to do is thank me."

"You kidding? You believed in me when none of them ever had. That means everything, Red, seriously."

Aurora twirled her finger in her curls. Her face started to match its scarlet hue. "Don't get all gushy on me."

Jason chuckled. "This is gonna be great! Once we're done, maybe you can be the new Skewer Bandits Captain."

Aurora stared at him blankly. "What?"

"Yeah. The strongest is always the leader. My dad was the leader before . . . he died. Then, Alicia became the leader."

"I, um . . . figured that. But Jason, I don't intend to lead you guys, or even stay here. Once I'm done, I'm probably going back to the castle with Polaris. There are . . . other things I have to master, too."

"What? But you don't have to, right? You'd fit in more with us half-demons. C'mon, friend."

Aurora was taken aback. "What did you call me?"

"I—uh—friend?"

She never thought she'd hear someone refer to her as that. Just thinking of it made her shudder. Sure, he was great to be around, as was everyone else, even Alicia. But she couldn't help but remember what happened to the last friend she had. That familiar warm feeling was coming right back. The same feeling she felt with Polaris the night before.

"Jason . . . thanks," Aurora smiled at him. "But, when we're training, just be careful. Don't get too comfortable with me."

"Whoa, Red, I understand your concern, but you're not my type."

She had the sudden urge to punch him. "That's not what I mean!"

"Sure, it isn't," he chuckled, rolling his eyes.

Aurora scoffed, turning away from him. Even still, she felt happy for the first time in a while. Atop it all, she was finally going to master that curse. Her ascent to be the world's strongest was back on track.

"Oh, by the way, Red," Jason started. "I don't know if I hit my head too hard or what but, I saw you fighting Camella. Did you use water magic against her?"

"SOLARIAAA!"

Just before Aurora could register what he asked, she heard a familiar ear-tearing screech. She turned to see Polaris sprinting at her at full speed, wearing a white tunic and black slacks. She had completely forgotten about her.

19
Emotions Aflare

Aurora giggled, twisting a loose curl in her hair with her finger as she leaned against the tree. "Hey. Good morning, sunshine."

Her sister got in her face with a quickness. "Don't you 'sunshine' me! Where in the blazes were you the past four hours?"

"Oh . . . ya know . . . around—"

"She helped us with a raid! You should've seen her, she was incredible!" Jason boasted.

Aurora's grin started to fail, the corner of her smile twitching. *Way to be a snitch, Jason.*

Polaris folded her arms, giving Aurora that hard glare she'd grown to despise. "Incredibly foolish, maybe. Since she knows good and well that her identity and face should be kept secret as much as possible!"

"Come on, Polaris, it wasn't that big a deal," Aurora continued playing with her curls. "I had on my hoodie the entire time, so no one could see my tattoo."

Polaris eyed her up and down, studying her closely. "You engaged in combat, didn't you? Tell me, what was the damage?"

Aurora's nervous grin morphed into a frown. It was Ria all over again. "I didn't lose control. Plus, Alicia and Jason looked after me. I'm fine. You have nothing to worry about."

The princess batted her eyes, remaining firm. "Did you engage with the Magic Militia?"

"No!"

Polaris cocked a brow.

"I uh . . . fought against Princess Camella," Aurora admitted.

"CAMELLA! Have you gone mad? Why would you engage with someone like her?"

"I—"

"Don't answer that. I don't want to hear it." Polaris took in a deep breath, and pinched the space between her eyebrows. "All right, we'll sort this mess and everything else out with Bishop Agura. We're heading home immediately. We've been gone long enough."

Polaris turned on her heel, prepping a quick exit. But now? Just when she was about to make some sort of headway on the very thing that plagued her most? Aurora lunged forward and snatched her sister's shoulder, turning her around.

"Wait, Polaris!"

Polaris swatted Aurora's hand. "What is it?"

Aurora fiddled with her fingers. "Well . . . maybe we can wait a bit longer before heading to the castle. Preferably a week?"

"I beg your pardon. A week? What's the meaning of—" Polaris gasped, her eyes darting between Aurora and Jason. "Is there something going on between you two?"

"No!" Aurora and Jason both squawked.

"Well, there's your answer. Now let's go."

"Hold on! You didn't even hear my reason."

"I don't much care. We've far exceeded the deadline. You've had your fun. Now it's time we left."

Aurora's eye twitched at Polaris's dismissiveness. "Look, Jason is going to train me to master my demon aura. Omni knows I need it, and as a half-demon, he's one of the only ones who can. I know you need me home, and I'm still coming to train with Euryale. But after I master my other curse, my demon aura. I really think if I do this first, it'll help everyone, ya know?"

"Now you want to master the power you've willfully avoided? Rich." Polaris tapped her foot impatiently. "Solaria, we don't have time for that. Sorry, you'll have to forget about mastering that power for right now. We're heading home at once."

Aurora was taken aback. Was she not even willing to consider it, especially after all they had been through? "But I need to master this! This is my best chance. Come on, Polaris! Euryale is in a council meeting set to last a week anyway, so it won't hurt."

"It doesn't matter! Did you forget everything that transpired in Verona? We need as much time to groom you as possible before she returns."

"Groom me? Seriously?"

"Enough. I have my mission, Solaria. I don't want to hear it."

~ She doesn't care about anyone but herself. Hell, she doesn't even care about you. She's just following mommy's orders. Soon as you're home, you'll be nothing but a tool at best. ~

Aurora flattened her lips. "So that's it. You're just following orders?"

"Pardon?"

Aurora stared at her feet, her fists now shaking. "You know how much my demon side affects me. You've seen it. The one chance I finally have to truly fix it and you're prioritizing your damn orders? Is it always about following commands with you?"

"It's never been about anything different!"

Passersby, including Alicia and the other bandits, stopped what they were doing after the outburst. Aurora felt their stares and heard their whispers, but didn't care. The only thing that existed was her so-called sister treating her as she had since they met: a prize to present to the queen.

"So. That's how it is. That's what your tears were really for. At the end of the day, you really are just the queen's daughter. For a second, I actually thought . . . never mind. Forget it."

Polaris gripped the side of her arm and shook her head. "Enough of this pointless argument. I needn't remind you of the entire purpose we sought you out to begin with. Staying here a second longer is hazardous as is. We're leaving."

"No. You're leaving. Alone."

"Excuse you? Did you not listen to a word I said? We don't have time for this!"

"We? You mean *you!* Do you ever think about someone other than yourself? You try to kidnap me, order me around, threaten me, and all for what? The Queen? That's such bullshit. You say we're blood, but you always treated me like a tool! At least here everyone treats me like a person. I thought you finally were, too. But I guess I was wrong!" Aurora shouted.

"Solaria . . ." Polaris bit her bottom lip, her brown face reddening. "You need to understand the situation we're in is already murky. Returning any later will just . . . it's not good for either of us. Not just me."

If she weren't already red-hot, Aurora may have even felt a twinge of sympathy.

"Losing control has never been good for me, but you don't seem to care!"

"Could you just calm down for a second?"

"No way! I have every right! You said it yourself that you're just doing it to be queen, right? That's why you care about that little crown thingy so much? Want to do everything perfectly for Euryale so you can sit on her throne?"

"Shut up."

"I'm guessing Serena was right about you. Maybe you did go to all those lengths just for that, so I shouldn't be surprised!"

"I SAID SHUT UP!"

Polaris's aura erupted, wrestling the leaves free from its branches above. They danced in the violent twirl of blue. Aurora took a step back. Her face loosened upon seeing a tear streak down her cheek.

"You have no idea what that woman is like! What being raised by a Demi-God is like! You had a wonderful God-sister who you claim loved you as if you were blood. I could only dream of that. It's always orders and expectations and always will be. That's a princess's burden, *my* burden! I understand you have your burdens and wish to be free of them, but don't think for a second that I'm doing what I'm doing out of pure aspirations for her title. I know of your struggles, but you know not of mine."

Aurora's jaw hung open. The princess couldn't have been more right. She had no idea what Polaris went through while growing up. All she knew was that the princess had deep scars on her back, and was always frightened about the prospect of either disappointing Euryale, or confronting her directly. She didn't have all the details as to why, but did it really matter? After all, right before her was a golden opportunity to gain control over something that ruled her through her entire life. She couldn't afford to pass it up.

"You're right. I don't understand, and I'm sorry for that. But I must do this right now. Right here with these people is where I belong."

Polaris sniffled and wiped her tears. "Seems we're settling this just as we did the first day." She snapped her fingers twice, and with a flash of aura, her sword and sheath appeared in her grasp.

What was this twisted feeling in her gut? Why did her hands suddenly feel clammy? She knew full well what she wanted. Mastering her demon aura was the top priority. She couldn't keep living a nightmarish life, where she always awoke to corpses. If that meant coming to blows with her sister again, the one who she wept for not even twenty four hours ago, then so be it. They fought once already, so why did she feel ants crawling all over her?

All it took was one good look at her sister's eyes to find that answer. The quick aversion of eye-contact. The quiver in her bottom lip. Even her sword rattled as she drew it from its scabbard, the metal hissing as it glided out. Even Polaris's stance was a far cry from the confident, elegant one she usually presents in battle. Polaris wanted this outcome as little as she did.

Aurora lived for battle. She was raised on it, to the point of learning to throw a punch before even learning to read. There was nothing that she loved more. For the first time in her entire life, Aurora raised her fists for a fight she desperately didn't want.

Jason jumped between them. "Whoa, hold it! Can't we settle this another way? Do you guys have to go all out here?"

Polaris's sword vibrated. "Sir Jason, please step aside."

Aurora grabbed Jason's shoulder from behind. She gave him a soft, defeated smile. "It's alright. I'll try to make it quick."

Alicia flashed in front of Polaris and pinned down her sword with her index finger. "Don't worry, JayJay. There won't be a fight."

"Stay out of this, Miss Alicia," Polaris protested. "Solaria is my responsibility."

"She is a Gorgon, but also a half-demon. So, in a way, she's my responsibility, too. Plus, you're starting a ruckus in my home. My land. I'm like the queen around here, and I decree that Ari gets to stay. If you have a problem with that," Alicia leaned in. "I'll escort you out personally."

"Th-that's absurd. You haven't the right to give me orders." Polaris's aura fizzled out and she took a step back.

"Last time I checked, the strongest call the shots. Let's see, Princess, between you and me, who do you think is stronger?" Alicia flared her aura, blowing Polaris off her feet. "Oh, and no lying."

"You wouldn't dare harm me! L'est you wish to face Mother's wrath."

"I dunno. You wanna flip that coin, then be my guest." Alicia shrugged. "But I imagine you wouldn't want the blood of yet another race on your hands, would you?"

Polaris shied away from Alicia's gaze, prompting the half-demon's smirk. The princess glanced toward Aurora, who simply refused to look back.

"Sorry, Ice-Devil. Ari is one of us for the time being. Don't get too down, though. She'll be back in your castle in a week. Maybe."

Polaris stood and dusted herself off. "Solaria . . . you're truly . . ."

"I'm sorry," Aurora muttered. "And for the last time, my name is Aurora."

Polaris looked defeated, appearing worse than when Aurora found her in the cave. Like she'd been weeping for days. Polaris sheathed her sword. "Very well. You can train, but I refuse to return home without you," she said softly as she turned her back to them. "If it makes you feel any better, I'm happy you've found a semblance of kinship."

Aurora watched her sister walk through the village and head toward an empty cabin.

Aurora's argument with her sister plagued her mind the entire night. As much as she wanted to tear her a new one, she had a feeling of how much getting to the Pearl Kingdom meant to Polaris. She buried her face in her pillow to ignore that thought. After all, Polaris just wanted her back for the Queen's sake, right? Aurora tried to forget how they had fought together in the black market. She wished she could forget the stinging pain of watching her die, and the joy when she learned her sister survived. She wished Polaris didn't look so apprehensive when trying to fight her earlier. She especially wished she could forget Polaris's tears raining on her face in the cave.

She started to question what it was all for if this was what came of it. What would coming home later mean anyway? She expelled the thought as soon as it came. Besides, her curse has been in her life longer than Polaris ever had. That comes first. Aurora comes first. Polaris only saw her as cargo anyway. And all Polaris was to her was an escort. She didn't need her to get to the Pearl Kingdom. She didn't need her at all . . . right?

The night came and went. Aurora wanted to distance herself from the thought of Polaris as much as possible. That following morning, she'd been given that opportunity to distract herself, with her training set to start. Under normal circumstances, she'd be salivating at the thought of gaining a new means of strength. However, the only thing she felt was an urge to punch something. She gobbled down her small breakfast and begged Jason to start training her immediately.

Together, they stood in the same field where Aurora had confronted Alicia the previous day. As expected, the field remained in poor shape, decorated with scars of blackened grasses and trenches, like a tornado burrowed through it. Craters and gashes were littered about, likely from Alicia's ferocious sparring sessions with the other bandits. Aurora even noticed the blot of burned grass on the edge of the field, courtesy of her lightning strike. She soaked in the spoils of this training field, ready to do some damage herself.

Jason stood across from her, finishing his cup of coffee as he sat in a rare spot of grass that wasn't ripped from the ground.

"All right, Red. Let's turn you into a powerhouse!" Jason exclaimed.

Aurora took a deep breath. She widened her base and raised her fists, ready to engage. "Yeah."

"Whoa! What's with the fisticuffs?"

Aurora relaxed her shoulders. "It's . . . my fighting stance? We are about to train, right?"

Jason chortled. "Yeah, but we aren't fighting. You're doing aura training, not combat training."

Aurora scratched the back of her head. "There's a difference? Aura is energy linked to stamina and strength, yeah? That's strengthened through fighting. At least that's what Blair taught me."

"Well, yeah that's true. But you're not trying to make your aura stronger. You're trying to control your demon aura."

Aurora scoffed at herself. "Right, right. Sorry." She rubbed her temple.

Jason frowned. "Everything OK?"

"Yeah. Everything's good. Let's start."

"Um . . . OK." Jason rubbed the back of his neck. "First, let's get you to activate your demon aura. We can see what you're struggling with, and we can go from there."

Ice invaded her veins. "You want me to activate it? Right here, and now? Just like that?"

"No, I want you to activate it tomorrow. Yes! Right now."

"Smart ass." Aurora closed her eyes, concentrating on her aura. Her chest tattoo brightened, as did her necklace, taking Jason's attention. Her green aura swirled around her in a powerful whirlwind. Her muscles tensed, fueled by her immense power.

She tried her hardest to concentrate. Yet, her mind was stuck on Polaris and their argument. How they fought when they met and all the shit she had put her through. Her irritation quickly sparked into anger. But she also remembered seeing Polaris's back scar, her fight with Serena, and their talk the other night. Her aura lost its ferocity, the twisting mist-like energy oscillating. That heated anger dwindled.

"Red, stop! Your aura is—"

Her green aura popped like a balloon, throwing Aurora to the ground. She panted, her chest tearing inside her. She never lost focus so much that her normal aura couldn't hold a shape. Jason ran over toward her and offered his hand.

"You okay?"

Aurora saw Polaris behind his scarlet eyes. She slapped away his hand. "I'm fine!" She stood under her own power.

"You seem distracted. Anything eating at you?"

"I said I'm fine. Let's keep going."

Jason folded his arms. "Do you have to lie?"

Aurora leered at him.

"C'mon, you can tell me. We're all friends here."

Something in Aurora snapped. Her charmed necklace radiated. "Let's get something clear here, Jason. Don't take this the wrong way, but I don't do 'friends.' I just need you to train me so I can beat your loudmouth sister. That's all this is."

Jason stumbled back, appearing pale. Immediately Aurora felt remorseful.

"Wait . . .sorry. I didn't—"

"That's a first." Jason rummaged through his pockets and pulled out a small, cracked pocket mirror. "Red, your eyes."

Aurora saw her scarlet eyes in her reflection. They slowly reverted back to green as her necklace dimmed. Any semblance of her demon aura faded the instant it surfaced.

"Well, we answered our first question! Your trigger to your demon aura is anger. We're already halfway done on the first try. Let's keep going, okay?"

Aurora stared at him, reluctant to return his enthusiasm, especially after what she just said. Was it right, her taking his kindness yet treating him as if he's just a means for her to get stronger? Just as she was a means to a mission for Polaris? Either way, she couldn't ignore that white smile reflecting the sunlight. She smiled back and they continued.

Aurora trained with Jason for several more hours to pull out her demon aura. Despite it mostly consisting of standing in place and bringing forth her aura, it was the most draining thing she had ever done. Amidst the migraines and numbing of her body, she could hold her demon aura just a fraction of a second more. She tried to keep her emotions constant, but it quickly drained her.

Aurora's body had never felt so sore. She could barely walk or move her tight arms. Her chest wouldn't stop hurting or glowing. She was afraid of what would happen if she took the necklace off. The necklace kept her aura in check, so she kept it on the entire time despite trying to bring that power forward. When Jason asked about Aurora's tattoo glowing, she claimed it was just a Gorgon thing. She was surprised he bought it. After training, they called it a day and returned to Jason's cabin.

On the walk through Furasaku Village, Aurora was again drawn to the half-demon locals. Off to the side of the dirt road, near one of the cabins, she noticed Alicia handing off a crate of goods to an elderly couple. Her radiant smile made her seem like a completely different person. It was a nice thing to see, but after witnessing Jason's saddened glance in that direction, she figured he didn't think the same way. He even flinched when Alicia looked their way. After handing off the food, she approached them with a hop in her step.

"Ari, JayJay, how's the trainin' going?"

"Good, actually. I'm bringin' it out little by little," Aurora said confidently.

Alicia laughed at her. "That's all? Are you sure you'll have enough to beat me by the end of the week? If you want, you can still back out. I won't blame you."

Aurora rolled her eyes. "Forget it. I'll have it down and I'm poundin' ya. Can't wait."

"I love that misplaced optimism! Even if it's a Gorgon thing."

Jason didn't share that same confidence or vigor Aurora did. His eyes were stuck to the ground. Aurora thought one of the siblings would say something to the other, but they didn't.

Aurora broke the silence. "Sooo . . . any raids today?"

"Nah, kid. We have what we need for right now, so I'm just sticking around. Also keeping a close eye on Sourpuss over there." Alicia pointed behind them.

Aurora gazed into the distance and her stomach turned. She saw Polaris sitting on the porch of the medical cabin, holding her chin in her hand. She and Aurora narrowed their eyes at each other before Polaris turned away completely.

"I see . . ." Aurora said.

"I'm looking forward to our fight though! Maybe I'll see you use that famous water magic trick again!"

Aurora's heart stopped at Alicia's words. Alicia's grin was unsettling, slowly dissipating. She forgot all about that mistake. Alicia mentioned she watched her fight with Camella and probably saw her use more than one element. What would she say? What lie could get her out of it? She stayed silent too long. Alicia was bound to know something.

"Well, bye now kiddies. Happy training!" Alicia said before skipping away.

Aurora was a statue.

"Uh . . . Red? You good?" Jason asked, finally breaking his silence.

Aurora just nodded and walked gingerly back to Jason's cabin. Her mind was in disarray. Why didn't Alicia ask about it? She always questioned her before. Was she trying to scare her? What was she plotting?

Amidst Aurora's internal panic, she and Jason returned to their cabin, where he grilled some boar meat for them to eat. The savory aroma brought back nice memories of hunting with Blair. It was almost enough to distract her from Alicia's earlier comment. She sat at his mahogany table, tearing away at the meat like a wild animal. Jason failed to mask his cringe, but Aurora didn't care.

"So, training wasn't too bad today. You're making some good strides." Jason started. "But, you know, you really are stubborn."

Aurora stopped munching and batted her eyes. "Okay, and?"

"You tried to bring that aura out but kept on that necklace. It's an aura suppressor, right?"

Aurora swallowed. "Yeah. My god-aunt Ria gave it to me because of . . .an incident. It's one of the only things she gave me that I'm thankful for."

Jason put his fork down. "You mentioned yesterday that someone usually dies when you use your power. Why is that?"

Aurora shrugged. "I thought all demons were that way. I mean, that's what all the books and stuff say. But after meeting everyone here, I figured that was wrong. But I know whenever I use my power, I lose control."

"Well, you didn't today."

Aurora stared down into her plate. Images of that final night with Blair and her fight with Reiya flashed through her mind. "Yeah, but I didn't really use it. It only surfaced."

Jason stroked his chin. "Lose control. What do you mean by that exactly? Like, is it overwhelming? Does your magic go out of control on its own?"

"No, not exactly. It honestly feels like someone else takes the driver's seat. Someone like me, but not me, ya know? I feel like a monster and when I black out, I awaken to corpses."

Jason's eyes widened. "Oh."

"What?"

"Nothing that's just . . . not at all what I expected."

Aurora backed away from the table slightly. "Really? No one else here dealt with that?"

"I can't speak for any of the new people we've housed here, but that isn't normal. Even if the aura is too much to control, I've never heard of a half-demon fighting while unconscious. Not one in the modern era anyway."

Aurora sank into her chair. "Not in the modern era?"

"Back when my dad was alive, he'd tell us stories of the Holy Rebellion, or what most people refer to as the First Great War, when half-demons and humans fought against the old Gorgon Empire. The Furasaku Clan was a part of that army, and he said that they witnessed the leader of the entire rebellion losing control and appearing like a different person when she used her power. Heard she was the same, if not worse in the Third Great War."

Aurora shot back up. "You're not talking about Medusa, are you?"

"Yeah. These were just stories though. No idea if they're true, but if they are, maybe it's a Gorgon thing." He laughed nervously.

That didn't make Aurora feel any better. "So, I'm just like the most dangerous monster in history? Great. May as well do to me what they did to her."

"No, no! Okay uhh—" Jason rubbed the back of his neck "— even if you are like Medusa, you're still good! You make your own decisions and are not a ruthless killer like she was. Besides, you brought it out today and didn't attack me. Even with the necklace on, that's something. We're making progress."

Aurora glanced up. "Wait, so you're not giving up on me? Even though my power doesn't work like a half-demon's should?'

"And let my sister win? Heavens no. We can do this. *You* can do this."

Aurora hid her grin behind her thick scarlet curls. There weren't many people that had that much faith in her. It would've been more off-putting if it didn't amp her up. "Thanks, Jason! Oh . . . and about earlier . . . sorry about yelling at you. Saying all that mean stuff . . . and—"

"Apologies aren't really your thing, Red."

Aurora grimaced at him.

"It's okay. You can apologize after you've beaten Alicia, okay?" Jason pointed his fist at her.

Aurora, again, was reluctant to return the gesture. She fist-bumped him anyway and felt good doing it. In the back of her mind, she wished Polaris had that kind of confidence in her that he did. Maybe she'd change her mind if she saw her progress. She dispelled the thought. So long as Polaris got her way, it didn't matter what kind of progress Aurora made.

Alicia's day was as busy, if not busier than Aurora's. After distributing more food to the cabins in the morning, she did a routine check of all the residences in their small village. She spent the afternoon playing with the children, keeping everyone all smiles. As the sky darkened in their small village, the girl headed for the hills and into the outer kingdom's forests.

Alicia ran through the tall, sharp grasses and leaped over the mossy rocks. She zipped past the pixies sprinkling sparkly gold dust as they flew. She ran to her favorite spot, an expansive, grassy meadow surrounded by oak and willow trees. It was almost as big as the training field back in the village. She looked up to the now starry sky, basking in the serenity. There were few things as peaceful as the sounds of the trickling of water from the nearby creek, or the rustling of the nearby animals through the bushes and trees. It was away from all the demands of the village and the chaos of the raids.

"Finally, alone time."

Alicia sat crisscrossed in the middle of the meadow. She closed her eyes, steadily releasing her aura as she blocked out all sounds. She desired to clear her head of everything, but the young Gorgon sisters invaded her thoughts. Aurora's unique powers were far too strange to ignore. Aurora's mastery of destructive lightning was weird enough, given how rare lightning affinities were and how it's the most difficult element to control, but water as well? Even if both her parents had it, it shouldn't have been possible for Aurora to inherit both. What was more bothersome was that Polaris defended her immediately. Not to mention Aurora's comment about people dying when she used her demon power. What were they hiding?

Alicia was so lost in thought, that she jumped at the sounds of one of the shrubs violently shaking. She sprang up and reached for her dagger. "Who's there?"

The rustling continued until two small rabbits trotted across the meadow, playfully chasing each other. Alicia sighed with relief and sheathed her weapon. She tried to shake off the thoughts and regain her peace.

The rustling happened again. This time, it was from all the shrubs surrounding her. The ground vibrated beneath her feet. Rabbits, along with deer, squirrels, pixies, and birds, ran from the bushes again. They all went in a flock together, fleeing from something as they zoomed past her.

"Please be anything but the Gorgon Queen," she prayed, walking towards the source.

A brown mane and a lion tail peaked just over bushes.

Alicia scoffed, unsheathing her weapon again. "We don't have jungle cats in this part of the world. Come out or I'll turn you and this entire forest to ash!"

Alicia stopped, feeling the tip of a blade touch her neck. For the first time in a while, she was caught off guard. But she didn't feel the presence of anyone behind her. She slowly turned her head just enough to see a familiar black katana suspended in midair, the blade's frigid edge resting against her throat.

What leaped over the bushes and into the meadow was no lion at all. The humongous, lion-woman wore a trench coat and a pentagram necklace dangling from her neck. She also had no left arm. As she stalked towards Alicia, her fur, mane, and claws vanished as she shrank. Her skin became pale and her eyes returned to their pink glow. Her long, black hair flowed, and her fangs became thin and pointy. Serena wore a delightful grin.

"Sorry I had to deceive you. I needed to sniff you out, so I borrowed some blood from an old colleague," the vampire said.

Alicia growled. She gripped her blade tighter. However, the floating blade pressed further against her throat.

"Don't move. Even half-demons can't survive decapitation. Besides, I'm not here to fight you. I just want to talk."

20
I'm Ready!

"Talk? If you're after the Gorgons, forget it. I won't let you make a playground out of my home," Alicia declared.

Serena glared at her. "You're risking that just by keeping the girl."

"Not for long. After a week, she and her annoying sister will return to the kingdom. After that, you can have at them. So long as I don't get interested in your high bounty again. Your head could provide some nicer beds for us. Maybe even plumbing!" Alicia chuckled.

Serena knew she didn't have that much time to waste. She had to get to them before the other Vipers got involved, especially those two Hatake had promised to send. "The only way you put your people at risk is by keeping the girl. Even as a half-demon, she's far more dangerous to you all than I am."

Alicia knitted her brow, but ultimately laughed at the notion. "Don't be ridiculous. She's not a monster like her mother. I've seen the chick fight. She'll be easy to put down."

"Have you seen her demon power?"

"No. Even with it, she wouldn't be much stronger. You sure weren't when you drank her blood."

Serena felt the urge to release Masamune and end her right there. But that would be wasteful. After all, she had her right where she wanted. "Solaria's blood is poisonous like Euryale's, that's why I fell ill."

"Mephion down under, your generation loves making excuses."

Serena took a deep breath, frustrated. "Her demon power, specifically when she uses it, could wipe out a village like yours in under an hour. She already claimed the lives of one of our subordinates."

"Oh? Guess you Vipers are a bunch of pushovers, huh?"

"Wretch! That girl has the power to wipe out an entire army, no, an entire kingdom if she wanted! Only the blessing of my blood magic allowed me to subdue her, otherwise, I'd be dead."

"Personal problem."

Serena squeezed the space between her eyes. She knew Alicia was intentionally being difficult. She tried her best to keep cool. "Fine. Even if you're so confident at taking her down in her demonic state, it would still be unwise to let her return to Euryale. The girl was created as a weapon, and that's the last thing that tyrant needs."

Alicia rested a hand on her hip. "Created? Like, she's a test tube baby? I mean, I can see it, but—"

"Fool! If you let her go, Euryale will have another Divine Sorcerer's Stone! Is that something you want to risk?"

Alicia's eyes widened. "Another . . . what?"

A grin stretched on Serena's face. She got her. "Didn't you know? Solaria has a Divine Sorcerer's Stone inside of her. It's the source of her elemental magic."

Alicia's face discolored. She scoffed, folding her arms while lifting her chin. "You're bluffing. That's impossible. Even the Demi-Gods can't use the stones so carelessly, let alone put them inside a person! Besides, it's infinite magic. She'd have annihilated everyone in her way with power like that."

"That's just the thing. I'm not sure how her stone works yet, or how she's able to use it."

Alicia rolled her eyes and let out a huff. "Sorry, Batsy. You should work on your lying. None of that's believable."

"What's unbelievable is a mortal having more than one type of magic affinity."

Alicia raised her eyebrows.

Serena knew that caught her attention. "You saw her fight, didn't you? If so, I know you saw her use multiple elements. You know as well as I do that—"

"No," Alicia interrupted. Her eyes darted in every direction, Alicia trying to rationalize Serena's claim. "That . . . that isn't due to a Divine Stone! Can't be . . ."

Serena paced back and forth. "Don't think her chest tattoo glowing is random. It's still unclear how, but the girl has a Divine Stone. With the one stone The Pearl Kingdom already has in their possession, from my understanding, they violate the Magic and Allied Nations' peace treaty and the Stheno Accords. Regardless, with that girl, Euryale will have a living weapon, which paired with her demon aura, makes her potentially the most dangerous person on the planet. Why do you think Polaris is desperate to bring her home as soon as possible?"

"Was it not to protect her from you guys?" Alicia said, now appearing frightened for the first time.

Serena muffled a laugh. She pulled up her sleeve with her teeth to reveal her snake tattoo. "I may have this, but I'm not loyal to these monsters. If anything, I intend to use the stone to gain my freedom from them. They don't know about the girl having a Divine Stone, and I intend to keep it that way as long as I can. But . . . I'll need your help."

"Is that right?"

"Thanks to your stunt taking my left arm, I can't fight the girl and capture her properly. Come a week from now, more Vipers will appear here to capture Solaria. They're under the impression that she's responsible for sinking one of our ships, and they want her dead. If they have to mow down your village to do so, they will happily do it."

Alicia stared off to the side in frustration. "Lemme guess, they're stronger than you?"

"Shiro Kitsune. Mordred Pendragon."

Alicia's jaw dropped. "Y-you're lying! Those two are part of your organization? And they're coming here?"

"Unless I capture Solaria on my own. So, you see how we can benefit each other."

Alicia's gaze fell to her feet. From Serena's vantage point, she was stuck in contemplation, likely going over all possibilities. Serena decided to give her one last nudge.

"You risk not only the Vipers coming and turning your little village into a parking lot, but Euryale one day using Solaria to slaughter you all either for your crimes or just because she felt like it. Trust me, I speak from experience. Do you really want to risk the lives of your people? The life of your brother?"

Alicia glared at her. Mists of red flared around her as her irises luminated. "I've heard enough."

"What?"

"I said *enough*. Vipers, Euryale, Ari, I don't care who or what threatens my village. So long as I breathe, no harm will come to them. So long as I have my team, no one will ever present a danger to us. And that includes you!"

Serena barred her fangs. "You're a fool, Furasaku! Kitsune and Pendragon's strength combined could rival a Demi-God's! Do you really want that at your doorstep?"

Black tendrils spewed out of Alicia's ankles and dug into the ground. Then, they sprouted back up and yanked down Masamune. Alicia swiped her dagger, and a wave of black flames flew at Serena. The vampire vanished in a gust of wind as the flames struck the trees behind where she once stood.

"Shit, she is faster," Alicia mumbled to herself.

Alicia turned around and saw that the blade of Masamune was gone as well. She ran around the meadow, trying to feel Serena's presence, but found no trace. She sheathed her blade and the black flames dissipated, saving the nearby trees from turning to complete ash. "If I see your face near my home, Batsy, I'm ending your bloodline! Heed my warning. That goes for your buddies, too!" Alicia yelled before walking off.

Serena hovered high in the sky, watching Alicia return to the village. Despite not getting her compliance, she laughed to herself joyously. She reached for her pendant and closed her eyes in prayer. "Lord Fraizen, the path you've set before me has been realized. Soon, everything will fall into place. Both vengeance and salvation are upon me. I pray that you give everlasting peace to the sacrifices I'll be sending to you. Amen."

The next morning, Aurora and Jason were back at it. Unlike the day prior, Aurora was far more eager to tackle training and gain a grip on her demonic aura. They wasted no time, heading straight to the field, where Aurora would use her emotional trigger to bring forward that red glow. To the duo's surprise, Alicia awaited them at the field.

"What are you doing here, Alicia?" Aurora asked.

Alicia was initially silent, her face made of stone. She almost appeared lost in thought. "Just wanna see your practice, Ari, that's all."

Aurora and Jason shared a glance, both questioning Alicia's motive. Aurora especially didn't know what to make of it. No trash-talk? No jab at her before their impending fight? She didn't even belittle Jason like she usually did. Something was seriously off.

Nevertheless, they resumed their training.

Much like the day prior, Aurora's demonic aura would only last a blink, getting just a fraction of a second longer each time. Doses of crimson was insufficient for battle however. An hour into the regiment, Jason took a different approach. Rather that continuing to emphasize emotional triggers to bring forth her demonic aura, he instead brought another blockade to her attention. One that he was adamant would accelerate her advances if removed.

"Take it off?" Aurora's fingers pinched the crescent moon pendant of her necklace.

"It's like you said, it's a suppressor for demon aura. Keeping it on would be counterproductive."

"But . . ." She shuddered to think about the times she had lost control, particularly against Reiya and Serena. "I could lose it. What then? No offense, Jason, but I don't think you could stop me—"

"If that's the case, we'll put the necklace back on. It literally won't hurt. You can bring it out a little with it on, but the enchanted necklace is like a seal. If you want to bring more out, you need to take off that seal."

Aurora rubbed her chin in contemplation. He had a fair point, but it was risky. While considering, she saw a blue blur in the corner of her eye. She looked to the far edge of the field and witnessed Polaris sitting on the steps of a cabin. Her gold irises peaked just over the horizon of the book. Those eyes vanished the very second they met Aurora's own.

Aurora sighed, deciding it may be the best course of action.

Jason gave Aurora a bit more space as she took her crescent moon necklace off and placed it in her pocket. Immediately, power jolted through her body. Her tattoo glowed and her hair stood up on her neck and arms. It was the first time she hadn't had the necklace on since she first received it.

Aurora closed her eyes, digging up any painful memory she could to trigger that power. Only one incident came to her mind. The sight of Serena tossing her presumably dead sister off that boat. Watching her bloody body fall through the air while Aurora was helpless to do anything about it. Her face and throat burned with the mere thought. Her muscles hardened as her teeth and nails sharpened. Her chest tightened and her head pulsated with the intensity of an earthquake. She grabbed her hair with her sharp nails as her scarlet aura flowed around her. Her thoughts became erratic as the thumping in her head continued. She recognized this feeling. That desire for destruction. That lust for blood, so insatiable that her mouth watered. Still, she remained vigilant. She couldn't let such urges control her! She quickly reached for her necklace and was about to put it on.

"No!" Jason shouted.

Aurora's head shot up in shock.

"You're in control, Red. It's your power! It belongs to you, you don't belong to it. Let it flow!"

Her hand shook while holding the necklace. She noticed her nails—or rather, their hue. They were white, instead of the usual black they would be whenever she used her demonic aura. She took deep breaths, relaxing her tense body as best she could. She did her usual reverse counting, and even took notice of her surroundings. She stared at the swelling grey clouds eclipsing the sun above. She felt the brisk wind ticking the back of her neck. She even counted the various craters in the training field. Anything to ground her. Opening her eyes, she the calm red swirl of her own aura. Jason wore a huge smile on his face, and Aurora matched it.

"You're doing it! Red, you're doing it!"

"I'm really in control! I can't believe—" She stopped.

Blood splattering. Screams. Raging flames. Butchered bodies. All these images flashed through her mind. The witch fell to her knees and her aura darkened. Blades of loose grass flickered in the air from the intense whirlwind created by Aurora's raging aura. Her mind slowly diminished, and that will to kill overtook her psyche at full force. The temperature fell like a stone in a lake, lightly frosting the grass at her feet.

Jason slowly backed away from the maroon storm in shock. Alicia rushed over and shielded her brother.

"This some new trick you taught her?" Alicia asked.

"No! I—I don't know. She was fine then—"

Aurora's sclerae turned black, as did her sharp fangs and claws. She let out a chilling, ear-rupturing screech that filled the entire village. Alicia whipped out her dagger in a hurry.

"Jason, stay back!"

"What are you doing?" he screamed at his sister.

Aurora's body tensed, her knees bending like a jungle cat prepared to pounce on their prey. She eyed the siblings with a hunger to match. The siblings backpedaled, both of them pale. They both flinched as Aurora reached into her pocket and put on her necklace. The crescent moon pendant shined a bright purple. Her darkened aura dissipated, and her features returned to normal.

Again, Aurora fell to her knees. She fought for air as she faced the ground.

Aurora looked up at the half-demon siblings and gave them a light-hearted chuckle. "Sorry about that. Don't worry, I'm still here," she moaned weakly.

She was all too familiar with that look. The look of terror. The shaking of Alicia's hand as she held her weapon. Her smile vanished. She could hear Ria criticizing her as a monster in the back of her mind. She could also hear footsteps fast approaching, only it wasn't in her mind. She turned to see Polaris slide to her side, creating a small dust cloud.

Polaris grabbed Aurora's shoulder. "Solaria, are you alright!? Are you with us?"

It was the first time she had spoken a word to her in two days. It was so abrupt, she didn't even know how to respond initially.

"Y-yeah, I'm good." Aurora tried not to look her sister in the eye.

"Are you certain? You're not in any pain? No daunting thoughts or anything of the sort?"

"I said I'm good." Aurora shoved Polaris's hand off her shoulder.

Polaris's lips pressed together. She looked away while they both stood.

"Um . . . progress!" Jason cheered awkwardly.

Aurora chuckled, appreciating the attempt to undercut the awkward air. Polaris turned her back to them, while Alicia's glare was still fixed on Aurora. Her stare made Aurora feel uneasy, as did the sight of Alicia's weapon drawn, and pointed in Aurora's direction.

"Uhh . . . Alicia? Is something up?" Aurora asked.

"Oh," Alicia realized her matte-black blade was still drawn. She sheathed it again. "Sorry, Ari. You're good." She laughed it off. "Carry on, kiddos. Happy trainin'! You'll need it." She winked and ran off.

Jason folded his arms. "Something is up with her. She'd never pull that weapon inside the village, let alone point it at someone living here."

Aurora lowered her head. "Oh."

"Ah! But you held it up for a while longer, which is good! I bet you were impressed, right, Polaris?"

Polaris grimaced at the two of them. She continued her silence, walking off back to the cabins.

Aurora sighed. She stared at the palm of her hand, and couldn't help but envision it covered in blood. "Sorry about that just now."

"About Blue? Nah, she's okay. She can be like that."

"No, not her. About losing it. I could've . . . it could've been worse."

Jason hesitated for a moment. He had that same look on his face but smiled through it. "Hey, you consciously put the necklace on, right? That's progress. See this as a win, Red. We're almost there, I can feel it."

Aurora smiled. "You're so weirdly optimistic." Despite herself, the half-witch did feel more at ease.

Aurora continued her training, gaining more of a grasp of maintaining consciousness while having the demon aura flow. Jason had her bring it out little by little and put the necklace on afterward rather than leaving it off the entire time. Aurora could maintain her aura's flow for seconds longer after each attempt, dispelling it before she could lose control. The hours passed, and Aurora's confidence grew. She grew closer to maintaining a stable flow of demonic aura for an extended period. It certainly warranted joy. Yet, while working with Jason on the field, her eyes and mind were stuck on her sister.

The pair wrapped up for the day, and Jason headed out to the forests to hunt while Aurora stayed behind and rested. She took a makeshift bath in a metal barrel in an empty room. She filled it herself with her water magic, then heated the barrel with flames. She sat comfortably in the steaming water, washing away a day's hard work. The nearly boiling water soothed her roaring muscles. All the while, she contemplated the day and everything up to this point.

The day she met Polaris and battled Reiya was the catalyst that set her on finding this demon village. Now, she was just days away from never having her power burden her again. Of course, as much as she didn't want to admit it, she would never have gotten this far without Polaris. The girl had gone through hell to get Aurora to this country, and what was she giving her? More time to wait while she urged them to get there as soon as possible.

Aurora shook her head and sank half her face under the piping-hot water. Even if Polaris was losing out, she only saw Aurora as a means to an end. She said it herself, multiple times. The half-witch wished she could think about literally anything else. The girl who constantly got under her skin since they met refused to leave her thoughts. Polaris clearly had her own agenda, but earlier at the field? After their encounter with Serena? Why? Why did Polaris care but say otherwise?

A knock on the bathroom door undercut her train of thought.

"Still bathing, Jason! Wait your turn," she shouted. What could he possibly want?

There was a brief pause. "Solaria . . . it's me."

Aurora's eyes widened. Polaris? Of course, she'd show up now of all times. Aurora didn't even want to respond to her.

"Worry not, you don't have to speak. I only want you to listen for now," Polaris said.

Aurora furrowed her eyebrows. Polaris was probably going to insist that they leave or even beg her. She was more than prepared to deny her again.

"I'm sorry."

Aurora stood up in the heated barrel. She wasn't prepared for that.

"For the other day. My actions were quite childish. I'm aware of how much this means to you. I've witnessed the horrors your power can inflict and—" Polaris paused momentarily. "You have every right to conquer this. It wasn't my intention to pry you from this opportunity. Uhm . . . you've made tremendous progress, too! I um . . . expected nothing less from my own sister."

Aurora held back her laughter. She never heard Polaris act so bashfully and at a loss for words.

"I'm aware you're still frustrated about what I've said, and the things I've done since we've met. Just be aware that I wish not to make you out as some sort of pawn or weapon. After all, I'm indebted to you. For several reasons—" Polaris stopped, sighing. "I'm getting ahead of myself. Best of luck with your training. I look forward to your duel with Alicia. Make our family proud."

Aurora listened to the echo of Polaris's heels fading away. Her face warmed, but not from the warm water. Tears formed in her eyes, and she grabbed her tightening chest.

That brief exchange lingered in Aurora's mind through the night and into the next morning. Perhaps Polaris cared more than Aurora realized. It was still difficult to fully accept her words, but it made things much more complicated in her mind. If Polaris meant what she said, what was Aurora doing for her by prolonging their return? It wasn't a matter of a petty grudge anymore. And if coming late meant upsetting Euryale, what would that mean for the young princess? Aurora shuddered at that thought when remembering the scar on her back.

Polaris's prior complaints through their journey all came to a head. Yet, Aurora couldn't pass this opportunity. There was still much to do in terms of training and to ensure Jason didn't lose his stake in their little bet. Aurora couldn't bear the thought of him having to leave the Bandits because of her weakness. She wished she could have the best of both worlds. Gain control, get home with Polaris, and keep Jason in good standing with his team. Alas, there was much to do.

Like every day up to this point, Aurora and Jason trained in the field, Aurora standing in place and using her emotions to bring forth the demon aura. Steel clouds stood overhead, blocking out any semblance of sunlight. Again, Alicia was sitting in the field, waiting for them.

"Don't you have duties to attend to or something? Stop spying on us!" Jason barked at her.

Alicia disregarded him entirely and locked eyes with Aurora. It almost felt like she was looking through her.

"Um . . . yes?" Aurora asked.

"Can't wait to see what you do next, Ari. Give us a show," Alicia said.

Aurora couldn't fathom what was up with Alicia. She tried her best to disregard her comment.

Without any further formalities, they jumped straight into it. Both with and without the necklace, bringing forward the demon aura demanded less of a mental strain on Aurora's part. For several hours, Aurora pushed the duration of her demonic aura flow. By noon, she could maintain a steady flow for a full minute. After a short break, she asked Jason to spar with her while she used it, taking Jason by surprise.

"Spar now? But you just got the hang of triggering it and maintaining its flow."

"I know. Which is why it makes sense to spar now that I can, right? This is meaningless if I can't fight with it," Aurora fired back.

Jason rubbed the back of his neck, shying away from her gaze. "I don't think that's wise. Not yet anyway. Maybe we should wait a while before we get to spar. Let's make sure you have firm control first."

Aurora recognized that face Jason made. It was nearly identical to Alicia's the day prior. To how everyone looked at her back in Westtown. Aurora gritted her teeth and scoffed.

Jason pulled out an old stopwatch from his pocket. "Okay. Bring your aura out without the necklace again. Let's see if you can maintain a flow for one minute and thirty seconds."

Aurora leered at her trainer. Reluctantly, she took off her necklace and closed her eyes. She relaxed her body and brought forth that scarlet glow. Her muscles tensed and bulked as her nails and teeth sharpened into fangs and claws.

"Good, good." Jason set his stopwatch.

Aurora's eyes flashed open as she pounced. She blitzed Jason without warning, swiping her claws at his face. Jason narrowly ducked, leaping a few feet backward to put some distance between them.

"What are you—" Jason was given little time to talk with Aurora rushing him. She tenaciously swiped her claws and threw her fists, forcing him to dance.

Aurora felt a few steps faster and a few notches stronger than she had in her bout with Camella. Her fist connected with his forearm, ratting the boy with intense force. He slid backward several feet, and a red lump formed on his arm for a moment before disappearing. Aurora flashed a smirk, reassuming a fighting stance and beckoning Jason with a finger.

Jason huffed, charging her himself. They traded fists, but Aurora had the upper hand. She broke through his defenses and landed bone-crushing blows in his chest and on his face. Her trainer tumbled through the grass before propping themselves back up.

"Forty seconds have passed. We have fifty more. Come on! Let's get serious," Aurora yelled, outputting more of her red aura. Her aura twirled around her rapidly, blowing the loose grass and dirt from beneath her.

Jason brushed aside the drop of blood from his nose with his thumb. "You asked for it." He charged his aura, matching Aurora's intensity.

The boy fired black spears out of his palms at her. Aurora zig-zagged around the speeding, bullet-like spears with ease. She charged at him with her witch-blade, glowing red instead of its usual green. A spear the size of a staff emerged from Jason's shoulder, and he wielded it as such. They clashed weapons repeatedly, but Aurora's ferocity was too great. Jason slid backward with each violent swing, and suffered small cuts as Aurora outdueled him. She barely felt the usual strain in her chest, or the pounding in her head. She only felt elation, and had victory in her sights.

With a final monstrous swing, she sliced straight through Jason's spear. The half-witch seized her opening, aiming her left hand, and *BANG!* Aurora fired a powerful lighting strike at point blank. Jason tumbled backward, covered in static, steam rising from his body. His skin bubbled as it regenerated. The boy slowly looked up to see the tip of Aurora's blade in his face. She panted but maintained a large smile as the stopwatch rang. Time was up.

Jason sighed, hanging his head. "I'll be damned. You're . . . amazing Red."

Aurora's witch-blade dissipated. She felt the pounding in her head resurface, but immediately put back on her necklace. Her claws and fangs vanished. The satisfaction of victory overtook her, filling her with unbridled joy. Aurora pumped her fist and cheered, "Yes!" under her breath. She heard the echoing of applause, taking her by surprise. She looked around and saw Polaris on the sideline, clapping with a bright smile.

"Great work, Solaria! Fantastic work," she cheered.

Blots of soft red formed on Aurora's brown cheeks. She hid her smile with her long curls. The clapping had an echo come from behind her. Aurora turned to the other side of the field and witnessed Alicia approaching them.

"That wasn't bad, Ari. You got some moves and got that power under control. In such a short time, too," Alicia gave Aurora a friendly pat on the shoulder. "Who knows, maybe my baby brother can learn a thing or two from you instead?"

"Thanks!" Aurora scratched the back of her head. She turned back to Jason, who still sat on the ground. Frustration was apparent through his frown, Aurora offered him a hand. Jason reluctantly took it and pulled himself up.

"Hey, that was a good fight! Sorry for springing myself at you. I couldn't help myself, ya know?"

"It's okay," Jason muttered. "You're super strong. You didn't lie about that."

"Thanks to you, man. Thank you for training me and letting me stay with you. It means a lot, Jason."

The boy looked up to her. He gave a half-hearted smile initially but then cocked his head to the side. "Hold on . . . don't go thanking me yet.

We still have three days. We're gonna refine your control and possibly do something with your lightning magic—"

Aurora held up her hand. "Again, thanks. But. . ." Aurora turned back to Alicia, who appeared just as confused as her brother. *Best of both worlds. Yeah.* "Alicia. Fight me. Right now."

21
Aurora vs Alicia

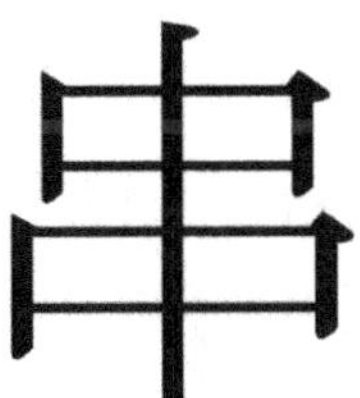

"Accepted," Alicia said without hesitation.

Jason leaped in front of Aurora. "Hold on just a second, guys! Don't be so hasty, Red. You aren't ready to fight her just yet."

Aurora glared at her trainer. "I was ready to fight her when I got here. I'm more than ready now. Step aside."

Polaris, who previously just watched the ordeal from afar, ran over from the sidelines and grabbed Aurora by the shoulder. "Solaria, listen to Sir Jason. You've only seen Alicia fight once. I've seen it numerous times. At your current level, victory isn't in your court."

Aurora saw concern and worry written all over Polaris's face. While part of her appreciated it, it was also infuriating. "Polaris, we're going home. After I beat her. Just worry about that, not me."

"Just forget about that for just a moment! I'm aware of what you wagered on this confrontation and think it wise to use all the time you have allotted to truly master this power. You only attained minimal control of that power, so challenging Alicia now is foolish—"

"Can you stop doubting me?" Aurora snapped.

Polaris backed away slightly. Aurora wasn't a fan of her scared, pitiful frown, but that quickly turned into aggression.

"Can't you just listen when someone else speaks to you? Just once? You aren't ready for her! I've seen your power and know you can wield much more than you did against Jason. That won't be enough against the likes of that woman!" Polaris pointed to Alicia.

"She's right." Alicia propped her hand on her hip. "But Princess, Baby Bro, step aside. Ari issued a challenge and I accepted. You two have no right to keep us from a duel, whether she's prepared or not."

"You can't be serious," Polaris muttered.

Aurora grinned. "You heard her, guys. Get lost. We'll need space for our battle."

Jason sighed. He grabbed Aurora's shoulder. "Red, look, I get it. You want to prove yourself. Hell, I want you to beat her. That's why we should use the three days we have left. Beat her the right way. Possibly learn some more ways to use your power more effectively. There's literally no reason to rush."

Aurora removed his hand. "You have a point, Jason, but I need you to trust me on this. I can beat her now. Just have faith in me, 'kay?" She winked at him.

Jason furrowed his eyebrows. "You're dead set on this, aren't you?"

"Yup!"

Jason rubbed the back of his neck and blew air from his nose. "Fine. If you're certain, I won't stand in your way. But I'm letting you know

now, if you can only use that much aura that you did against me, Alicia will have her way with you."

"Really? Good thing I held back."

Jason backed away slowly. "Y-you're bluffing."

"Am I?" Aurora walked past Jason and toward Alicia.

Jason shook his head. "What about you, Alicia? You're eager to fight her hastily?"

Alicia stared at her brother for a moment before responding. "I want to confirm something, so fighting her now helps. Besides, the sooner they leave our village, the better."

Jason squinted his eyes as he walked off the battlefield, appearing weary of Alicia's comment.

Alicia assumed her fighting stance, baring her claws. "You sure are confident and reckless. You remind me a lot of my father. You do know what happened to him, right?"

Aurora assumed her fighting stance. "I'm not him, so don't worry."

"The mouth on you. You're Ice-Devil's sister all right." Alicia's eyelids lowered and her grin dissipated. "You're also a liar."

"W-wha—"

Alicia rushed in before Aurora could finish and whacked her in the face, ripping into her cheek with her sharp claws. Aurora slid through the dirt and loose grass. Her face stung, bathed in red as she picked herself up. She hissed, not being the biggest fan of Alicia's sucker punch. The bleeding claw marks on her cheek closed right up and her eyes flickered red. Her necklace shined, but she removed it and shoved it in her pocket. A scarlet vortex rushed around her, flickering up loose grass and dirt in its wake.

Polaris and Jason fled to the far sideline as Aurora's aura continuously swelled. It dwarfed the amount she used against Jason, and Aurora loved it. With how much she could put out now, she expected Alicia to be shaking in her boots with a jaw halfway to the ground.

Alicia, much to her surprise, remained stone-faced, her stance strong and her focus unwavering. She didn't even entertain Aurora with any quips or flexing that she'd become accustomed to. The woman was quiet, and that notion ticked Aurora off. Aurora rushed to her and swung her claws with much more velocity. She followed her claw swipes with swift jabs, and even a few kicks. None hit home. Alicia was a blur, and Aurora struck nothing but air. Even when feinting an uppercut, and following up with a hook, Alicia dodged with impeccable finesse. Despite her apparent increase in strength and speed, Alicia toyed with her. Aurora saw flashes of her fight with Camella, again unable to land a scratch, which only infuriated her more.

Fuck this! She fired her go-to lightning bolt and struck Alicia point blank. *BANG!* The thunderclap echoed through the whole village, drawing the other half-demons out of their homes in concern. A dense dust cloud from the blast obscured Alicia, and seemingly ceased all movement. The corners of the half-witch's mouth curled up. *I win, bitch! I win!*

The dust cleared, revealing Alicia on one knee and stabbing her dagger into the ground. Sparks of electricity channeled through the dagger and into the dirt. She was completely undeterred by the blast. Aurora's confident grin dissipated, and an agape jaw took its place. *When? How'd she react so fast?*

Alicia withdrew her blade from the ground and dusted herself off. "A tip: don't use strategies your opponent has already seen."

Aurora's eyebrow twitched. She snarled, her aura erupting once again.

"I'll show you the difference between me and my brother."

BAM! Alicia's fists slammed into Aurora's face before she could even raise her fists. She stumbled back, grabbing her pulsing, bloody nose. The moment she looked up, Alicia was right on top of her.

She instinctively dodged to her right, narrowly avoiding Alicia's left hook. She had no choice but to block her strikes, her palms stinging with each punch her hands caught. She backpedaled from the intense blitz and could not fire an elemental attack of her own, let alone throw a punch. Then, Alicia opened her hands and swiped at Aurora's arms, leaving bloody claw marks. She shrieked and lowered her guard, with searing pain from her bloody arms taking precedence, even with her regeneration. Two more punches to Aurora's abdomen rocked her, bringing her to her knees and making her gasp for air.

Alicia's foot pressed down on the back of her head, something she was becoming annoyingly familiar with. Aurora wasn't having any of it. She erupted with aura and forced Alicia off.

Aurora's body burned like a furnace, and her chest caved in and out. Her heart ran faster than Alicia moved. Her hands shivered with pure rage. Even the drops of rain from the murky sky couldn't cool her boiling blood. She could only wonder what it would feel like to strike Alicia down. To ram her fist through her face, or even better, tear her claws through her flesh. Aurora staggered, hearing the faintness of a white noise and feeling her head pound.

Alicia folded her arms at that. "You're even sloppier than Batsy. I haven't even used my magic yet."

"Shut the fuck up!" Aurora roared.

She sprung back up and attacked again, this time creating a crimson witch-blade. She clashed with Alicia's dagger over and over, swinging with all her might. Aurora grunted with each swing, parry, and jab, but again couldn't as much as graze Alicia.

As their exchange went on, Aurora lost steam. Her breathing picked up, her muscles tightened, and her head rang like a bell. As if her situation couldn't have worsened, Alicia's trademark tendrils emerged from all over her body. The black wisps wrapped around Aurora's wrists and ankles, keeping her in place. She huffed, trying to wrestle her way out of their grasp, but their grip only tightened. *Fuck, fuck, fuck, fuck!* Aurora flailed to no avail.

"You're done, Gorgon." Alicia said, jumping into the air and launching both feet into Aurora's chest.

Alicia's tendrils released Aurora at the last second, and Aurora flew across the field before tumbling on the ground, collecting grass and dirt along the way. Aurora coughed up blood, pain permeating from her chest. Aurora fought for air, her eyes bulging out of her head as her face lost color. She placed her hand over the point of impact, feeling an unnatural dent in her chest cavity. She felt several of her ribs shatter just from the impact, and while she was no doctor, she was certain Alicia ruptured a lung. In all the fights she'd had up to that point, never had anyone hit her with such force. Her intense wounds gradually healed, and her breathing eventually stabilized. Though she remained on the ground, her deathly glare locked onto Alicia.

Polaris, who stood by Jason as they watched from afar, gritted her teeth in frustration. "Enough of this." Polaris marched toward the battlefield before Jason could try to stop her.

Aurora saw Polaris approaching in the corner of her eye. She nearly popped a vein as she picked herself up. "Back off, Polaris! We're just getting started!"

"Enough of this nonsense. Your little 'duel' has reached its conclusion. Put on the necklace at once. You're already starting to lose it."

"How many times do I have to tell you to stop telling me what to do? I'm not your *soldier*, I'm not your *maid*, and I'm not your *slave*. So, get the hell out of my face!"

"Actually," Alicia interjected. "Princess is right. This fight is over. I've learned what I wanted and continuing is pointless. Sorry, Ari, you weren't ready."

"W-what?"

"You're burning aura at an alarming rate by healing the intense damage and you're clearly out of stamina. Fight any more and we could do some damage. Well, more so me to you. You remember our deal though. This fight is over, so you and the princess and run back home now—"

"No!" Aurora screamed.

"Ari, seriously." Alicia folded her arms.

"I'm not tired. I haven't lost. I can still fight! I can still beat you! I will beat you!"

Alicia's palm dragged down her face. "Okay, now this is getting sad. Princess, please get your sister."

"No need to echo it," Polaris snatched Aurora's wrist. "I understand you're frustrated but you must reel back. The fight is over. It's time you called it quits."

Aurora glared at Polaris. Someone like her, grabbing her wrist? The nerve. Her aura didn't come close to hers. If she weren't her sister, she'd— Aurora shook her head. Her thoughts were too erratic. She had to focus on the task at hand.

"I'm not done. I'm still awake, I'm still breathing, so I can still fight." Aurora whipped out her red witch blade.

"You do remember Moro Town, don't you? You're exhibiting the same behaviors. Cease this nonsense!"

The drizzling picked up. Aurora's nails felt like they were tingling as if she were grinding them against the rugged surface of a chalkboard. "It's not nonsense! Back away before I do to you what I'm about to do to her!"

Polaris reached into Aurora's pocket and yanked the necklace out. She tried forcing it around Aurora's neck. "Put it on, now!"

"No!" Aurora swiped her blade at Polaris in a knee-jerk reaction, forcing her to leap away. The aura blade cut right through the crescent moon pendant, splitting it in two. The two pieces glowed for a moment as they hit the ground. Any semblance of light flickered out, and while Polaris was unscathed, she looked as if Aurora just gutted her.

"Wh–what have you done?" Polaris mumbled as the rain started pouring down.

Alicia and Jason shared Polaris's concern. Alicia gripped her blade and got on her guard.

Aurora stared at the broken charm for a moment before sucking her teeth. "Who needs the damn thing anyway? This fight is mine," she said in a rugged voice, charging her aura even more.

"Damn. Polaris, back away! I'll knock her out before this gets crazy," Alicia called out.

"Alicia, hold on! There's possibly another way—"

"No! Your sister has made her decision. Don't worry, I'll make sure not to break your precious Divine Stone."

"Wait, the what?" Jason asked.

Polaris was taken aback. "You knew?"

Without warning, Aurora swiped her blade at Alicia's head. The girl narrowly ducked the swipe before tackling Aurora to the ground. The witch kicked Alicia right off. They locked and clashed blades repeatedly, dancing in the flickering red aura and the calm rain.

Gradually the warm rain cooled. Aurora's swings grew faster, fiercer. Alicia matched her growing strength. Her tendrils spewed out of her back and lashed at Aurora once again. This time, Aurora batted the tendrils away with the swipe of her blade. She wouldn't let herself be ensnared again. Alicia took a different approach, instead lashing Aurora with the swift swipe of her whip-like tendrils. Despite the stringing pain and her blood spraying all over the wet grass from each strike, Aurora refused to let up. The girl only grew more ferocious, grunting like a wild beast as her swings came down on Alicia harder. Alicia retreated, but Aurora pounced at her, unrelenting her attack. Still, Aurora couldn't land a hit on the elusive girl, even with the muddy terrain. Upon noticing, and idea struck.

Aurora aimed one hand at the ground while forcing Alicia to dodge her witch-blade once again. Alicia, as expected, leaped backward. However, the bandit's feet sank into the mud, and all movement stifled. Mud rose to her ankles, causing an immediate panic.

"Earth magic?" Alicia muttered.

"Not my favorite to use, but good in a pinch!" Aurora snatched Alicia's dagger-wielding wrist and squeezed it with her left hand, popping the joint. With her right, Aurora punched her square in the abdomen with all her strength. Alicia hunched forward, vomiting blood on impact.

"Y-you—" Alicia muttered, barely able to breathe.

"Hurts, right? Feeling all your ribs crack like that." Aurora boasted a devilish grin. Her chest glowed green and sparks streamed down her arm. "Now it's over."

CLAP! Aurora fired a powerful bolt of lightning that tore straight across the training field. When the dust cleared, a giant scar was left in the middle of the field, with Alicia lying at the end of it, fifty yards away from Aurora. Aurora's slow chuckle erupted into hysterical laughter.

Jason walked up next to Polaris, hugging himself to keep warm from the downpour. "Damn. She did it. I have never seen anyone overpower Alicia. She must be happy."

Polaris stood there wide-eyed. Her bottom lip quivered as she stared at her sister's back.

"Red won. Aren't you happy?"

"No," Polaris mumbled. "She didn't."

Aurora's aura erupted again, shooting into the sky. This time her aura's hue was darker than blood. The bloody aura turned the sky from steel-gray to a daunting maroon. Thunder roared and lightning blared in the sky. Rain whipped and lashed around as if a monsoon engulfed the village. The nearby cabins and houses leaned from raging wet gusts.

Both Jason and Polaris shivered. A thick mist swirled around Aurora, and the rain surrounding her froze to miniature flakes. The pouring rain slowed down and turned to dark snow. Crimson flakes swirled around, creating a bloody blizzard. The half-witch slowly turned toward Polaris and Jason, wearing the grin of a true demon.

"Who's next?"

22

Demon

Polaris quaked, and not solely from the dramatic drop in temperature. Her sister's blackened claws, and fangs to match. The darkening of her eyes. That sadistic, twisted grin that made Aurora the spitting image of their mother. It happened again. Her sister was gone, and this animalistic beast was back in the driver's seat. Polaris swore under her breath over and over. Why hadn't she pushed back against her harder? If she had just forced Aurora to put on the necklace, even if it meant being rougher with her like how they first met, they wouldn't be in this mess. Moreover, Aurora wouldn't be marching her and Jason down with a murderous glare. Polaris instinctively stepped back with every step the demon-witch took toward them.

"S-S-Solaria. " Polaris struggled to utter words. "It's me! Your sis—"

Aurora rushed her like a feral beast. *SLASH!* Blood splashed into the air, but not Polaris's own. Jason shielded the princess at the last moment, taking claws to the chest in her place, and grabbing Aurora's wrist with both hands.

"Red, wake up!" Jason groaned as his bloody chest regenerated.

Grabbing Aurora's arm proved to be costly. Aurora instantly overpowered him and continued her assault, slashing at Jason like a wild animal. She tore through his chest an arms with ease, prompting terror-ridden screams. Jason wouldn't allow himself to be mauled for long, blocking one of Aurora's strikes before launching his feet into Aurora's chin. He rolled away while Aurora recoiled, then jumped to his feet, his wounds repairing themselves.

The boy dashed around the wet field, firing projectile-like spears at her from a distance. Aurora evaded the spears with ease, then zipped to Jason in a blink, forcing him to slide to a stop. He slipped in the mushy field, trying to brake but it was too late. Aurora pounced on him once again, pinning him down with her knee before tearing through him again with her claws. Jason fought tooth and nail to bat her strikes away and protect his neck, but Aurora was relentless. His blood dyed the puddles beneath them, and all Polaris could do was watch on in horror.

At this rate. . . he'll—Cassie flashed into the princess's mind. *No. Not again!* Polaris sprinted toward them and blasted her sister with her hydrant cannon of water. The blast launched Aurora across the field, freeing Jason. Then, she closed her fist, and the water engulfing the demon solidified into a thick minature glacier. Polaris exhaled, her extended hand quaking. Even from a distance, she could see her sister's feral expression beyond the ice. She wasn't entirely sure why, but this latest rampage of her sister felt different from the others. Her aura was much darker, and colder.

The princess redirected her attention to Jason, running to his side as he struggled to push himself off the ground. The lacerations on his body healed on their own as expected, albeit slower than normal. At the very least, he appeared more distraught than hurt.

"Man, I'm glad to be a half-demon," he said with bated breath. "But seriously, what the fuck?"

"Are you well?" Polaris asked.

"Mostly, but that girl! Blue, what is she? She's a total freak!"

"Don't say such things. She's a half-demon as you are. She just struggles in controlling her aura—"

"No, Blue! That isn't just a lack of control. No half-demon acts like that!" Jason yelled. "Not since. . ."

Thunder roared above them. "Surely that's . . . fictitious. Solaria is all the proof you need. The girl just needs more time and that aura-suppressing necklace."

"That *thing* needs to be put down," a rugged voice interrupted them.

Alicia limped toward the shaking pair, fury fueling her gaze. Though most her her wounds were gone, her scorched, tattered clothes and disheveled hair were a clear indicator that she was not willing to deal with Aurora's antics a second longer. Alicia whipped out her dagger and aimed it directly at the miniature glacier containing Aurora. Aware of what would happen next, Polaris slid over and stood in Alicia's path.

"Move it, Princess!" Alicia yelled.

"Under no circumstances! I won't sit here and watch you incinerate her."

"She must be dealt with now, or she'll do much more than just hurt us," Alicia claimed. "If you're that worried, I'm sure the flames won't eviscerate the Divine Stone. You can collect and high-tail it home after I've vanquished this monster."

"You keep mentioning that. What's this about a Divine Stone?" Jason asked.

"Ari has a Divine Sorcerer's Stone inside of her. That's how she's able to use more than one element. I know you've noticed it too, Jason. And those two have been hiding the fact that that's why those Vipers are hunting them," Alicia hissed.

"Wait, seriously? Those jewels of infinite magic that everyone goes to war over? She just casually has one inside of her?"

"Bingo. Let her get loose in that state, with the power of the Divine Stone, and she'll turn not just our village, but the entire Pearl Kingdom into a crater."

Polaris was reminded once again of the Alucard incident. She knew of the dangers of a threat like that. Even so, it was her mission to bring Solaria home. Failure would yield devastating results for the princess. More than that, the thought of her sister getting hurt, or even killed. She couldn't stomach the thought.

"Sorry, Miss Alicia, but I cannot allow you to do this. We must find another way to calm her down and—"

"And what, Princess? Bring her back to normal only for her to snap again later?"

Polaris paused. She averted her gaze and bit on her nail.

"This ain't the first time she's been like this, is it?"

Polaris remained silent.

"Sorry. I can't afford to let this thing present a danger to my home. Now or later. Besides, those Vipers will snuff us out so long as that rock is here. I'm using the flames and ending this."

Polaris panicked. "Jason? You wouldn't let her? You and Solaria bonded recently, yes?"

Jason clenched his fists. He couldn't meet Polaris's eyes. "It's not right, I'm with you there, Blue. But . . . I don't know."

Polaris remembered everything Aurora ranted to her about throughout their journey, including the scene of her struggling on the boat while she fought Serena. If only she heard her out more, and truly understood the horror she wanted to avoid. She hung her head.

"I'm sorry it had to come to this, Princess. I should've never accepted the girl's challenge. But I can't allow her to go off like this anymore. Your mother would do the same," Alicia said.

Polaris continued staring at the murky puddles on the ground. Just how could things have gone so wrong? Even with Aurora's curse, they were still supposed to be catching Aurora up to speed as a princess at the castle. Not only were they late, but now her sister had become so out of control that she had to be killed right then and there. It was all her fault. Everything she'd done, everything she couldn't do, going all the way back to dealing with Reiya, led to this. Polaris immediately thought of her mother. *Of course! Mother can fix this. Surely, she has some spell or ability to subdue Solaria. If I can get to a wyvern and fly back to Neo-Camelot, surely she's to know the solution and*—Polaris paused, thinking on Alicia's last statement—"Your mother would do the same."

The Princess thought back to Cassie and the rest of Serena's people. How they were laid to waste, and how she ended the poor girl's life on her own, all because of the potential threat they caused. If Euryale were to see Aurora now, she would probably kill her and start the experiment over. All the same, would it even be wise to bring danger to the kingdom?

It was her responsibility to learn how to keep the kingdom safe. Polaris rustled her stringy, wet hair, torn on what to do. But she was out of time.

Alicia pointed her dagger, Alighieri, to the heavens and set her sights on the iceberg. As she swung her blade downward, Polaris tackled Alicia to the ground. The flames zipped right past the iceberg, turning the grass to rising ash and evaporating water surrounding it.

"What are you doing!?" Alicia yelled.

"Let's not be hasty. We can figure this out a different way!"

"Damn, you must really want a living weapon that bad, huh?! Do you ever do anything that isn't ordered by that scorpion she-devil?"

"I've caused enough damage as-is and won't lose what I've fought all this time for!"

Alicia popped up and snatched Polaris by her collar. "You caused damage? What a coincidence, so has she! She'll cause more if we don't kill her now! I'm trying not just to help my people, but yours too, and you're stopping me?"

"People will die but . . ." Cassie flashed through Polaris's mind, along with Aurora's obnoxious laugh. "So will she . . ."

"Why the hell do you care? She's just a tool to you anyway!" Alicia barked.

Polaris felt as if she were pierced through her chest with a blade. Aurora's words from when they met, their talk on the boat, and the aftermath of beating Serena, flooded Polaris's mind. All this time Polaris prioritized a mission, a duty, over a person. The same person that fought for her circlet when she didn't have to. The same person who refused to sell her off to Vakari in the black market. The same person who fought Reiya after she tried kidnapping her. A person who desperately wanted to avoid the situation she was currently in. Polaris was doing the same thing Ria did to Aurora but in a different way. She could only imagine, if the girl were somewhere in there, she must be suffering. Suffering the same way Polaris did during the Alucard incident.

All that Aurora had done for her, and Polaris was just going to let her die? Still prioritize an order over her, just like she did with Cassie? Treat her like a tool, just as Euryale would? What kind of sister was she? What kind of princess would she be? Who was the real monster? Her face flared and her eyes welled with tears.

Alicia raised her hand to swipe again, but Polaris jumped in front of her. She drew her sword and aimed it at Alicia.

"If you so much as aim that wretched weapon at her again, I swear from Echidna above to Mephion below, I'll execute you where you stand," Polaris warned.

Alicia glared at the princess, aiming her dagger at her. Jason yelled at his sister to stop, but his plea fell on deaf ears.

"If you continue protecting her, you're just as dangerous as she is. Even if that she-devil hunts me the rest of my life, I refuse to let my people die because of *two* selfish monsters." Alicia's blade flickered with black flames.

"Alicia! Jason!" someone called out.

Alicia stopped and everyone turned around. They rest of the Skewer Bandits and several villagers ran onto the field.

"We heard lighting and felt a surge in aura. What's happening out here?" Fasha asked.

"No, no, no," Alicia muttered. She turned toward her people. "We can discuss this later. You and everyone else go back to your homes. This storm will be over soon."

One of the children emerged from the crowd, pointing at the ice. "Why is Miss Aurora frozen?"

Fasha stepped forward, her eyebrows furrowing at the sight of the black flames in the distance. "Are those . . . Cap', you used Alighieri? What's going on? And why are you all beat up?"

"Guys, please! Just return to your homes and—"

A loud crackle echoed through the sound of surging wind and rain. Polaris turned and saw the ice melting away from the heat of the black flame. The ice changed in hue from a blueish white to a pinkish red.

"No, no! Not here! Not with everyone here!" Alicia raised her blade again.

"No!" Polaris swiped her arm and submerged Alicia's dagger-wielding hand in a thick coating of ice.

"Bitch!" Alicia screamed.

"Blue, what are you doing?" Jason yelled.

"Saving my sister!"

The iceberg exploded, blowing an icy mist in every direction. When the fog cleared, the burgundy aura flowed again, darkening to nearly black. Wintery wind mixed with ice flakes blew past everyone, freezing the water around them and causing everyone to panic. What emerged from the dark mist was almost unrecognizable.

The red-haired half-witch now bore muted, bubbly skin akin to a salamander, along with a single horn curling upward on the right side of her forehead. She stood a few inches taller than before, and her muscles were bulkier and more toned. Her claws were almost the length of her forearm, and she had longer, sharper teeth, akin to an angler fish. Pointy spikes stood on her shoulders. To top it all off, a long, scaly scorpion tail spewed out from her backside and lashed around.

Polaris marveled in terror at the razor-toothed demon that once was her sister. The half-demon villagers all gasped and muttered in shock and fear. The monster released a contorted screech akin to the tearing of metal and the screaming of bats.

"So . . . laria?" Polaris mumbled.

"That's a demon," someone shouted from the crowd. "A full demon, straight from Tartarus!"

"No way. What's one doing out here?" another cried.

"Everyone, get out of here now!" Alicia screamed to the top of her lungs.

Aurora's giant talon-like claws ruptured Alicia's stomach. The demon rushed toward her without Alicia realizing it. Alicia hunched over and spewed blood from her mouth.

Greg and Fasha swooped in and kicked Aurora away from her while everyone else fled in a frenzy. They helped Alicia up as her wound repaired itself. Aurora sprang back up, now on all fours, ready to charge.

Alicia huffed, fighting for air. "Jason, Jack, and Zai, evacuate the other villagers as far away as possible. Take the wyverns if you need to."

Zai and Jack nodded, but Jason hesitated, staring at his feet with apprehension. "But—"

"Don't argue, just go! They need you right now, Jason! *I* need you. Please!"

The siblings met eyes. Jason nodded. "I'll do my best."

"I love you."

Jason paused for a moment, flashing her a smirk. "Don't be weird. Just handle her!" He ran off with Zai and Jack.

Polaris froze, staring at her demonic sister and the red ice flakes swirling around her. That crooked, saber-toothed grin sent chills down her spine. Polaris had to do something before the Skewer Bandits killed her. Before she or the bandits could act, Aurora leaped away and ran toward the fleeing villagers on all fours.

"NO!" Alicia screamed.

What Polaris saw next was utter horror. Aurora zoomed through the fleeing half-demons. Anyone caught within inches of Aurora was torn by her sharp claws. Bright beams of fire launched from Aurora's mouth, engulfing several stragglers amongst the chaos of those that fled. The beast even fired streams of lightning that tore through the ground and decimated the village houses and anyone unlucky enough to get caught in its path. Screams and moans rang through Polaris's ears. It was the Alucard massacre all over again. She couldn't so as much as lift a finger during the ensuing carnage.

Zai and Jason rushed the transformed witch. Jason dug his hands into the ground and his aura flared. Giant black spikes erupted from the ground, forming a barrier around the fleeing villagers who ran away unscathed. Zai and Jack recovered the injured who weren't completely charred or mutilated. Even for the survivors being half-demon, their wounds barely regenerated.

Jason's arms vibrated and he winced while yanking his hands out the ground. He stared at Aurora from behind the spiky barrier, giving her a look of contempt before turning around to assist in rescuing the villagers and fleeing.

Aurora stared at the spiky spear barricade in confusion. Before she could swing her claws at the structure, Alicia tackled the monster to the ground. Alicia tried to pin her down, but was struck in the face by Aurora's tail. The beast leaped back onto her feet, letting out another horrifying screech.

Alicia spat a wad of blood out to the side, Greg and Fasha rushing to her side. "You're not killing anyone else!" Her voice ragged.

The trio cornered the beast. Polaris expected to have to run in and stop them from hurting Aurora, but the three bandits combined were lambs to the slaughter. She tore through their flesh and tossed them around the training field and toward the cabins. Alicia provided the most pushback, swinging her long tendrils and spraying black flames, to at least keep Aurora on the defensive.

It all meant nothing. Alicia couldn't so much as touch Aurora. She broke through Alicia's defense with ease before sinking her claws into her stomach once again. Rain and puddles froze as they dyed a bloody red.

Though their respective wounds were regenerating, their painful wails grew harder to listen to. The princess remained still nonetheless. The utter terror of what her sister had become overtook her. Polaris started to consider if Alicia was right.

After she smacked Alicia away with a swipe of her scorpion tail, Aurora set her sights on Polaris. She foamed at the mouth, crawling toward her on all fours.

Polaris treaded backward. No words could escape her throat. Just when she thought Aurora would pounce on her, laughter filled the air, taking the beast's attention.

Alicia slowly rose again, chuckling and wiping the blood from her mouth and face. She shuddered and her knees wobbled. Polaris never could've imagined seeing someone like her in this state.

"We're half-demons too, Ari. You won't kill us that easily," Alicia smiled through the unimaginable pain. Her wounds were healing slower than normal, and her aura flickered like a candle in the wind. "Guys, Formation F," she muttered as she raised her fists.

Fasha popped up and spewed dragon wings from her back. She flew up in the sky and fired flames at Aurora from above. However, their effect on the demon overall was nothing more than an irritation. Aurora screeched and leaped into the sky at Fasha.

"Greg, now!" Fasha yelled.

The hulking man leaped in and tackled the monster out of the air before she could reach Fasha. He suffered her immediate wrath, Aurora carving his back and shoulders with her claws as they crashed to the ground. However, Greg managed to get behind her. He wrapped his bulky biceps around her and squeezed her in a bear hug with all his might. Veins bulged all over his bald head and biceps, and his aura exploded. Despite all his valiant efforts, Aurora was breaking his bind rather easily.

"Captain!" Greg yelled.

Before she could completely break free of his grip, Alicia rushed in and thrusted her dagger at Aurora's heart. However, Aurora caught her wrist with her scaly scorpion tail, stopping the blade just inches from her chest. Alicia pushed forward with all her strength, trying to pierce her heart and end Aurora. Alicia's effort didn't even faze the beast.

"She's conscious enough to protect her heart?" Greg panicked, still trying his best to bind Aurora.

"Survival instinct, even when feral," Alicia panted. "But it won't matter. She'll be an ashtray soon! Greg, let her go, now!"

Greg released her, leaping back as Alicia twisted her blade in Aurora's grip, sparking black flames that engulfed the demon completely.

The monster roared once again, this time feigning agony. Her wails and cries reverberated in Polaris's head. Her sister was dying. Polaris's heart sank, and an initial wave of sorrow overtook her. She, in essence, did this to her. She wanted to scream and run out to her but saw a shining green light.

Strands of Polaris's hair lifted and pointed toward the action, and then she noticed she was being literally pulled toward it. Alicia, Fasha, and Greg were also magnetically pulled toward Aurora. They each tried to run away but were all being sucked in along with Polaris. As the flames raged on, Aurora's tattoo beamed brighter.

"What the hell is happening?" Alicia screamed, pulling out her aura and trying to pull away.

Polaris slid on the muddy, murky grass. Water, dirt, debris, and wind all flew toward Aurora, and the green light as it shone. Green sparks shrouded the burning witch, and her wails only intensified. Polaris recognized the feeling of this energy that was pulling them all. The Divine Sorcerer's Stone was surging. Its brightness reached a peak and *BOOM!* Polaris was launched into the air before banging her head on the wood of a cabin door. She lost consciousness on impact.

Ringing filled Polaris's ears as her blurry vision cleared. The black snow continued to fall, along with dark pieces of ice and debris. She felt numb to the bone from the frigid air. Polaris slowly picked herself up, not recognizing where she was. She scanned the area, seeing nothing but dirt, ice, specks of flames, and wood. That's when it hit her. The slope of the land caving in. The lack of houses and trees. Polaris was inside a giant crater that spanned the size of what was once Furasaku Village. Her head pulsed as the ringing noise faded into the sounds of burning wood crackling.

Polaris looked around frantically before spotting Fasha lying amidst debris and Greg near her. Both were severely burned and bloody. Polaris ran to them to feel their pulse. They were alive, but their heartbeats were fleeting. She spotted Alicia further away, her dagger tight in her grasp. Her burns were the worst. Most of her skin was either charred black, or completely melted off. Even half of her skull was revealed. The girl flinched and groaned in pain, her eyes shut. Just as Polaris moved to check on her, a powerful gust almost blew her off her feet.

She turned to the side and saw that green light again. The dust settled and Aurora emerged, howling in agony. Her burn marks from the black flames were mostly gone, but the monster had glowing green streaks surrounding her body. She writhed and rolled on the ground. Flames and electricity erupted around her, spreading out and tearing the soft ground. Blasts of water and wind flew out around her, along with dirt and rocks. Polaris saw tears streaming out from the girl as she destroyed everything with elemental blasts—or would have, if there was anything left to destroy.

Was it always like this? Have you been keeping this bottled up inside your entire life? Solaria . . . I . . . I let this happen to you. I disregarded your plea and now . . . no. You must still be in there. Polaris squeezed her fists and ran toward the screaming, raging girl.

She dodged the roaring flames and streaming lightning. She leaped over the water blast and eluded the stones and boulders flying at her. Her thighs tightened and her knees buckled, but she didn't care. She pushed ahead until she was close enough to reach her.

"Solaria! Do you hear me?" Polaris screamed.

Aurora screeched. She cocked her arm back and swiped at Polaris. However, Polaris caught her giant claws and pushed back against her with all her strength. Her arms roared, and her hands burned and bled. The heat from the surrounding flames made her sweat, and the rumbling ground beneath caused her knees to buckle further. She winced as her cold blood streamed down her arms. But seeing the pain in Aurora's teary eyes was enough for her to press on.

"I won't . . . allow you to . . . " Polaris choked on her words. "I won't allow you to remain in this fiendish state."

Polaris yanked Aurora's clawed arm forward and wrapped her arms around the screaming beast. Aurora's screaming stopped upon feeling her embrace. Polaris felt a stab in her back, courtesy of Aurora's scorpion stinger. Pain permeated from the piercing, but Polaris locked her grip.

"I lost a sister once. I turned the other against me. I refuse to lose another." Tears rolled down her cold cheeks. "I'm sorry for kidnapping you and for ignoring your plea. You can flee from this country. Become the warrior you desire to be. Commit any crime you see fit. You can do whatever you please, but Solaria, please come back to us. You're no monster; you're no demon. You're . . . Aurora. Aurora Salem, raised by the Amethyst Witch! But you're also my sister. This isn't you, far from it. Remember who you are!"

The blackened aura swirled around them, and the green light shimmered from Aurora's chest. The frigid air smothered the princess. Polaris snapped her eyes shut, hoping, praying that her words would reach through. But, part of her thought she would suffer a quick end at the hands of her sister, since she lacked the same regeneration as the half-demons. In the face of that, she smiled. At the very least, her sister could be held in the end. While not much, that provided some comfort.

Abruptly, the dark aura dispersed. The glowing stopped, and Polaris felt Aurora shrink to normal height. Her claws dulled, and her scorpion tail vanished. She pushed Aurora away from her, meeting her eyes. The crimson glow was replaced with that emerald shine she desperately missed, and tears accompanied it.

"Po . . . laris?" Aurora muttered.

Polaris grinned from ear to ear, wiping her wet face. "Welcome back!"

23

Sisters

Aurora woke to a migraine and a burning chest, as she often did. Mushy sludge surrounded her, with small fires dancing about. She noticed the destroyed, charred wood and pieces of torn metal hanging in the curved earth surrounding her and Polaris.

"Did I . . ." She raised her blood-covered hand. Her eyes widened as flashes of her rampage flooded her mind. She shoved Polaris in a panic and backed away. "No, no, no, no. I did it again! I hurt you. I hurt them. I hurt everyone I—" Aurora rustled her hair, hyperventilating.

Polaris walked toward her. "That wasn't you. It's okay now."

"NO!" Aurora yelled at her. "Get away from me! I'm a monster!"

Polaris yanked Aurora into her embrace, taking the girl by surprise. "You're NOT a monster! You're not a demon. You're not evil nor malicious. You're you, and I don't want to hear another word about it!"

There it was again. That familiar warmth. The same warmth that brought her back to consciousness. It was as if Blair had returned from the grave. Aurora hugged her back and broke down, bawling into her sister's shoulder.

"I'm sorry! I'm sorry!" Polaris's shoulder muffled Aurora's cries.

Polaris gently rubbed her sister's back. "It's not your fault. You needn't apologize."

Aurora sniffled, squeezing the back of Polaris's shirt as she embraced her back. "But it is! I rushed the fight and I cut the necklace. I just wanted to try and get us home faster, but I wasn't thinking. I did this. It's all my fault."

Polaris stared off to the side. "So that's why. You challenged her for my sake," she mumbled. "Forget about Mother. Forget about the castle and my mission for now," Polaris released Aurora, looking her in the eye. "I don't wish to burden you further. If you wish to return to Westtown, you may do so. I can make arrangements for you to head back east before Mother returns. This nightmare of yours can be over."

Aurora stared off to the side. "But . . . won't she hurt you again?"

Polaris sighed, brushing the blue strands of her hair from in front of her eyes. "You figured that out, have you?" She shook her head. "You needn't worry about my well-being. And I'm sorry for—"

"I know. I heard you apologize already." Aurora never imagined Polaris would let her go free. She could return to doing things her own way, free of people. Free of anyone getting too close and her potentially losing it. But did she really want that, especially after coming all this way?

"Hey!" A voice called out to them.

Alicia approached them with a scowl and teary eyes. She gripped her tagger tight, steam emitting from its hilt. Aurora got on her guard before she finally noticed the extent of Alicia's wounds. Deep gashes and sever burns decorated her from head to toe, and part of her skull was still exposed. Worst of all, none of her injuries were regenerating, and Aurora couldn't see even a spec of her aura. Aurora's heart sank. Alicia was at death's door, and it was all her fault.

"You're not leaving alive, *monster*," Alicia groaned.

Aurora rubbed her arm, avoiding Alicia's gaze. "I'm sorry I—"

"Sorry? *Sorry*? Look what you've done to my home! My family! What the hell is *sorry* gonna do? And you, Ice-Devil, brought this thing to us! Is this some fucked up way for Euryale to wipe us out?"

"Miss Alicia please, just . . ."

"Just what!?"

Polaris's lips thinned. "It wasn't Solaria's intent to let any of this happen. Nor mine, nor mother's. We can compensate you and restore your village, I promise, just please."

"Bribery won't save you—" Alicia stumbled, dropping her celestial weapon, and falling to her knees. She screamed in frustration, yelling, "How dare you! How dare you! *How dare you!*" The yelling morphed into a tearful whimpering. She dug her claws into the soft ground. "Why does this always have to happen to us? To Mom . . . Dad . . . and . . ."

Alicia's fury and anguish radiated from her. Aurora bit down on her lip to fight off tears. Even though Polaris tried to reassure her, Aurora was sure she'd never be rid of this curse. Perhaps it was best that she stayed alone, just as she had for the past six years.

Polaris placed her hand gently on Aurora's shoulder, grabbing her attention. "Summon your broom, Solaria, let's get out of here before—"

A black object blurred past the sisters, moving fast enough for wind to accompany it, breezing through their hair. The pair of them froze, hearing a painful yip before they could fully register what they saw. A sword pierced the left side of Alicia's chest, blood seeping from the wound. Aurora's pupils shrank, recognizing the blackened blade of Masamune right away. Polaris shrieked. Alicia's mouth hung open, blood spewing out. Her scarlet eyes lost their glow, fading to black.

Can't be. She can't still be alive! Aurora quaked, blinking over and over, hoping she'd wake up from this bizarre nightmare.

"That was meant for Polaris. My bad," a familiar voice echoed from the sky, confirming her hellish reality.

The witches looked up and watched Serena descend to where Alicia lay. Sure enough, she was in near perfect health, aside form her right arm still missing. She snatched the half-demon by her hair and jerked her head toward her.

"Can't heal? Wonder what that must be like, Furasaku." Serena grinned, yanking Alicia's head closer to her own. "That said, I have to thank you. I figured planting the seed of Solaria's origin would bring you two to blows, but I never could've imagined this! It was a pleasure doing business with you."

Alicia couldn't as much as utter a word before Serena sank her fangs into her neck, draining her blood as if she were sucking through a straw. Alicia's skin drained of color, becoming prune-like.

Aurora rushed her without a second thought and tried to manifest her witch-blade. The Divine Stone within her surged, burning the middle of her chest. The stone's energy pulsed through her already tired body, causing her knees to buckle. Her muscles, especially those in her forearms, strained with intensity, a damning symptom of exerting more aura and magic than her body could handle. Similar to what happened on the boat, she couldn't utilize her aura. Her body was so numb and her muscles too tight, as if her body was rejecting the Divine Stone. She groaned and grabbed her chest as her muscles inflamed.

Polaris took the initiative, charging at Serena with an icicle of her creation. She thrust her icicle at her, but Serena zipped out of sight, dropping Alicia's shriveled body. The princess caught Alicia, checking her pulse at once.

Polaris covered her mouth, her eyes glossing. "This isn't real. Alicia, you can't be—" she choked up.

Serena flew back into the sky, her aura swelling, bathing the clouds red. Her missing arm had regenerated in its entirety and her muscles bulked and toned. Her nails sharpened into claws and her pink eyes turned scarlet.

"I gotta thank you, too, Solaria. Thanks to you, every real threat here has been removed. Now, I'll finally be free."

Aurora gritted her teeth. The half-witch wanted to tear Serena apart for what she did. But, what could she do? She couldn't infuse magic and was in far too much pain to move.

Serena made the first move for her. She swooped before her in the blink of an eye and rammed her hand into Aurora's chest. Aurora froze. It felt like all her muscles were collapsing at once. She could feel Serena's claws tearing through her sternum and pulling her Divine Stone out. Aurora gradually lost feeling throughout her body.

"SOLARIA!" Polaris screamed, sprinting to her. However, Masamune flew out of Alicia's corpse and shot right into Polaris's abdomen.

The vampire yanked the green, spherical stone out of Aurora's chest, pulling through the stretchy, bloody flesh. Aurora dropped to the ground. She lay motionless, watching Serena marvel at the luminous jewel, covered in green static. Aurora's body temperature fell like a weight. Her demon aura wasn't repairing her wounds. She struggled to breathe. Her vision faded. Polaris screamed at the top of her lungs, but Aurora couldn't hear a sound.

The emerald sphere scorched Serena's hand. She winced but still maintained a smirk. "Such overwhelming power. It's more than enough to deal with her." Serena called for her sword, which flew out of Polaris's stomach and into her grasp.

Aurora's vision distorted as Serena ascended to the black and red clouds above.

"Farewell, Gorgons."

Serena disappeared in the distance, leaving the sisters for dead.

Aurora's breaths grew shorter and shorter. Her heartbeat faded. She saw a blurry vision of Polaris crawling toward her and crying. However, her eyelids grew heavy and eventually shut.

Aurora snapped open her eyes, finding herself floating in a pool of scarlet blood and underneath a dark sky. The blood felt like an ice pool. She glided her fingers over an empty, gaping hole that sat in the center of her chest. Aurora stood and walked around aimlessly. Her eyelids were half shut. Her monstrous reflection mocked her in the blood beneath her. Corpses rose to the surface. She always envisioned her end to be like this. In a graveyard. She released a heavy sigh, waiting to die. That was until she heard a familiar voice.

"Yo, kiddo!"

Aurora turned around and her jaw dropped. Blair sat on a stump before a campfire, the flames a bright green. A second tree stump emerged next to Blair. She patted the top of the stump invitingly.

"Don't stand there lookin' crazy. Come sit. We needa' chat." Her smile hadn't changed even a little bit from back then.

Aurora was hesitant, but sat on the vacant stump, feeling the light warmth of the emerald flame. Her eyes were fixated on the small, dwindling flame, threatening to flicker out at a moment's notice. Aurora hung her head, sighing.

"Ya just gonna sigh this whole time, kiddo? We haven't spoken in seven years. Talk to me," Blair said.

"Why? You're not even real. Even if you were . . . it doesn't matter."

The flame teetered even more, becoming candle-like.

"Ain't you all doom-and-gloom? That ain't the Aurora I know and raised. Chin up, kiddo."

Aurora cut her eyes to Blair. "Chin up? For what? Being a weakling? Screwing things up? Nearly killing everyone I get close with?"

"Is that entirely true? You shut people out so much, did ya really get 'close' with anyone?"

Aurora's shoulders tensed. The still blood pool fizzled at her feet. "You know why I couldn't get close to anyone!"

Blair frowned.

Aurora's eyes watered and her throat burned. "Ya know you could've told me I was a half-demon. You didn't have to hide that from me! And did you hide that stone that was in my chest too?" Aurora reached over and yanked Blair by the collar of her jacket, pulling her within inches of her face. "You found me when I was born so you knew, didn't you!?"

Blair stared at her with eyes full of sorrow. Aurora dropped her and turned her back on the witch.

"I'm sorry," Blair uttered.

Aurora raised her head in surprise.

"For not being upfront with you growin' up. You were young, but old enough to know the world's truths. If I could tell you that, I should've shared the truths about you. Your nature. Where you came from. I just didn't want you to bear the burdens of those truths, ya know?"

"See how that worked. Everything's fucked now."

Blair hung her head. "Omni knows if I could, I'd go back and change the past. I'd change it all." She twirled her finger in her lavender curls, a habit Aurora adopted from her. "But ya can alter ya future and move forward."

"How can I move forward knowing I'm just a literal killing machine? On top of which I have a stone that the whole world wants! Or . . . I did." She sucked her teeth. "None of that matters anymore. I was too weak then and I'm too weak now. Won't be long before I die anyway if I haven't already."

Blair stood from her stump and grabbed Aurora's shoulder. "You're not weak, kiddo, far from it."

Aurora's eyes were stuck on the red liquid and the monstrous reflection below. The demon smiled back at her, its scorpion tail lashing behind her. "What makes you say that?"

"Through this whole ordeal, ya never stopped doing the one thing that truly makes people strong. Always fightin'."

Aurora scoffed. "Really? I've lost almost every recent fight I've been in, at least the ones I've been wholly conscious for. Plus–" Her bottom lip quivered, recounting her life since Blair died. "Fighting hasn't done shit for me but destroy homes and create graves! I wanted to keep your dream alive, I really did! I wanted to even surpass the Demi-Gods, but all I've done is . . ." She buried her face in her hands.

Blair hurled with laughter. Aurora turned to her in confusion. "Kiddo, you missed the point of what I told ya back then. I told you to never stop fightin', but I didn't just mean magic and fisticuffs. I meant never stop movin' forward. That's where true strength lies. Omni knows I did a long time ago, but you? You never did, so don't stop now just 'cuz of the setback."

Aurora's jaw loosened. She rose her head from her hands, but not a sound escaped from her lips. The green campfire flame grew slightly in size.

Blair folded her arms. "Anotha' thing. I don't think that's all that's eatin' at ya. If all you cared about were winnin' fights, no way you'd rush your duel with the Furasaku girl."

Aurora looked away from her.

"You care a lot about your sister, but you must love keepin' a distance from her, right?"

Aurora tightened her fists. Her tears were warm on her face. "Of course not! You know why I can't. You saw what I did to the village. You saw what I did to you! Time and time again I end up doing the same thing. I'm a monster, and they're all right to see me as such. They're all better off without me. Hell, the world is—"

Blair slapped Aurora in the face, catching the girl off guard. "Stop fillin' ya head and heart with that bull! Yeah, sure, you're different. Blame that skank Euryale for that. And yeah, some people fear ya. But that girl, your sister? Well . . ." She pointed up to the sky

An echo filled the void. Aurora heard Polaris screaming and crying out for her name, begging her to wake up. The Princess bawled, wishing for her sister back. The heat from the flame grew higher. Aurora was left stunned.

"She witnessed you transform into somethin' even you don't recognize, and just like she always has, she still considers you a sister. Think of all the times y'all interacted after y'all fought. Has she once ever called you a monster?"

Aurora clenched her fists and bit down on her lip. Her face got wetter and warmer.

Blair grabbed Aurora by her shoulders. "Kiddo, trust I wish I could've survived and been with ya through this hell. But ya not alone. Power and physical strength are all well and good, but you can also find strength in others. Trust me from one loner to anotha', it's okay to lean on a friendly shoulder. Don't make the same mistake I did and make power your only comfort."

The flame spiraled and boomed, warming Aurora right back up. Even so, the tears wouldn't stop flowing. "Yeah but . . . it doesn't matter! I'll be dead soon and never see her again."

Blair gave Aurora her signature smile, one she hadn't seen in over seven years. "I'm not so sure."

Aurora felt something in her chest—a faint, but hard beating. A pink light glowed in the black void above. The diluted blood beneath her cleared, leaving crystal blue water as far as Aurora could see. As the blood cleared, the demonic reflection in the water was displaced with her natural one, green eyes and all. The flame reached its peak.

"Stubbornness must run in the family. No, both families. Ya should get back to your blood." Blair smiled brightly as she began to fade into golden particles.

"Wait, Blair, don't go again! I still need—"

"Don't worry. Ya have your sister. So long as you have at least one person who loves you, you're never alone. Those who don't care if you have claws, wings, or a stone in your chest."

Polaris's crying grew louder. Aurora rushed quickly to hug her god-sister one last time. She missed her embrace. "Thank you."

"Try to keep it a while before we meet again. Oh shit, I'm a dud! One more thing!" Blair separated herself from Aurora and stared at her intensely. "Watch out for the woman with the eyes—" She completely vanished. The pink light in the black void radiated to its peak, blinding Aurora.

Aurora struggled to open her moist eyes. Her body still felt numb and cold from the soft, slushy dirt. Dark, red clouds still loomed overhead, with a sleet mix raining down around them. However, her chest felt warm, albeit still wet. The pink light eclipsing her vision emanated from the nevma-shard water mix Polaris casted over Aurora's chest. The princess bawled so hard she could hardly open her eyes.

"Please don't take her, too. Please, Grandmother, have you not punished me enough? You mustn't allow Solaria to pass, please!" she whimpered.

Warmth and color returned to Aurora's body. She regained feeling in her limbs again, numbness dissipating. She raised her arm with a slight shiver and wiped the tears off Polaris's face. The princess flinched, gawking back at her.

"S-sup?" Aurora managed a weak laugh.

Polaris gasped. She pulled Aurora into her embrace and cried. She rubbed her sister's head softly.

"Curse you, Solaria! I thought I-I-I'd lost you!" Polaris wept.

"What can I say . . . I'm stubborn. But thank you, Polaris . . . for everything." Aurora's body got much hotter. She could feel her fangs and claws growing back, but not to the point of her mind deteriorating. Atop of that, the demon aura flowing through her was minuscule. She sat up and felt a scar over her tattoo and chest. The wound hadn't been completely repaired, but that didn't matter much at the moment. "We have to catch Serena, now."

Polaris backed away and wiped her face. "Hold on, now? We should get you medical attention before any action is taken. Furthermore, you're in no condition to take her on right now."

"You didn't hear me, Princess. I said *we*, not *I*."

Polaris blinked at her. "We?"

"Look, the further Serena gets with that stone, the more trouble it will be for us and maybe everyone else. We need to find and capture her.

Even with her speed, she probably hasn't left the continent yet. We can't afford to dawdle anymore."

"You're so . . . decisive. And . . . using your head? Who are you and what have you done with Solaria?"

"Shut up." Aurora weakly blew a whistle into her fingers, summoning her broomstick. Aurora struggled to stand. Her legs stiffened and her knees wobbled. Despite that, she managed to mount her broom and offered Polaris her hand. "I know I wasn't the best. I gave you shit, and I most likely nearly killed you. But I can't beat Serena by myself, and I don't know this land. Can you help me, sis?"

Polaris's eyes watered. Without hesitation, she hopped on the broom behind her. "You needn't apologize for anything. To the skies, Solaria. Serena headed due east."

As they ascended, Aurora looked back at the gaping crater she had left in Furasaku Village. Some half-demon villagers and bandits returned to the wreckage, including Jason, who had a distressed face that shrank the higher they got. Aurora ground her teeth, reminded of how she couldn't save Alicia and left Jason without a sister. Both could've been her friends had things gone differently. Her face burned with fury. She was determined to take Serena down and correct her folly.

The witches flew over leafy forestry, scanning the area. Thus far, there was no sight of Serena.

"She most likely hasn't gone very far. Not at this time of day," Polaris said. "We need to find a nearby cave. That's where she's likely hiding out."

"What makes you say that?"

"Simple. Your battle with Alicia was at noon. Only a few hours passed. Serena operates at night given her vampire nature. She only got the drop on us due to this storm. Sunny days are most detrimental to her kind."

"Got it. Either way, the two of us should be able to beat her, especially if we catch her off guard."

"Your magic is significantly weaker, is it not?" Polaris asked.

Aurora raised her hand. Infusing her aura could only form a witch-blade. She couldn't conjure any elements at all. "It is, but we're out of options. You've known her for a long time. Anything you know that we can exploit?"

Polaris was silent for a moment. "She only just discovered a portion of her abilities during our childhood, so I never had the opportunity to grow accustomed to her battle habits during our… friendship. However, we both tangoed with her once already. If we can limit her mobility, victory is assured."

"Okay, Princess, what's the plan then?"

"Firstly—"

BOOM! In the distance, a green beam shot in the air, blowing trees and debris high in the sky. Birds flew away from the explosion site in a hurry.

"Of course! The stone is unstable! Head that way immediately, Solaria. I'll explain along the way."

"Right!"

24

The Divine Sorcerer's Stone

Aurora and Polaris hovered high above the explosion site. All forestry within a quarter mile radius were blown away, as if a comet had touched down. Trees were ruptured, buried in patches of raised earth. Bushes and all other forms of greenery were completely mangled, unrecognizable, and some of them scorched. It wasn't too unlike the state Aurora left Furasaku Village in, only on a much smaller scale. The glowing stone sat at the center, with Serena quaking beside it. The vampire had seen better days, gripping her bloody ribs and missing one of her arms yet again. Her injuries quickly repaired themselves however, with her red aura bathing her body as her arm re-grew. Aurora sucked her teeth. Serena having Alicia's blood was a big issue. So long as Serena could regenerate, the sisters were in for an arduous battle, and they knew it. Polaris checked the pouch in her pocket, finding only a single nevma shard inside.

"Drats! Only one remaining, so we must execute our strategy as efficiently as possible. Descend slightly, Solaria. I must be in closer range for phase one."

Aurora nodded, descending but remaining high enough not to be seen.

Down below, Serena slammed her fist on the ground and screamed at the top of her lungs. "Damn it, damn it, **_DAMN IT!_** How can I kill her if I can't even transport this thing? How is that girl able to harbor this much power without evisceration? Even with me harboring demonic blood, it still . . ." Serena stared down at the glowing stone as green static surrounded it. She tried picking it up again, but her hand scorched immediately. Serena dropped the stone in a heap. She stared at her trembling arm as her scorched hand healed, eying the snake tattoo with an insatiable ire, and longing for it to disappear. "Lord Fraizen . . . I ask you . . . how much longer until this suffering ends? How much more do I have to bear until that fiend draws her final breath? How much longer until I'm free?" She buried her face in her hands.

The vampire was so distraught she didn't even register the rumbling beneath her. Serena turned quickly, witnessing a colossal tidal wave crashing in from the desolate forest behind her, washing away trees, shrubs, and loose soil. Serena sucked her teeth, scooping up the stone and ascending. The waves curved upward around her, forming a bowl shape before closing into a dome.

"What the hell?" Serena shrieked.

The shimmering dome of water crackled violently before solidifying into a massive, frigid shell of white ice. Aurora and Polaris hovered at its peak for a moment before descending, their feet touching the frozen ground with a soft crunch. Beneath them, the icy sphere had swallowed the landscape whole, snapping trees and burying shrubs beneath its thick, glacial shell. Jagged formations jutted from the surface, making the interior feel less like a frozen barrier and more like the heart of an ancient iceberg—or a cavern trapped in the ice age. Each breath they took spilled out in wisps of cold vapor. Their bodies trembled against the relentless chill, the ice seeping into their bones. Serena however wasn't phased a bit, only staring at the sisters with contempt.

"Both of you just refuse to die. Tsk." Serena brushed a loose strand of her hair from her face. "Creating this snow globe was unwise, Polaris. You know the cold doesn't affect my kind at all. I can also tell it was costly."

Sure enough, Polaris panted rigorously, her hands on her knees. Aurora wasn't sure how much aura her sister had left. Nonetheless, Polaris wore a confident smirk.

"What was costly was stealing the property of the royal family. No, of my sister." Polaris whipped out her sword and pointed at the vampire. "We can strike a deal. Return it, you gain freedom from this cage. Resist, and it becomes your tomb."

Aurora nodded. She just hoped Polaris's plan would work.

Serena smirked, but her hand started smoking and crackling again. The vampire dropped the stone to the icy ground. The bright emerald sphere melted through the icy surface, creating wisps of vapor in its wake.

Serena snarled and glared at the sisters. "You made this ice cage to keep me from fleeing, but the only ones trapped here are yourselves."

Her grin washed away. "Until I use the stone to wipe her out, I'll never truly have freedom."

That line again. Aurora recalled Serena's words in the cave about wanting to destroy someone stronger than Euryale. Who was Serena referring to? Regardless, Aurora didn't have time to ponder. Serena zipped past Aurora and launched her knee into Polaris's stomach.

The moment Aurora reared her head around, she received a whopping kick to the face. She skidded across the spiky, cold surface until she crashed into the remnants of a fallen tree submerged in prickly white ice.

Her face pulsated and burned as she pushed herself off the ground, holding her swollen cheek. She was decorated in cuts from trampling on the rigid ice, but they healed rather slowly alongside her cheek. The vampire stood between her and her sister, who was in a similar state. The princess held her stomach and ground her teeth. Even from a distance, Aurora saw a red blot grow on Polaris's tunic.

Damn! She struck Polaris there purposely and re-opened that wound. Aurora thought as her eyes went to the stone just across from her in the opposite direction. She scurried toward it, slipping and struggling to gain traction on the icy ground. Serena appeared before her in a heartbeat, aiming Masamune at her face. Aurora slid to her knees to stop before the blade could pierce her.

Even from that short exchange, Aurora felt her lungs on the verge of collapse. Her legs were numb, and her entire body dropped in temperature. She stared into Serena's scarlet eyes, which brightened in her scowl.

"Lord Fraizen has brought the two of you to me alive for a reason. Turns out you both may be lucky." Serena lowered her blade, allowing Aurora to stand.

"Let me guess, you desire more negotiations for the Divine Stone's power?" Polaris asked from afar with a strained pant.

Serena looked back to the glowing emerald stone, shining as it melted through the ice. The vampire exhaled, releasing cold vapor from her mouth. "It would bring me great pleasure to bury you both under the ashes of your kingdom, right alongside your mother. But the stone has a much greater purpose for me. Until I can use it, and understand how it works, killing you isn't in my best interest. It would only be quick gratification. Solaria couldn't provide me with the answers I wanted. Maybe you can, Polaris?"

"As if I'd even consider informing you about its use," Polaris objected. "Whoever else you have a vendetta against is none of my concern."

"Polaris is right," Aurora added on. "You don't deserve that kind of power, considering all those lives you took, at least the ones we know about. Alicia, and even your own partner!"

Serena snickered, propping her hand on her hip. "Still finger-pointing? Have you already forgotten about turning that village into a bomb site? Knowing your history, whatever lives you claimed there weren't your first. And I know the Ice-Devil is no stranger to taking lives either."

Both witches averted their eyes for a moment, feeling the brunt of Serena's words. Aurora balled up her fists, in spite of those words hitting so close to home. "I know I've done some terrible things, whether I was conscious or not doesn't change what happened. However, letting you have that much power? I may as well rampage for my entire life. I'd only be costing more lives by letting you escape with that power."

Serena's eyebrow twitched. "Stubborn even when locked in the jaws of a predator. Fine. You both may be more cooperative with fewer limbs." Red aura surfaced around her in a violent spin, creating a frigid current.

Aurora shielded her eyes from its intensity. She met eyes with her sister. Upon seeing her give the nod, she nodded back. Aurora formed her witch-blade just as Polaris rose and charged with her own sword.

"Dumb!" Serena threw her katana at Polaris, while a tendril spewed out of the palm of her hand at Aurora.

Polaris blasted Masamune with a hydrant from her palm before freezing the sword in place, while Aurora smacked the tendril away with her witch-blade.

Being pressured, Serena flew out of the way before the witches converged on her with their blades. She stood across from them once again, this time without her sword.

Aurora smirked. *Just as Polaris predicted. Good. Now for phase two.*

Serena zipped in with tendrils lashing from her body. Aurora charged back with her witch-blade and the two clashed.

Much like in her fight with Alicia, Aurora couldn't touch Serena with her blade, striking her shadow while the vampire punished her. If she swung at her left, Serena appeared behind and lashed her back with a tendril. If swung at her feet, Serena lunged up, feeding her knee into Aurora's nose. Blood spewed from her nose as she stumbled back. Serena thrashed her with her whips, ripping through her skin from all directions. Even so, Aurora remained upright, and kept a smirk that made Serena growl.

"Is your devastation so amusing, Solaria!?" Serena hissed, swinging two tendrils at Aurora simultaneously from both sides.

Aurora quickly snatched both before they could strike her, gripping them tight. She yanked them forward, catching Serena by surprise as she stumbled forward. Aurora then launched her foot into Serena's mouth with all her strength. She couldn't help but snicker as Serena stumbled back, grabbing her bloody lip.

"What's wrong, Serena? Got a mouthful of your own blood for once?" Aurora asked as her lashings healed. "How's it taste?"

Serena hissed, her aura erupting again as her vein nearly popped on her forehead. Aurora retreated without haste. The witch kept Serena in pursuit of her, sliding through the ice. Serena overtook her in a heartbeat. Yet, a white blur flew past Aurora's face and grazed Serena's arm.

She stopped, looking around in a frantic panic. Serena's eyes widened at the sight of an ice sickle submerged in the ground below. Aurora took advantage of her trepidation, slicing Serena in her chest with her witch-blade and following it up with a solid left hook to her jaw.

Again, an icicle darted to Serena, this time from above. She evaded it but received another kick to the face from the witch. Serena was the one tumbling this time.

"What is this?" Serena seethed, gripping her burning, pulsing face as she jumped up.

Aurora wasted no time charging back toward her. The icicles flew faster, like bullets from every direction. The vampire struggled to dodge them and combat Aurora at the same time. Now she was on the defensive, flying around with Aurora on her tail.

Serena quickly caught on, seeing water droplets peel off the ice dome and freeze before firing at her. She even spotted Polaris waving her arms, directing the ice sickles. Serena immediately launched a tendril at the princess. Much to her surprise, it bounced off an aura barrier shielding her, Aurora's aura barrier.

"What?" Serena shrieked.

Aurora eclipsed her vision and drove her witch-blade through Serena's torso. Blood spewed from the vampire's mouth, and she finally remained still.

"That was for Alicia." Aurora returned the vampire's glare. *The plan worked! She's done.*

Serena spat out blood to her side but still managed a demonic smile of her own. "You miss the bitch? You won't be apart for long."

"Solaria, get out of there!" Polaris shouted out to her in a panic.

Serena snatched Aurora's blade-wielding wrist, her claws piercing her skin and drawing blood. Aurora shrieked in pain. Serena yanked Aurora's blade in deeper to draw her close, then, many thin tendrils spewed out from her body. The tentacle-like tendrils pierced Aurora all over her body except her head and heart. It was as if she were pierced by a hundreds of daggers. Her insides bled and burned. Blood seeped out of the holes left in her. Aurora's witch-blade dissipated, while Serena's wounds healed.

"Alicia's anatomical magic is rather useful, isn't it?" Serena's tendrils retracted into her body and Aurora fell to the ground.

Aurora could barely move. Her demon aura dwindled as her wounds barely healed. She saw her sister standing across from them, seething in anger as she squeezed the handle of her sword. Aurora weakly reached her hand out to her. "Don't . . . stray from . . . the . . . plan."

Serena grinned before turning Polaris's way. "So, how about it, sis? Are we feeling more cooperative? Or should I do to you what I did to her?"

"Insolent wretch!" Polaris sprinted toward Serena with her sword.

Aurora crawled with her shoulders, straining her screaming muscles as she squirmed forward through the frigid ice. She grunted and groaned, her body throbbing with intense pain. Her skin gradually lost color the more she lost blood, and the colder she got in the ice prison. Her breaths drew short, and her throat collapsed. Through the intense pain, Aurora realized she was squirming the wrong way. She turned around toward the radiant green shine of her Divine Sorcerer's Stone that sat in the melted ice. The twenty feet between her and the stone felt like miles.

All the while, Serena overpowered Polaris, zipping around her and scratching her with her demon claws. Polaris couldn't so much as attack, even with her sword. However, with her free hand, the princess directed more icicles to Serena to separate them. Polaris tried as much as she could to keep Serena off balance, firing the ice skewers from all directions. However, Serena smacked them away with the tendrils sprouting from her back. Polaris was forced to flee but wasn't as elusive. One of Serena's tendrils shot out of her hand and wrapped around Polaris's ankle, grazing her skin as Serena yanked the princess off her feet. The princess tumbled to the ground, grabbing at her bloody ankle.

Aurora stopped crawling toward the Divine Stone, witnessing her sister fall. "Polaris! No!"

Serena descended to the ground, laughing gleefully. Aurora heard the crackling of ice. At first, she assumed the dome around them was about to collapse. But then she noticed the small structure of ice that contained Masamune. The sword inside was glowing red and the ice was swiftly melting away. Her heart sank. Polaris was a winter rabbit, helpless in the jaws of a wolf.

The sword burst through the iceberg and flew into the vampire's grasp. She slowly approached Polaris. "So, sis, about the stone."

Polaris lay there, panting. Her aura was minimal, the princess being at the height of exhaustion. Despite that, she readied her sword in defense. A sphere of water formed at the tip of the blade.

Serena knocked the sword out of her grasp with a powerful swing. "Strike one! Solaria, you can feel free to chime in!"

Polaris huffed through her heavy breaths. "I'll never tell you anything and neither will she! Solaria, get the stone immediatel—"

Serena swiped Masamune again, this time slicing through Polaris's hands. The wound was deep, seeping to the center of both of her palms. Aurora winced at the sight of Polaris's nearly dismembered hands, covered in her own blood. Polaris cried painfully to the peak of her lungs as she writhed painfully on the icy ground.

"Strike two! Talk, or next is your head!" Serena cocked back her sword, prepared to swipe again.

Aurora's eyes widened in horror. Déjà vu struck her. Polaris being thrown over the boat, and Blair's fight against Shoto; she was going to relive it all. She refused to watch it again. Refused to sit by unable to do anything again. After all they had been through, losing her would make it all meaningless.

"No, wait!" Aurora called out.

Serena looked her way. "Yes?"

Aurora bowed her head, glancing back at the stone for a moment. "I know you can't carry the stone but . . . I can. You can take me with you to carry out your vendetta and use its power when the time is right. But only if you let my sister live."

"Solaria, have you gone mad?" Polaris whined through her tears.

Serena squinted her eyes at her. "And I'd do that, why?"

"You can't carry the stone very far. Even if you knew how to use it, it's too unstable. Otherwise, you'd have been long gone, right?"

Serena leered at Aurora.

"You want to kill someone right? Worse than Euryale? Are you willing to do it without the stone?" Aurora asked.

Serena pondered for a moment before sheathing her sword. She walked toward Aurora. She yanked the witch up by her red hair, tugging her scalp. "Don't try to swindle me. I'll behead you the moment you do and take my chances with using Polaris as a hostage. I'll cut through and kill whoever I have to in order to gain that power. To gain my freedom."

Aurora squirmed as she was dragged to the stone. "W-why?"

"Why what?"

"It's always kill this and cut that. Why do you? Even if it's your friends?" Aurora asked, trying to buy time.

Serena glared at her for a moment. "I was conditioned to kill by the very one I need power to assassinate. Lord Fraizen put obstacles before me in order for me to remove them from the world. To end their paths. Me killing them is purely his design, providing me opportunities to attain my freedom. Also, I don't do 'friends'."

"What kind of crap is that?"

"Come again?"

"That Fraizen guy doesn't sound like any god I'd like to follow."

Serena snatched Aurora by her hair to raise the witch to her eye level. "Whether you follow him or not is irrelevant. The fate of all is by his design, including your own. You should be grateful that you and your sister may have a future after I get what I need. That is, if I'm feeling merciful."

"How can you even say that?" Aurora's voice creaked. "By your logic, your family's massacre was fated, right?"

Serena's brow twitched. Her mouth curled upward, showing off her fangs. "You don't know what you're talking about!"

While Serena's own anger distracted her, Aurora stuck her fingers into one of the regenerating holes in her back. She grunted but tried to ignore the pain as she dug into her own flesh, coating her fingers in blood.

"Was it fate to lose your sister, your parents? To be all alone?"

Serena's eyes threatened to leave their sockets. It was obvious she was reliving some painful memories. That moment of hesitation was all Aurora needed. She yanked her bloody hand out of her wound and launched it into Serena's mouth. The vampire gagged and backed away, spitting out Aurora's hand. She released Aurora, who fell to the ground next to the stone. The sphere's shine intensified the closer Aurora got to it.

Serena clawed at her throat, heaving and coughing to the point of her pale skin turning red. She dropped her sword and fell to her knees.

"What did you do—" she hissed. Her skin bubbled and steamed. "It's like before—" Her aura faded in and out. Her toned muscles deflated. Her demon aura sputtered and her eyes lost their scarlet shine, returning to her normal pink color. As her demonic features completely vanished, she vomited black liquid.

Aurora panted, grabbing her bloody chest as she watched Serena writhe on the ground in tremendous pain. It was as Aurora predicted. She glanced over to her injured sister, giving her an assured smile, despite being covered in blood.

She couldn't waste any more time. Aurora reached for the Divine Stone. Its radiant heat and dense energy prickled the skin on Aurora's palms. An intense jolt surged through her body, making her spasm upon grabbing it. She dug her claws through her chest, wincing as she made an entry-way through her sternum and inserted the stone inside. She couldn't fully insert the stone inside of her, as its magic was too potent. Intense energy shot through her body, contracting, and tearing apart her muscles. She fell to her knees. Blood leaked from her eyes and spewed out of her wounds and mouth.

Polaris gasped as she witnessed the bloody horror. "Solaria? What's wrong?"

Glowing green streaks stretched on her skin, spreading from the tattoo. Aurora screamed in agony, her pain far eclipsing anything she ever felt before. Her howls reached a peak as she hunched forward, her body pulsating.

"Solaria!"

Aurora looked up, seeing her sister kneeling in front of her. She forgot her own pain for a split second as she saw her sister's wounded, shaking hands holding the single remaining pink nevma shard. Before Aurora could get out a word, Polaris shoved the lone nevma shard in Aurora's chest. A thin, pink water coating surrounded Aurora's body.

"You've suffered through worse. Much worse. You can handle this," Polaris said.

"But you need it, Polaris," Aurora said in a rugged voice. "Your hands and ankle."

Polaris shook her head. "Remember, you don't have to do this alone. Allow me to do this for you."

Polaris pushed the stone deeper into Aurora's flesh, along with the nevma shard. Aurora squeezed her eyelids shut, feeling her skin boil and her muscles cramp once again. This time, however, she got a familiar headache. Her claws darkened, along with her sclera. Her mind was numbing. "Polaris, get away—"

"Absolutely not!" Polaris winced from her own pain. Yet, she smiled at her. "You won't lose yourself. I've complete faith in you. You control your power, demon aura, and Divine Stone alike."

Aurora closed her eyes tight and ground her teeth so hard they could shatter. Jolts of energy shot up to her brain, sending various odd images into Aurora's mind. She saw a glowing arrow, a levitating woman with flowing scarlet hair in a white dress, blood spillage from spears, and various magic. A faceless, glowing being towering over a man with white hair. The last thing she saw were seven glowing jewels, each a distinct color.

Her red aura wrapped her and Polaris. Her eyes and claws returned to normal, and her scorpion tattoo glowed. The stone merged with Aurora's flesh and her chest wound regenerated completely. She could feel her muscles reforming and returning to normal. Her crimson aura shifted to emerald and swirled around the both of them ferociously, clearing up all of Aurora's wounds and shaking the ground beneath them. Aurora's eyes finally were the normal green glow.

Her stone was back, and her aura was replenished. Aurora stood back up, helping her sister up as well.

"Thank you, sis." Aurora smiled at her.

"Of course, but don't celebrate yet."

Serena shivered as she stood, wiping blackened blood from the corners of her mouth. Her eyes were bloodshot, staring daggers at the two witches. "You two just keep getting in my path. Again and again, you make things difficult! Lord Fraizen will see to it that I strike you down!" She aimed her hand at them again, but her claws were gone. She realized in that moment that she no longer had Alicia's magic at her disposal.

"Look at that. I've learned your powers better than you now." Aurora snickered, folding her arms. "The moment you ingested my blood, you lost Alicia's power. And my blood is poison to you. Serves you right, always using shit that ain't yours." She assumed her fighting stance. "You want to take me so bad, do it with your own power, *Batsy*."

Serena screeched at the sky. "You Gorgons are just set on ruining my life! I've had enough! I don't even care if the stone is eradicated! This here will be your grave!" She picked up Masamune and aimed her blade at them.

The sword glowed red, and a mass of white energy swelled at the end of the blade. Aurora and Polaris felt themselves being pulled in by its energy. Aurora knew well what came next.

Serena laughed to the heavens. "Try to dodge this!"

"Please." Aurora whipped out her witch blade, but Polaris sprung forward, sprinting at Serena.

"Polaris, stop!" Aurora ran after her.

Serena's feet left the ground. Thinking quickly, Aurora sprayed water at her feet and froze it before Serena could get a full foot off the ground. The vampire was stuck.

Polaris knocked the blade out of the vampire's hand. Masamune flipped above them before firing its beam into the sky. The ice dome shattered from the intense blast. Ice crystals sparkled and rained down from the sky, mimicking the inside of a giant snow globe.

Polaris tackled Serena down to the ground, pinning the vampire's wrists with her cut-open, bleeding hands.

"Get off me, you devil!" Serena yelled.

Polaris seethed through her teeth and squinted her eyes. She froze the blood around her hands, also freezing Serena's wrists to the ground. Serena couldn't budge.

"What are you doing, Polaris?" she panicked.

"Solaria! Incinerate us both!" Polaris shouted.

Aurora froze. "W-what?"

"So long as she draws breath, she'll be a danger to our people along with many others. This is our chance! She's finally immobile and you have your magic back. So do it."

"Polaris, no! I can't kill you!"

"Please! It's my atonement!"

Aurora was taken aback. She saw the tears in her sister's eyes.

Polaris looked back to Serena, who still squirmed and struggled to escape. "Understand I never desired nor did I take pleasure in taking Cassie's life. She was as much of a sister to me as you and Solaria are. I loved you both, Serena."

Serena's face reddened with fury. "Shut up. Shut the hell up!"

"I don't know who your vendetta is against, but I'm deeply sorry you've suffered for so long. We both have suffered tremendously. We've both been conquered by our demons, so it's fitting we die together, isn't it?"

Serena's eyes watered. Her lip quivered and she shook her head over and over. "No. No, no, no. You're dying alone!" Serena reached to sink her jaws into Polaris's neck.

Polaris cocked her head back before slamming her forehead into Serena's. The golden headpiece shattered on impact, sapphire and all. Blood streamed down both of their faces. Serena's eyes nearly went to the back of her head. Aurora could only stare in shock.

"What are you waiting for? Do it before she recovers and flees!" Polaris screamed.

Aurora sighed, looking up to the sky. Her eyes burned and she clenched her jaw tight. For a moment, she thought she had been forced to be on her own again. Forced to kill a loved one for a second time. The rain from the storm came down on her face softly. Looking up at the cloudy sky, she remembered something important. In a hurry, she blew a whistle through her fingers and summoned her broom. The witch boomed toward the sky.

I won't lose you Polaris, but I am ending this, Aurora thought as the cold wind and rain smacked her face the further she went up. She flew into the dense, dark clouds before seeing the blue sky above. She stopped, hovering inside the thick cloud, and taking a deep breath.

I know I put you through hell, body, but I need you. Not for me, not for the win, but for her, and everyone else Serena has hurt. Please work. Aurora took a deep breath and counted backward from five.

First, she brought out a bit of her demon aura, growing claws and fangs. Then, she concentrated on her Divine Stone. Her scorpion tattoo glowed bright green as she drew as much of its power as possible. Her chest tore apart, and the rest of her body cramped. With a powerful jolt shooting through her arms, she surrounded herself with streams of wind firing from both hands. She waved her arms in a circular motion, and the stream circled her ferociously, getting faster and faster. The clouds turned and circulated with the wind, forming what looked like a hurricane from below. Her eardrums rang from the sharp whistling noise the wind made. Her body screamed as did her ears, but she ignored it as much as possible. She had to infuse more power. Green sparks surrounded her arms as the wind grew faster and her aura grew more powerful. Soon, the clouds parted, forming a hole that exposed the open sky. The sun beamed through the hole, shining down on the forest where Polaris and Serena lie.

Polaris witnessed the bright sunlight from above, as did Serena. Her skin sizzled once it contacted her skin.

"No, NO!" Serena screamed in agony.

Her skin ignited. Polaris's icy hands melted enough for her to pull away before she caught fire too. She backed away and watched the vampire scream and squirm.

Aurora ceased her aura flow, and her demonic features vanished. Her head throbbed, as did her body. She snatched the stick of her broom to keep herself from falling off of it. She smiled, seeing her plan work. Polaris was safe and Serena was finally down for the count. Aurora descended from the clouds to Polaris's side.

"You . . . are unbelievable," Polaris said to her.

Aurora beamed from ear to ear, twirling her finger in her crimson curls. "I know, right?"

25

The Pearl Kingdom

The sun shone overhead in the eye of the storm. Serena howled painfully, rolling on the icy ground trying to put herself out. Aurora cringed at the sight, but not of contempt. She formed a shady dome over Serena using her earth magic. Once free from the burden of the sun's rays, the burning stopped. The vampire heaved and quaked, with most of her pale skin charred and melted off, revealing a horrific blend of black, pink, and red. Her long hair was half burned off, similar to her condition during her bout with Aurora on the ferry.

"Solaria? Why?" Polaris asked.

"You heard her? She's in far too much pain. No one deserves to suffer like that, not even her." Aurora could vaguely remember when she was in a similar state herself just hours prior.

Aurora knelt in front of the crispy vampire. Serena's bulgy eyes quaked with terror.

"S-s-stay away. Stay away!" Serena pleaded with a squeal.

"Relax. I'm not gonna kill you. Like I told you before, we aren't the same."

Serena scoffed, still wincing in pain. "That weakness will cost you greatly one day. You'd be better off killing me. I'm sure your sister would love to end my life right now."

Aurora looked to Polaris, who gave Serena a solemn stare.

The princess sighed. "If we can properly contain you, you're hardly the threat that warrants death. I wish not to make the same mistake twice, regardless of whose command I'm under. But we will have to place you under arrest. You will be interrogated and tell us everything you know about these Vipers. Then you'll spend the remainder of your days locked away."

Serena sucked on her teeth. "I suppose that fate is greater than going back to those—" She stopped, and her eyes widened again. Aurora saw Serena's right arm, despite the skin being melted away, glowing, taking the shape of her snake tattoo. "No . . . no, no, no, no, she can't be here!"

"Who can't? What are you talking about?" Aurora asked.

"Kill me! Kill me right now please!" Serena panicked.

"What? No, I told you—"

"I don't care! Please, you have to end my life! End my path! End my suffering!" Serena cried and begged, disturbing the two sisters.

Aurora and Polaris took a step back. Something appeared in the corner of Aurora's eye, startling her. It was a small snake. The witch's heart sank as she backed away.

"Ew, ew, ew! What IS that?" Aurora freaked out.

"It's just a snake. We're in a forest. Plenty of reptiles and critters inhabit this land. Although, it's strange it's so close to the blast site."

"Get rid of it! It's so gross and scaly and slimy!" Aurora shrieked.

"Quit your stupid squabble! Kill me before it's too late! She's already here!" Serena screamed.

"Who are you on about, Serena? Who's here—" Polaris stumbled, finding another large black snake slithering past her injured ankle. "What in Echinda's good name is happening?"

"Where are these things coming from?" Aurora whined.

One by one, more snakes slithered in from all around them or emerged from underground. Eventually, these serpents smothered the entire battlefield, leaving no trace of the ground visible. They converged on the injured vampire, making a collective, loud hissing noise that clawed on Aurora's eardrums. Seeing every slimy scale on those slithering creatures made Aurora's face drain of color and her pupils dilate. Serena howled, buried under the serpent pile.

"This is a nightmare. Just what on earth?" Polaris uttered.

A powerful purple aura erupted from the writhing snakes, its sheer intensity unlike anything Aurora had ever felt. Its crushing force slammed into her, as if gravity itself had doubled, yanking her toward the ground. She stumbled, her legs giving out beneath her. Polaris collapsed beside her, both sisters buckling under the aura's suffocating weight.

Aurora's vision blurred as blood trickled from her nose. Every muscle screamed in protest as she fought to lift her head. Through the haze, she saw the mass of serpents coiling over Serena, swallowing her in an overwhelming tide of darkness.

Then—just as suddenly as it appeared—the writhing pile of snakes vanished into thin air, taking Serena with it. The oppressive aura dissipated, the suffocating weight lifting from their bodies. Aurora and Polaris gasped for breath, sprawled on their backs. Aurora's hands trembled. Her entire being quaked. She had faced countless horrors before, but nothing like that.

"What. The hell. Was that? Where's Serena?" Aurora caught her breath.

Polaris couldn't stop trembling, her breath shaky. "That aura...belonged to a Demi-God. Only a Demi-God has an aura so dense that it pulls. And those snakes . . ." Polaris huffed, sitting upright. "Can't be. It's absolutely impossible."

Aurora sat up as well, still trying to regulate her breathing. "What is?"

"I . . . I . . . " Polaris's eyes slowly shut and she fell over to her side.

"Polaris!" Aurora scurried over and scooped Polaris into her arms. She quickly realized the severity of her sister's injuries. Polaris's hands were completely cut open, bloody and swollen with a plum hue. Her ankle was in a similar condition. Her soft brown skin muted, drenched in sweat. She was losing too much blood. Aurora pressed her ear on Polaris's chest, hearing a weakening heartbeat. "We need to get you to a doctor. Polaris, where can I take you? Polaris?"

Polaris's breaths were short and swift. "The castle . . . the kingdom . . . fly straight north and you'll . . . see it."

Aurora wasted no time summoning her broom and placing her sister behind her. "We'll get you there as fast as possible. Let's go home."

Aurora's broom launched into the sky, heading north toward their destination.

Aurora zipped through the dark clouds as fast as she could. Polaris hung on to her back, barely conscious. They flew for about an hour, Aurora growing more concerned with each passing second. "You better not die on me, Polaris. Hang in there, will ya?"

"Below," Polaris mumbled.

Aurora glanced down, spotting a golden-orange light piercing through the thin veil of clouds. Before she could admire the sight, a powerful gust of wind roared in from the right, nearly tearing her and Polaris from their broom. She gripped the handle tightly, her heart pounding. Then came a deep, resonant bellow, haunting and thunderous, like a whale's song echoing across the sky.

She turned, and her breath hitched. A colossal dragon, twice the size of a warship, soared beside them, its massive wings beating with an earth-shaking force as it ascended high above. Aurora's grip tightened as she dipped below the clouds, her eyes widening in awe. Below them, a kingdom bathed in brilliant light stretched endlessly, its vastness breathtaking. The sky teemed with movement, small dragons gliding between towering spires, airships sailing through the air, and pixies flitting about like living stars. The buildings, far grander than those in Moro Town, boasted red-tile roofs and pristine white-bricked roads, their sheer scale rivaling entire villages.

But it was the castle at the kingdom's heart that truly stole Aurora's breath. A massive, ivory fortress dominated the landscape, its walls sprawling across a space as vast as Furasaku Village itself. Dozens of towering spires pierced the sky, each bearing the banner of the Magic Nation—a shimmering crystal cluster enclosed within a perfect circle. It was a vision ripped straight from the pages of a fairytale.

Yet there was no time to marvel. Polaris needed medical attention, and fast. Clenching her jaw, Aurora urged the broom forward, determination burning in her chest.

Aurora flew directly over the thirty-foot gates surrounding the castle and into the mile-long path leading up to the castle's entry. Aurora spotted two guards–a centaur and a reptilian man with a lizard's tail stretching out of his backside–flanking the massive door, both wearing red and gold uniforms similar to Polaris's when she first arrived in Westtown and armed with halberds. Both of them raised their guard as Aurora landed.

"You were better off hovering above. Trespassing at Gorgon Castle warrants execution. Go back home, girl, if you value your health," the centaur called out.

"What also warrants execution is treason, which is what you'll commit by not allowing us to pass," Polaris groaned over Aurora's shoulder.

"Polaris, save your strength," Aurora whispered.

The lizard man gasped. "Princess Polaris!" He zipped before them in a blink and aimed the pointy edge of his halberd at Aurora's neck. "State your name, witch! And you best have a good explanation for the princess's dire condition!"

Aurora's eyebrow twitched. She wanted to snap the thing over the lizard man's head. But she swallowed her frustration. She never imagined she'd ever utter these words. "My name is . . . Solaria Gorgon. The oldest daughter of Euryale Gorgon."

The man's face discolored, along with the centaur's. "You're Solaria?" he freaked. Both of them knelt. "We apologize for our rudeness, Miss Solaria," they both said in unison.

"We don't have time for this! Take me to a medic now or you'll both need one more than she does!" Aurora demanded.

"Right away, Miss Solaria!" The lizard man rushed to the door and opened it.

The dazzling light from the grand chandelier nearly blinded the girl as they burst into the castle. Everything was a blur—golden glows, polished floors, towering walls, rounded arches. Before she could process any of it, they were ushered up a sweeping staircase and down a vast corridor, their hurried steps echoing against the marble. There was no time to admire the grandeur, and no moment to breathe.

Aurora sat on a plush, velvet couch outside the castle's medical ward, her gaze locked on the intricate white-and-gold patterns engrained in the marble floor. Her mind spiraled through the roller-coaster of events that led her to that spot. Discovering her true lineage, being hunted by a nefarious terrorist organization, and even discovering the true nature of half-demons like herself. Never in her wildest dreams, not even in her years with Blair, could she have imagined going through all that.

And yet, amidst the bloodshed and chaos, she gained something she wouldn't trade for all the power in the world—a friend. No, a sister. She couldn't help but smile at the fact.

Her world of thought shattered with the creak of the ward's door. A man emerged, his brown hair tied in a loose ponytail. Aurora jumped to her feet, her pulse escalating. Crimson stains decorated scrubs and latex gloves. Despite his medical mask obscuring most of his face, it couldn't fully obscure his frown. Aurora noticed the name tag embroidered on his chest. *Dr. Asclepius.*

Dread formed a pit in her stomach. She braced herself for the worst.

"Well?" Aurora asked, impatient.

"As for good news, we were able to stop all bleeding and fully restore the miss's ankle with nevma. There was no permanent damage, so walking wise, she'll be just fine. . ."

Aurora wasn't a fan of his sudden pause, paired with his scrunched eyes. She balled up the bottom edge of her tattered shirt in her hand.

"However, the young miss has permanent nerve damage in both her palms. Even with the nevma, the magic receptors in her palms may be beyond repair, with those nerves having been damaged for that long."

Aurora's head hung. She blamed herself. If she didn't let Serena grab her, Polaris would've never got her hands wounded and frozen. But an idea struck her mind. "Wait, what about my blood? You can transfuse her blood with mine, right? I'm . . . well, a half-demon. If her blood mixes with mine, she can regenerate with no problem, right?"

"Half-demon?" Asclepius raised both eyebrow, his voice pitching high for a moment. It was likely that he had no idea of Aurora's true nature. She wished she didn't even bring it up. "Well, even if you both had the same blood type, mixing demon blood with witch blood is dangerous. You could risk numbing the brain or destroying the body by doing something like that. It would likely do more harm than good for Her Highness."

Aurora sighed. "Fine, fine. Can I at least sit with her?"

Asclepius stepped aside, allowing her to pass.

She sat in a chair next to her sister's hospital bed. Polaris's hands were wrapped in gauze and an IV tube extended from her right arm, filled with luminous magenta liquid. Her burgundy scrubs had specs of dark stains, likely born of her own blood. The dark circles under her eyes stood out, her exhaustion apparent. Aurora stifled her tears, softly grasping her sister's arm.

"Are you okay?" Aurora asked softly.

Polaris's eyes swung toward her sister. "I . . . I'm no brawler like you. But even as a princess, my combat prowess was something dear to me. It's vexing that it won't be commonplace anymore."

"Hey, don't say that. Things look rough now, but there may be a way to heal you. Or maybe you can adapt to a new fighting style. You don't need your hands to hit something."

"You do need them to infuse magic properly. Even if I somehow regain the ability to manipulate water again, changing phases may be out of the question. I'll be useless in battle. I'll likely revert to being a simple diplomat if anything."

Aurora hadn't seen Polaris so somber. She rubbed her neck. If only she defeated Serena earlier. Her sister should've never had to sacrifice her hands.

"But that doesn't mean I regret my actions," Polaris said.

"What?"

"What we did brought us both back alive and kept your stone safe. All things considered, I can smile at that fact. Indeed, it will be a while before I can draw a sword again, if ever. But you're here. That makes it all worth it."

Polaris gave her a smile that pierced through Aurora's heart. Her tears finally broke through. Aurora quickly wiped her face off and returned the gesture. "Thank you."

"I should be thanking you. You got me here rather quickly. And the way you stood against those peons we call guards was stellar. I must be rubbing off on you. You're becoming more of a royal already."

Aurora twirled her finger in her hair and blushed. "Ah don't go there. I'm nowhere near as insufferable as you, yet."

"I beg your pardon? I'm far from insufferable, Aurora!"

"Oh please you're the wor—" Aurora paused. "Did . . . did you just call me 'Aurora?'"

"I . . ." Polaris's face turned red. "I-uh . . . I-I have no idea what you're talking about! You must've misheard!"

"Holy shit you called me by my name! Look at you finally learning. Ahhh!" Aurora bear-hugged her squirming sister.

"Solaria, let go! That hurts!" Polaris cried.

Aurora sang in tune, "*You said my name. You said my name!* Yayy!"

A knock on the door brought them to silence, followed by someone clearing their throat. Aurora jumped up, startled to see a tall blue goblin standing in the doorway, wearing a Magic Militia uniform, but with several more badges than what Reiya had. The goblin man squinted his golden eyes. It was the same young goblin that Polaris called back in

Moro Town, Bishop Norman Agura. His entrance washed a nervous look onto Polaris's face.

"Bishop Agura. A pleasure to see you." Her eyes floated away from him. "Whatever brings you to the medical ward?"

"To attend to you, obviously! I do wish you had given me all the details about your crisis. Had I known, I'd obviously have made arrangements to—" Norman sighed mid-sentence, pressing his fingers onto his forehead. "You both are safe, and that's what matters. But her grace requests the presence of both of you in the throne room at once."

"Mother is here?" Polaris freaked. "But the Council Meeting should last another three days, should it not?"

"There was an early suspension upon . . . Agh, just please hurry. You know she isn't the patient type. Good day." He bowed and scurried off in a hurry.

Polaris sighed, starting to rise from her bed.

Aurora stopped her. "Hold it! You can't go. You just got treatment; you should be lying down."

"And keep her waiting? Trust me, Solaria, my health is at far greater risk the longer we stay here." Polaris stood up, wincing and grunting from the pain in her hands. "This is quite embarrassing but . . . could you be a dear and assist me in changing into my royal uniform?"

Aurora nodded but felt that if the queen wanted to talk so badly she should come to them, especially if she knew her daughter was injured. She begrudgingly helped Polaris get ready, eager to meet this Queen she had heard so much about.

Aurora and Polaris stood before the towering marble doors, their sheer size imposing. Etched into the center was the sigil of the Pearl Kingdom—a burgundy shield bearing a golden scorpion, with two gleaming swords crossed behind it in an 'X.' The sight alone sent a shiver down Aurora's spine. She had yet to meet *the* Gorgon Queen, but dread coiled in her gut like a tightening knot. Everything she had heard about the Demi-God spoke of malice, a being whispered about in fear. And yet, here she was, about to stand before her, seeking training.

Aurora wasn't thrilled about it. But then again, how many people had spoken of *her* in hushed, wary tones? Back in Verona, her name carried a reputation, one that likely stirred fear just as easily as respect. On top of which, Euryale's legacy was only spoken by her enemies in the Allied Nations, as far as Aurora remembered.

Beside her, Polaris stood rigid, her head bowed, a deep frown etched onto her face. Aurora placed a gentle hand on her sister's shoulder, offering a small but steady smile.

"Everything will be fine," she reassured softly. Whether she truly believed it or not, she couldn't be sure. But Polaris needed hope.

And so did she.

"A warning, Solaria . . . allow me to do the talking. She should hear everything from me," Polaris said.

"If you can handle it, sure."

Aurora pushed open the massive doors, stepping onto a plush red velvet carpet that stretched endlessly ahead. Golden columns flanked her path, their grandeur interrupted only by crossed spears mounted beside them, a silent warning of the power within these walls.

The walls themselves were adorned with opulence, draped in scarlet with intricate gold diamond patterns, their brilliance contrasting against the stark white marble that peeked between them. Overhead, grand chandeliers glittered like constellations, their countless lights and flickering candles casting a warm yet haunting glow across the vast chamber.

A vast mural hung overhead above the chandeliers, featuring a colossal woman with crimson hair flowing in ever direction and her arms stretched out over the other beings depicted in the painting. Although the woman's face wasn't distinct, Aurora was certain she recognized her. Three other women hovered beneath her, one with the wings of a moth stretching from her back, another with a scorpion tail, and the third with snakes for hair. Droves of people were underneath them, bowing and offering blue spheres of energy to the beings above. Aurora assumed the blots of blue to be some depiction of magic. Underneath them all, at the very bottom, masses of men linked together by chains and shackles.

While not having had a formal education, Blair taught her just enough for Aurora to recognize the mural as the former regime of the Gorgon Empire, which once reigned over the entire planet.

The throne room may have exuded elegance unlike any other, but all of it, paired with the mural, made Aurora grimace. However, her eyebrows furrowed even further when she looked toward the throne atop the raised staircase and spotted her mother for the first time.

Queen Euryale crossed her legs while sitting on the velvet and gold throne, her scorpion tail hanging on the end of it. Her scarlet hair was wrapped in a bun and a golden crown rested on her head. She was covered in jewelry from head to toe, shimmering gold bands and bracelets on her arms, ruby studs on her pointy ears, and a sapphire necklace resting on her neck. Aurora desperately wanted to believe that she wasn't staring at her biological mother. She took notice of Euryale's skin, several shades paler than that of her own and her sister's. However, Euryale's scarlet hair, while not sharing Aurora's natural curls, was enough of a visual confirmation that they were indeed bonded by blood. Not to mention the golden eyes that mimicked her sister's, like piercing daggers.

"Kneel," Queen Euryale said.

Polaris knelt right away. Aurora glared at her but reluctantly followed.

"Mother, a pleasure," Polaris greeted.

Euryale waved them off, allowing them to rise. "So, we finally meet, my darling Solaria."

Aurora felt her throat burning and her bones shaking. She wasn't in any immediate danger, but her body was in fight-or-flight mode. Also, something about her felt . . . familiar.

"Polaris, I see you've disgraced me yet again. You not only injure your hands beyond repair, but you also seem to have lost your royal headpiece."

Polaris's head dipped down. "Forgive me mother . . . the circlet was badly damaged in—"

"Oh, this should be rich. Let me guess, was it when you both got an entire Militia squad slaughtered? Or how about when you were in a lowly Verona town, destroyed an underground market, and desolated an entire town block!"

Aurora and Polaris shared a brief glance.

"You . . . knew?" Polaris asked.

"Knew? *Knew?* Hard to not know when you were all over the news in the Allied Nations!" Euryale jumped out of her throne and her aura erupted with a gold shine.

Her aura brought the sister's to their knees, crushing them both with its divine weight. Aurora's suspicions were confirmed. It was just like back in the forest.

Euryale approached them while they were being pulled into the ground. "Because of you two bloody lollygagging, I had to explain to the other Demi-Gods—my colleagues—why my daughter was running around with the most notorious half-demon in the Allied Nations. Do you know how embarrassing it was to leave a council meeting early to clean your stupid messes? Those Allied Nation swine threatened us since they assumed you, Polaris, were in league with the fabled 'Crimson Witch.' It was quite the chore to convince them otherwise! Luckily for you both, Icarus believed their wanted half-demon still resides in their borders and is in hiding."

"My deepest apologies, Mother! A lot happened and we were forced into several unfavorable situations! And we didn't want to disturb your Council meeting nor make the situation worse by—"

Euryale's tail smacked Polaris across her face, knocking her to the ground. "Excuses."

Polaris spat blood from her mouth, and Aurora's breath was zapped straight from her own. Her eyes turned scarlet, and without a second thought, she launched forward and swung her fist at her mother.

Euryale caught her punch with little resistance. She squeezed Aurora's fist, cracking the knuckle before effortlessly tossing her aside. Aurora rolled down the velvet carpet before springing back to her feet, shaking out her stinging hand. The pain didn't keep her eyes away from her birth mother.

"Bitch! She's injured and you attack her? She's your daughter! You didn't even hear her out. The hell is wrong with you?" Aurora fussed.

Euryale scowled at the young girl, looking down at her. "I can see it. That devilish glare paired with your foul mouth. That lowly thief, Blair Salem, raised you after all, didn't she?"

Aurora's expression loosened for a moment. "Don't change the subject!"

"Though I can't say I care for the shouting much or the recklessness of an attack on your mother. You should be grateful to be in my presence after spending your entire life on the streets. Yet you try and strike me?"

"Forgive her . . . Mother," Polaris picked herself up and wiped the blood off her face. "She knows not of our ways yet. I assure you, in due time she shall."

"Pray to Goddess Echidna for your sake she does."

"W-what?" Aurora freaked. "You're joking, Polaris. How are you not pissed right now?"

"Quiet, Solaria. Mother hasn't finished speaking."

"I won't! She's blowing hot air anyway and I refuse to listen to her after she struck you for no reason!"

"She's our Queen, Solaria, and our mother. If she sees it fit to strike us, it shall be," Polaris replied shakenly.

Aurora saw the slight quiver in her sister's lips. How often did this happen? Her jaw tightened. "If she's willing to strike us, she's willing to get punched in the mouth." Aurora faced Euryale again, clenching her fists and getting closer. "I don't care if you are a Demi-God. I'll die before I let a bitch like you walk all over me."

Euryale's aura flared even more. Her aura's pressure bared down on Aurora once again, but she remained standing tall and kept her gaze fixed. She clenched her jaw as hard as she could.

"All this over a strike? Why is it you show such passion over something so frivolous?" Euryale asked.

"Because my sister isn't *frivolous!* She's a person, dammit, not a tool!"

"She had orders and not only accomplished them late but caused a stir in enemy territory and lost six of my men in the process. Or, perhaps you wished to be struck in her place."

"Lose six men? You're kidding! One of them was a Viper spy responsible for this all happening. She couldn't control that!"

Euryale's aura dissipated. "Did you say Viper spy? One of *my* men?"

"Yeah. And he wasn't the only one after me. After us," Aurora rubbed her stiffened shoulders, thanks to the Queen's aura.

"She's correct, Mother. They hunted us every step of the way," Polaris added.

Euryale gripped the space between her eyebrows. "Mother, my almighty Goddess, they are a threat after all, aren't they?" she groaned under her breath. Euryale walked back to her throne and sat, burying her face in her hands for a moment. "Tell me everything that happened. I want a full report, now."

26
Gorgon

Aurora and Polaris told Euryale everything—from their first encounter with Reiya to their final bout with Serena. Euryale had her maid, Matilda, pour her red wine while she listened to the girls' story.

"Reiya. An Alucard survivor. Black market merchants. To think those slimy little snakes slithered their way into our ranks. Who knows how many of them there are now, " Euryale griped.

"So, you've heard of them, too?" Aurora asked.

"The Council meeting was centered around them. The group is young, but members seem to pop up everywhere from working in stores to working for local police forces in minor nations. We don't know who they are or what they seek, but they only appeared to be a small cult until you provided this vital information. One infiltrating our Magic Militia is a threat to our national security, and to have ranked criminals amongst them as well?" Euryale took a sip of her wine. "But, thanks to your effort, we now know this group isn't loyal to either the Magic or Allied Nations. Solaria, you were wise to end the life of that traitor quickly. Yet, if you had done the same with the Alucard, we might be in much better shape. Nonetheless, you did spare the Magic Nations a potential loss, so I'll acknowledge your triumph."

Aurora wasn't sure if that was some type of praise or not. Initially, she didn't know how to react until she looked at her sister. "I wasn't alone. If it weren't for Polaris, I'd be dead, or worse."

There was a brief silent stare between Euryale and Polaris. She didn't address her directly at all. "Did either of you learn anything else from those terrorists?"

Polaris's eyes fell to the ground. Aurora felt the urge to wail on Euryale with all her might. But she decided to let it go and answer her question. "We think their leader may be a woman. Serena may not be loyal to them as we thought. She killed her partner, along with several other Vipers on a cargo ship. She kept saying she needed my stone to kill 'her' but wasn't clear on who 'her' was."

Euryale stroked her chin. "A traitor amongst their ranks? In which case she might have provided useful info through interrogation." She looked to Polaris. "You were once friends with the girl, weren't you? Let me guess, it impeded your efforts in detaining her?"

Polaris bit down on her lip and looked away. It looked like she was fighting every fiber in her body so as not to curse her out loud. "No, ma'am. She was just more powerful than I. That's all."

Euryale scoffed, taking another sip of her wine.

Polaris's eyes widened and she gasped. "Actually, Mother. There is one more thing. After we bested Serena in combat, millions of snakes slithered over to collect her, and they all vanished."

"And that's important, why?"

Aurora shivered just thinking about it. "An aura surrounded these snakes, and it felt a lot like yours. Smothering, dense, and full of malice."

"Hold on, are you insinuating that there was a Demi-God that cast some sort of spell—" Euryale stopped.

Both girls witnessed a sense of fear and dread on Euryale's face for the first time. Her eyes twitched. "That's . . . not possible. No. It can't be."

"Mother, please don't tell me you think it's . . ."

Euryale's hand tightened around her wine glass until it shattered, spilling the red liquid on the ground. "Snakes, Demi-God aura, Vipers? It has that whore's name written all over it. But that can't be! Not even Mother could've survived such a thrashing! And it's been over twenty years!"

Aurora looked between the two of them confused. "Wait, who are you guys talking about? Do you know who it is?"

Euryale sank into her throne, covering her face. "My sister. Medusa Gorgon."

Aurora's stomach bottomed out. She recalled the horror stories Blair told about that woman, especially how she murdered Blair's parents along with millions of others. "Medusa? No way. I thought she died in the Third Great War."

"As did I. The Council and I saw to it personally!" Euryale slammed her fist against the throne arm, severing it from the chair. "If she is alive, then it's the worst-case scenario. Although, if it was her and they were seeking the Divine Stones, there's not much reason for her not to take you both herself. Why let you run free?"

"Perhaps to send you a message . . . letting you know she's returned," Polaris muttered. "It doesn't make sense though. What's she after?"

Euryale sighed. "Children, worry not of Medusa and the Vipers for now. I shall arrange a Council meeting and work with them to snuff out the bastards as soon as possible. In the meantime, you both are dismissed. Polaris, you can show Solaria to her quarters and inform her of the castle rules. Even you shouldn't manage to botch that task."

Polaris bowed before heading in the other direction. Polaris didn't even seem as glum after the surgery as she appeared now. Aurora wanted to console her, but somthing still lingered on her mind.

Aurora remained standing before Euryale, still frowning at her. Polaris called for her, but she wouldn't budge.

"What are you gawking at, child? Are your ears not functioning properly?" Euryale asked.

Aurora took in a deep breath. "You mixed my blood with a demon's and inserted the Divine Stone into me. Why did you experiment on me with these things? Because of you, I've been hunted and my power has been unstable for as long as I can remember. I wanna know what purpose you had for me."

Euryale muffled a laugh. "Purpose? Simple. I designed you to be a potential weapon in my arsenal and to see if such a feat was possible. I'd have used any child for it, but what better genes to utilize than my own?"

Aurora stared at the ground for a moment, processing that answer. She should've known that's how Euryale would respond. "I refuse to be your sword."

"I beg your pardon?"

"I won't be at your beck and call, so you can forget that shit. Still, I won't leave. I'll stay here so long as my sister is here. Also, I want to train under you to use my powers properly. All of them."

"Solaria, no! Don't speak in such a way to her," Polaris freaked.

Euryale stood up from her throne and marched to Aurora. Mere inches separated them. From such a close proximity, Aurora felt the shackles of imminent death strangling her. Just a flinch would be all it took to have her head roll. Aurora didn't care. She didn't care if Euryale was a Demi-God, the queen, or her mother. She never flinched before overwhelming power, and she wasn't going to start now.

Aurora saw her own reflection in Euryale's rigid gold irises. "You've got some nerve making such declarations and demands. Give me one good reason I should adhere to this nonsense and not remove your head from your neck?"

Aurora shared a glance with her sister. For a moment, Blair popped back into her mind, her remembering their most recent talk.

"Simple. I still wanna get as strong as I can be, and you'll want a strong witch on your side. Don't get me wrong, I won't fight for your cause. But . . . the Vipers have been tormenting me and the people I love for a long time, and I assume they'll threaten you soon too. I don't know about you, but I ain't willing to just stand by and let those clowns do whatever they want. So, you keep me around and help me get stronger, and I'll crack your sister's skull myself." Aurora smirked, cracking her knuckles. "So, what's it gonna be . . . Mom?"

Euryale was taken aback, but much to her surprise, she laughed. "You, take on Medusa? *Ha!* Such a ridiculous notion! You're without a doubt a product of Salem's teachings. That witch greatly intrigued me, and so do you."

The Queen paced away, reliving Aurora of her immediate presence. Despite her declaration, breathing became much easier without the threat of Euryale's stinger being so close.

Queen Euryale returned to her throne, picking up her wine glass again and taking another long sip. "Fine. If you are willing to take on such threats, I'll grant your request for power. That said, you are not to leave this castle until further notice."

"What? Why the hell not?"

Euryale snapped her fingers, summoning a manila folder full of documents that she tossed down the stairs. Aurora scurried to pick them up, finding they were a blend of flyers and newspaper articles. One of them was a newspaper with the headline reading, "*Local half-demon burns cultural hotspot. Fifteen confirmed dead!*" Guilt wrapped around her tight, and squeezed tighter once she found her wanted poster amongst the scattered papers, with an updated price tag on her head.

If she found this out a mere week earlier, Aurora would've jumped for joy. Now, however, the price tag hindered more than helped.

Euryale folded her arms. "The United Military is a large army, and with a bounty that big, they are likely to seek you out. With the Viper issue, along with the public, if word got out that The Crimson Witch and my daughter were the same person, my kingdom would become a war zone. I cannot allow that under any circumstances. Not to mention the Magic Council has no clue of your identity either. Your identity and whereabouts are meant to be top secret and shall remain that way, understood?"

"But . . . I can't just be trapped here—"

"Understood?" Euryale's frightening aura flared up again, nearly pushing Aurora off her feet.

Aurora reluctantly nodded.

"Get out."

Polaris guided Aurora to a bedroom suite perched high in one of the castle's towering spires. The space, much like the rest of the castle, radiated luxury, drenched in rich hues of gold and crimson. From the thick, lavish comforter on the large bed to the ornate trim lining the walls, every detail exuded the grandeur expected from royalty. Aurora sat on the king-size bed, immediately sinking into the comforter's cloud-like embrace. She laid back, enveloped in it's divine softness. Out were the days laying atop cardboard in a Westtown city alley, or on a bed of autumn leaves in Eden's forests.

Aurora stretched her arms and legs out. "Man, I can get used to this! You sleep in this every night?"

Polaris said nothing as she strode toward the balcony door. Curious, Aurora left the bed and trailed behind. As the pair of them stepped outside, they got a great look at the dazzling kingdom, brimming with life beneath the night sky. A gentle breeze swept through, rustling their hair as they leaned against the railing, their gazes lost in the kingdom lights.

Polaris broke the silence. "Solaria, you're a strong witch. You are aware of that, aren't you?"

"I mean I can hit pretty hard, have a lot of powers, so, kinda?"

Polaris elbowed her in the arm. "Dolt. I didn't mean your physical or magical prowess. I meant how you just stood up to her. Without a second thought, you pushed back against her. Nobody I've ever known has been able to push back against her. How were you not terrified?"

"I was terrified."

Polaris arched a brow.

"She's a Demi-God. She beat Blair and could probably kill both of us easily if she felt like it. She's every bit as terrifying as those damn snakes." Aurora hugged her shoulders. She perked up quickly however, showing off her radiant white smile. "But that doesn't mean I'll cower or quake. Or let me or you be disrespected. Besides . . . I know if things go left, you're there to fight with me."

Polaris cracked a weak, half smile. "I envy you. Even after everything, you're still so assured. Though, I wouldn't make a habit of relying on me. My weakness cost me my hands, and likely my mother's respect . . . or what little of it I attained at least."

Aurora punched Polaris in the arm. "You're not weak, jackass. You came all the way to Verona, an enemy to you guys, just to find me. You pulled me out of my berserk state when no one else could. And you survived plummeting to the ocean, and all the craziness with Serena. You were even willing to take her life for your people's sake. After it all you're still here pressin' on, ya know? I don't think I could handle all that, even on my best day. To be honest, Polaris, you're the strongest person I know. Even if Euryale doesn't see it, I sure do."

Polaris's face lit up, her gold eyes shimmering as tears welled. She gazed down at the vast kingdom below, the wind catching her tears and carrying them away. "How many times have I thanked you now?"

"A lot. But don't thank me too much. Since your mom put me on lockdown, you're stuck with me. You know I'm a handful so . . . be ready," Aurora snickered.

"So long as you don't go around destroying mother's busts for a good laugh, I believe I'll manage." Polaris wiped her face with her arm. "Are you prepared for training? Mother isn't as lenient or easy as Jason—" Polaris paused, her frown becoming apparent.

Aurora sighed as well, upon realizing it. With the intense aftermath of their fight with Serena, she nearly forgot about Furasaku Village, and the poor state its people would be left in without a home and leader. "I wish I didn't . . . ugh. Alicia . . . and who knows how many others. They didn't deserve that."

"I know. Actually, it may be for the best you stay in the castle for a while. The Skewer Bandits may seek you out soon enough for the village incident. You'd be safer here."

Aurora gazed at the sky, the dark clouds finally parting, revealing vibrant stars dotting Omni's blueish-purple canvas. She reached up to the sky and formed a fist. *Blair . . . Jason. For what you both taught me, I'll see that it doesn't go to waste. And I'm sorry I couldn't save you, Alicia.*

Dragons screeched overhead, passing by no differently than airplanes would back in Verona. Aurora giggled at the sight. She hadn't been there long, but The Pearl Kingdom was already so different than anywhere she'd been in Verona. She wondered what other fantastical sights and people The Magic Nations had in store for her.

"A lot of strong guys out there. Plus, you owe me a rematch. Heal up so we can have that bout, okay, sis?" Aurora winked at her.

Polaris smiled. "Don't expect revenge. I'll have you frozen, just like at our first encounter."

"Nope. In fact, you won't even scratch me when we spar again."

Polaris gasped. "Not scratch you? You dare insult my ability? Simpleton!"

"Prissy."

"Arrogant wretch."

"Asshole."

"Swine!"

"Bitch!"

Aurora and Polaris stared daggers at each other before bursting out into laughter.

"Road to gettin' stronger. You ready, 'heiress?'" Aurora asked.

"As ready as you are, sister."

Aurora aimed her fist at Polaris. Polaris raised her hands wrapped in gauze, her left eye twitching. A fist bump was out of the question.

"Oh. Shit. Sorry."

Serena's mind swam in haze, fragments of memory drifting through the mist. She saw herself rushing through the snow with ragged breath, fear fueling her every step. A shadowed figure emerged—a woman with an outstretched hand and a reassuring smile, a beacon in the storm. A sharp noise shattered her vision and her eyes flew open.

Serena jumped up off the cold hard ground, each breath rougher and harder than the last. She felt her face in a panic, feeling smooth, soft skin. She wasn't scorched anymore, and felt no immediate pain. Her limbs remained intact as well. "Am I . . ." She turned her arm over and saw the snake tattoo was still there. She sighed.

Sinister giggles filled the void, reverberating around her. She looked around in a frenzy, finally taking in her new environment. She awoke in a shadowy underground cave, the air thick with an eerie stillness. Along the jagged walls, candles flickered with ghastly purple flames, their soft glow casting dancing shadows across the cavern's rough surface. Said shadows grew more defined from the seven statues of various humanoid creatures that stood around her, all sharing an expression of agony. Even that didn't freeze her as much as the bulky throne made of stone that stood in the center, a mere six feet away from her. Serena shook her head, crawling away from it. She was brought to her throne already?

Laughter rang again, forcing Serena to her feet in a panic. *Wait. That voice. Can't be her.*

A middle-aged woman wearing a white and red kimono with cherry blossom patterns approached her. Her slik-like, white hair stretched down her back. Her white fox ears twitched atop her head, and nine fox tails lashed behind her. *Shiro Kitsune. Shit.*

"So glad to see you back, Ally! Are you okay, my little traitor?" Shiro said in a sweet, bubbly voice.

"Traitor? Please, you have no proof of anything, rodent," Serena fired back, dusting herself.

Shiro poked her lips out and frowned. "Aw, but hon, you're so sloppy, you gave us all the proof we needed. You were the only one at Vakari's ship when he and all the other no-names went offline. You blamed my babies, Skewer Bandits, but that's just too convenient, isn't it?"

Shiro's honeyed voice made Serena's skin crawl. She couldn't bear it for much longer. "I gave my report to Hatake already. I do not need to explain myself to you."

Shiro smiled. "Then maybe you can explain why every single one of their recovered bodies was either without heads or cut open? Almost as if it were done with a katana."

Serena's eyes widened. "One of the demons had a sword, what of it?"

"You've worked with us for seven years. We know your style of assassination and your lying pattern, even though you're sloppy at both."

Serena reached at her hip and ice invaded her veins. She didn't feel the comfort of Masamune's hilt. The weapon wasn't on her anymore.

Shiro busted into laughter. "Look at you, all rarin' to go! It's so cute!"

Serena growled at her.

"Awww, now you're getting mad? I could just pinch your cute little cheeks clean off. Don't get too mad, we just cleaned you up. Can't have you combusting again."

Serena trembled out of fury and fear. "Save it! Pendragon isn't here to back your ass up. If it's just you, I'll take my chances turning you into my pelt!"

"You must still be concussed, thinking you can fight me. Euryale's daughters must have hurt you pretty bad." Shiro poked her lips out. "You poor thing. Remind me what your mommy looks like so she can give you a hug," Shiro teased, extending her arms.

Serena bared her fangs and her aura flared. "I'll skin you alive, you furry relic!"

Shiro's whimsical expression faded. Her cheery tone lowered to more of a stern one. "That's exactly your problem, Ally. You're too easy to get worked up. You were trained to be an assassin and you have all the talent in the world, but it's wasted by your uncontrollable emotion and how much you cling to your family's corpses. *My family this, my god that.* Worry about those things so much and the next time you come back, it'll be in a body bag."

Serena's aura erupted in a pink frenzy. Her hands quaked with fury, and her blood ignited. "How about I put you in one instead!"

"Shiro, did you forget what I said about provoking the others while I'm around?" an ominous, chilling voice pierced her ears. Serena's blood froze. She remembered how she ended up there in the first place and panicked internally.

Shiro and Serena bowed at once as a deathly woman appeared out of thin air, sitting in the stone throne. Soft purple light reflected from the onyx scales of serpents made that a home of the woman's head, their sleek bodies shifting and coiling. She was clad in a flowing black dress, but gauze wrapped tightly around her only arm, as well as half of her face. Her luminous gold eyes burned like embers in the dim cave light. The mere sight of her grimace shot raw terror through the vampire's veins.

"You may rise," echoed Medusa Gorgon, the leader of the Vipers.

Serena and Shiro did so, the former keeping her eyes glued to her feet.

Medusa stood from her throne and walked toward the girl. Soft hissing echoed off the cave walls, radiating from Medusa's serpents. "Serena Alucard, my dear girl. Several things have happened since you left HQ. Reiya's dead, Vakari's dead, several of our men are dead, our cargo ship sank, and you seemed to be in the center of all of it." Medusa's voice was as calm as it was chilling. She leaned in closer to Serena, her breath tickling the back of her neck. "Then I see you come in contact with a Divine Sorcerer's Stone."

The hissing grew louder with each second, making Serena's skin crawl. She felt the sensation of many snakes slithering on her bare body, tightening their grip as they all coiled around her. Serena refused to raise her eyes. She couldn't. Only death befell those that met that woman's gaze, a constant reminder whenever she'd spare a glance at those statues.

"I-I-n-no . . . no. I don't know what you're talking about," Serena stammered.

"The moment Vakari brought it up to you, the poor man lost his life. You were there. Probably the one responsible, weren't you?"

How did she know? What was she forgetting? What end did she leave loose? "I don't know what you're talking about ma'am."

Medusa closed her fist. Serena's snake tattoo expanded on her skin and coiled around her entire body. She howled to the top of her lungs, feeling Medusa's magic assault her from the inside. It felt as if her internal organs were being seared and ripped apart at the same time. Her veins pulsated, threatening to burst.

"Lying to me? I didn't teach you that, did I?"

Serena's voice became hoarse. Medusa opened her hand, undoing her curse. The young vampire collapsed, finally relieved of the pain, her breaths ragged and short. Medusa snatched Serena up by her cheek-bones, bringing to her eye-level. Serena snapped her eyes shut to avoid Medusa's glare.

"I'll let you in on a little secret. The crystal balls I lend all my subor-dinates double as open communicators. I can listen to everything you all say whether you're on a call or not." Medusa's grip tightened. Her claws drew blood, and began to crack Serena's cheekbones, making her wince. "You killed my men and attempted to withhold information. Explain yourself before my patience runs out."

"I . . . I—"

Medusa dropped the girl abruptly. The Demi-God stumbled back, grabbing her stomach and groaning. Her purple aura sputtered around her, weighing Serena and Shiro down. Blood erupted from her mouth, and she collapsed to a knee. The white gauze on her face and arm slowly turned red before dripping blood onto the ground. "Damn it all!" She groaned, her serpents swaying wildly on her head.

"My lady? My lady, there you are!" A voice called out to them, echoing from the darkness. Another Viper, Hatake, emerged from the lower levels of the cave, rushing to Medusa's side with nevma-shards in hand. "You mustn't displace like that without at least taking a shard or two! You know the consequences of overexertion."

"Don't lecture me, Fekoku!" Medusa snarled, making him flinch.

She snatched the shards from Hatake's grasp and poured them down her throat. Her quaking stopped, alongside her bleeding. She wiped her bloody chin, . She took a few deep breaths and revitalized her calm demeanor. "Damn that Council for ruining me! Soon as this body is restored, they'll get what's coming to them. Speaking of which . . ." the injured Demi-God set her sights back on Serena.

"Wait, boss I—"

The snakes in her hair hissed loudly, buying Serena's silence. "You remember the day I found you, fresh after you lost everything? Tell me again why you took my hand and joined me?"

Serena swallowed her saliva. She felt the weight of a million boulders collapsing on her all at once. "You . . . promised power. Strength."

"And?"

Serena didn't want to utter another word. She didn't want to utter the lies she was fed all those years ago. "Ch-change this world and make it safe for . . . for me. F-f-for people like me."

"Exactly. And to achieve that, I need you to complete whatever task I give you, just as I need every single one of our members. Everyone here was chosen for a reason, even beyond their magical prowess. Our combined efforts will tear down the world the Demi-Gods built on the blood of the weak. I allow you all to do whatever you please so long as you contribute to that cause. If you aren't contributing, you're a liability. So, give me one reason I shouldn't add you to my collection right now."

Serena quaked, low on options, and having no means to combat her. She rummaged through her pockets and pulled out Aurora's schematics, which only sustained singed edges. "Boss, take this. It's how your sister created the Crimson Witch with a Divine Stone."

Medusa snatched the documents from her hands, skimming them momentarily. Serena remembered how its text was illegible. She bowed her head, knowing her path may truly be at an end. But, upon seeing the corner of her boss's mouth curl upward, Serena's inner tension eased.

"Well, Serena, you may have bought yourself more years of life," Medusa said.

"R-really?"

"My sister is clever, writing it in ancient Gorgos so no one would be able to decipher it. The language may be dead to the rest of society, but unbeknownst to her, our old tongue lives on through me! Her presumption of my death will be her undoing, along with the rest of those wretched Demi-Gods. With this, we can create something of our own with the Divine Stone we possess."

"Create . . . our own?" Serena mumbled. "Will you use me as a base for this power?"

Medusa shot a glare at Serena, making her face the ground once again. "For you to use against me? No. I theorize that a Demi-God's genes are necessary, and she likely used a lot of demon blood to keep that stone in check. Luckily, my seed still resides in one of our hideouts. Shiro, contact Salem and arrange for my child to be sent to me."

"You want to bring back *that* one? Are you sure that's wise?" Shiro asked.

"It is an order of mine. That's all the wisdom you need."

Shiro's busy fox tails curled around her as her ears flopped downward. "Boss, forgive me but, it was reported that Zeus was spotted near that hideout last month. If he's near there again and discovers the kid, no one from that hideout will survive, not even Salem! Maybe we can call

Mordred back from Zerex to join Salem and me! With the three of us, we could—"

Medusa grimaced with an intensity Serena was glad wasn't directed at her. She marched over to Shiro, who cowered and bowed. "Firstly, I'm not risking three of my vanguard in the event there is such a threat. Second, rest assured, even if he is around, he doesn't have the stomach to interfere with us. He has habitually kept his nose out of any strife in the last decade. If that changes, alert Salem and everyone else at that facility to flee on sight. Relocate to any of the other bases if necessary. Otherwise, don't mention anything concerning that man to me again. Are we clear, Kitsune?"

"Yes, boss! Consider it done." Shiro bowed over and over.

"Get to it."

Shiro took off in a hurry, leaving Medusa alone with Hatake and Serena.

"Now, where were we?" Medusa yanked Serena up by her black hair. "You were and still are a valued asset due entirely to your talent and my teachings. Because of that, I'll allow you to live and continue serving me. But the next time I find out about any treason on your part, well . . . to give you an idea." Medusa launched her knee into Serena's stomach. She felt half her ribs shatter from the blow. All of the vampire's breath was yanked right out of her.

"There's far too much at stake for insubordination. Whatever aspirations you had by doing this, abandon them. Our cause is much bigger than you and your selfish desires. Defy me again and I'll confirm to you if your god Fraizen truly exists or not." Medusa marched back toward her throne. "Hatake, lock her away. We need to keep an eye on her for a while. Once my experiment is done, he should be a nice fill-in for the little traitor within my vanguard."

"Ma'am. " He threw the paralyzed girl over his back.

As she was being carried away, Serena could only think one thing, the same thing she had thought for years: murder the woman who brought her here—the one who had tortured her constantly for years and made her life a living nightmare. Medusa Gorgon was as much her target as she was her master. But Aurora's words lingered in her mind. Was this all just Fraizen's will? Was there a means to combat absolute power? Is this all just her fate? Her eyes watered at the thought. But what hurt most of all was knowing that she likely had failed the family she lost, including the little sister she was too weak to protect.

Acknowledgements

There's just not enough I can say about the people in my life who I would've never gotten this far without. Firstly, my wonderful parents, Shawntell and Richard North, who not only raised me in a healthy environment but supported me in all of my life's endeavors. Thank you for allowing me to pursue my dreams and aspirations, and I couldn't be more grateful to be your son. My amazing sisters, Rickell North and Kianna Edwards, who I grew up with and who also helped to raise me, thank you both for always looking out for me and supporting me through thick and thin. I wouldn't have gotten anywhere without you two in my life. To my other lovely siblings, Richard North III, Julius North, and Brittney North, though we may not have grown up together, you three always inspired me to move forward and showed me that love and loyalty doesn't need close proximity to exist. I'm glad to have you guys as role models. I love my family and I'm so grateful to each and every one of you!

To my best friend, Faith Mbadaugha, I thank you for all your support as a friend and when it comes to my writing career. I sincerely believe that I wouldn't have kept this passion of mine had I not have you read my first written content all those years ago. To Cameron Geer and Raisa Sohel, I thank you for giving me inspiration for this series as well as helping me with ideas during the production of this book. This story wouldn't have existed without you guys' input and without you guys just listening my idea spills. To my great friends Clifton McFarlane, Andrew McFarlane, Nina Palmeri, Darryl Bentley, Nia Campbell, Omalola Solaru, Youssef Mourad, and Zephia Cannon for all of the support for me and this story, even back in its conception stage many years ago. I'm grateful to have such a great support system and great lineup of friends backing me.

A special shoutout to Nahal Naib for beta reading my story and to Sadie Anderson for helping me create and manage promotional content for this story. You two helped immensely in the later stages of this story's production and it wouldn't have been possible without you. Also, a special shoutout to the immensely talented Adrian Doan Kim for the stellar book illustration and interior character artwork! I'm so honored to have the opportunity to share a snippet of that talent with the world.

To all of my family and friends who I have not mentioned, I thank you for all of the unconditional love and support you've shown me both before and during the process of writing this story. To everyone I have mentioned and who has been in my life, this story, this series, is written for you!

2